# The Bathory Bride

A.P. Raven

THE BATHORY BRIDE

Copyright © 2025 A.P. Raven

Cover design by: Getcover

Printed in the United States of America

ISBN: 979-8-9919095-1-8
Hardback ISBN: 979-8-9919095-2-5
eBook ISBN: 979-8-9919095-0-1

For all my original readers who followed me here

# CONTENTS

# CHAPTER 1

I smiled at the cab driver in his rear-view mirror as his eyes roved over my body, focusing on my abundant cleavage suspended above my black corset.

"This the place?" I looked out the back window at the Bathory Estate for a moment. It was just as Vladimir had described it to me. The mansion of a house boasted large white columns interspaced between the wrought iron railing of the upper and lower porches. A long driveway with a cul de sac welcomed you to the front of the enormous estate. Manicured gardens and a fountain completed the look that felt more like you were stepping out into the Regency period of England than small-town America, just as Vladimir preferred his residences. I knew there would be a sprawling European-inspired garden in the back and extensive staff maintaining it and the mansion.

My gaze returned to the mirror, "Yes, this is it."

"Do you need help with your bags, Ma'am?"

I sat on the edge of the seat and whispered, with my blood-red lips in his ear, "No, but I could use your help with something else." His mind was practically melting with my closeness.

"Yeah?" He managed to get out with a breathy whisper.

"Yes," I drew out, whispering in his ear, before lowering my lips to the base of his neck.

His breath caught as my fangs pierced his flesh, and blinding pleasure took him at the first draw of his blood into my mouth. His head fell back against the seat, and his hands tightened on the steering wheel as a guttural moan escaped his lips. I drew from him again, and his jaw fell slack with the pleasure. My eyes roved down the rather good-looking man and landed on the evidence of his arousal. I couldn't stop my eyes from rolling before I closed them and focused on the pleasure of the man's blood flowing over my tongue. He moaned again as I pulled even harder, consuming more of his blood. At last, I withdrew my fangs and licked the wound clean, sealing up the holes I had made there.

I kissed my way back up to his ear, whispering, "Thanks. Now forget." I

1

entered the man's mind with my power, obliterating what had just happened.

I stepped out of the cab, satiated momentarily, and took my two massive suitcases out of the trunk. I paid the man, easily pulling the suitcases behind me, and turned toward the beautiful mansion that belonged in a Jane Austen novel, not my horror story. Each suitcase weighed as much as a horse, but with my strength, I had no problem. I lifted them and carried them up the steps to the ornate front door.

I pursed my lips, hearing the Governess giggling upstairs with one of the coven brothers. That was going to stop. Vladimir had given me explicit instructions that the endless flow of Governesses, maids, and housekeepers running through this coven was to stop; the brothers had been fooling around with them too much, and it was beginning to draw attention and become a notorious thing.

Vlad had also given me instructions on the other problems with the community here, the coven brothers; they were out of control, and he had sent me to get them back in line. I would deal with the Cavaliers, the werewolves, and the Blackwood witches. Hard ass? Maybe. Spoilsport? Absolutely. I was a controlling bitch with the power and skill to back up my attitude; it was why Vladimir had 'acquired' me in the first place and why he kept me instead of killing me for his own gain; he had designs on using my skills and on my future. It was why he had decided to send me here. To deal with his sons, who were drawing far too much attention to themselves. No more.

The Cavaliers, in particular, had gotten too bold in their devout anti-supernatural activities, and their numbers had grown to where they were becoming more than a nuisance. Vladimir had growing concerns about them harming his precious, gifted coven brothers. The Blackwood witches were the other concern for harming the coven as they hated Vladimir and anything he touched; a botched past romance with the matriarch had ensured decades of feuding. The werewolves were growing in numbers too, but so long as they didn't see the coven as a threat, the group was less of a problem than specific individuals in it, like the rumors of a wolf hanging around the coven grounds and the mansion itself.

I didn't bother knocking on the door. It was Vladimir's home, not theirs. I opened the door and pulled my two suitcases inside the entryway. They could hear and smell me instantly, just as I could them.

Niklaus was down in the study, and my vampire sight tracked him as he ran to stop the intruder that had just entered "his" home. His chocolate hair with natural auburn highlights brushed his jawline as it flew out behind him as he rushed toward me. His moss green eyes zeroed in on me, turning red, as his broad shoulders squared up the threat, prepared to attack. He wore knee-high leather boots over riding pants and a long-sleeved tunic, complimented by his black vest trimmed in green with a dagger on his hip. He would have looked intimidating to another, but it was merely amusing to me, as he was no threat.

The youngest of the brothers, Jaxon, came flying down the stairs in much the same manner, and I heard Eben telling the Governess to be quiet and that

Jaxon would be right back. Eben obviously was staying upstairs to protect the weak human and the brats Lucy and Lucian.

Jaxon rushed at me with his trim but muscular frame, accentuated by the jeans and muscle shirt he wore. A gold chain glinted around his neck, matching the gold of his eyes. He had spikey light blonde hair that was cropped close on the sides of his head, complimenting his high, sharp cheekbones and thin lips, which were currently curling up at me.

I stood there picking at my nails, looking as bored as I felt, as Jaxon snarled at me with his red eyes. Niklaus, too, had red eyes and fangs descended as he entered the room, though he was more under control. Jaxon snarled louder as he came at me. I looked at him but didn't move an inch.

My power slammed into him, throwing him back onto the stairs while I said, "That will be enough of that, Jaxon." I could feel Niklaus trying to enter my mind, and I slapped him away mentally. "And enough from you as well, Niklaus." Niklaus stood there shocked, looking at me. He was trying to figure out how I knew their names and how I had blocked him and Jaxon.

"Who are you? What are you doing here in our home?" Niklaus demanded of me. His gaze traveled the length of me from my dark brown, almost black hair down to my black corset that covered a blood-red full skirt and finally landed on the two huge suitcases I had drug in with me.

His gaze returned to my black eyes as I answered, "I am Sasha."

"What are you doing here?" Niklaus demanded of me again, his eyes narrowing.

"I belong to Vladimir, and he sent me in his place."

Niklaus hissed displeasure at Vladimir's name, but both brothers calmed considerably at my revelation; even their eyes returned to normal. I knew they weren't fans of their coven father, but mentioning his name made me less of a threat. Instead of fear, curiosity radiated out from them now. Jaxon stood and walked towards me, trying to intimidate me by getting close.

"Why would he send you, Sugar Lips?" Jaxon asked, cocking his head and wearing a mischievous half-smile. His eyes openly perused me but in a much different manner than his brother had as he stood over me. His eyes lingered on my cleavage before he met my gaze. My eyebrow raised at his heated gaze, and I felt his twinge of surprise that I hadn't blushed at his gaze. I smiled at him, matching his playfulness for a moment.

I leaned toward him, walking my pointer and index fingers up his chest, whispering, "Because you've been naughty." My fingers reached his neck, and I reached up to run them along his strong jawline towards his chin, flashing him an alluring smile. His eyes practically caught fire as he unconsciously leaned farther toward me, following my fingers as they left his jaw. I reached up and quickly flicked him hard between the eyes, breaking the spell, while I rolled my eyes and drawled, "Apparently, you need a babysitter, so here I am."

Jaxon had jerked his head back in response to the hard flick I had given him, taken off guard. "As I said, Vladimir sent me."

I waved my hand at Niklaus just as his cell phone buzzed and sang from his pocket. He answered it, turning from me. My vampire hearing could hear a muted Vladimir on the other end of the line, explaining who I was and that he had sent me. Niklaus walked into the study, talking on the phone and leaving me alone with Jaxon. He was still staring at me. His mind revealed that he wasn't used to being the one that was toyed with.

"Do tell your brother upstairs that he can come down. I promise I won't eat the Governess just yet."

Jaxon growled a little at me over that comment. So, he was the one currently screwing her; typical. He looked me over again and disappeared upstairs, leaving me to look around. The mansion's interior matched the overall feel of the outside, fresh and white, decorated in a bright but traditional way with rich textiles and beautiful artwork. The grand staircase with white railing gave the large entryway a magnificent feel of grandeur, lacking any gloom and dank atmosphere one might expect from a vampire such as Vladimir; he saved that for his European castles.

Vladimir Bathory was no mild-mannered modern vampire like this coven he had sent me to. He was born of the Original vampire, Elizabeth Bathory, the world's most notorious female serial killer to the historical records and who secretly was a witch. That magic and her obsession with blood eventually transformed her into the bloodthirsty creatures we now are. She wanted to live forever and achieved her goal after bathing in the blood of her virgin victims while delving into the dark arts. Virgin girls were sampled and soaked in until mortality with bloodlust fell upon Elizabeth; the historical records only know about over 600, but I learned from my time with Vladimir that Elizabeth had had thousands of victims. That was the woman who had birthed Vladimir and raised him into the sadistic, evil tyrant that he was, ruling him with an iron first up until the day he killed her and stole her power.

He was the most powerful vampire in existence, and his lust for power was even more potent than his lust for blood. He had covens all over the world that he had created and established, including this one, where he sent his more 'gentle' acquisitions, who preferred to feed on the local wildlife instead of humans. Each member of this household was intensely gifted, which gave Vladimir the patience to deal with them until he could convert them to his ways. He managed to convert one of the coven brothers, Otis, who now lived with him in Europe, but the rest remained firm in their distaste for this new afterlife and Vladimir himself. You could even say they hated their coven father to varying degrees. If they hated him so much, they should have behaved better to prevent him from intervening, which is how I ended up here now.

Niklaus, the now-scholarly acting head of the family, returned, still talking on the phone, just as the rest of the household appeared at the top of the stairs.

Eben, the middle brother below Otis who hated Vladimir the most, descended the stairs first but stayed far away from me, hooking his hands onto his jean pockets, quietly relaxed, and chewing his lip pensively as he examined me. His simple black t-shirt did little to hide his tattoos poking down past the sleeves and the V neckline, giving glimpses of them on his neckline. His jet-black hair hung in his eyes, longer than Jaxon's but just as neatly cropped on the sides. The black studs in his ears complimented the black rings he wore, one with a deep red jewel glinting at me. His dark blue eyes appraised me with caution as I appraised him back for a moment before switching my gaze to the Governess and then Lucy and Lucian.

The Governess wore a pair of daisy dukes and a crop top with a half-frightened, half-irritated gaze while she clung to Jaxon's arm. Hardly a uniform for the benefit of the witch twins.

My eyes turned to Lucy and Lucian, who were hidden behind Jaxon's leg on the other side. They looked like they were about seven years of age, but I knew they were ancient, even older than me. They favored black and white, Lucian in black pants, a white shirt with a ruffled collar, and his sister in a black frock with a white collar and striped tights. They stared at me with black eyes, making them seem even more pale than the rest. They were Vladimir's first acquisition ages long ago in his lifelong quest for power; their power is typically a rival for the average vampire. Good thing I wasn't average.

Niklaus hung up the phone, and his gaze caught my attention. "Seems you are who you say you are. Vladimir has instructed me to get you settled in," he cleared his throat before finishing, "In his room." The other two brothers' gaze snapped to Niklaus as he finished. I could hear all three of their minds speculating at what that meant.

"Well then, perhaps you could show me the way?"

Eben slowly approached me and reached for one of the suitcases as my gaze switched to him, towering over me. He was broader than the other two, though only marginally over Niklaus. I evaluated Eben for a moment before handing the suitcase over. He was the quiet one, the gentle one, they all said. My eyes turned to Niklaus as he took the other one from me. Niklaus was now the calm head of this gentle coven, but he had once been a fearsome werewolf hunter. He sighed and turned down the hallway, sprawling past the study, kitchens, parlor, and dining room.

I took one last look at Jaxon, with both girls hanging on him and Lucian standing behind watching. I flashed him a mocking half smile with a snort that Governess couldn't pick up with her human senses. My silken curls, which cascaded from the top of my head to mid back, bounced as I turned on my heel to sashay after the other two brothers down the long hallway towards Vladimir's and now my room.

None of them were happy about my presence here, but that was something I had anticipated. The Governess was particularly unhappy; she was practically raging in her mind, feeling threatened. She should. I was about to destroy her and her little game.

The two brothers entered a room at the end of the hallway, and I followed them inside. It was a vast room, decorated in all black, boasting a fireplace with a writing desk and small library on one end, opposite the massive black four-poster bed at the other end. A large private bathroom was also attached to the room that boasted a small pool for a tub and a rain-head shower. Another door led to a walk-in closet. The two brothers wheeled my suitcases near the bed and watched me as I perused my new quarters; they were far different from the mansion's bright, cheery entryway and public spaces.

I looked at them momentarily before looking down to take off my black lace gloves, revealing long black fingernails, as I said, "Thank you." Niklaus was dying to ask me questions but was ruling in his curiosity in favor of being a gentleman. "We can talk later, Niklaus, after I have had a chance to unpack and get settled. I will find you in the study if that suits you?" He came to the correct conclusion that I could hear his thoughts and was disturbed that he couldn't hear mine; typical of every other mind reader I'd ever come across, however extra gifted Niklaus was.

"Yes, that would be nice, thank you," Niklaus said.

I gave him a dismissive nod before I turned to Eben. Niklaus left the room. My gaze made Eben more wary, but he held his ground as he looked at me. "My name is Sasha, Eben, since you missed my earlier introduction while guarding the others upstairs." I refused to call Jaxon's plaything a 'woman,' as she sounded too much like a preteen drama queen in her mind. She was probably a scratching slapper in a fight, too.

Eben simply nodded at me, biting his lower lip. Eben was the quieter, gentler, gifted with the ability of empathy to literally feel those around him. He expressed himself deeply in music and poetry, despite his wilder look and propensity for riding a Ducati. He was the least trouble in this house, and I could tell we would get along just fine.

I gave him a genuinely friendly smile, saying, "I appreciate the help, thank you." He nodded, looking to the side. "Eben, you don't have to stay until I dismiss you, you know. I know I make you nervous, so I'll be straight with you. As long as you don't make trouble, we will get along just fine, and out of the three of you brothers, you have the least to worry about." His vibrant blue eyes met mine, narrowing in evaluation. I gave him another friendly smile, and he seemed to settle down a little bit. "So long as you don't make trouble, we will get along just fine." He didn't really know what to make of me. I gave him a knowing smile as I walked up to him. I studied him for a moment as he looked back down at me.

"Why did you really come here, Sasha?" Eben asked. "Normally, if Vladimir has a problem, he just calls."

"I guess he thought it wasn't effective any longer since things haven't changed after numerous calls."

"Is that really the only reason?" Hmmmm, Eben was observant and could see into the emotional side of things well. I expected that from Niklaus, but Eben surprised me. His gift was more potent and more valuable than previously thought.

"It is the reason that matters. Now, tell me. How long has Jaxon been sleeping with the current Governess?"

# CHAPTER 2

I unpacked my things, taking my time to really get settled. I would be there for a long while and detested living out of a suitcase longer than needed. I pushed Vladimir's suits to the back corner of the walk-in closet and began hanging up my extensive wardrobe. After finishing, I moved my items into the bathroom, again sweeping Vladimir's things to the side. He was meticulous but would have to share the space, especially while he wasn't here. I threw my now empty suitcases on the top shelf in the back of the walk-in closet, dusting off my hands.

I walked out to look around the room. It was all black, elegant, and stunning. It needed some touches of red, though, in my opinion. I sighed and turned to walk down the hallway to the study to meet with Niklaus, as I had promised. The Governess was messing around in the dining room, getting herself something to eat as I passed by. I continued down the hallway to the study. I walked in the open door to see Niklaus pacing in front of the windows that overlooked the tailored gardens in the back of the manor. His thoughts were dwelling on not taking care of things well enough that Vladimir had sent me. Damn straight.

"Niklaus," I said, getting his attention. He stopped his pacing and looked up at me.

"Sasha, thank you for being willing to come and speak with me." I simply blinked my acceptance of his words.

"You had questions?"

"Vladimir didn't fully explain all that he wanted you to, ahem, 'fix' when we talked on the phone. What exactly are his concerns?" I sneered at him. How could he not know? I stepped farther into the room, looking at him.

"You really have no idea?" I could feel his probing attempts at gaining entry to my mind once again. "Really?" I asked incredulously. He smiled calmly, trying to soothe me with his power. We looked at one another in silence for a few moments.

"Really, Sasha. I would like to understand," he nodded.

"Well," I huffed, throwing my arm out toward the study door, "that, for starters." The door slammed shut, sending the snooping tramp of a Governess sprawling out on her exposed butt, causing a few other passing staff to look over. I had heard her sneaking down the hallway from the dining room to listen in on our conversation. Niklaus gawked at me. "Oh, come now, you knew as well as I that she was snooping. That can be a very dangerous trait to have in this mansion. The hired help shouldn't be snooping around where she doesn't belong. Vladimir will come for her if she ever does get too nosy."

"Sasha, what is your relationship with Vladimir, exactly?" Niklaus asked, looking at me. I just smiled at him.

"He turned me if that's what you're asking. It was a very long time ago, much longer than your conversion, though not as long as the twins." The witch twins were the oldest in this house, followed by myself, then Niklaus, Otis when he had resided here, Eben, and the Jaxon being the newest edition to the coven a decade ago.

"How did we not know of you then?"

"You think Vladimir shares all of his secrets with you? He kept me in Europe for his dealings there until now, using my skills as he saw fit."

"And what skills are those? You obviously are a witch of extensive power." I smiled a mocking smile at him.

"Mmmm, yes, well, let's just say he kept me secret for a reason."

"What is your full name, Sasha?"

"Sasha Genovese, though I suppose you could also change it to Sasha Bathory, as you all have switched yours because of Vladimir." His mind began trying to determine whether I would be considered a sister. Listening to him, I couldn't stop the laugh that erupted. "No, Niklaus, not even close. Let's just stick with Sasha Genovese for now, shall we? What can you tell me about the Cavaliers?"

Niklaus leaned away from me, crossing his arms. His silver bullet pendant caught my attention, drawing my eyes to his throat for a moment. My eyes came back to his, and he was watching me intensely.

"Your diet may be a problem for fitting in around here, Sasha."

"You let me worry about that, alright? I'm here to fix problems, not make more of them by being reckless. There are plenty of ways of getting what I need without drawing unwanted attention." Niklaus pursed his lips.

"You will not bring your victims in the house. Jaxon struggles enough as it is without you bringing anyone here. The last thing I want is another Otis happening." Otis was now comfortably living alongside Vladimir in Europe, indulging in blood, women, and riches. He had caved to Vladimir's influence, but resisting him was the real challenge.

"That shouldn't be a problem. My question is, if Jaxon struggles so much with control, why do you allow him to screw around with the Governesses and maids so much? From what I understand, he's already had several slip-ups." Niklaus frowned at me, still with his arms crossed.

"You try holding him back when the girl throws herself at him, especially with his gifting. It's impossible." I sneered. The golden playboy with a bizarre gift for luring and attracting others beyond the standard abilities of our kind. He also had increased reaction speed to things like a physical attack. Personally, I believed Vladimir had acquired him to bring on the substantial fortune he had inherited the year before his conversion.

"Oh, I intend to spoil their fun. Even if I need to dismiss her and find a Governess that has 'less appeal' than the current ones you've been hiring. He might not be so inclined to go to bed with the Governess if she is a 60-year-old woman, don't you think?" Another scowl. I could hear his frustration at not being able to listen to my mind. I stepped up close to him. "You love your brothers, Niklaus," his face softened at my words, "but you have been too lenient with them in certain areas." His scowl returned. I flashed him a patronizing smile, saying, "Understand that if you don't want Vladimir coming back here, inserting himself in your lives, and putting you under his considerable influence, some things will need to change around here." He still wasn't happy with me but weighed my words. "Do you need some time to think about it?" He looked at me, trying to figure me out.

"And what about you, Sasha? Are you under his considerable influence?" He asked me. My chin rose in response as I drew in a breath. He was wise and perceptive even without his mind reading.

"Perhaps," though I didn't really believe it. Vladimir had been my second master, and out of the two, he offered me a better deal than the previous one ever had. They were all the same anyway; men, always out for what they could take. Funny, Niklaus actually looked concerned about me. "I can handle Vladimir, don't worry." His eyebrows shot up at that, and his arms unfolded as he leaned in closer to me, scowling out of concern instead of scorn like he had been earlier.

"Those are bold words." I blinked, showing my lack of concern.

"Tell me about the Cavaliers."

"Well, their influence in the city is growing, and they have become bolder, shooting us with vervain bullets, even in our own forest. They have connections at the college and seem to be training and selecting some of their newest recruits from there." Perfect. I loved a youthful mind that could easily be manipulated.

"Then I will start my search for them at the college. What about the werewolves, specifically the Professor? Vladimir seems to think that you've been 'consorting' with them on his land." "If you mean consorting by living peacefully alongside them, then yes, we are. Most keep to their own, but we interact with Professor Payne and the occasional youth at the college."

"Payne, did you say?" That grabbed my attention.

Niklaus nodded, "Professor Sebastian Payne."

"You're letting him run unchecked on Vladimir's land?"

Niklaus had no reply for me on that one. His thoughts evaluated the situation for me, cluing me in. The wolf had been around at different times, mostly showing interest in a couple of their female staff but not with the current ones. He wasn't about to start a bigger problem over the wolf running through their woods on occasion. One thing was certain: Vladimir hadn't given Niklaus's wisdom enough credit. Nilaus wasn't just skilled in dispatching werewolves as once was his occupation; he had the wisdom of when to pick his fights during times of peace. I suspected that wisdom would overflow into other areas.

"And you know this werewolf?"

"Yes, he is the Folklore and Mythology professor at the college." Real monsters teaching humans about monsters always amused me.

"The college again? Seems to be a hub for problems. And what is this I hear about befriending Blackwood witches?" The Blackwood witches were one of several powerful covens in the area. The Blackwoods, in particular, were the prominent coven led by a matriarch who detested my master.

"Sabella Blackwood has 'befriended' several of our staff, including the last Governess. There was a period when her closeness with the one Governess was encouraging," he paused, looking for the right word to describe the relationship. "Mutual peace in close proximity with the Blackwoods. It has been an Olive Branch, though a weak one."

"I see. And she has been in the manor?"

"Once or twice." I scowled my disapproval at his answer. "That stops now."

"That shouldn't be a problem. Our current Governess isn't attending college and isn't friends with her. She's been rather occupied with Jaxon."

I gave a light snort, saying, "That, too, is going to change. Who is 'closest' with the witch?"

"None of us are close; we are at peace with her in ways, but she doesn't think too much of us. I suppose Eben has had the most exposure to her." I nodded my acceptance of his words; I would check in with Eben later about the witch.

"How do you plan to satisfy your 'diet' requirements, exactly?" Niklaus asked, looking intently at me.

"I'm assuming the Governess is 'off-limits' in your book?" I couldn't help but goad him a little; he was so calm and under control. I heard a hiss escape his lips as his arms came up to cross across his chest again. I gave him a sarcastic half-smile, showing him that I was kidding. His eyebrows furrowed, and he almost smiled. My attention was drawn to the bullet pendant once more. Hunters of old wore the silver bullets of their first kills to bring them luck. He had set that life aside but still wore the pendant, interesting choice. "I have my ways; don't concern yourself over me. Remember, I'm here for you, not the other way around."

"Sasha," he said, confused, like his entire being rejected my previous words. I suppose with how much of a gentleman he was known as he would have issues with that statement. There was that concerned look on his face again as his mind tried to reassure me that he could be trusted. I mentally fanned my mind, wafting the vapors of his gifting away from my senses. I wasn't about to be manipulated by this suave vampire.

"Save it, Niklaus," I said, reaching up to touch the pendant he wore before dropping my hand and turning away. I walked across the room and said over my shoulder, "I'm not one of the seemingly helpless girls you like to employ as

Governesses. I don't need your help."

I heard his mind disagree as I opened the door, strolled out, and returned to my room.

I entered the decadent room and went to find my cell phone on the nightstand where I had left it. It had only one number, which I dialed. His voice rolled out over me, demanding an update on how things were going.

"It is worse in some areas and better in some than we expected. Seems the witch and werewolf are not as big of problems as you presumed them to be. They stem from the different staff members who have passed through the manor. I'll shore things up, but it won't take much, I don't believe." He spoke for a while about his sons' recklessness; I waited him out. Just like my previous master, he needed to feel powerful and influential; it was why he wanted me in his cache. "I assure you; it will be dealt with Vladimir." The sound of my door being opened had me ending the call lightning fast.

The little Governess had worked up her courage it seemed to come and confront me about things; to mark her territory. Foolish child. She had no idea who she was messing with or how much danger I posed. Unlike her boy toy and his brothers, I had zero qualms about feeding on humans. It was all I did. Her knowledge of vampires was tame. The little hussy balled up her fists, actually shaking with anger as she stormed across the room to raise her hand to point her finger at me.

"How dare you!" She shouted at me, grasping for drama. I turned in her direction, my eyes darkening as I bared my fangs at her, hissing.

Her eyes widened as her hand dropped, and she realized how big of a mistake she had just made.

# CHAPTER 3

I advanced on the now-frightened Governess, baring my fangs at her. She had started to back away from me, and I felt the predatory pull to follow her. I would have launched myself on her from across the room if I hadn't just fed on the cab driver.

"How dare I what?" I hissed out as I stepped closer. She seemed to have forgotten her complaint as she backed away from me. She bumped into one of the large armchairs and gasped as she looked behind her to get her bearings. I took the opportunity to move up directly in front of her quickly before she had even had a chance to turn her head back around.

When she did, I was right in her face, standing over her, eyeball above eyeball. I could feel the burning heat in my gaze as my vampire eyes lit up to crimson. She froze with wide eyes and a beating pulse that was so tempting.

I whispered just loud enough for her poor hearing, "How dare I what?" Each word was dripping with danger. I could hear them coming; two of the brothers had realized their pet was missing and were searching for her. She squeaked in an attempt to answer me. "You think you're brave, living with five vampires, don't you? Don't fool yourself into thinking I'm like them, Barbie. I have the traditional diet plan and will have no issues making a meal out of you."

Her eyes widened, and her heart sped up even more as I leaned over, dropping my red lips to her ear, pressing the point of one fang into her neck as I whispered, "If you ever enter my room uninvited again, I will tear your throat out and then lick your blood from my fingers." I heard her whimper and smiled. "Your reign in this household is over, Blondie. I have no issues with cock-blocking. You either start doing what you're paid for instead of whoring, or I'll make you disappear." She gasped, and her anger slowly took back control of her frozen limbs. I pricked her neck, drawing out one drop of blood that welled and then rolled down her neck. I raised my face to look back into her eyes with my crimson ones. The brothers were there, at my door, taking in the scene.

They could smell the blood.

I heard Jaxon's growl and turned my face to look over at him and Eben. An amused smile tugged at the corner of my lips. Jaxon's mind couldn't decide if he was feeling more protective or turned on at the moment. He would be the type to get off watching a couple of girls fight. I had the feeling that Jaxon would even take deep pleasure from watching me feed on her. There were a lot of things he would take pleasure from watching; he was the type.

Eben stepped toward me, "Sasha, please." I pulled my head up slowly at his words, turning my body towards him. He disapproved of Jaxon screwing the Governess, but he also was the type to not want her to get hurt.

Eben nervously glanced between us, walking up close to us slowly. I stood up straight to meet him. So, he was the peacemaker of the group. I guess I had known that already.

"Then take her, Eben. Walk her back to her room and make sure to explain things to her. You might not be around to save her next time." Eben's eyes took in my face as he wore a sad expression that touched his eyes. Where Jaxon was aggressive, Eben was gentle. Had Jaxon used his approach, I would have instinctually matched his aggression, and his play toy would have been collateral. Eben's simple plea and sad eyes bought the brainless bimbo her unscathed freedom.

I didn't move as Eben walked up to us, almost inserting himself in between us, still looking at me. The desire to gently caress his face surprised me. He was curious about me in his thoughts but wasn't going to miss the opportunity to get the Governess away from me so he could stick around to puzzle me out. He pushed the Governess to the side and then out in front of him as he took her back to her room. The sound of their footsteps grew quieter as they crossed the house and went upstairs.

My eyes shifted to Jaxon, who now leaned in my doorway. He was measuring me up, trying to decide if I would have actually done anything to the girl.

"I have self-control Jaxon, but make no mistake, I also have follow-through." He smirked as his mind applied my words to other areas besides terrorizing the Governess. He liked what he heard. My power reached out and touched him, like my fingers had in the entryway, running a tingling sensation along his jaw. His eyes widened ever so slightly as they met mine.

"Come in, Jaxon. We need to have a chat, you and I." He pushed off the door frame he had been leaning against with his shoulder and came toward me. My gaze started to cool as my eyes faded back to their usual black. His mind almost seemed disappointed that they had. "Shut the door," I stated. His eyes sparkled and his grin returned as he did as I asked. I moved around the other side of the armchair that the Governess had backed up against and sat down.

I leaned back, lounging in the chair at an angle as I watched him close the door and come over to join me. He sat in the other chair near me, looking interested.

"What exactly do you see in that bimbo?" I asked him, genuinely curious.

He laughed as his mind revealed the simple answer; she was amusing, available, and eager.

"She has her qualities," he said, letting his eyes rover over my body once again.

"Like a nice ass and no brain?" His raised eyebrow and delighted eyes gave me my answer. "I didn't take you for a lazy predator, Jaxon. Don't you think you could do better than the easy pickings set before you by Niklaus?" His smirk grew into a full-out, delighted, flirtatious smile.

"And what would you suggest?" He asked me, perusing me again very pointedly. I just couldn't help myself around him; his flirtatious attitude bidding me to mess with him. I gave him a smoldering look, raising my eyebrow as I placed my elbow on the armrest of my chair and brought my hand to my face. I framed my chin between my thumb and index finger, with my pointer finger tipped in a long, black, sharp nail running up the side of my cheek. His excitement mounted at my silence.

"I think you should find somewhere else to plow the field." I let my smoldering look fade to a more serious one, saying, "You have an entire college of girls to get your kicks from. You don't need to bother with the little bimbo down the hall from you. You have ample opportunity every week at the college, and during weekends at the parties, you like to go to. Keep it in your pants when you come home to your hallway."

"What about across the house?" I ignored his implication, dropping my hand from my face and resting my arm on the chair.

"Your most recent mistake filled me in on your little love shack in the woods while Vladimir had her in Europe after he cleaned up your mess. Take them there if you need to bring them back here, but stay away from the Governess, got it?"

"And what should I do when she throws herself at me? That would just be a waste." I stood up, and he tracked me with his eyes. I stepped to his chair until my shins touched the front of the chair between his spread legs. I leaned down with a hand on the back of the chair near his head, giving him a good view. I narrowed my eyes at him, leaning in close to his face, almost touching him.

"You'll think of something, I'm sure. Either you do something about it, or I will, got it?" His eyes flared red, scenting the recent blood on my breath, enabled by our close proximity.

I stood up straight, drawing my nails along the upholstery as I went. "You can go," I dismissed him.

Jaxon rose up out of his chair, maintaining eye contact and brushing up against me as he did. He was almost a full head taller than me as he stood over me, so I angled my head to look at him. He was eating me alive with his gaze, both from irritation as much as arousal.

He leaned in closer, whispering, "You sure you want me to go? If I didn't know any better, I'd say it sounded like you wanted me for yourself." I glared at him but couldn't stop the smirk that pushed my blood-red lips closer to his.

The idea of luring him away from the Governess was momentarily intriguing, but I knew my place and purpose in being here. The bedroom door flew open with a gust of wind that whipped around us, giving him his answer. "Your father wouldn't approve, I'm afraid."

"Is that so?" He asked me, genuinely intrigued as the smirk faded from his face. "What exactly are you to him, anyway?" I let my eyes wander over his face, studying his features while they weren't smirking for once. His amber eyes drifted down to my lips, so close to his, and I could hear the temptation they presented him with being so close.

We were similar creatures, him and I, but where he lacked self-control, I had never had that luxury in my difficult life as I matured. Once I was old enough, I learned how to control others, much to my master's delight and tutelage. Vladimir had been no exception when we had crossed paths that first time. It was why he had returned for me, to claim me as his own. To bring my power and skills to his arsenal.

My eyes softened, and my smirk disappeared from my contemplation. An honest moment came over us, devoid of our previous games. We sat in silence, staring into each other's eyes. I slowly reached up, capturing a segment of his light blonde hair, running my fingers down its length, feeling its softness. The tip flitted through my fingertips, and they came to rest on the side of his face. Jaxon was a playboy, but I discovered his depth at that moment; there was more to him than the flirtatious ladies' man he paraded around as. It seemed we both hid below the surface, revealing only what we wanted others to see.

His eyebrows twitched as they came together. His mind was contemplating my silence at his question, our closeness, and our complacent moment. I could see his question burning in his eyes, the slightest flicker of concern buried deep in them. A bitter smile flashed across my face as I let my fingers start to drop from his face. His hand shot up and captured my wrist, holding it in place as he implored me to answer him with his eyes.

"It doesn't matter," I whispered. He was dying of curiosity and intrigue inside his mind. "Now, if you don't mind, I'm going to get some sleep after my travels. His grip on my wrist lessened, and he finally released me.

"Sleep well, Doll face." He finally moved away from me, leaving my clothes feeling drafty where his warmth had soaked into them from our long moment of standing close; we were the same temperature, after all.

He closed the door behind him with a click, and I turned to undress and take down my hair. I changed into my sheer black nightgown and made my way over to the massive black four-poster. I pulled back the blankets and slid into the silken sheets. They smelled of Vladimir. I sighed, closing my eyes, and my thoughts drifted to the blonde vampire. I silently sent a word of thanks to him and his lack of self-control. If Jaxon hadn't had so many 'slip-ups' in the recent past, I wouldn't be here and I would have found myself in Vladimir's bed with him there. Missy warmed it for him, and for that, I was grateful. She had been a welcome blessing, just in time, too, after Vladimir had tired of the previous one. But he would tire of her too, eventually. And then he would come to claim what he intended on making his.

# CHAPTER 4

I felt him draw his hand down my body, gliding his fingertips down my face, neck, over my shoulder, and down over my waist and hip. An open-palmed caress over my thigh caused a shiver to run the length of my spine. It was a shiver of repulsion, not pleasure. My eyes flew open, and I sat up on a gasp, looking around the black room with my vampire eyes. His translucent form smiled before fading away as I stared at him. Vladimir. He had been thinking of me there, connecting with me in the physical here. I drew in a breath and swallowed from dread. I let my breath escape, cleansing me from the feelings.

The house was still but not silent. The very gentle melody of a piano sang out through its empty corridors. I rose and pulled on a black silk robe to cover my nightgown. Silently, I walked across my room and out the door to the entryway. I followed the sound and listened in the hallway outside Eben's room.

"Sasha." It was a whispered acknowledgment of my presence. His vampire hearing would have picked up on my footsteps, and he could undoubtedly smell me. I smiled and pushed his door in, entering his room. I shut it behind me to mute the piano once more and looked over at him.

He was bent over his piano, playing out his miseries. So sorrowful. I studied him as he played until he looked at me over his shoulder. His sad smile showed, reaching his eyes.

I walked over to the edge of his bed closest to the piano and sat down. His mind was a typhoon of melancholy thoughts tempered with kindness. I listened to his mind as much as I did his piano for a few minutes as I looked around his room. It was dark, with various posters on the walls and several full bookshelves, and the corner next to the piano he played was dedicated to an electric guitar and violin, both on a stand.

"Did you need something, Sasha?" I didn't smile at him, but my eyes held a kindness in them. Eben was going to be a natural chink in my armor, I could tell. "Did you sleep well?" He asked, turning back to his piano.

"Until Vladimir woke me, but yes," I stated, emotionless.

His fingers stilled on the porcelain keys at my admission, and his head turned to the side, towards me, absorbing what I had just said. He swung around on the piano bench to look at me. I waved away his concern and let a self-assured smile stretch my lips to hide behind as I laid back on his bed, my shoulders resting on the headboard. He was back to evaluating me and the situation in his mind, puzzling me out mentally.

His mind was beginning to draw some correct conclusions, so I moved us in a different direction, "Tell me about the Blackwood witch." He seemed surprised for a moment before his look darkened.

"What about her?"

"Well, Vladimir seems to be under the impression that you're friends." His dark, irritated look remained.

"Hardly. Sabella was friends with a few Governesses and maids who passed through this house."

"Including one you were involved with as well?"

"For a while. It was the only reason I was ever near Sabella. She doesn't care much for us, just like the rest of her family doesn't. She hasn't been around me since that Governess left. You can hardly call that a friendship, Sasha."

"So, there is nothing I need to worry about concerning her then?"

His mind ardently confirmed my question as truth as he said, "No." I gave him a smile. I knew he would be the least troublesome brother.

His mind returned to his previous pondering. His thoughts dwelled on Vladimir being a tyrant and evil. Well, I couldn't argue with that.

"How did Vladimir wake you, Sasha? Does he call often?" I lightly laughed.

"You could say that." His brow wrinkled with confusion, but he stayed quiet. Eben's quiet concern rang out, threatening that armor I wore. I decided a taste of the truth would satisfy his mind, so I reached out with my power. I mentally ran the back of my hand over his cheek, like I had thought about doing earlier in my room, saying, "He makes his presence known when he is thinking about me, concentrating on me wherever he is." Eben's surprise was shown in his bright blue eyes, and he looked at my hands lying at my sides on the bed.

I blinked a confirmation at him with a sad smile before I rose up off his bed. I turned to leave, but Eben stood and walked close, causing me to turn back to him.

"What has he done to you?" His question hung in the air, but its multiple meanings were not lost on me. It was a question of the immediate waking, but it also demanded of the past.

"Besides turning me, you mean?" His dark scowl returned, and I could see a blue flame of anger in his eyes, meant for Vladimir. Sweet, dark Eben. I gave him a smile that unmistakably was set in bitterness as I laid my palm on his cheek, stroking him once with my thumb. I removed my hand and then myself from his presence, leaving him standing in his room looking after me.

I walked back toward my room, thinking about what I needed to do that day. The sound of a crackling fire coming from the study announced Niklaus's awakening. It was early, but it didn't surprise me that he was awake. He heard me pass by as I continued on to my room.

I dressed in black boots and a black skirt just above my knees in the front but fell to mid-calf in the back. A dusted purple corset and black choker completed my ensemble. It was what the modern age might most readily call 'steampunk' but was true of one of the eras I'd lived through, though a little more revealing. I pinned my hair up in large curls that fell in a waterfall down my head and neck to tickle my shoulders. I matched my lips to the dusted purple of my corset but left the rest light. The prey I had in mind today couldn't be too intimidated.

I dipped the slightest touch of scent on my neck and wrists and left my room to go see Niklaus in his study.

The Governess was just coming down the stairwell in her cute little sweater and short shorts. The contrast between her and I could not have been more pronounced. I smirked at her before turning toward the study as she walked toward the kitchen. Niklaus looked up from the book he was holding open in one hand in front of him.

"I'll be heading to the college today to shore up a couple problems."

"Would you like my number in case you need help with anything?" He offered.

I smiled at him, "I'll be fine, Niklaus. Directions are the only thing I need."

"You could just walk there with the Governess if you'd prefer an escort." The other brothers obviously hadn't filled him in on what had happened the previous day.

"I don't think that would be the best of ideas." He looked up from his book towards me.

"Oh?"

I sneered at him again, "Unless you want me to use her for breakfast, I'll walk alone."

"I'll drive you, Doll Face," a whisper into my ear. Jaxon's breath on my neck. I smiled at him over my shoulder.

"Very well. Are you ready?"

"Come on," he said with a hand coming to the small of my back. I met Niklaus's scowl with an impassive glance. He disapproved of Jaxon's closeness. There was a promise in his mind to talk about it later. Fine with me.

I allowed Jaxon to guide me out of the study and toward the front door. I opened it for myself before he could bother and walked down toward the sports car waiting for us. He actually beat me to the car door, holding it open for me with one arm while leaning on the vehicle with the other, effectively boxing me in.

He perused me with his eyes and spoke through his smirk, "You're not exactly going to blend in at the small-town community college looking like that. What do you intend to do?"

"What I'm good at." I flicked him lightly with my power before sinking into his car. I heard him growl low before he shut the door, but it sounded different from pure irritation.

I looked out the window, swinging my foot, which was suspended in the air from crossing my legs. He glanced sideways at my legs, where my skirt had slid up from sitting. I let him and met his eyes when they lifted. He gave me an unabashed smile and turned back to the road. He parked and came around to let me out, standing so close I had to brush up against him to stand up. He reached over and shut the car door.

"Happy hunting," he whispered while lightly pressing me up against the door.

I raised an eyebrow and leaned in close to him, "You too." I gave him a meaningful look, reminding him of our previous conversation. I heard an annoyed sigh escape him. It was Friday night, so he would have more opportunities that night if he went out.

I put my hand on his chest and pushed him back. I stepped around him and headed off towards the college. I smiled. I could just smell the hormones flying all over the place. I took in the various male predators mixed in with the less impressive specimens, stalking various prey. A few pairs of their eyes noticed me as I passed, but most turned back to their easy prey of brainless cheerleaders or insecure victims.

But there he was. I had plucked him from the minds around me in the mansion. His predatory blues flared to life as he looked at me coming towards him. I met his eyes and let him see me peruse him with my eyes, traveling down and then back up to meet his gaze again. I flashed him an appreciative smile at what I saw, turning my head a little to maintain eye contact as I walked past him.

His body instinctually turned toward me as I passed. I felt his eyes follow me as I entered the building. I needed somewhere quiet to stage my trap. He would come to me like a moth to the flame in a matter of seconds. I walked down the hall looking for an empty classroom when my eyes landed on a door labeled 'library.' That would do.

I slipped inside, stealing a glance down the hall to make sure he had seen where I went. I moved through the tables in the center of the room towards the back area where we wouldn't be overheard but stayed in sight. I picked up on Eben's scent; he must spend quite a bit of time in here for it to linger so. I heard the door open and the predator's measured footsteps as he slinked up on his discovered prey. I could smell my little Cavalier coming to me as I perused the electronic catalog for a pretend book. He was closing in on me in the quiet library.

Just before he could slide up next to me, I looked at him casually and flashed him a friendly, innocent smile, and then I returned my gaze to the screen long enough to point like I had found my book.

I turned, leaving to wander deeper into the library's stacks. I led my little lamb to the slaughter as I ventured deeper and deeper away from prying ears and eyes that might enter. I finally found a dark aisle and entered it, pretending to search for a needed volume. My vampire sight took in his silhouette as it filled the opening of the aisle.

I looked up toward him like he had startled me, "Oh!" A delighted smile crossed his features as he reveled in the assumed fact that he had taken me by surprise.

"You're new here, aren't you?" He came up to me, wearing a half-friendly but still predatory smile.

"You could say that, I guess. I'm just visiting."

"Checking out the college to attend?" The possibility excited him.

"I'm visiting a few friends that are living here in town, staying with them for a time. I came to the college to see Professor Payne and got distracted with this amazing library."

"Who are the friends?"

"The Bathorys."

"Oh." He was taken aback for a moment. "And you say you are friends with the Professor?"

"We go way back, but he's not really my type." I let my eyes drift to his mouth quickly and looked away like it was a stolen glance, but he noticed. He moved closer, stretching his arm to lean against the bookshelf over me, moving into my space.

"So what's your name?" I could smell his blood heating as his eyes landed on my cleavage when I turned toward him.

"Sasha."

"Sasha," he tried out my name, "My name is Blake." I gave him an innocent smile as I forced a flush to my face. His eyes darkened. It was time to stage a moment. I pretended to get wide fawn eyes as I bumped into the bookshelf. My power brushed a few books off the top shelf that fell close behind me. I jumped toward him, gasping in surprise. I was now within arms' length. Blake looked up at the top shelf, and I pushed out another large volume that was directly above my head, letting it slowly slide free, heading right for my head. His hero complex kicked in, just like I predicted, and he reached out and pulled me to his chest, out of the perceived harm's way.

The book crashed to the floor behind me as I splayed my hands on his broad chest, letting out a breathy gasp. I angled my head to look up into his intense gaze, widening them in mock shock and surprise. I let my hands shift just slightly so he noticed them there.

"Thank you for saving me." An amused smile crossed his face like he could taste my innocence. "How could I ever thank you? It would have knocked me out for sure!"

"How about you come out with me tonight and let me buy you a drink, as a thanks?"

I forced another blush like I was overwhelmingly flattered and stammered, "Ok." I gave him another interested but timid-looking smile as I 'dared' to reach out and touch his face like I was enamored with my hero. The predator smiled down at me, not realizing that he was now caught in my web.

# CHAPTER 5

The bell disrupted Blake's moment of attempted seduction, and he had to leave for class, but I had what I wanted. I would meet him at one of the local bars tonight and work my magic on him. My thoughts turned to my next target as I wandered my way out of the library, passing through the tables there. Eben was sitting there, and he looked up at me. He gave me a guarded look, having heard my little interlude in the back. I flashed my fangs at him, smiling.

"Normally, I'd warn you away from that one, but perhaps I should warn him away from you instead." Eben's mischievous look surprised me, and I gave him one back in response.

"No love between the two of you, I take it," I stated, looking at him. His look faded into a simple one of kindness for me. I liked Eben more, discovering he also had a playful side. He simply nodded as an answer.

"Where are you headed to now?"

"I'm going to drop in on our professor and have a word with him."

His eyebrows crinkled, and his mouth turned down before he spoke, "You sure that's a good idea?" He was worried about me again; how cute.

"You worry about me with the Professor but not Blake?"

His mischievous look returned as he said, "The latter you could make a meal of, eating him up. The professor is another matter." I raised an eyebrow at him and leaned close with a hand on his shoulder.

I whispered in his ear, "Speak for yourself." I stood, and we exchanged another smile before I left the library to head to the professor's classroom.

I followed a group of students who were running late and slipped up the side to the back corner of the classroom. The professor was at his whiteboard writing down some reading assignments he had for the class. I saw his shoulders stiffen as my scent reached him and he stood up ramrod straight. He finished what he had been writing and turned to look over the seating, searching for me. His eyes locked with mine, and I flashed a fang at him, winking. He tried to hide his smile from me, but I caught it. He turned to his class, doing his best to ignore me, and started his lecture. I sat in the back watching him, amused at all the girls whose hormones revealed they would whip their panties off for him in a heartbeat if he asked. He always had been good looking, for a wolf. Tall and broad, shaggy black hair that stood out in spikes where it wasn't cropped shorter like on the sides. Handsome thin lips that commented his high cheekbones and piercing golden eyes accentuated by dark lashes. He was clean shaven and had an air of unstated confidence that didn't need defending.

Finally, the class was over, and the students shuffled out of the room. A group of girls converged on him at the end of the class, drawing out a small, amused chuckle from me that the hoard couldn't hear. The professor's eyes snapped up to me, evidence that he had. He smiled at the students around him and patiently answered their questions. At last, they left him standing there alone. His lips pursed for a moment before he turned and walked into his adjacent office. I used my vampire speed to beat him inside, settling into his office chair and folding my boots up on his desk, my skirt sliding up a little to reveal my thighs. He drew in an irritated breath as he closed the door behind him. He turned and looked at me from across his office.

"Been a long time, Sebastian. How ever did you find your way to this little town that also happens to house the Bathorys? No coincidence, I think." He gave me an amused, albeit somewhat irritated, smile.

"Yes, it has been a long time, Sasha." His eyes took in the length of me, starting with the boots on his desk and coming to port in my black eyes. "You haven't changed a bit," he observed. I rewarded him with a smile before flashing across the room right up to him. His eyes held an emotional wariness as he looked at me.

"Did you miss me?" I whispered, sliding a hand around his collar. He laughed, reaching up to grip my wrists and remove them.

He leaned close and playfully whispered, "Hard to miss a viper." I hissed at him, flashing him my extended fangs. He moved around me to sit at his desk as I took up the comfortable chair in front of it, lounging and watching him work. "What do you want, Sasha? I'm busy."

"Heard there was a wolf running around unchecked on Bathory property, and I've come to 'deal' with it." He looked up at me and smiled as he shook his head.

"And where did you hear that from?"

"Vladimir." He looked up at me, alarmed.

"Is your master so well informed that he knows it was me?"

"No, he just knows there's been a wolf around." He looked back at the computer screen.

"Well, you can report back to him that it's been dealt with. I have no more motivation to come around there anyway."

"That so?" He looked up at me and gave me an amused smile.

"Well, I had thought. The current Governess isn't a student and couldn't interest me less, but I hadn't known they had other 'guests' staying there."

"MmmmHmm," I said. I looked at him before looking around to take in his office. "You seem content and settled at last," I observed while I took in the surroundings. My gaze returned to his and I asked, "How have you been?"

"You mean since the last time I saw you in Moscow?" His eyes flared at me, burning with anger. I smiled at him, amused that I could still evoke such emotions in him.

"Mmmm, I would have thought you'd be over that by now, Seb. But you're not one for letting sleeping dogs lie, are you?" His eyes narrowed at my chosen expression, glaring at me, making me laugh. He sighed, but I saw the amused smile cross his features.

"Why *are* you here, Sasha? Surely Vladimir wouldn't send you all this way just to check up on me running through his woods in one of his numerous covens."

"You were only one of the mentioned issues he wanted me to deal with. I'm here to get the Bathory brothers back in line before Vladimir is forced to return himself. You know very well that would be unfortunate for this town in many ways."

"What are the other issues you're *dealing with*?"

I stood, saying, "I have a little witch to deal with and the Governess."

"That's it?"

"And the Cavaliers, but I'm already progressing in that area." He stood and came around to me.

"You had better know what you're doing with them, Sasha. They're not amateurs at dealing with my kind or yours. They're dangerous, even for you." I gave him a patronizing look.

"I always know what I'm doing, Seb." I turned to leave, and he pulled me back to him. His mind was dwelling on the past.

"It is good to see you, Sasha, even if you do tend to bring trouble with you." I smiled at him.

I reached up, put a chaste kiss on his lips, and whispered, "For old time's sake." I pulled back from him. "Now, unless you want to study 'the Vampire's Kiss' more with me as you once did, I will leave you." Desire flared in his eyes, but he let me leave his office. I heard him sigh as I left the classroom to return to the estate. I had noted how to get there from the drive with Jaxon that morning, so I knew my way back.

I moved at a quick human pace, not enjoying the sun's rays overhead. I made it back to the mansion without issue, though one bar patron, drunk before mid-morning, attempted to heckle me. He was lucky we weren't in Europe; otherwise, I would have left him for dead. Here in small-town America, the news would spread like wildfire, drawing attention.

I entered the manor, and Niklaus appeared in his study doorway, inquiring, "Well?" I smiled at him but ignored his question and headed down the hall towards my room. I was almost there when I heard him follow me. I left the door open for him, and he followed me inside. I went to my nightstand, picked up my cell, and pressed the 'send' button.

Vladimir answered immediately, "Sasha."

"The wolf is no longer a problem, and I am making progress on the Cavalier issue. I should have more information on that front by tomorrow. Jaxon should be under control very soon," I let my eyes drift to Niklaus's as I said this. He stood in the middle of the room, listening, watching.

"Will I need to come for the Governess?" Niklaus's alarm showed on his face at Vladimir's words.

"No, Vladimir, not at this point. I'll let you know if she needs to be picked up." Niklaus was relieved. He knew I could have thrown them under the bus at that moment.

"Excellent, Sasha. I'm pleased; keep at it, my minx." The line went dead, and I hung up the phone, still not breaking eye contact with Niklaus. I finally turned to set the phone down; it's home was my nightstand.

"You wanted to discuss something with me, Niklaus?" I looked up at him again, walking up to him. "If you have concerns over Jaxon, you should bring them to him, don't you think?"

"I always try to encourage my brother to make good choices, but he lacks self-control, and you are too much of a temptation." I raised an eyebrow. He hadn't qualified the statement by saying 'temptation for Jaxon.' He had just left it at temptation. Was he tempted? I would have to test the theory and try to get under that calm and collected surface.

"Am I?" I flashed my fangs slightly as my lips parted. His eyes caught the movement.

He was dying to know why he couldn't hear me, under his irritation with Jaxon's obvious interest in me. "You can't hear me, Niklaus, because I don't want you to; it is as simple as that. If I let you in, you would hear me like everyone else around you." He released an irritated sigh. "You're not used to not having access, so you can play your mind games, are you?"

He crossed his arms and scowled at me, "Mind games?" I gave him a taunting smile.

"Yes. You enjoy listening in, don't you." He was silent, but his mind wished it could see in mine so he could figure me out.

"Not so easy is it when you can't hear what isn't meant to be heard." His mind was mulling over what he had overheard on the phone.

"You still haven't said what you are to him."

"He is my creator, like yours, and he chooses to do with me what he wants. Right now, that means coming here to crack down on your brother, babysit the Governess, deal with the Cavaliers, and I have already dealt with the wolf."

"And how did you manage that exactly?"

"Look, as much as I'm loving our little chat, I have a date tonight that I need to get ready for."

I didn't wait for him to answer; I just started taking my hair out and then my jewelry, throwing everything on the bathroom counter. I sat on my bed, unzipped my boots, and tossed them into the closet. He hadn't moved.

"Does this 'date' have to do with the progress you've made with the Cavaliers?"

"Yes. I have a date with Blake this evening."

"You need to be careful."

"Because I need to be careful around him or with him, Niklaus? Are you so worried that I will draw attention?" He scowled at me. "I am not your brother, Niklaus. Plus, I can easily manipulate his memories if I need to."

I didn't care that he was there; I just walked into the bathroom and started stripping. He cleared his throat, turning away. I started running a bath and added plenty of bubbles. My clothes dropped to the floor, and I slid into the tub. He was still there, trying to figure out what to say.

"You are too used to Jaxon, Niklaus, who is out of control when he feeds. I am not that way." He stormed into the bathroom. The bubbles of my now-full tub covered me from the chest down; only my shoulders up and the bottom part of my legs could be seen, where I had them propped up on the side of the tub.

"They are still people, Sasha."

"Mmmmm, yes, and they taste so good." He walked up to the side of the tub, still scowling in scorn at me.

"You really don't care at all?" He asked.

"I have never been allowed to care. So unless you're offering, I'll stick with my methods." He dropped his arms and his mouth opened slightly; he was shocked by my attitude and proposition. Sadness at my past entered his mind. "I don't need your pity, Niklaus."

"Pitty? No, I just wish you would let me in," he gently touched my temple, "so I could help you."

"I don't need that either."

He laughed humorlessly, "Vladimir has warped your mind. You need help more than you'll admit."

"What makes you believe he has warped my mind?" I snapped at him.

"His cruelty emanates from you, but you weren't always that way; no one is born that way, Sasha." A bitter smile, and I closed my eyes to ignore him. I hadn't been born this way; no, I had been created and molded by two different men's machinations.

"I am what I am." His gentle fingers slid down the side of my face to hook under my chin and turn my face up to him. I looked at him like he wanted, wearing a guarded expression.

His words were quiet, "If that were true, you wouldn't work so hard to hide. What are you afraid I will discover if you let me in?" The truth.

"There is nothing to discover, Niklaus. Now, if you're not offering your vein, you'd best leave so I can prepare to go find one."

# CHAPTER 6

I walked down the dark street, holding the small clutch as my red heels clicked over the sidewalk. I had put on a form-fitted black number that came to mid-thigh and had a corset bodice with off-the-shoulder sleeves. My clutch, heels, bangles, and choker were all red. Large black chandelier earrings, smoky eyes, and matching red lips finished my look. My hair was up in a French twist, held to my head by red chopsticks. I gave knowing smiles to the men who turned to look after me as I walked past the various bars.

Ahead of me was the bar that Blake had asked to meet me at, and there, leaning against the lamppost in its light, was my prey. He was looking at the bar and hadn't noticed my approach. I reached out and slid my hand over his shoulder and down on his chest as I walked around to his front, plastering a charming smile on my face. He turned his head at my first touch and tracked me as I came to stand in front of him. His smile grew wider as he ran his eyes over me.

"Well, there you are. I was beginning to think you weren't coming."

I smiled, "Sorry I'm late." His eyes twinkled.

"Forgiven," he whispered, motioning to the bar while placing his other hand on the small of my back.

The bar looked like a popular establishment boasting a long bar, dance floor, lots of tables, plenty of pool tables in the center, and booths in the back corners for those wanting quieter privacy. I smiled over my shoulder at Blake as we entered, and my eyes looked up at him, flirting.

I could smell them the moment I entered the bar, and my gaze turned to land on the brothers at the far pool table in the back. Eben was bent over, taking a shot, but Jaxon was staring at me with his head at an angle, using his pool stick to lean on. Had Niklaus sent them, or was this just a coincidence? I held Jaxon's gaze until Blake slid into my line of vision. I looked up at him to give him a winning smile. He took my hand and gently pulled me toward a booth in the back.

He let me slide into one side of the booth and then bent close, asking, "What can I get you to drink?" Oh, if he only knew. I licked my lips, and his eyes took in the moment.

"You pick." He left for the bar to go get our drinks.

My gaze wandered over from Blake's back to where Jaxon was standing, now facing the booth looking at me. I raised an eyebrow at him. He was irritated, but his mind didn't give away exactly why. I watched Eben take another shot and then stand up to say something to Jaxon. Eben's gaze followed Jaxon's and landed on me. It lingered for a moment before he turned back to Jaxon and elbowed him so he would turn and take his shot.

Blake returned to our table and slid some fruity little drink over to me. Cute. I smiled at him, tilting my head, pretending to be absolutely pleased with his choice. He sat down and slid into the booth beside me, putting his arm around the back. I angled my head slightly, giving him the view he was trying to see over my shoulder.

"So, Sasha. How long are you planning on being in town?"

"I'm not sure exactly," I turned my face toward him, angling my body toward him. "I guess it depends on how interesting things get for me here. I would need a pretty good reason to stay."

"Yeah?" He asked, and his face lit up a little with his reply.

"We'll see if I find one," I whispered, letting my eyes travel down his chest before turning to my drink.

"So you live with the Bathorys?"

"That's right, but we shouldn't talk about them. I want to know more about you, Blake. You're a Senior at the college?"

"That's right."

"And you're a football player?"

"Quarterback." Ahhh, so that explained a lot to me.

"Quarterback! Really?" I said in a convincingly amazed voice. Acting surprised, I laid my hand over his, resting on our table. "And how does the starting quarterback from the college not have a girlfriend he's going out with on a Friday night? Seems like you would be pretty popular." I rolled my eyes inwardly at the responding hubris; he practically puffed his chest out at my flattery, soaking it up. There was also a twinge of irritation with another girl pictured in his mind.

"Yeah, well, I haven't found a girl yet that I want to get tied down over."

"Oh," I looked down, putting on an air of disappointment. He took the bait.

"Well," he hesitated, "I think I may have." I brought surprised doe eyes back up to meet his, following that with a blush. I turned back to my drink, fiddling with the straw, pretending to be nervous.

"So, do you have family here in town then, Blake? Are you from the area?"

"Yeah, I have family." His mind turned to his family and the Cavaliers they were a part of. Perfect. Born into them and raised by them, he would be an even more significant source of information than I had initially predicted.

"Do you live with your parents, or did you move out when you started college?"

"I live in an apartment near them but not with them, no." His mind showed me an apartment building on the other side of town inside of a gated community. Was this the Cavalier headquarters, then?

"How close? Don't tell me you live in an apartment in your parent's basement, right?" I gave my tone an abhorred sound, ending with a laugh.

He laughed before leaning in close, whispering, "No. It's in the same community as them but is totally separate. Why, you want to come over sometime?" I smiled at him.

"I was just checking to see if that was the real reason you didn't have a girlfriend," I winked at him. He laughed again; my teasing was exciting him. I now knew where their headquarters were, but I wanted to see what other information I could wring out of him. "So, you must be a frequent party-goer, being the quarterback and popular." He gave me another pleased grin at the compliments.

"There are always parties going on, and I enjoy them."

"Do you ever throw them yourself at your apartment?" His mind revealed that security at the compound was tight, and a party at his place would never happen because of his association with the Cavaliers.

"Private ones, sure," he winked at me suggestively. I blushed and looked down like he would expect.

"So, since you grew up here, can you tell me a little more about the town? Are there any legends, landmarks, or places I should avoid? Being new in town, I don't really know my way around that well." His hero complex rose in him a little bit.

"You mean besides where and who you're living? The Bathorys are infamous for their lineage." That was most certainly true, and he probably only knew the half of it.

"Mmmm, yes, the Blood Countess, also called the Countess Dracula. The rumors of Countess Elizabeth Bathory bathing in and drinking virgins' blood back in the late 1500s. A reputation and heritage of that sort does tend to linger, when surrounded by rumors." Vladimir's mother was known as one of the world's most notorious female serial killers to the general public, but what they didn't know was that she was a vampire with a cruel streak, just like her son.

"Substantiated by witnesses."

"Yes, besides that," I implored.

Blake laughed, "You should, of course, avoid alleyways downtown after dark, and there are a few places on the outskirts of town that are best avoided." Bingo.

"Like what, Blake?" I asked in an 'alarmed' hushed tone, moving a little closer to him. He drew in a breath at my closeness.

"Well, there are a couple of houses that are reportedly haunted and a few that are old and very unsafe." His mind sorted through the houses for me, showing me the ones that were reportedly haunted and two others that were

29

old and abandoned-looking but were a point of interest for him.

"No one owns the old houses? They just sit there run-down? How sad. I've always loved old houses."

"Someone owns them, but they aren't safe," he insisted. His mind again revealed that they were used by the Cavaliers. Perfect. I could tell he was getting slightly irritated, so it was time to move on. I turned my gaze from him to the dance floor as the song changed to a pulsating, sexy song.

"So tell me, Blake, do you dance?" His predatory smile spread, and he slid out of the booth, offering his hand. I took it and let him pull me along through the tables to the floor, where we flowed into the crowd of dancers. I started moving my body to the rhythm, standing close to him, purposely letting my body brush his.

I gave him a smoldering look that lit a flame in his eyes. I ran my hands up his chest to wrap my arms around his neck as we undulated to the music and lights. He brought his hands to my waist to hold me while we danced close, heating as he touched me. Perfect. I preferred my blood nice and hot when I took it from the vein. I smiled at him, eating him up with my eyes. The looks that started to cross my features didn't need to be faked as I watched the vein in his neck pulsing to the beat and his growing arousal. I was lusting after the blood flowing through his body, which he happily interpreted as he wanted. I whipped my head about me as the rhythm picked up, exciting him even more. With the amount of alcohol he had the bartender put in my drink, he would be expecting me to be more than buzzed by now.

He leaned his face over me with those blue eyes boring into mine, sneaking looks farther down. That predatory grin returned as his hands slid their way down to pull my hips up against his.

I heard a vampiric hiss from the pool table across the room, drawing my eyes. Both brothers were watching us. Both were irritated mixed with other emotions; Eben was irritated but also amused and fascinated whereas Jaxon was more intensely irritated with a mixture of arousal and disgust and . . . Was I picking up on jealousy? Interesting. I flashed him a taunting smirk before returning my attention to my little Cavalier and soon-to-be meal. We stayed on the dance floor for a few songs before I felt like he was hot and bothered enough.

I pulled on his hand toward the back of the bar, leaning in close to his neck to whisper, "I need to use the restroom." He nodded and followed me. I flashed a triumphant smile toward the pool table and led Blake off the floor towards the back. I rewarded Blake with a quick smile before stepping into the ladies' room to complete the ruse. I looked in the mirror, arranging my hair a little.

I exited the restroom and saw Blake waiting for me in the dark, completely out of view from the rest of the bar. I licked my lips in anticipation of what was coming. I moved close to him, running my hand up the length of his arm, over his shoulder, and onto his neck. His tantalizing pulse throbbed under my fingers. I could feel another part of him throbbing as I leaned against him.

I pulled him down to whisper in his ear over the music, "Did you want to dance more, or did you have something else in mind for tonight's festivities?"

His pulse quickened, calling to me like a siren as his hands came to me and pulled me up against him. He leaned in close and kissed my neck. I faked a sigh for his benefit, caressing him with my hands. When I responded favorably, he became more fervent. He pulled back to look at me before leaning down to capture my lips with his, kissing me enthusiastically. Two more seconds, and I would sink my fangs into his neck when his attentions returned to my neck. I was so thirsty. I was in the middle of bloodlust.

That's when I heard a feral snarl from right behind me and was yanked away from my prize as a white fist slammed into Blake's face, once, twice and he collapsed to the floor on the third, out cold.

I was furious. My meal had just been stolen from me. I snarled and turned to face off with the unwelcome interruption. Jaxon's eyes glowed red and his hold on my wrist didn't let up as I snarled at him, baring my fangs. He snarled back and pulled me to him.

I snarled at him again, growling out, "You just cost me my meal!" He didn't say anything; he just smiled at me, pleased. I growled at him again, frustrated with his interference. "I guess I'm going to have to go find another willing party to get what I need! Damn you," I shouted over the thundering bass pounding the room.

I turned to stomp off and find my new victim when I was yanked back up against his chest again. His arms surrounded me, and he captured my lips with his in one movement, stepping forward to force me up against the wall.

# CHAPTER 7

Fire. Fire all around me, in me, burning. Flaming, scorching, consuming desire. Jaxon's mouth and hands on me lit me up, desire spreading through me like wildfire. My body moved of its own accord, responding to him whether I wanted to or not. His dominating kiss demanded that I give in, that I allow him entry, as his body pressed me hard against the wall. It stole my breath and self-control. My fingernails dug into his shoulders through his shirt as his tongue finally was granted entry. His taste was perfection. Nothing had ever created such a response in me before besides bloodlust. It was why I didn't bother pursuing human men for anything other than blood.

Blood. I had been about to feed and was in the middle of bloodlust; it was why I was out of control. I had self-control to a point, but no vampire could deny the bloodlust, especially when that moment had been so close. I was breathing heavily, as much from Jaxon as from the consuming need for blood.

Jaxon broke away, pulling back to look at me with a smirk laden with desire. His flaming red eyes flashed before he bent his head to ravish my neck and shoulders with his talented lips. I moaned from need, the need for him to stop, the need for him to carry on, the need for blood. His exposed neck was there, pulsing in front of me. What the hell. I snarled and pulled him up against me more, sinking my fangs into his neck.

His breath hitched, and his breathing became shallow as the white-hot pleasure flowed through him. I heard him moan on the second strong pull while he continued kissing my neck. His blood hit my tongue, flowing down into my system with its intoxicating, spicy flavor. It was one of the most complex and wonderful flavors I had ever sampled, and I wanted *more*. I pulled him tighter to me, still with my strength that would have been too much for a human. His growl in response was entirely approving. I continued to feed on him until I knew I had to stop; even if he was a vampire, we didn't want him passing out when I drained him. I'd hate to have to carry him home.

I stopped pulling on the wound, but I refused to release him from my jaws just yet. I still held him tight against me as my lips were on his neck, my fangs in his flesh, savoring the last red drops resting on my tongue.

"What the hell!" Eben's hissed surprise and admonition met our ears. I released Jaxon suddenly, being caught out, allowing him to pull back and bore his red eyes into mine while he ignored his brother. A drip of his blood slid down over my bottom lip, creating a red line down my chin. "You were supposed to just come and check on her, Jaxon!" Jaxon wore a smug look as he leaned over and, with his tongue, slowly licked the blood from my chin and lower lip.

His lusty eyes never left mine as he answered his brother, "I did come and check on her."

My bloodlust was quite thoroughly satiated for the moment, but the rest of me was still on fire. Despite that, my ability to think returned, and I remembered. Fear swept through my being with its icy grip, smothering out the flames burning more potent than ever before. Vladimir. If he knew. My pulse stopped entirely for a few beats before doubling down into the frantic fluttering of prey caught right before the kill strike would come. The brothers could hear it. They could smell the fear wafting out from me. I pushed Jaxon away and walked over to Blake's slumped body. I ignored the two brothers watching me, trying to figure out what I was so terrified of in their thoughts.

"Sasha?" Eben quietly asked, just loud enough for my vampire hearing to pick up over the music.

"I need to take care of Blake," I stated like that would satisfy his question. Jaxon whizzed in front of me, picking up Blake's limp body, and sped off with him into the bar, throwing his slumped body onto one of the benches of a back booth. He looked like he had had too much and was sleeping it off.

Eben turned to look at Jaxon's handiwork, allowing me to beeline out the back exit that led into an alleyway. I didn't stop; I sped my way through the shadows of Pine River, running back to the mansion, running from what I had just done.

I flew in the front door and down the hallway to my room, shutting the door behind me. Niklaus wasn't in his study as I had feared. He must be up in his room or with the twins, Lucy and Lucian. Good. I didn't need him coming after me. But the other brothers had. They were only a minute behind, coming down the hallway for answers. Oh god. If Vladimir got wind of this, he would come. Terror pulsed through my body. He would do much worse to me than kill me. Fear seeping out. He would snap Missy's neck and come to take me away. Trepidation.

"Sasha! Open up!" Jaxon growled, but it was Eben who opened my door. As the two brothers pushed their way into my room, Eben's sad, concerned eyes looked at me, looking down into my soul.

"No, you need to leave. Both of you. Get out." Eben's brow wrinkled with even more concern. He slowly approached me as Jaxon turned and shut the door; he didn't want Niklaus getting on his case. It took everything in me to hold my ground as Eben finally reached me.

"What are you so frightened of, Sasha?" My heart sped up again. His mind went to Niklaus since he was always scolding Jaxon, but he dismissed that as quickly as it had come. His eyes strayed to all around us for a moment, roving over the room we stood in and then back to mine with the answer. "Vladimir."

I swallowed with the truth discovered in his mind and spoken from his lips. Renewed fear seeping out of my pores confirmed his conclusion. I could feel Eben's anger at Vladimir, half rooted in what he saw in me and half in what Vladimir had done to him, to us all.

I could hear in his mind how the brother's close bonds had been forged in the beginning by the commonality of their creator but also the desire to not be like him or live life his way. Jaxon's mind repeated the sentiment. I could hear the same sense of closeness that they felt for me. The desire to protect one another from Vladimir was slowly drawing me into their fold; I was becoming 'one of them' in their minds. No. This had to stop, or I would never recover from it. I couldn't belong to their family in that sense. I belonged to Vladimir, and caring for the brothers would only bring trouble.

Eben's hands came to my shoulders, and his blue eyes were gentle as they delved into mine. And then I was afraid for a new reason as Eben slowly drew me to him. He was going to hug me. Kindness. That was almost as frightening as the idea of Vladimir coming for me. I shook my head at him, desperate to get away.

"No, Eben, don't." Eben paused as another knock at my door sounded. Eben's hands dropped from my shoulders at the sound. Oh no. Niklaus. That's all I needed; another concerned look aimed at me from Niklaus, now. What was with these brothers in this soft coven!?

"What's going on?" Niklaus asked through the door. He was concerned in his mind; he could smell the fear and blood and hear the brother's thoughts about Vladimir.

"Go. All of you, get out." I commanded weakly. I opened the door with my power but blocked Niklaus's entry. I pressed against the two brothers in my room, forcing them to back up towards the door. "You need to go, now." I released them, hoping they would make the choice to leave. They just stood there looking at me. Niklaus's worry. Jaxon's protectiveness. Eben's gentleness. "Please, leave," I asked, my voice breaking. I was cracking. My manifested armor was no match for the three of them. I had never been around men like this, ones who were concerned for my welfare instead of what they could get out of me and how they could use me.

"Sasha, what happened? What's going on?" Niklaus asked. His brothers' minds filled him in on what he had missed. His scowl aimed at Jaxon could have killed, when the attack and subsequent kissing were revealed. I watched his expression change to shock as he saw me feeding on Jaxon in his mind. Niklaus's eyes flitted to mine, and I set my jaw, drawing in a breath before looking away. And then came the fear and the truth of Vladimir.

"You can go over what happened with them in your study. You don't need to do it here in my room." My irritation with Niklaus's reaction strengthened my voice and helped me reign in the rest of my emotions that had almost slipped. It had been a close one.

I pushed at them again, forcing first Jaxon and then Eben towards the door. The moment was ended, and my armor had survived. I advanced, pushing them out of the door and into the hallway. I shivered from the resilient emotion of fear. They looked at me, and I looked at each of them in turn, ending with Eben in my doorway. God, those blue eyes were pleading with me. He saw the flash of mine softening before my hard mask returned.

"Good night." I closed the door and turned the lock, sending them all the blaring signal that it wasn't open for discussion. I leaned my forehead against the door and listened to their footsteps finally fall away. Eben stayed longer than the other two, but eventually, he followed.

I breathed a sigh of relief.

I closed my eyes, feeling the prick of tears that wanted to come. I had never felt so torn before. It was easy to keep your armor strong around men like Vladimir because they demanded it. My old master before Vladimir had never wanted to see what was truly below the surface. He had rescued me from certain death at a young age and trained me to be the controlling, manipulative bitch that I had learned to be. He had spent extensive time teaching me how to mold others around me, to do what I wanted them to do, and how to get my way so I could then serve his purposes in keeping his men in line when they needed it or peddling me out to reward them when he thought they deserved it.

I'd so rarely experienced such passion or genuine caring in my life as I had in the last hour. There had been a couple, one in particular, a very long time ago, but I had fled before he could get under my skin's steel facade, choosing to face Vladimir's wrath instead of staying to manipulate him. I couldn't stand what I had been doing to him back then, so I had run to save him as much as myself. Now, it was happening again, threatening my resolve. I had to build my walls back up; I knew the price of failure by fleeing, but I also knew that the ramifications would be indescribably worse if Vladimir ever discovered what had happened with Jaxon. I belonged to Vladimir.

I would have to clear things up with Jaxon to ensure that it would never happen again and that Vladimir wouldn't find out. The memory of Jaxon's tantalizing, spicy blood rolling over my tongue and his soft but demanding lips on mine had me flaming to life again. No. Never again. If I ever tasted him again, I would never be able to get enough. I wouldn't be able to stop. I wouldn't be able to stop myself at just him, either.

I had been dead inside when I walked through the manor door, but in only a few days, they had awakened something deep inside me. All three of them, with their caring way of looking out for you, were a temptation I hadn't anticipated. I hadn't anticipated having the ability to care for them. I hadn't anticipated wanting to. I hadn't anticipated that a touch could evoke such feelings inside of me. I hadn't anticipated wanting them. So much for self-control.

# CHAPTER 8

"Yes, Vladimir. That's right, a couple of houses on the outskirts of town. No, I was planning to check them out today to see what I could find out. Of course, I'm always careful. I wasn't planning on bringing any of them, no. MmmmHmmm." It was morning, and I was heading down the hallway toward the front door with the phone to my ear when I heard a disturbance from upstairs.

"What is that?" Vladimir asked me from the other end of the line.

"I'll call you back." Eben and Jaxon had already left for their classes for the day so that really only left two options. Following the screaming, I walked up the stairs, and the problem became crystal clear. The twins were throwing one of their colossal fits, and the Governess was having trouble handling them again.

I walked into Lucy and Lucian's room and saw them throwing things at the Governess using telepathy, a lightning storm just below the ceiling of their room. The problem with the vampiric witch twins was that they had been turned too young in Vladimir's haste for power, and now their power was left aggravated by the aggression of our kind. It was why he had sent them here in the first place, hoping his "soft" coven could 'tame' them. I rolled my eyes.

"You little selfish brats!" The Governess screamed back at them, throwing a stuffed animal at Lucian's face, enraging the little beast. Why Vladimir had been unable to wait and turn the children was beyond me. Perhaps he did have a father complex? It evaded me, but then again, he never had been a patient man; asking for a decade before securing their power would be asking too much.

Lucy and Lucian screamed their rage at the Governess, their eyes turning a vibrant red and fangs descending. Simultaneously, they sprang at the Governess, pouncing on top of her and knocking her to the floor, intending to bite her. The Governess was screaming and flailing, trying to avoid the multiple sets of eager fangs. The situation was amusing, and although I had no qualms

36

with feeding on humans, I knew the brothers would have serious issues if either of the twins fed on the Governess. That and it would probably cause other problems.

I sped across the room, grabbed two fistfuls of dark hair, and yanked just in time to prevent their fangs from sinking into the Governess's neck. Two loud snarling screeches ripped out of the twin's little throats, more vicious than any wild animal. I pulled them off of the Governess by their hair, baring my fangs, snarling at them even more viciously than they were. The Governess was screaming in the background, but I ignored her, focusing on the black and white gothic brats. My snarl quieted them, but they still struggled against my hold on the back of their heads.

I got a patronizingly friendly smile on my face as I said sweetly, "Now Lucy, now Lucian, is that any way for a little lady and gentleman like yourselves to act? Tsk, tsk." I shook my head at them, still wearing my smile.

Both of them struggled all the harder against my iron grip and hissed again, moving so they could bite me while screaming. I released them both and gave them each a swift slap across their faces simultaneously, shutting them up and effectively ending their attempt to bite me. The twins stopped their struggling, and both glared up at me.

I bent close to them and whispered, "The Governess is not on the menu and if you don't stop acting like a spoilt brats, a little hair pull will be the least of your problems." I batted my lashes at them, plastering my patronizing smile on again, "Mmmmm-K pumpkins?" I looked between the two, holding my smile. Lucy and Lucian stared at me momentarily, then slowly nodded. I stood up straight, saying, "Now get ready for school. You're late and your tantrum has made your room a mess." A raised eyebrow had them skipping off to do as I said. Children recovered quickly, vampire or human.

I turned to the Governess, still lying on the floor in her pajamas. I looked her up and down, not saying anything.

"What is going on in here!?" Niklaus filled the doorway.

I turned to him, saying, "It's under control so long as the Governess doesn't go into shock. Excuse me." I pressed past him and started down the hallway. I heard Niklaus checking in with the Governess, helping her up and checking on her emotions using his telepathy. I walked back down to the entryway and dialed Vladimir.

"So?"

"It was a minor altercation between the Governess and your witch twins, but it's under control." I looked up and saw Niklaus coming down the stairs toward me. "No, Vladimir, I'll ensure it doesn't happen again. Yes, I'll head out soon to check out the first house. Yes, I'll call you when I return to the manor." I still couldn't call it 'home.'

Niklaus watched me from across the entryway, listening in on my conversation.

"You will be careful."

"Yes, Vladimir."

"Very good, my pet." Niklaus's eyebrows shot up at that, and I met his eyes. "Call me soon or I will visit you again," he warned. I closed my eyes, swallowing at the threat.

"Of course, Vladimir." I heard his breathy chuckle on the other end of the line.

"Perhaps I may anyway. I miss having you at my side, Sasha." Not good. My eyes flew open, and I swallowed again, steadying my voice before answering.

"You have Missy, and I am needed here, as you heard with the twins. You sound like you're going soft on me," I let my smile be heard through the line. He growled in response, which was what I wanted.

"Call me after you visit the house."

"Yes, Vladimir." The line went dead, and I dropped the phone from my face and took a deep breath.

My eyes went to Niklaus. He hadn't moved or looked away from me. I got a wary look on my face, absorbing the concern flowing out of him. He had gained much by listening in on that particular call. He walked toward me and I had to fight the desire to walk away from him; backing down was not the best way to maintain control of this household, so I stood my ground.

His moss green eyes were so intense, imploring me to confide in him as he asked, "What did Vladimir mean when he said he will 'visit' you, Sasha? Is he coming here?!" He stood next to me, so close he was looking down at me. What would the truth hurt in this instance? It might make Niklaus reevaluate Vladimir's power so he wouldn't bother me.

"Vladimir comes to me at night like this," I said as a translucent form of myself appeared next to us. Niklaus blinked in surprise and I backed away from him, making room for my translucent double to move in close to him. My physical hand reached out into the air, and the double did the same but made contact with his hand. I had the double take hold of his hand, raise it up, and lace its fingers with his. I could feel his palm on my physical one, heating it through our connection, as he could feel mine through the translucent image of me.

He gazed in wonder at the magic before him, forgetting momentarily about his concern with Vladimir coming to me. He looked into my double's eyes, and I looked back through them at him, in a sort of double vision that was strange; usually, you cast this image when you weren't present.

I closed my eyes to just see through my double's. I had my double reach up with her other hand and lightly touch the silver bullet around his neck, then wander to his neck to run its fingers through a section of his chin-length hair.

"Niklaus." The ghosted image whispered to him as I thought his name.

Slowly, he reached out with his free hand, fascinated, and touched the cheek of the image there. His fingers went through the image somewhat as it wasn't truly a full physical force, but I could feel the tingling caress on my real one. I watched his eyes shift to the real me, and suddenly, his mind remembered that he had asked about Vladimir. I opened my real eyes to meet his and let the ghosted image fade away.

"Now, if you'll excuse me. I have somewhere I need to be." I walked to the front door, but he caught my hand and pulled me back.

"You mean he comes to you that way and can physically touch you, speak to you, even though he is halfway across the world?"

"It is the same as what I just showed you, though it is exponentially more difficult and less effective when he is this far away from me. It can't be maintained very long and the touch is always lighter than what you felt. I need to go," I pulled on my arm, but he wouldn't let me go.

"How? I didn't realize he was so powerful as that. Why would he not use it to check up on us then?" I sighed, impatient with his questions.

"Because it is not so much him as it is me. He has a connection with me when he really concentrates on me and can cast his image there, through me in a way."

"Sasha, please come and sit and explain this to me," he pulled on my hand, and I gave in and followed him to his study. He sat me down on the couch, sitting next to me. I noticed he didn't release my hand. "What do you mean he casts it through you?"

"Well, it's difficult to explain, but basically, through his established mental connection with me, he uses my power as a mental beacon to cast the image."

"You're saying he has a hold over your mind?"

"In a way, but it's much less serious than that."

"How could it be not serious?"

"It's kind of like a dog being chipped if you will," I explained as he scowled at my example. "The chip is there, unseen, not controlling the dog or harming it, but it can be used for a simple function of storing information. Vladimir has a mental 'chip' there, if you will, that allows him to establish a connection with me for brief periods of time, checking up on me."

"Maintaining his hold over you." I said nothing in reply. "Sasha, how long does this connection last? Is it indefinite, or does it 'time out' after a while?" His intimate knowledge of the mind was evident.

"You are correct. It will fade, and eventually, the connection will be lost if he doesn't reestablish it."

"And how long does it last?" Niklaus asked.

"I'm not really sure. Vladimir would always sit me down a couple of times a month to link with my mind. The longest I've ever gone without him shoring it up was a month."

"And how long has it been since the last time he connected with you?"

"He has to be with me, so maybe a week?"

"Does it bother you?"

"The actual link? No, because I can't sense it until he uses it."

"No, when he *visits* you. What does he do?" The wary look returned to my face. I couldn't hold his gaze and looked down away to the side. He was waiting me out. I sighed, irritated with his silent persistence.

I didn't want to talk about this, but Niklaus's patience was wearing down my resolve. What could I say about Vladimir's visits? That he touches me just enough to remind me that I belong to him? That he steals a kiss when he is pleased and slaps me when he isn't? The thought made me squeeze my eyes shut and wince in pain. Niklaus saw it. His gentle hand slid onto my face, raising my face so I would look at him.

"Yes, it bothers me when he *visits,* but that is his purpose, reminding me that I belong to him." He looked into my eyes for a long moment, trying to draw conclusions without insights into my mind.

"Would you like me to remove it, Sasha?" His offer had me sucking in my breath, surprising me. It unsettled me so much that I dropped my hard exterior because the infection of hope entered my mind.

"You could do that?"

"I think so if you would let me in." If I let him in, I wouldn't be able to stop him from discovering whatever he wanted about me. It was too risky. He saw the fear in my eyes and spoke softly, "I won't go snooping, I promise. I'll only move through what I must to find and destroy the link."

"You can't Niklaus. He would know. If he thought for one second that you had removed it he would be here on the next plane. Removing it would be very bad for all of us. I'll just have to deal with it."

"What if I didn't remove it, Sasha? I believe I could simply locate it and weaken it to the point that he will experience it like it's just faded, timed out, after a short while."

"He may want to come for real then." Niklaus thought for a moment.

"Do you think you could convince him he didn't need to?"

"He was planning on having me just check in more often once it happened, but not needing to move to that so soon. Maybe. Probably. Yes. I've never been this far from him, so perhaps he will believe it is because the distance puts extra strain on the link. He's used me mainly in Europe."

"Do you want to be free?" Free? I would never be free of Vladimir. But I could put some distance there for a treasured time.

"Ok."

Niklaus reassured me with his eyes as his hands came up to gently hold my head, centered over my temples. I took a deep breath for courage and then let him in.

# CHAPTER 9

My eyes closed as I felt Niklaus enter my mind, his warm, soothing hands on my head. My lips parted with a silent sigh as my mind was no longer protected from his calming, reassuring gift. He was looking at my mind as a whole, probing for any mild flavor of Vladimir's presence. The difficulty was that Vladimir was a part of me in many ways. He had stolen me from my previous master, wanting me for himself.

"Where would he hide the link, Sasha?"

"I honestly don't know." Niklaus pressed into my mind toward my memories of Vladimir.

"Don't resist me, Sasha," Niklaus whispered. I had pulled back mentally from him, fearing what he might see. I sighed and relaxed, giving in.

The image of the first time I had seen Vladimir came to the surface. I was transported back to the ball thrown by my master. He had radiated power to match my own, even from across the great hall, drawing my eyes instantly to his dark, smoldering countenance as he observed the fanfare around him with disinterest until his eyes landed on me. His eyes were blacker than the night, complimenting his ebony hair and symmetrical masculine features set with confidence and an agelessness I had yet to recognize for what it was. He was timeless, powerful in essence and frame, and the most beautiful man I had ever seen.

Vladimir crossed the ballroom, staring at me as I stood behind my master's throne on the dais. My master considered Vladimir an ally at the time and reluctantly granted his request to dance with me. I waited until my master stood from his throne, coming to unlock the chain connected to the collar around my neck. And then Vladimir held out his hand as I descended the steps, his mind revealing his immediate decision to make me his. My hand slid into his and he twirled me away onto the floor, unable to look away from me, enraptured with me. The memory faded as Niklaus moved further into my memories of Vladimir, searching.

Another memory surfaced, transporting me to Vladimir's home in Europe.

"I can't, Vladimir! I won't go back to him. I can't do this to him!" Vladimir's marble hand crashed into the side of my face, sending me sprawling to the floor.

"You will do as I say, Sasha. He is an important part of my business deal with Darius. The wolf was the price, and you will return to set the trap, to finish making him care for you so he comes."

"No." Vladimir drug me up by my hair, snarling in anger.

"You will never forget the price for telling me 'no,'" he promised as he sent me sprawling to the floor again, and then he reached down and dragged me from the room by the hair as I screamed. The memory faded as I gasped where I sat on the couch.

"Hang with me, Sasha. We are getting close. I can feel the link just a little more," Niklaus reassured me.

Another memory played, a more recent one.

"If you will agree to my terms, then we have a deal," Vladimir said as he stood before me.

"I have your word? You won't make me do that anymore?"

"Yes, you have my word, but there is something I need you to take care of for me first."

"Vladimir," it was a frustrated and impatient tone.

"It shouldn't be too hard for you. I want you to go to Pine River and fix the problems with my coven of 'soft' sons. The Cavaliers have a strong presence there." Groan.

"Can't you just call?"

"No, I need the best on this. Go, fix things, and then come home to me, and I promise you, I will make good on our bargain."

"Alright. When do I leave?"

"Tomorrow." I turned to leave his office, but Vladimir stopped me.

"Take this with you to remind you of our deal," he said, handing me a small black velvet pouch.

I could feel Niklaus's concentration as he mentally gasped at finding the link at that moment. He reached out with his mind to the link and weakened it considerably, just as the memory faded with me dumping something from the pouch into my waiting palm. I jerked my head out of Niklaus's grasp before the memory could complete itself.

Niklaus opened his eyes to look at me sitting close to him, breathing heavily. I swallowed down the emotions, but my eyes still turned glassy, and I shivered from the dread the memories had brought out in me. Niklaus's reassuring calm wrapped me up in a blanket of comfort, and for once, I welcomed it.

"Thank you, Niklaus," I whispered, meeting his eyes.

"You're welcome, Sasha. I'm sorry for Vladimir's treatment of you," he whispered back, gently stroking my cheek with the back of a finger. He wanted to hold me; he was practically aching to take me into his arms and comfort me.

Oh no. Not again. I felt my walls beginning to crumble a little with his kindness. I stood suddenly, needing to escape him, heading for the door.

"Sasha." My back stiffened at him saying my name.

"Yes?" I asked, not looking at him.

"It's ok to let people in once in a while."

"Only for people who are free to care, Niklaus." I looked at him then. "For those of us who drag around our invisible shackles with us, caring is like a poison, one that seeps in, debilitating our ability to deal with the reality of those shackles that we have to face. You and your brothers would seep into my life if I let you, and then I would still have to return to Vladimir. No, Niklaus, it's dangerous to let others in, especially you and your brothers." I turned on my heel and left him sitting there thinking about all he had seen in my mind and my parting words.

I left the house, unable to shake the feeling of Niklaus's touch. He had touched me on more than just a skin level, and I was struggling to escape him. I had wanted to let him hold me as much as I had wanted to flee in that moment. A dangerous desire. But oh, how I ached to taste the comfort he wanted to provide, even if just for one moment, to know what it would be like.

I gave myself a mental slap to the face and turned my attention to my focus for the day; surveillance of the two houses that Blake had given me info on in his mind. I headed toward them to see what I could find out.

Later that day, I wandered back to campus. I needed to reconnect with Blake in case I needed him in the future. I had found him quickly and acted all delighted to see him, spinning some tale about a drunk hitting him that started a bar fight and about how the barkeeper had gotten me out of there quickly and into a cab to go home so I would be safe. He had bought my story and seemed soothed for the time being. We promised to see each other soon, right before some blonde had come up to us to pull him away from me.

I had snorted in amusement before walking through the parking lot to head home. Jaxon had been there, ushering some other blonde into his car. I was torn between feeling irritated over it and relieved he was doing as I had asked and wasn't going for the Governess.

I returned to the manor, closing myself in my room to give Vladimir his promised phone call. He picked up immediately.

"What do you have for me?"

"Hello to you, too."

He gave a quick laugh and said, "Alright. Now, what have you found out about the Cavalier houses?"

"They are occupied by small groups of Cavaliers and are used at outposts to their main campus where they do more *shady* activities like interrogations."

"How do you plan to proceed?"

"I think I'll just start making the Cavaliers themselves disappear, one by one, thinning their population. The operations are done mostly by men, so it shouldn't be a problem."

He almost growled but said, "Very well. How will you pick them off?"

"I'll use the houses to watch and select targets before seeking them out in the local nightlife as I can. I'll lure them away and use them as my source of needed blood. Two birds with one stone."

"Don't bring attention by leaving bodies around my town, Sasha." His arrogance knew no bounds. He had covens stashed all over the world, and simply by having one in a given place, he believed that place belonged to him. I doubt the local covens or packs would agree. Even his own coven didn't, not this coven.

"I know how to make the bodies disappear, Vladimir. You taught me that. I just need to gain some information on where I could dispose of them, and I'll be good to go." A growl of approval this time.

"When do you start?"

"Tonight. There are a few bars that I will peruse tonight, looking for familiar faces."

"No funny business, Sasha. Stick to draining them." I rolled my eyes. Like I would be interested in human men anyway. Little did he know the biggest threat was inside his very own coven house, in the form of his three 'soft sons.' I couldn't help taunting him a little, though.

"Don't inhibit my appetite for fun, Vladimir. I need to get *something* out of the whole affair." A snarl. Mmmmmm touchy.

"Remember who you belong to, Sasha. I didn't take you from your last master who handed you out like a party gift, just to have you out messing around." This time, it was me who snarled at him, making him laugh.

The line went dead, and I put the phone down momentarily before using it to call another number. He picked up, surprised, and I asked my favor.

That night, I put on a deep purple dress that showed off my curves, hugging them in just the perfect way. I was the lure and the bait for my quest to make at least one Cavalier disappear that night. I put my hair up in a lovely updo, slipped on some jewelry and stilettos, and left the manor for the bar I had been at with Blake. It was already dark out as I slipped inside.

Instantly, the spicy aroma of Jaxon accosted my senses. He was here *again!* His smirk at seeing me cross the bar to him only widened the closer I got.

"What are you doing here? Are you following me?" I accused him in a low voice so others couldn't hear.

He smiled, and an arm snaked out around my back to pull me up against him. My hand instinctually landed on his shoulder as I bumped up against his hard frame.

He leaned in close, still smirking with those beautiful amber eyes, and teased, "I was here first, which means you're following me, Sugar Lips." His eyebrow shot up as he said, "Maybe you decided you want another taste?" I smiled back at him, playing his game, and slid the hand on his shoulder to his neck to pull his face close. Our faces were almost touching as we looked at one another.

I whispered through my smile, "Not on your life." And then I reached up quickly with my free hand, pulled the hat he was wearing down over his eyes, and freed myself from his grip. He laughed in enjoyment as much as frustration.

I left him standing there and went and sat on a stool at the bar to wait. I couldn't get Jaxon's spicy blood off my mind, so when the barkeep asked what

I would have, I ordered a stiff bloody Mary. I took the first draught and played with my straw while waiting. I smelt him as he entered and came up behind me, but I didn't turn.

A warm pair of hands slid around my waist to the front and wrapped me up in a pair of strong arms as his face came to my ear, saying, "You called?" I turned my face to look at him and smiled. He wanted to kiss me, his mind weighing how much he would suffer from it later. I reached out and touched his face, angling my head slightly to brush my lips against his for the briefest moment.

I heard him sigh before he drew a deep breath and pulled away to slide onto the barstool beside me. He was in a suit, having come from working late on campus. My vampire hearing had also picked up a noise of intense surprise followed by a low growl from across the room. Jaxon had each arm slung over a girl, but he still reacted to me being touched. I ignored him and angled my stool to face Sebastian. He ordered himself a drink before looking over at me.

"So what did you need, Sasha?" I waited until the bartender gave him his drink and wandered down to the other end of the bar, away from our secluded corner. I spoke with a low voice his werewolf hearing would be able to pick up.

"I need some information. You run the surrounding woods, and I'd like to know the best place or places to start stashing bodies."

He growled and got up to leave, but I caught his arm and pulled him back down, saying, "Hear me out before assuming I'm going to be randomly draining the town." He reluctantly sat back down and crossed his arms, giving me a disapproving look. "I'm going to be thinning the Cavaliers, starting tonight, and will need places to put them that their comrades won't discover." His disapproving scowl softened and then turned to one of concern.

"Is this Vladimir's doing?" I rolled my eyes at him.

"The only reason I'm here at all is because of Vladimir. He doesn't like them running around his town unchecked, and it's not like he expects his soft coven to go to war with them. My understanding is that they're too preciously gifted in his eyes and value human life too much for much more than self-defense. I'm going to thin the population. Will you help me?"

"This is a bad idea. They're dangerous, Sasha." I simply stared at him in askance. He sighed, saying, "You got a map?" I slid my phone to him and moved closer to him so we could talk.

Another low growl, too low for even the humans next to him, came out of Jaxon as Sebastian's arm slid around my hips, and he picked up the phone with the other. Might as well lay it on thick to piss the blonde vampire off. I put my arm around Sebastian's neck, slid between his gapped knees, and sat on his thigh. Sebastian gave me an amused smile, half-irritated and half-humored.

He whispered in my ear, too quiet for anyone else, "Why exactly are you trying to piss off the Bathory, and why are you using me to do it? Not that I mind, Sasha. I've missed you." I knew I was walking a line with him; I didn't want to actually hurt him again.

"He cost me a meal the other night and deserves it." He laughed and pulled me up higher on his lap. A hushed snarl from across the room made us both smile.

# CHAPTER 10

Sebastian entered several places in my phone, enjoying irritating Jaxon with his hands on me simultaneously.

"There you go, that should get you started," he said, handing me my phone.

I tucked it away on my person, smiling at him, saying, "I don't suppose you want to go dig the holes for me, too?" He laughed in my ear.

"Mmmmm, then you'd owe me."

"Careful, Seb," I said, stroking his face. "One might think you want to play with fire again." He looked at me with a feral grin.

"Want me to stick around?"

"I have to hook a Cavalier, sorry."

He laughed, "I won't interfere."

"Some other time. Thanks, Seb."

"You owe me a ride." Jaxon's snarl was a little louder on that comment.

"I'll let you drive me home on your Harley some other time, Seb. I'll be busy tonight. Actually, how about you pick me up after I'm finished?"

He stood, "Alright, Sasha." He bent and kissed my cheek before dropping a bill for his drink. "See ya soon." And with that, he left, much to Jaxon's relief.

I finished my drink and scanned the bar. There were two Cavaliers that I had spotted at the house. One was around a table laughing with his buddies over the sports score on the TV. The other, a rather good-looking man, sat at the bar sipping scotch, facing the dance floor. Bingo.

I walked over to the dance floor, molding into the crowd dancing there, joining in on the collective rhythm of dancers. I strategically positioned myself in his line of sight. I ignored him for a couple songs, dancing to show off my curves. I heard Jaxon's mind as he watched and looked around to determine who my target was. He figured it out when my eyes lifted to briefly peruse the man. The man was looking at me and I met his eyes for a second. I then turned and ignored him for another song. A sensual song with deep bass rolled out over the dance floor, and I started moving my body, looking up at him again,

47

calling to him like a siren.

His eyes were dark and dilated as he looked at me. I looked at him again then, traveling the length of him and meeting his eyes. An alluring smile and I turned to him, openly flirting. He smiled back, and I set the hook, angling my head in challenge.

He came to me slowly, reading the signals I was sending him. He was tall and broad with dark red hair and handsome features. His wranglers and t-shirt did him credit. I would enjoy this hunt. He reached the edge of the dance floor, and I started dancing toward him, flashing him a smile. He gave me an appreciative smile and moved in close. We danced near each other for a minute before I slowly reached up, running a hand up his arm to settle on his shoulder, smiling.

He accepted the inviting touch and reached out to me, capturing my waist to dance together to the pulsing music. We danced, slowly getting closer and closer until our bodies were pressed up against one another, and I wrapped my arms around his neck. One of his hands wandered up my back, and the other slid low to settle on my ass. I caressed the back of his neck with my fingers, looking at him with desire.

His leg slid between mine as he leaned into my ear and whispered, "Want to get out of here?" I pulled back to smile at him in a naughty way.

We turned and started heading to the exit with his hand on my lower back, guiding me out. Jaxon caught my eye as we made our way out of the bar. His chin came up, and his eyes were hard. A corner of my mouth tugged up in response before I turned and left with the man. The man guided me to his car and helped me in.

"Your place or mine?" the Cavalier asked. I gave him a smile that hinted that I liked it kinky.

"Let's go park somewhere in the woods." He flashed an approving smile and took off out of town.

We made it off onto a secluded dirt road in record time, and he parked at an old, abandoned campsite. He turned the car off and the lights and turned toward me. I gave him a feral grin and leaned over, giving him a good view as I reached the lever to lay his seat back. I crawled over to straddle his seat, sitting on him as his hands came to my thighs, pushing my dress up. His touch did absolutely nothing for me, but I faked my enjoyment. I leaned down, kissing him, sucking his lip into my mouth until he moaned and cupped my breast with his hand.

I let his hands wander as I worked him up with my kisses.

My lips went to his ear, "I'm going to bite you, big boy, and you're going to like it." He sighed his approval and turned his head as my teeth lightly nipped down to my goal.

My fangs descended as I located his pulsing carotid. I bit down, and he moaned, being so overwhelmed with pleasure that his little Cavalier brain couldn't process that a vampire was feeding on him. Draw after draw, I took from him until he started to weaken. By the time he realized something was wrong, it was too late. I held him down, finishing him off as his blood entered my system. I felt his life go out as he dried up, and I pulled back. How disappointing; his blood was bland compared to the blonde vampire I had sampled last.

I flopped his body onto the passenger seat and drove farther into the woods toward a site Sebastian had marked out for me. I carried his body there and buried it deep. I then drove the car two towns over on the highway and pushed it over a dam outside the town. Brushing my hands off, I called Sebastian to come pick me up, telling him where to meet me.

Sebastian pulled up on his bike, a classic Harley Cruiser. I noticed he had changed out of his suit into tight jeans and a leather jacket. I openly admired him, flashing him a smile, which he returned. He held my hand as I hopped on the bike behind him. I wrapped my arms around him, and he took off, opening up the throttle once we reached the highway.

I held him close as we zipped by the two towns and slowed upon entering Pine River. He drove up to the estate mansion and steadied the bike with his legs so I could climb off. The bike idled under him as he looked at me for a second.

I approached him, and he wrapped an arm around my legs, "So, were you successful then?"

"One down, 349 to go." He laughed.

"That's pretty exact," his other hand came to the side of my face.

"Small goals, right? Thanks for the ride, Seb."

"Anytime."

"Really? You dying to be an accomplice that much?"

"The Cavaliers are a problem for all of us, Sasha. I'm game to help."

Just down the long driveway, a white form was walking toward the mansion. Jaxon's mind hardened when he saw me there with Sebastian. Sebastian smiled at me, smelling Jaxon just like I could.

*"Wanna make him mad?"* His mind teased. I smiled at him, nodding. Jaxon was going to regret stealing my prey.

Sebastian pulled me close, grabbing my ass with both hands, closing any gap between us. I grabbed his face with both hands and kissed him from above, inserting my tongue into his mouth, ravishing him. It worked, and Jaxon was raging in his mind. I pulled away before Jaxon could reach us.

"Night, Seb. Thanks for the *ride.*"

Sebastian laughed and took off on his bike before the seething vamp could reach us. I ignored Jaxon and walked toward the mansion's sprawling porch. I could feel his angry steps close behind me. He followed me all the way to my room. I shut the door behind me, but he just burst inside.

"If you think Vladimir is mad about that wolf running around our property, what will he do when he finds out you're fooling around with him?" Jaxon asked me. I flashed him a patronizing smile and laughed.

"Vladimir doesn't need to know, Jaxon. You go ahead and tell him and see what happens. You want Vladimir here less than me, so go ahead and call." He walked up to me.

"How do you even know Sebastian? You couldn't possibly be that close from just one visit to his office the other day."

"Seb and I go way back. We have history and possibly a little bit of future, too."

Jaxon snarled and reached for me, but I evaded him and went to sit on my bed to take my heels off. He set his jaw and stormed over to me, not pausing before forcing me back on the bed with his body, settling on top of me. He looked at me for a long moment, smoldering, while his thoughts flamed at the knowledge that I had been taunting him.

"You're still pissed about that kiss, huh? Wanting to punish me for it?" He jeered. I smiled at him.

"You stole my meal in the middle of bloodlust; you deserve it. Now get off of me and out of my room." He didn't move, so I shoved at him. His smirk captured his face. He started to bend his face to kiss me, but I covered his face with my hand and pushed him up and off of me, forcing him to stand. I released his face but used a hand on his chest to force him back and out of my room, shutting the door in his face.

"You wouldn't try to punish me that much just over a simple vein, Sasha," he whispered through the door before leaving. Damn, he was right. I resented that I desired him, that he had ruined others for me.

I changed and slipped into my nightgown, and flopped down on Vladimir's bed, smelling both the faded scent of him and the fresh waft of Jaxon. Damn him. I fell asleep, breathing him in.

Vladimir was there waiting for me in my dreams, in an assault on my mind in the form of memories. My drudged-up memories from earlier and the evening spent with Sebastian had my tortured mind focusing on the memory of returning to Vladimir, telling him I wouldn't manipulate Sebastian any longer. My nightmare picked up where my memory had faded last time, Vladimir dragging me from his office by my hair while I screamed in pain.

Vladimir dragged me through several rooms of his castle into a room with no windows and only one door. Vladimir threw me to the center of the room by my hair as he removed his jacket and shirt. He stood over me, his glowing red eyes burning with anger like never before. He tore my clothes from me and suspended me from several large meat hooks on chains from the ceiling, using the skin on my back.

I screamed in my nightmare and in real life, sleeping on Vladimir's bed, the pain of my dream so real. My arms were shackled out to the side of my body, and he used a dagger to slowly slice my wrists and other places on my body, bleeding me out slowly as his overwhelming power restrained any attempts to fight him. He pulled my hair, yanked my head back, and sank his fangs into my neck. His feeding purposely brought pain instead of pleasure, and I screamed again, a second scream echoing down the corridors of the mansion.

Somewhere in the stillness across the entryway, a violin melody stilled.

# CHAPTER 11

My nightmare raged through my mind, the memory of Vladimir's torturous cruelty drawing out cries and whimpering from me as I lay on his bed. I saw his red eyes glowing brighter as he pulled back from my neck after feeding, my blood running down his chin.

He didn't release my hair as he growled at me, "You will never forget the cost for telling me 'no,' my pet." And with that, he drove the dagger he had used to cut me open into my side, towards the back.

Another piercing scream rang out through the manor as my head flew back on the scream of agony in my memory.

"Vladimir, please!" He smiled cruelly at me and turned to walk across the room. I watched in dread as he removed the rest of his clothes and crossed back to me. He grabbed my hair as the tears began to flow down my face. And then he grabbed the knife, using it and my hair as leverage to force himself into my body.

"Sasha! Sasha, wake up!" I woke with a start, my eyes flying open wide with terror as my entire body trembled and streams of tears ran down my face. Eben's blue eyes were alarmed as he knelt by the side of my bed. A sob escaped me, and his gentle hand came to my face.

"Sasha, what is it? Did Vladimir come to you again? Was it a nightmare?" I closed my eyes and nodded. His other hand touched my shoulder in concern, and he could feel me trembling from head to toe. His mind was taking in my state, wondering how a nightmare could evoke such a response in me. My haunted eyes revealed the truth, and he sighed, anger at Vladimir rising. I swallowed and wiped the tears rolling down my face with a shaking hand.

He released me, only to pick me up and move me over, sliding onto the bed next to me. I didn't have the emotional strength to fight him, so I let him wrap his arms around me and pull me close. His comforting touch had me closing my eyes. I breathed deeply, trying to calm my shaking as he held me.

Sweet Eben, even his scent was slightly sweet in the best way, like pure decadence. He shifted to lay on his back and pulled me with him to lay partially over his chest and shoulder, still holding me. My hands rested on his side and chest as my head settled in the crook of his neck. Slowly, his warmth soaked into me, and my breathing and trembling settled at last.

I took another deep breath, finally calming, breathing in his scent. I could see his vein pulsing, being so close to him. I knew that, like Jaxon, he would taste even better than he smelled, and for a moment, I was tempted.

Eben didn't say anything; he didn't have to as we lay there. I just accepted his comfort, enjoying the closeness my vulnerability forced on me. I reached out and gently hugged his chest, showing my appreciation, and he responded with a light kiss on the top of my head. I closed my eyes at the caring touch so foreign to me.

"You're safe, Sasha," he whispered in the dark. Safe for the moment. "Sleep, I'll wake you if you begin to have another nightmare." I sighed and closed my eyes, drifting off to sleep in his arms.

I woke in the same place, having slept soundly for the rest of the night. I pulled myself up to look at him. His eyes were kind as they looked at me. I swallowed, suddenly feeling guilty for accepting his comfort.

"Eben, thank you," I said, looking down, embarrassed. I had never let anyone in like that before, and I was uncomfortable.

He said nothing, but I could feel him looking at me. His mind was seeing me, into me, and for the first time in my life, the raw, miserable creature in me was laid bare before another. He had seen the tortured, frightened, trembling little girl that lay within during the night, and she was there under my blushing cheeks as well. Underneath it all, he saw himself in the pain that Vladimir had brought on us both.

I closed my eyes at his thoughts and felt him raise my face to look into my eyes. I opened them, black and glassy from unshed tears, and his blue ones caressed my face with a glance. He stroked my face with his thumb, drawing out a sigh from me as my eyes closed again. So this was tenderness. He drew my face to his, resting his forehead against mine as he slid his hand around to cup the back of my head. I trembled again, but not from fear this time; my heart started to bleed. I had to pull away, or I wouldn't be able to recover from this; I had to get away from this man's touch who was a chink in that armor I wore. I opened my eyes, meeting his, and started to pull away.

"No, Sasha. Don't shut me out. You don't need to be alone anymore. We are all here for you," he whispered lightly, holding my head gently but firmly.

"Eben, I can't," I choked out as my hands on his chest shook.

"Real strength is carried here," he whispered again, touching my chest over my heart. A small sob escaped me, and my lips trembled. His hand returned to the back of my head, holding me close against his forehead again. We lay like that, Eben just giving me the time I needed to think about his words.

His mind revealed his past to me as we lay in silence. Eben had always been a loner, except for his brother, Ian, in his mortal life. Ian had been older, but their relationship had placed Eben in the protector role, defending his disabled brother. Eben had always been in tune with Ian's emotions and learned a manner of communicating with a person's soul from him, where words weren't required. Eben's giftedness in music also helped to soothe Ian when he would have dark episodes of despair. It was Ian's doctor who had pushed assisted suicide into Ian's head, and despite Eben's objections and pleas, Ian went ahead with the appointment. At the last moment, Eben could sense Ian had changed his mind, but the doctor had refused to listen to Eben. Ian's unnecessary suicide, now murder, had sent Eben into a dark rage where he had murdered the doctor and fled. The taste of murder, death, and despair had haunted him ever since, giving him a deep hatred for any authority pushing things on another. Just like Vladimir had on him only days after crossing his path on the run. Just like Vladimir had on me.

I sucked in a breath and ran a hand up his chest and neck to cup his face for a second, and then I swept his black hair to the side.

"I was wrong about you, Eben." He looked at me, surprised. "You are going to be the most difficult brother to handle in this house." He gave me a smile as he laughed and stroked my cheek. My eyebrows wrinkled at the touch, the gentle, loving touch. "Eben," I shook my head, trying to reject his tenderness again.

"So stubborn," he whispered in response. Now he had me laughing? How was I going to resist this dark angel? I started to pull away again. He gave me a scowl and tightened his hold on the back of my neck gently.

Eben silenced my complaint when his lips gently met mine, carrying me away on the most tender, slow-burning kiss I had ever experienced. My hand on his face gently slid up into his black hair. My heart bled for him, for his gentle kiss. He pulled his lips from mine and rested his forehead against mine again, resting in the moment.

What was I going to do now? I had let him in and was bleeding out, unable to stop the change that swept over me. How was I ever going to go back to Vladimir after tasting this?

"Sasha, what was your nightmare of?" He gently asked, looking into my eyes. I swallowed.

"It was a memory, actually. The memory of what Vladimir did to me the one time I dared to tell him 'no' to something. He had told me I would never forget the price for doing so, and he was right." I closed my eyes in pain.

Eben rubbed my back, comforting me again. I could hear his heart breaking for me. For me. Breaking for me. He pulled me into him, laying his cheek on my head and wrapping his arms around me.

I clung to him, breathing him in again, and my eyes fell on his neck. I swallowed, so tempted. I reached out and touched the throbbing vein just below his soft skin. I wanted to taste him.

He gave a breathy laugh at my touch and whispered, "Thinking about using me as a pacifier, are you?" I could hear his teasing and sat up on an elbow to look at him. That mischievous look was back. I smiled back at him and laughed.

"Thinking about it, yeah. Sorry," I admitted. Eben's look stayed as he gently pulled my lips to his again with a finger under my chin. This kiss was still gentle but held a heat the first hadn't; smoldering passion had me sighing into his mouth, granting him entry, as he ran his fingers up into my hair. He pulled back and looked at me, his blue eyes darker than before.

This secret side to Eben lulled me into a sense of peaceful intimacy. He pulled me onto his chest, stroking my hair. How had this happened? How had I gotten here, laying on Eben's chest in such a tender, intimate moment? His eyes studied me a little, deciding his thoughts about letting me taste him that way. Listening to him had my thirst rising, and my eyes lit up red, burning with a growing need. Eben looked at me, taking in my eyes with fascination, as his response matched my own. Eben was a gentle, sensual vampire, but he was still a vampire.

His qualms with feeding on people didn't really extend to other vampires; it was more the intimacy that he was weighing. There really was no going back from that. Just like I couldn't get Jaxon's spicy blood off my mind, we both knew I would crave Eben if I fed on him. I also knew it would break the dam for my self-control concerning him and his brothers.

A wariness mixed with the desire in my crimson eyes. It was too late. I'd already let Eben in and would never be the same. I should have run when I had the chance. I closed my eyes and let him hear my thoughts. I would leave the decision with him.

His arms tightened around me, bringing me to his lips for another smoldering kiss. And then, with his eyes locked on mine, he ever so slowly tilted his head to expose his neck to me. I looked intensely at him to make sure he was serious. A rub up my back was all the encouragement I needed. I took a moment to kiss my way down his neck, making him murmur a little. His pulse was throbbing in anticipation under my lips. My fangs descended, pressing their points into his neck, and he sucked in a breath. My hand came to the other side of his neck, and then I bit down.

His head fell back at my first draw, and his arms tightened against me. I added more pressure to his neck with my hand as his blood hit my tongue, moaning with exquisite pleasure.

I had been right; he tasted better than he smelled. Eben was the most perfect dessert I had ever tasted; a perfect balance of sweet and rich. I would never be satisfied with any other sweet-blooded person again. I fed on Eben in a slow, savoring way compared to the fast and hard feeding I had taken from Jaxon at the bar. I wasn't going to cheapen this moment between us by being animalistic. Eben's soft sighs and moans met my ears as I took my time with his decadent essence. I pulled back and looked at him.

"You've ruined me, Eben," I whispered to him. He pulled me to his lips, kissing the blood off of mine. The kiss deepened as a smoldering but intense heat of desire built up inside of me. This was only the third man I had ever kissed in my hundreds of years who had awakened this type of hunger inside me.

Eben rolled us over without breaking our kiss, pressing me down into the soft bed. My hands traveled down his torso to hook under the bottom of his shirt and pull it up over his head, revealing his trim waist and beautiful chest. My eyes briefly took in the black ink tattoos on his upper arms, shoulders, and chest. He was beautiful. My nails dug into his back as I held him to me, sighing his name, riding the waves of deep need and pleasure that were rising up in me.

Such passion was foreign to me. Even my time with Sebastian had been limited by the shield I had kept in place, but Eben had broken through, tearing down every ounce of distance I had put up between me and others. This dark angel had ruined me utterly; each kiss and tender caress destroyed more and more of my armor. His hands gently pulled my nightgown up, bunching it below my breasts, and he bent to freckle kisses over my stomach. I gasped, burying my fingers into his soft, dark hair and dragging him back up to my mouth. He kissed me and moved down to my neck, and then I felt it. A single fang point pricking my neck as he went still, resting his lips on my neck, waging the war to sample me for himself or not.

I felt him move, preparing to bite down when a shrill ringing from Vladimir's cell phone filled the room as the phone buzzed on the nightstand.

# CHAPTER 12

I had to answer the call; there was simply no choice in the matter. Eben sat us up and I reached for the phone, bringing it to my ear as Eben stayed silent.

"How did last night go?" Vladimir demanded. He was asking about the Cavalier, but my mind wandered to how I had slept in Eben's arms.

My eyes met Eben's as I answered, "Perfectly." Eben's eyes softened, and he reached out to pull me onto his lap, leaning back against the headboard to hold me while I talked with Vladimir.

"Were you able to dispose of the body, then?"

"Yes. I had a local source on where to hide the bodies that will shortly be piling up. One down."

"You will go out again tonight." It was a command, not a question.

"Yes, Vladimir." I closed my eyes as Eben's gentle hold tightened a little.

"Very good, my little minx. You followed my instructions?" He was referring to not 'playing with my food.'

"Yes."

"Good. Never forget that you are mine, Sasha." I could feel Eben tense below me, working hard to hold back a growl that threatened to escape. I looked at him and put a finger to his lips. I didn't reply to Vladimir. I just waited to see if he would say anything else. "Report in earlier next time." I looked at the clock, and it was almost 11am. I had lost track of time with Eben.

"Yes, Vladimir." The line went dead, and I returned the phone to the nightstand.

I released a heavy, frustrated sigh and lay down on Eben's bare chest. My heart was aching. I hugged Eben, and he hugged me back.

"What instructions did you follow?" I sighed and sat up to look at him, getting an ironic smile on my lips.

"He instructed me not to 'play with my food,' if you will."

Eben's mischievous look returned, and he pulled me to his lips, savoring me. I ran a hand down his torso to his waistband and then back up, actually making him growl lightly. His hands began gathering my nightgown up to pull it up over my head when another interruption sounded with a knocking on my door. I heaved another impatient sigh. Eben groaned, letting his head drop back against the headboard, thunking, as he pouted. I laughed at him before getting up to go see who was at the door.

I opened the door only wide enough for half of my body. Jaxon stood there, smoldering at me.

"Yes?" I asked with a bit of sass. "Need something?" His eyes sparkled at my question, and he moved up closer.

"Well, I came to see if you knew where Eben was because I needed to confirm if we were going out tonight, but if you're offering something else, I'll bite." His eyes traveled down my nightgown, returning to my face with a suggestive eyebrow raised.

I glared at him momentarily before an evil grin spread across my face. In his mind, he thought I might actually be taking him up on his proposition before I stepped back, opening the door wide enough for him to catch sight of a half-naked Eben lounging on my bed.

Jaxon's chin dropped in shock, then pushed into the room, snarling at his brother as much as at me. I shut the door with a self-satisfied smile on my lips. Nothing could have goaded Jaxon more, and I hadn't even planned it. Eben remained impassive at first.

"You get on my case for kissing her at the bar and then this?" Jaxon almost shouted at him. Eben couldn't help but look away from his brother, go a little pink, bit his lower lip, and try to hide his half-smile. I walked up to Jaxon and got in front of him, poking a sharp finger in his chest.

"Leave Eben alone. He came to me when I was screaming from a nightmare and comforted me; he didn't interrupt me during bloodlust to steal some kisses."

Jaxon's look smoldered with desire, and he reached out to pull me up against him.

"And just how much comforting did he provide you with?" Eben's chagrin turned to irritation.

"Almost enough, but you interrupted us," was my bold, taunting answer. I purposely breathed into Jaxon's face so he would smell Eben's blood on my breath; Jaxon was irritating me. He looked at Eben's neck pointedly and snarled. I made a sound of amusement and pushed him away, even if his touch caused flames to lick up in my body.

"Go pick up your kicks from that bar you're going to tonight, Jaxon."

"Like you did with that Cavalier last night?" I saw Eben react slightly to that.

I huffed, irritated, and sarcastically drawled, "Jealous?"

Jaxon whipped me around up against him and claimed my mouth with his possessive, burning kiss. He backed me up to the huge black pole of the four-poster, demanding absolute cooperation with his speed. I heard a vicious snarl come out of Eben that surprised me. Vampire indeed. Jaxon held my wrists to his chest, holding me. I was burning up inside, hating that he had this effect on me. The problem was, before Eben, I had had my protections up, but now I was there in Jaxon's arms, unable to deny that I was attracted to him, that I was developing strong feelings for this flirtatious, demanding vampire.

Before Eben could even rise up off the bed to intervene, Jaxon pulled from my mouth and buried his fangs into the base of my neck. White hot pleasure burst inside of me, flowing from his lips on my skin there to engulf every fiber of my being. I couldn't prevent myself from fisting his shirt in my hands and moaning as my head slumped forward against his shoulder.

"Jaxon!" Another roar sounded from across the room, announcing Niklaus's presence. I barely heard his angry footsteps approach over the pleasure gripping my system.

Jaxon turned his face to Niklaus, releasing me from his jaws but not his arms. I gasped at the loss, still fisting his shirt. My lidded eyes lazily turned to Niklaus.

Niklaus pulled up short, his eyes landing on Eben, who stood up from my bed. There was enough of Eben's scent in the room and on the bed to make it obvious to any vampire that he had spent the night there with me, albeit tamely. He also had a little dried blood on his neck, and the scent of that, along with my fresh blood, was hanging in the air.

"WHAT is going on!?" Niklaus demanded, looking at the three of us, each in turn, ending with me. The fog of pleasure was just starting to clear, but I was still feeling drunk from it. I laid my head back against the post behind me with a naughty little smile on my lips, twinged with bitterness.

"Well, at least it's not the Governess this time, right, Niklaus?" I asked as I lifted my head to look at him.

It was a jibe at him as much as at the rest of us. Niklaus took a slow breath and then let it out slowly, calming down. He scowled at the three of us, crossing his arms, waiting for someone to say something.

"I guess you could say things have gotten," I paused, turning to look at Jaxon and then Eben, "Complicated." Jaxon turned to look at me with an admiring smirk. He appreciated that I didn't just fold and deny things under Niklaus's scrutiny. Niklaus's thoughts were irritated, but there was a twinge of something I couldn't place coming from him. Disappointment? But it wasn't the 'fatherly' disappointment based on actions. It was a disappointment that I hadn't opened up to him.

Niklaus was still waiting, arms crossed, scowling. I looked at Jaxon briefly, our faces close as he looked back. I gently pushed him back and turned to Niklaus.

"Do you want the long version or the short?" Niklaus glowered at me briefly, wishing he could read my mind. I saw his head tilt slightly, his eyes shifting to the side as he listened to his brother's thoughts. "I guess you'll get the long version silently," I stated.

Niklaus listened silently for a few moments, but I could hear the replay in his mind from both brothers, including what had happened at the bar. Niklaus's scowl intensified at Jaxon's piece of the equation before us, but it softened more and more as he listened to Eben's piece before it fell away completely.

I could hear Niklaus's mind remembering what little he had seen in my memories of Vladimir's treatment toward me when I had said 'no.' Eben's mind had revealed that my nightmare had been of that, and Niklaus's eyes softened as they looked at me. I couldn't hold his gaze and looked away. He approached me, holding my shoulders until I looked at him again. Jaxon had moved a step back, giving his brother room. He was the least clued in of all the brothers, only knowing I had had a nightmare.

"Sasha," Niklaus said softly, "Exactly what did he do to you?" He had heard my screams through Eben's memory of coming to me in the night. I started shaking my head, trying to pull away from him. "Sasha, please. Bearing things alone doesn't make you strong; it just makes you alone."

I looked down and away, whispering, "It can't be unseen, Niklaus. It's horrendous, shameful," my voice broke, and my cheeks flamed, "I don't want your pity."

"Empathy is not pity, Sasha. Vladimir has hurt us all in different ways. None of us understand your relationship with him. I only have tiny pieces from what I waded through in your mind."

"Then share those with your brothers, but don't ask to see this one. It's much worse than you can imagine, I'm sure." He squeezed my shoulders until I looked up at him.

"Try me." A shiver ran down my spine, and I closed my eyes, showing him the whole, complete memory from the argument in Vladimir's office to even beyond where Eben had woken me, days of extended torture and forcing himself on me. I didn't look at him or open my eyes.

I was gently enfolded in his arms as I felt a gentle probing at my mind; he begged me to let him in. I opened my eyes, looking at the silver bullet that hung next to my face. Taking a shaky breath, Niklaus's rich, savory scent filled my lungs as he held me. Eben's words about true strength challenged me to finally open my mind to Niklaus. His caring, soothing peace washed over me from head to toe, and I sighed, closing my eyes. I felt him mute me out of his mind and the others in the room for a brief couple of minutes, sheltering my mind from having to watch yet again. He was sharing with the other brothers all that he had seen in my mind both in the study and just now. I didn't need to hear the replay to know; the resounding snarls from the other two coven brothers were proof enough when Niklaus reached the nightmarish memory that Eben had awoken me from.

Oh, how my face burned while he held me. My instinct to pull away and hide overwhelmed me and I started pulling away from Niklaus. His calming aura intensified, and he started stroking my hair, calming me, reclaiming me to his chest.

"Sasha, look around you. You are not alone anymore." I closed my eyes with the sweet pain of his words. I wanted it so badly but the truth remained; I belonged to Vladimir.

"You really don't understand. None of you do. I belong to Vladimir."

Niklaus gave me a kind smile, still not comprehending, and then he planted a kiss on my cheek, only pulling back a short distance so he could look at me as he said, "Being controlled by Vladimir is not the same thing as belonging to Vladimir, Sasha. We have all been controlled by Vladimir at one time or another, but we don't really belong to him."

I felt sick. I reached up and ran my fingers through his hair, tucking it behind his ear while a sad smile crossed my face.

"Your words apply to you and your brothers, Niklaus, but they don't apply to me, I'm afraid." He made to protest, and I laid a finger across his lips, saying, "You don't understand."

I pulled out of his arms and walked into the bathroom, searching for what I needed to explain things to them all. I came back out of the bathroom and walked up to him. In my hands lay the black velvet pouch they had all seen in the cut-off memory.

"That's what Vladimir sent with you to remind you that you "belong" to him after whatever deal you made with him?" Niklaus clarified. I nodded at him.

Jaxon angled his body more towards me, and Eben walked over from the bed to join the circle to see. I looked down at the small bag resting in my open palm, and nausea swept over me, causing bile to rise in my throat. My heart was pounding, hard, and rapid. I was terrified to show them. I was falling for them, all three of them. They were as close as I had ever come to a family and each had shown me moments of love in their unique way. Niklaus's wisdom and concern. Jaxon's playfulness and protectiveness. Eben's sensitivity and gentleness.

Oh god, I was falling in love with something that could never be mine; they could never be mine. They all could hear my fear, smell it. I hadn't shut Niklaus out of my mind, but he had heard. His intake of breath at my admissions had the other brothers looking at him. He shared all that he had heard with his brothers, who seemed to move in closer to me, offering their presence as a comfort.

I looked down at the small black velvet bag resting in my hand, which felt like it weighed a ton. My hand went to my mouth to contain a gag before I reached down and grabbed the bottom corner of the bag, tipping it up and letting the object inside slip out into my waiting palm. All three brothers took a collective gasp at what they saw resting there. A cold, sparkling engagement ring.

# CHAPTER 13

Shock. Utter shock. Confusion. Deep-rooted anger at Vladimir. It all swirled together in the room from the three coven brothers standing around me, staring down at the ring in my palm. No one spoke for a long time. The question hung in their minds; no one could utter the words.

"You're Vladimir's Bride?" Niklaus, at last, spoke what they were all asking. I took a deep breath, exhaling before I could answer.

"Not yet." Relief. More shock. And then I felt the hurt.

"You're engaged to Vladimir?" Eben asked with a pained voice. I looked up to meet his sad blue eyes.

"Not right now. I will be once I have to return to him, or he comes to collect what's his." I had said the last with such bitterness and pain in my voice it trembled. They were still trying to process what all this meant. "Victor stole me from my previous master, rescuing me from him, but he too turned around to use me for his purposes, to further his hold over the underworld in Europe. He would send me all over the place to 'work my magic' and slowly build him an empire through manipulation, seduction, and," my eyes dropped down to the heavy ring in my hand before I finished, "and assassination." The brothers shuffled, anger at Vladimir mixing with grief for me. "I was his ultimate weapon for the underworld leaders, always kept hidden, secret, when I wasn't on a specific mission for him. It's how I know Sebastian so well. Vladimir had sent me to him to seduce him, making him fall in love with me so Vladimir could lure him out to pay a blood price to another associate."

"Then what was the 'deal' you made with Vladimir?" Niklaus asked, confused. I took another breath, dying inside as my freshly exposed heart bled.

"The deal was that he would no longer send me to do that to others, to be his weapon, but only if I became his Vampire Bride, his queen." I closed my eyes as the tears started streaming down my face, looking down at the eternal prison represented by the stone I held in my hand. I slowly took the ring and slipped it on my finger, trying it on for the first time. All three brothers stared at it, twinkling on my finger. I gagged again, bringing my other arm up to my lips to hold it in. Swallowing down the bile, I continued, "When 'I'm ready,' I'm supposed to start wearing it, and then he will no longer send me out to do his dirty work."

"But he came and took Missy. Why would he do that if he wants you?" Jaxon asked with anger in his voice. What could I say? How did I state the truth of the matter?

"Missy is just a plaything to pass the time, like the last one and the dozens before her. They are there to keep him amused until he tires of them. I have always been there; through the years, Vladimir has become 'attached' to me. As close as that monster can come to loving someone." My chest was starting to physically ache, and I crossed my arms over my body, trying to hold my heart together. "If. When I become his Bride, the deal was I become a more willing participant and don't resist him when he comes to me. I am to drink exclusively from his bitter, acrid vein. I -" My words cut off with a sob as my hands covered my face from the horror of it.

And then I was surrounded, on all sides, by pairs of strong arms offering their comfort. Niklaus and Eben each rested against a shoulder, and Jaxon at my back as I cried. And now they knew. I now feared they would leave me to Vladimir's mercy. Forever was a very long time to be the Bride of an evil tyrant like Vladimir. Especially now that my heart had been touched, beating and bleeding for the taste of love that I had sampled. How could I ever return to Vladimir now? I couldn't. Not alive. I had this time here, but then I would be his; his forever. Unless.

"Sasha! No." Niklaus had heard. He grabbed my wrists and pulled my hands away from my face. I looked up at him through my tears. He turned me to him and brought his hands to gently hold my face.

"Don't ever think that again. Not ever. We have some time. All is not lost. We will find a way." And then he smiled a smile so beautiful my breath caught as he leaned in close to whisper, "You are not alone anymore. We would never abandon you to Vladimir without fighting for you first." My eyes closed at his words washing over me, my lips parting at the thought of being with them instead of Vladimir. My heart ached. I should never have let them in; it would have been so much easier if I had never even - My train of thought was silenced as Niklaus's lips met mine.

A sigh so full of a myriad of things escaped me; surprise, peace, desire, longing, love. He released my lips, and I slowly opened my eyes to look at him. He was trying to judge my reaction, listening in on my mind. I reached up to lay a hand on his face to look into his eyes, and then my gaze fell to the ring there. My face contorted from the mask of peace and love to a pained and destitute one.

I drew in a breath and removed myself from his arms, backing away from the three of them. I frantically ripped the ring from my finger, stuffing it back in the black velvet pouch, walking away to stash it back in its place in the bathroom.

I splashed water over my tear-streaked face before returning to them. I stood there, looking at the floor, but inside, I was frantically working to build my wall again. The hard set of my jawline was the only evidence of it. I was destroyed inside, so raw, and trying to rebuild my emotional wall was like trying to build with hands that had the skin burnt off of them. I shut Niklaus out of my mind.

"Sasha, don't," Niklaus pleaded, but it was Eben that came to me. He raised my chin with a finger, making me look up into his beautiful blue eyes. A hand gently placed over my heart with a meaningful look had me crumbling again. I abandoned my efforts, and I felt Niklaus with me once more. Eben kissed my forehead and pulled me into his arms to lay against his warm chest. I sighed and let him hold me.

I clung to him, and my eyes opened to meet Jaxon's gaze. His eyes were soft and caring. I snuggled against Eben, but my eyes caressed Jaxon. He gave me a small smile devoid of any sarcasm or even playfulness. I knew it would return soon enough; I loved him for it, but at that moment, he let me see inside of him, just as I had for them all. It was that depth that I had glimpsed on the first day. I died at the thought of leaving Eben's arms, but I didn't feel whole not being touched by Jaxon, being caressed by Niklaus. I reached a hand out to Jaxon, and he came to me, eyes so intense on mine. I turned in Eben's arms, staying against him, but I reached out and pulled Jaxon to me.

He stood over me, sandwiching me between him and Eben. I gave a sigh and wrapped an arm around his waist. There it was, a little smirk pulling at the corner of his lips at my touch. He bent and kissed me. It wasn't aggressive, but it was most definitely possessive. His full smirk returned when he pulled back, making my stomach flutter.

"Screw Vladimir! You're mine, Doll Face." I bit my lip, trying to contain the smile that he was rousting out of me. The irritated growls rumbling out of Niklaus's and Eben's chests had my smile erupting. Jaxon's eyes twinkled, and he chuckled, "Well, you're ours, then." The rumbling settled, and I laughed, and my heavy feelings started lifting. I was theirs, even just for now.

I pulled him back down for a kiss and whispered, "Yeah, for now."

Jaxon wanted to hold me, I could tell, but Eben wouldn't release me. And then Niklaus was there. He lifted my face with a gentle finger and gently kissed my lips.

I wanted to soak up their closeness, so I pulled Niklaus and Jaxon along as I moved. Eben came with me, with his arms still around me. I climbed onto the enormous black bed, and Eben came with me. I laid down with him beside me and reached out towards the other two. Niklaus almost blushed a little? It had me smiling at him as he lay on my other side. I reached out for Jaxon and pulled him to lie with his head in my lap. I sighed and breathed them all in, savoring the closeness. Their scents slowly started to drown out Vladimir's from both the bed we lay on and my heart.

My forehead rested against Eben's, and Niklaus's head was behind mine, his hand tickling my shoulder as I reached behind to hold his head. My other hand played with Jaxon's hair, raking through it, as his head rested in my lap. I pulled in a deep, cleansing breath and finally felt whole. I rested in the moment, at peace for the first time in my life. My dark angel. My spicy challenger. My soul searcher. I would fight for them, to be with them. My eyes stayed on Eben's, letting him in to see my vulnerability. We all stayed like that for a time, unwilling to move away, to break the connection we had found.

Niklaus's arm came around my waist, pulling me against him, causing my stomach to flutter with his caresses on my abdomen.

Jaxon growled at the shift but consoled himself by running a hand up the length of my thigh, teasing, "I think I got the best deal." I laughed and yanked on a fistful of blonde hair. He laughed back but didn't stop his caresses, slowly setting me on fire.

Eben held my face and kissed my lips quickly before replying to Jaxon, "Not a chance." He leaned back in, making love to my lips, causing me to sigh. Niklaus brushed my hair away from my neck and kissed me there, causing my hold on the back of his to tighten. I was burning up.

I wanted to stay there with them all day, but I had to pull away from Eben's lips to say, "I have to go."

Vladimir's demand that I go take care of another Cavalier that evening had to be met. If I wanted more time with my vampire brothers, I would need to make sure I continued to appease Vladimir. I sighed and then sat up, pulling away from all of them. I walked into my closet to get changed for my evening out.

I had spotted two Cavaliers at one of the houses that I had selected as my target for the night; I knew exactly where they would be, but I needed to play the part. My tight evening dresses weren't going to cut it this time. I needed a specific look to fit in where I was headed. I heard the brothers climb off the bed, waiting to see what I was up to, though Niklaus could still hear my thoughts.

I changed into short jean shorts that were frayed on the edges, knee-high black boots that had studs and buckles on them, a worn black tank top that had 'Hard Rock Cafe' printed on it with a guitar, thick leather wristbands that had matching studs, a skull pendant on a chain, and silver hoops in my ears. I completed my look with deep red lips, black smoky eye makeup, and tousled hair that fell about my shoulders in voluminous waves. I added a little scent at key points and looked in the mirror, flashing myself a satisfied smile that stayed as I walked out to face the brothers.

I took in their reactions all at the same time. Niklaus's eyebrows shot up in lustful surprise. Eben's mischievous look took hold of his features, delighting at this new image of me.

Jaxon made a noise like he was pained and looked up at the ceiling before shifting his eyes back down to me, saying, "Damn, Sugar Lips. You really are a chameleon, aren't you? Is there anything you don't look good in?" I laughed and walked over to my nightstand for my phone, dialing the number.

"You ready?"

"Yeah. I'll be there in 10." I tucked the phone into my pocket. I kissed Eben, stroked Niklaus's face, and turned to say goodbye to Jaxon.

"Can I walk you out?" Jaxon asked.

I smiled, "Sure." He came up to me and reached down to hook his hands under my ass, lifting me up around his waist, holding me to him like that. I locked my ankles around him, wrapped my arms around his neck, and smiled at him.

He turned to carry me out the door like this, as I laughed at him so hard my head flew back. He kissed my neck when I exposed it. He let me slide down him as we stopped at the front door. I reached for the door, and he growled his displeasure.

"I'm going to follow you around." I raised an eyebrow and narrowed my eyes at him.

My pointer finger was in his face as I said, "You will not interfere, Jaxon. If you can't handle watching me hunt, you'd best just steer clear of my hunting grounds. Besides, I thought you were the type to like watching?" He growled in response as the other brothers walked up behind him.

I opened the door at the sound of the Harley pulling up the cul de sac in front of the porch. I walked down to the walkway, flashing one last look over my shoulder, before turning back to step up to Sebastian's motorcycle.

Sebastian's appreciative whistle was heard as he looked me over from head to toe. He flashed me a feral grin, and I returned the look, stepping up close and planting a kiss on his cheek. He wrapped an arm around me, much to the displeasure of the three vampires watching.

"Hey," I said. Sebastian's mind showed that he could smell all three of my vampires on me, which surprised him a little.

"Making nice with the blondie, huh?" He said after a sniff. I laughed.

"That mean our game is over?" He winked at me.

"Not at all," I returned the wink. His eyebrow shot up as his hand slid low to pull me close using my ass. Jaxon growled from the porch, making us smile. I turned and got behind Sebastian, wrapping my arms around his leather jacket. I flashed the three brothers a feral grin as the bike roared to life and revved, speeding off into the evening toward my prey.

# CHAPTER 14

Sebastian cruised easy through Pine River, but as soon as we hit the highway, he opened up the throttle, and we sped along, leaning easily into the curves. One blessing of being supernatural was the quicker response time, so we made excellent time traveling to a specific bar a couple towns over, weaving in and out of the traffic. Sebastian slowed as we entered the town and got close.

I had plucked this specific bar from the minds of my targets. I kissed Seb quickly on the neck and jumped off the bike as it moved, landing discreetly in the dark. I needed to show up to the bar alone, but Sebastian would be there if I needed him for any reason.

I walked down the street that seemed to be missing several lamp posts, unconcerned about any shady characters that could be lurking around; I was the real predator here. I turned the corner, and a long row of motorcycles came into view, and I couldn't help smiling. It was a popular biker bar that my victims frequented.

As I neared the entrance, I flashed smiles to different groups of men leaning up against their bikes or the bar wall. After a quick perusal of the row of bikes, I spotted the two I was going to focus on. One of the Cavaliers was leaning against the bar wall, across the sidewalk from his motorcycle, smoking a cigarette. I walked along the bike row casually, looking them over with my eyes but not touching them.

I would stop in front of one that was particularly impressive here and there, walking around the bike to look it over as I meandered toward my real goal. I pulled up in front of the two bikes I had been working toward and stood there, openly admiring them. I circled them as I checked them out, smiling in admiration or leaning close to look at detailing here and there.

I ignored the Cavalier, who was discreetly watching me admiring his bike, a pleased smile tugging at his lips as he took another drag on his cigarette. And then I did the naughty. I crossed a line to get a response from the man watching me; I very discreetly reached out and touched his bike, running my fingers along the leather seat.

He stood up straight, flicked his cigarette to the side, irritated, and walked over to me. I looked up at him, acting surprised and then guilty like I had been caught out. He moved into my space, still irritated.

I flashed him an apologetic smile and whispered, "I'm sorry, I just couldn't help myself. It's one of the best here. Did you do the detail work yourself?" He was still irritated with me, but my running compliments had a pleased twinkle come to his eyes.

"Yeah, it's a custom job by my brother and I. His has something similar."

"It's really excellent work." I spoke through a smile before turning back to look at the bike. I made a point of looking at him while I clasped my hands behind my back, showing him I wouldn't touch this time, and I bent over to look closely at the detailing. I strategically positioned myself so he would get the best view as I bent over. My vampire hearing picked up the quietest murmur of approval as he checked out my ass. I slowly sat up and turned back to him to smile in a flirting manner.

"Impressive specimen," I said with a double meaning as I looked him up and down. His look darkened just the slightest as he picked up on my innuendo. He was a brawny man with blonde hair and blue eyes. I took in his jeans with black leather chaps over them, a tight black t-shirt with a leather jacket, and a silver chain hanging around his neck. I brought my arms to my sides and then reached up to casually scratch my neckline with my black nails, drawing his eyes.

"Well," I said through my red lips as I looked him up and down once more, "Thanks for letting me look." I moved toward the bar, maneuvering by him and 'accidentally' brushing my breasts against his arm as I passed.

I walked to the bar door that a bouncer held open for me after giving me an approving glance over. I smiled for him, angling myself so the Cavalier watching could see my smile and how my eyes flicked back to him for the briefest second before I entered the bar.

I perused the bar, looking for my second target, and spotted him at a classic jukebox. I walked by him, flashing him a look, and went to sit at the bar on the far end that was empty. I ordered a whisky on the rocks and just waited as I nursed my drink. The Cavalier brother at the jukebox looked up and caught his brother's eye as he entered from outside, looking for me. I smiled down at my drink but otherwise ignored them both, looking at the TV above the bar.

The brother from outside jerked his head in my direction to the other brother, who turned to discreetly look me over. They shared a communicative smile and started advancing on my position at the bar. The brother from outside sidled up next to me.

"Hey, I forgot to ask you your name outside."

I looked up at him and lied, "Tiffany. What's yours?"

"Tyrone, and this is my brother," the other twin leaned against the bar behind me.

"I'm Tyler," the jukebox twin said. I looked behind me, openly admiring him for a second before turning back to Tyrone.

"Would you let me buy you a drink to apologize for being rude outside?" He asked.

"Sure," I said, hauling back my whisky in one draught. Both brothers gave me an approving look.

"So I've never seen you here before," he trailed off. I smiled at him.

"Yeah, I just moved into the area. I'm trying to get out a little since I don't know anyone here yet."

"Well, now you know us." I gave him a big smile.

"I guess I do." We sat at the bar making small talk; all the while, I was flirting with the two of them, sending them the right signals. They had steadily moved in closer until they were brushing up against me on both sides.

It was time to hook them, so I casually dropped the inflammatory question, "So which of you has the better bike?" They answered 'me' simultaneously, and I laughed at them. "Sure," I drawled out.

"You looked at them outside. Which did you prefer?" Tyrone asked me.

I openly looked him up and down as I answered, "It's not all about how they look; it's about how they ride." That did it, and they both converged on me even more.

"Well, Tiffany, would you like to go for a ride?" I gave him a feral grin, getting close.

"I don't know. I'd have to ride both to compare before I could say which is better." I felt Tyler's hand reach out to my hip and caress me there.

"Then I guess we better get outta here if we're going to have time for you to decide."

He took my hand and led me out of the bar toward his bike, with his brother following. He hopped on his bike and helped me on the back before starting it up. He pushed it back out of its parking space and waited for his brother to do the same.

I saw Sebastian watching us. He would follow us.

Tyrone turned his head, asking, "So where to?"

"How about we head up the mountain highway? I love the winding highway up there and the view."

"You got it," he answered and took off. His brother followed us up the winding road away from civilization. My vampire hearing could just make out the sound of Sebastian following us at a distance.

We slowed as we approached the pull-off area for the lookout, which featured plenty of empty parking spaces and a cinderblock outhouse on one side. My driver pulled up and parked in the middle of the lot, and we all got off the bikes.

"So? How did it ride?"

I gave him a lustful look, answering, "I don't know yet." He stepped into me and pulled me to him, kissing me. I pulled away, pulling on his hand and stopping at his brother. "I'll decide which one I prefer after I sample both." He grinned and leaned on his bike, watching us disappear behind the outhouse wall.

I let Tyrone bend and pick me up around his waist, backing me against the wall, and almost immediately, I sunk my fangs into his neck. I knew that Tyler could hear his twin's moaning because I could hear his heart speed up in anticipation as he listened. He liked what he heard, and his anticipation heightened.

I drained Tyrone, catching us as he fell, and stashed the body inside the outhouse. I called the other twin over, telling him his brother had gone into the outhouse to clean himself up. I challenged Tyler to try to outdo his brother while his brother listened from inside. He growled his approval, taking ahold of me, and was soon lying lifeless at my feet as well.

I put my cell up to my ear and called Sebastian, who was just down the road waiting. His Harley pulled up into the parking lot, where I waited.

"Where do you suggest we put the bodies out here, Seb?" He slung a twin over his shoulder and led the way. I followed with the other, and we buried them deep in the woods, returning to the parking lot to dispose of the bikes. "It really is a shame that we have to trash these; they really were great work," I announced regretfully as we pushed them toward the edge of the lookout. The bikes fell into the black abyss below to smash into an unrecognizable scattering of parts all over the mountainside.

We walked back to his bike. I turned to Sebastian, thinking about how much I had changed over the last few days.

He saw my look and pulled me to him in an easy, friendly, but intimate way and asked, "What is it, Sasha?" He leaned us back against his bike, half sitting on the seat. I reached up and touched his face, looking at him and thinking about the past.

"Seb, I just wanted to say that I'm sorry for what happened between us and for hurting you. I honestly fled, leaving you there because I couldn't stand hurting you." His eyes ghosted over with old wounds but still held an affection while he looked at me in the present.

"You never did tell me why you really left, Sasha. You just disappeared in the night, leaving that note saying you were returning to Vladimir."

I wrapped my arms around his neck, hugging him as I repeated, "I'm sorry." I pulled back and looked into his eyes to explain. "Vladimir was using me to manipulate your emotions, Sebastian. He was planning on using me to lure you to Darius, who wanted your head as the asking price for some business deal."

"So none of it was real for you?" He asked, a sad look crossing his features.

"That's as far from the truth as possible, Seb. It's why I left. I had started to care about you too much to be able to continue. I didn't want to be the cause of your death; I didn't want to hurt you. I'm sorry I wasn't able to fully let you in, to love you like you deserve." I smiled at him and affectionately swept his black hair to the side of his face.

He smiled down at me and brought me in for a caring hug, resting his chin on my head and whispering, "Well, it seems I was wrong. You have changed,

Sasha. Thank you for finally explaining after all these years. It's nice to have some closure." I hugged him back. "What changed for you, Sasha? Why apologize now? I mean, what happened?"

"The Bathory brothers happened, Seb," I looked up at him then.

He looked at me for a moment and then whispered, "They got under your skin, didn't they? Are you.....," he let his question die off as he looked into my eyes. He found his answer there. His hands came to my face, and he kissed my forehead. Pulling back, he just looked at me. I could hear his mind wondering where we stood; were we friends? Could we go on being friends?

"Yes, we're friends, Seb. If you are, I'm comfortable continuing as we have these last couple of weeks." He gave me a half smile and brushed my hair back with his hands, holding his face close to mine.

Almost to himself, he whispered, "Lucky bastards." I laughed and pulled back so we could get on his bike to head home.

Sebastian dropped me off at the mansion with a quick hug before he left. I turned, headed inside, and pulled out my phone to report to Vladimir immediately so I wouldn't forget.

"Ahhh, my pet, so soon? You really are a minx."

"Two more have disappeared and won't be found."

"Two, my my." I reached my bedroom door and paused just outside to finish my conversation quickly.

"I should probably wait a little while before hunting anymore. I don't want too many to disappear at once, raising suspicion."

"Very well, but I expect you to continue in a few days."

"Yes, Vladimir."

"Very good, my pet. Call me again soon." The line went dead, and I sighed. At least I would have a few days of peace. I put my phone back in my pocket and entered my room.

A hand shot out from behind me, shutting the door as I was pressed up against the door, and my lips were captured. A spicy aroma washed over me at the kiss.

# CHAPTER 15

Jaxon pressed me against the door, ravishing my mouth, his hands slipping under my tank top to pull me against his hips before he pushed me back against my bedroom door. He nipped his way down my neck, drawing out a gasp as I heard the lock on my door click. No lock would stop a vampire, but it sent a clear signal; he was about to make me his.

I reached up and grabbed his hat and tossed it onto one of the armchairs, the heat building inside me. He was back to my lips, forcing his way inside to take possession of me as I reached down to peel his shirt up over his head, breaking our kiss for only a second before crashing back together.

I was already moaning from his bold hands, deliciously running themselves all over my skin. He was back to my neck, and my hands went into his hair to hold him there as I started breathing heavily. His hands wandered down to squeeze my ass before he hauled me up around his hips, pressing me to the door even harder. Delicious pressure. And then, in one swift jerk, my jean shorts were shredded and tossed to the side. The flames inside me roared up, burning me from the intensity of the need he had ignited. His hands slid up my thighs, over my hips with a quick squeeze, and up my waist. I felt him start to fist my tank top.

My hands released his head to stop his hands, and I hissed, "Don't you dare ruin my favorite tank top." I felt him smile at the base of my neck as he laughed. He pulled it over my head instead of ripping it from my body and tossed it on the armchair where his hat sat.

I heard his approving growl as his tongue drew a trail down my neck to my breasts, making me gasp as goosebumps broke out over my skin. One hand dug into his shoulder as the other wandered up into his blonde hair. My bra soon joined the shredded clothes on the floor, and Jaxon had me gasping and throwing my head back against the door as he drove me crazy with his mouth there.

I wasn't about to let him have all the fun, letting my hands wander down his muscular back and sculpted chest. I reached between us and undid his belt, pulling it free before it fell to the floor with a chink. I undid his jeans and used my power to slide them free of him; his breathing was turning shallow, just like mine. His hands ran up my thighs, and his fingers hooked my black lace panties before pulling out to the sides to rip them from my body as well with a possessive growl. A deep moan tore itself from my throat as his fingers slipped up inside my heat to curl and drive me to abandon, as he left hot wet patches all over my chest with his mouth.

A gasp, and I sucked in a deep breath as an orgasm flowed out over me, causing me to squeeze his hips tighter with my legs wrapped around him. He captured my mouth again, and I felt him shuck the rest of his clothes.

He pulled back to look in my eyes then, with that sexy smirk. His amber eyes were burning with desire as they delved into mine, which mirrored his. He watched me as he pressed into me at last. I gasped and used my legs to pull on him, filling me completely. We released a collective gasp and looked into each other's eyes, breathing heavily, not moving for a moment. His hands came to hold my jaw in a moment of tenderness as he kissed me languorously.

The moment he started to move, all tenderness faded once more; hunger replaced it, and we abandoned ourselves to it. A growl rippled out of him as I moved with him, digging my fingers into his shoulders. He was exactly what I needed, what I wanted, in that moment; hard and fast. The slow build-up over the last few days had peaked in me, and I would not have stood for anything less in that moment. He had me snarling with just the right angle as he thrust into me, hitting just where I needed. Just. One. Gasp. More. And then my head fell back against the door as the most intense orgasm I had ever experienced ripped its way through my body, bringing out a scream. One more thrust, and I felt him find his.

Before either of us could come back down, I decided to bring us even higher. I pulled him to me and, with a vicious snarl, buried my fangs in his neck, drawing his spicy blood into my mouth. Jaxon's head flew back as the most sensual moan tore its way from him, his eyes rolling back up into his head in pure ecstasy. I drew again, and his chin came back down to snarl and bury his own fangs in my neck, bringing us even higher. We fed from each other, taking possession of one another in every way possible, moaning deeply as we did.

At last, I stopped pulling on the bite, as did he, but we just sat there, staying still in the moment. Locked in each other's jaws, him still inside of me, pressed up against the door and breathing heavy, nostrils flaring. After a minute, I finally released him from my jaws and pulled back to look into his flashing red eyes. His smirk was back, colored with deep, sated satisfaction. I grabbed his face and brought his lips to mine, kissing him as the blood on our lips mixed to create a whole new intoxicating flavor we both savored. With a grunt, he pulled back to look at me again, smirking.

He was about to pull out of me, and I wasn't ready to feel the loss, so I tightened my legs and my hold on him inside. He growled out a moan, staying where he was.

His husky voice whispered in the dark, "You do that, Sugar Lips, and I'll keep you busy all night." Flames shot through me at his threat, a delicious proposition I desperately wanted him to carry out. I flashed him a feral grin and tightened the pressure around his impressive length just enough that he had my answer. A deep, loud growl of approval and rising arousal filled the room and possibly the halls of the manor; we hadn't been quiet even for human ears.

His hands rested flat against the door on either side of my head, caging me in as he looked at me.

"I couldn't get you off my mind, Doll Face. I went out tonight to my usual bar and couldn't think straight for wanting you so bad. Knowing that you were off somewhere, possibly being with another man, had me going crazy. I had to come and wait here for you to come back. I waited in the dark for hours; it was pure hell."

I rubbed his neck and chest, caressing him as I answered, "I have no interest in my human prey, Jaxon. Even their blood is bland next to you and your brother. Probably brothers. You never need to worry when I'm out on a hunt. I'll always come home after."

A genuine smile spread across his face, touching his eyes at the pleasure of me calling the manor my home. It was home now. Earlier in the day, when I had lain on the bed, surrounded by all three coven brothers in that quiet, intimate moment, it had become home. My home. He leaned in and kissed me tenderly. It slowly built into a flaming hot kiss of growing need again, and my hands went back to his hair, which was still messy from our lovemaking. His arms came around me then, and he lifted me away from the door and carried me to the massive black bed on the other side of the room, moaning as I kissed his neck.

He laid us down on the bed and reached down to unzip the boots that I still wore. He tossed them into my walk-in closet with an amused look as he turned back to me. I looked at him, unable to hide the overwhelming sense of love for this beautiful blonde vampire, as I looked at him. Our kind falls hard and fast when it does, and I was no exception.

Jaxon pressed me into the bed with his body, and I saw an echo of my own heart in his eyes. He brushed my hair from my face and kissed me, murmuring something about how it was going to kill him to share me. His gentle caresses at that moment showed me the softer, sensual side he hid below the surface, under his demanding, playful one.

Jaxon had been the only son of a wealthy couple who had gotten rich generations ago, bolstered by the oil industry. Growing up, Jaxon had been doted on by his mother when the cameras were pointed their way but swiftly dumped with the latest nanny their father had chosen to have an affair with. His parents were cold and ignored him, and the nannies were often neglectful or straight-up abusive, creating a revolving door of loveless hired help. Jaxon had learned to hide his pain behind humor and sarcasm as he slowly began to despise his parents and their money. He disappeared as soon as he was of age, not looking back until the police came to inform him that his parents had been mysteriously murdered on their yacht. He was the sole heir to their massive, growing fortune. An investigation ran cold, and when things were finally settled, Jaxon found himself face to face with their murderer, who had come to claim both Jaxon for his unique giftings in seduction and influence over others and his amounting fortune. Vladimir's acquisition was swift and final. Jaxon's entire life had been devoid of what he had wanted most of all until he had arrived here in this coven to discover a brotherhood with the others and now a deeper love than he could have ever imagined with her.

I swallowed from the emotion in the confession of his memories, looking into his eyes and whispered, "Love you."

He smiled and kissed me again, whispering over my lips, "Love you." And then his hands raked into my hair to start making good on his threat.

Only as the sun had just started rising we finally settled down in the sheets of the great black bed to sleep. He held me to his side as he started drifting off, and I tickled his stomach with my fingers, making him mumble and capture my hand in his so he could sleep. I smiled into his shoulder and closed my eyes, breathing in his scent and our lovemaking. The scent of Vladimir was all but drowned out by it, and I remember thinking about how wonderful a sensation that was before I fell asleep in his arms.

"Alright, you two! Open up in there. It's midday already." I laughed at Eben's teasing voice coming through the closed door. I could feel Niklaus's mind as he walked up behind Eben, amused.

I got off the bed and went to the bathroom to rake my fingers through my messy hair. I went to my closet to put some clothes on. I heard Jaxon doing the same with his jeans on the other side of the room, before he opened the door to his brothers, annoyed. I laughed at his grumbling and walked up next to him. He put his arm around me as we faced off with his brothers, who filled the doorway, both looking amused.

I looked from one to the other for a short moment, a genuine blush spreading across my cheeks at their teasing but amused looks they wore. Jaxon wrapped his arms around me and pulled me back against his bare chest, nuzzling my neck. My eyes drifted close at his touch, even though the other brothers stood right there. Jaxon chuckled in my ear, hugging me to him very lovingly. I loved his softer side.

"Alright, you greedy jerk," Eben laughed, "You've had her all night, and you're just laying it on thick now." I laughed looking over at him as he smiled and teased. His blue eyes met mine and softened as we looked at each other.

Niklaus's fake scowl twitched as he tried to hold back the smile working its way to the surface. I gave him a knowing smile, and my eyes narrowed. Finally, he laughed and let his arms drop to his sides before he put a fist on a hip and gripped the door jam with the other. I finally stepped out of Jaxon's arms and went to them. They turned toward me when I reached them and started affectionately caressing me. I reached up and kissed Eben's lips as his azure eyes delved into mine. I turned to Niklaus and wrapped an arm around his neck to hug him as his hands came to my back to hold me there for a moment.

He buried his face in my hair and whispered, "I'm glad you're home." I died a little inside at him saying it. I was home. Here, with the three of them, I knew where I truly belonged. I had no idea how I would escape Vladimir's grasp, but I knew where I wanted to be. Right here with my three beautiful, wonderful, loving vampire coven brothers who had changed my heart and taught me how to love.

The ringing of my cell phone shrilled out across the room; the damn thing. I really hated it. I released Niklaus and went to answer it without looking; it was always Vladimir.

"Hey Sasha, it's Blake. I was hoping you might be up for going out with me again tonight?"

# CHAPTER 16

My eyes met Jaxon's as I held the phone to my face. Blake was waiting for my answer.

"Sure. Did you want to meet at the same place?" Jaxon's eyes turned hard, and I saw the muscles along his jaw tighten. He was going to have to deal.

"Yeah, that'd be great. See you at seven?"

"See you then, Quarterback." I heard him laugh on the other end before he hung up. So much for my break.

I put the phone back down, and when I turned, Jaxon was right there, pulling me up against him with an irritated growl. I brushed my fingers through his hair with an affectionate smile. I ran my fingers down his jaw with a playful smile and gently flicked him, as I had when we first met. He gave me a growl and pulled me tighter against him.

"Guess I'm going out tonight." I moved out of his arms to pick out what I would wear. I was in the middle of a dilemma. I needed to keep Blake on the line for a source of information, but I wasn't going to be able to dispose of this Cavalier; he was the starting quarterback of the local community college, which was way too high profile to not be noticed if he disappeared. Which meant I was going to have to walk a fine line.

I pulled on a tight pair of jeans and a black corset with built-in straps. I left my hair loose and put silver hoops in my ears. Deep red lips and smokey eyes, and I was ready.

Walking out, they were there waiting for me. I looked at Niklaus; I hadn't blocked him from my thoughts, and he could hear the dilemma. He came up to me and rubbed my upper arms.

"Would you like Jaxon and Eben there with you?" I smiled at his concern.

"I'm not sure that Jaxon could keep his fists to himself. I'd better just go alone. I've always been able to take care of myself," I reminded him.

"Doesn't mean you should have to, Sasha," he said, brushing his hand through my loose hair with a look of affection. I couldn't help but smile and bring a hand to caress his neck. I saw his eyes darken ever so slightly, so I planted a kiss on his lips. I could hear he wanted me to bring them just in case I needed them.

"If your brother can promise not to interfere, they can come." Niklaus looked up at Jaxon and gave him a look that communicated that he needed to behave. Jaxon just smirked.

"It's early for you to be leaving," Eben observed.

I looked at him and answered, "I'm going to head to the Cavalier houses first to see what else I can glean. I might even run by their headquarters to scope things out. I'll be back to the bar on time to meet Blake."

"In that case, I'm coming with you myself," Niklaus said, returning my attention to him. "Jaxon and Eben will be waiting at the bar when you arrive."

"Alright, let's go."

We sped out of the house with our vampire speed, but Niklaus still managed to hold the door for me on our way out. He followed me along the streets of Pine River until we arrived at the edge of the town where the first house was.

We watched and listened to the Cavaliers there before leaving to observe the second operations house. Their operation had grown even more than Vladimir had feared. The Cavaliers were becoming far too powerful. Niklaus and I communicated our observations in total silence, using our minds, which also felt more intimate. I enjoyed having him with me.

After observing the houses, I followed the mental images I had gleaned from Blake to the Cavalier headquarters. Niklaus and I snuck up a water tower decently close to the compound to observe. We stood to the side where we could just look around the tower to see but not be seen.

We observed the gated community with guards stationed around it as casual loiterers; a jogger, a homeless man leaning up against the wall, and an artist on the corner. It was a gated community with a guard booth where anyone going in and out had to sign in. We took note of the guard schedule and pattern for a while, also observing where there seemed to be important buildings inside the compound. There were plenty of residents and individual houses. The apartment building was in a back corner, and my eyes darted to Blake as he exited his unit. He was heading to the bar we had agreed to meet at. Ugg, I would need a nice long soak in a bubble bath after this one.

Since I wasn't hunting him and just appeasing him, it could be a long night, especially if he wanted to take things too far. Maybe Jaxon's fist would come in handy if it came down to it. I heard Niklaus chuckle next to me, and I smiled at him.

I turned my eyes back to the figure of Blake walking across the compound, greeting guards and other Cavaliers here and there. I would have to keep my bloodlust under control, too; I couldn't draw suspicion by feeding on this one after others had already started disappearing. They might be out of their mind with pleasure during the feeding, but if I left them alive, they would come to the correct conclusion; since I couldn't kill Blake, I wouldn't be able to feed on him.

Dang, I should have fed on Jaxon before I left. Maybe I could sneak off with him or even Eben at the bar for a few minutes? My eyes were lighting up with the thought as they tracked Blake. Turning my head to continue to track him, I caught sight of Niklaus's beating pulse on his neck. I swallowed down the desire to sink my fangs into his neck; he smelled too good, just like his brothers. I looked back to Blake's confident gait.

I felt Niklaus's hand snake out, coming around my waist, turning me toward him, and he rolled us along the tower wall, out of sight of the compound. He pulled me up against him, embracing me, slightly lifting me to his tall frame.

"Sasha, all you need do is ask." His eyes communicated as clearly as his mind that the idea of me feeding on him was more than appealing.

His hands went up into my hair, combing it back from my face, turning my face up to look into his eyes. I reached up and ran my fingers over his lips; I knew Niklaus would always try to be my 'white knight,' even in something as simple as this. If I needed him, he would do anything for me.

I removed my fingers and replaced them with my lips, kissing him slowly as his hold on me tightened. His hand wandered to my hip to pull me up tighter against his. His other hand stayed in my hair, holding the back of my head as he kissed me back. He had me sighing, reading my mind while he kissed me, knowing exactly what I liked. I was erupting in a flaming need of him, for more of him.

I wanted to stand Blake up and stay right here in Niklaus's skillful hands, but I knew I wouldn't be able to repair things with Blake as easily as I had the last time I had to go. Niklaus released my lips but not his hold on me, gently pulling my lips toward his neck as he leaned his head to the side, offering up what I needed. I ran a hand up his chest and slipped it into his collar to hold his neck, drawing out a sigh of pleasure from him, and leaned in close. His scent was mouth-watering. I kissed his neck and then bit down as he hissed.

He gently held the back of my head to him as I fed from him, his other arm coming around my waist to support me. Where Eben was the dessert, Niklaus was a five-star course. His fascinating complexity rolled over my tongue in the most deliciously savory rich blood I had ever consumed like a world-famous chef was purposely trying to surprise my pallet. I heard him give a moaning sigh as he enjoyed the pleasure that was rolling through his frame, consuming him just as I consumed him. I would never stop craving him now. He and his brothers really had ruined me for all others.

I pulled back on a satiated sigh, and his face turned to look at me, his eyes lit up red in the dark. He pulled me to him for a heated kiss that held promises to be fulfilled later. I was frustrated that I had to leave him; I wanted him right then and there, but I knew that was not his style. I could wait. He gave me a smile while his lustful eyes looked me over.

I gave him one last kiss and sped away; if I didn't leave him quickly, I might not be able to. I slowed just as I turned around the corner toward the bar. I licked my lips to make sure they were clean of blood, and then I opened the door to the bar and entered.

I saw Jaxon and Eben playing pool at their usual table and gave them a smile and a wink as I entered. I turned to look for Blake and saw him standing in a corner, surrounded by a couple of girls; one blonde girl in particular was hanging on his arm, trying to get his attention. I rolled my eyes and pretended like I hadn't seen him. I wandered through the bar, acting like I was looking for him but not finding him. I meandered up to the pool table, flashing my boys a smile that they returned.

"How was your afternoon?" Eben asked, referring to my reconnaissance.

"Productive, thanks." Both of their eyes flashed to my mouth and sparked red for just a second; they could smell the blood. Eben's mischievous look crossed his features.

Jaxon smirked, saying, "Did you actually do any reconnaissance of the Cavaliers, Sugar Lips, or just our brother?" I gave them a wicked grin back.

I leaned against the pool table to watch them play while I stole glances around the bar. Blake finally noticed me when the brothers and I were talking and tried to free himself from the blonde, but she was clinging to him.

"Hey, Sasha," he smiled at me, walking up. I looked at the blonde hanging on him and turned my eyes back to him, letting them appear cool. I could use her to my advantage. If Blake thought I was the jealous type, it would keep him more interested and would give me an excuse to draw a line on how far I was willing to go.

"Hey," I said in a cool voice, stealing a glance at the girl on his arm before meeting his eyes. The blonde seemed pleased that she was 'irritating' me. How pathetic. I could eat her alive if I was actually jealous.

"You wanna go dance, Sasha?" Blake smirked at me, self-assured.

I flashed another glance at the blonde and then turned my eyes back to watch the pool game as I replied, "Seems you're busy."

"Awww, don't be like that, Sasha. This is just Natalie Lane," he explained, gesturing toward the insecure bitchy blonde. I turned my eyes to Natalie and gave her a tiny glare before looking at where she had her arm through Blake's.

I turned to him and said, "Seems you already brought a date, so if you'll excuse me, I'm going to go dance by myself." I turned and walked past him and headed to the dance floor, where I melded into the crowd of singles dancing, ignoring him.

I saw him trying to free himself from the blonde again as another exceptionally handsome man came dancing up to me. I smiled at the man and crooked my finger at him. He eagerly started dancing in my space, and I turned around to dance with my back against him, looking at him over my shoulder as we pulsed to the music. The man's hands held my hips, keeping me against him as we moved. I made sure to steal a glance at Blake as my arm reached up behind me so I could caress the man's neck. The man bent down close to the side of my face in response. Natalie was pulling on Blake again, so I turned my eyes on the brothers. They watched me closely with their vampire eyes but appeared casual to a human observer.

My body and hands were on the man behind me, but my eyes were on them, flirting and practically undressing them with my eyes. The man took his hand and ran it down the length of my body, starting at my elbow, up by his neck, and ending on my hip again. Jaxon's impulsiveness flared, and he moved to come to me, but Eben's hand around his wrist held him back. I turned my eyes from them to Blake, glared at him for a second, and then turned my eyes back to the man behind me. My peripheral caught Blake finally freeing himself from Natalie, saying something harsh to her that had her going red and looking to the side, finally releasing him.

Blake came straight for me and jerked me to his chest from the man. The man was going to give a retort, but Blake silenced him with a look while his arms came around me. He took the man's place dancing with me, and I turned back around to watch the brothers as we danced; they seemed more irritated that it was Blake than a stranger this time, but I could see both of them were having a good look. Eben continued to keep his brother under control, but his eyes were darker as they watched me.

Blake leaned down and whispered in my ear, "Hey, I have something I wanted to show you. Can we get out of this place?"

I turned and whispered in his ear, "I don't think Natalie would approve of you showing me that."

He laughed, saying, "I meant that I wanted to go show you one of those haunted houses you were so interested in, and she won't be there, so if you want to see what else I have to offer, she won't get in the way. Come on."

# CHAPTER 17

I followed along after Blake out of the bar, flashing the brothers one last look. I noticed Natalie raging at us in the corner. Blake led me down a street, and we crossed several alleyways. I could hear his mind wanting to turn around and push me up against one of the brick walls, but he decided to be patient and wait until the 'haunted' house. I rolled my eyes. How exactly was I going to get out of this one? I might not have minded so much a few weeks ago; he was good-looking, but I had absolutely no interest in any other men now that I had tasted my Bathory brothers. Besides, Vladimir would be pissed, not that I would tell him.

We finally reached the outskirts of Pine River, and he led me toward one of the houses I had seen in his mind before. We crept up the porch steps, and he pushed the door open, which creaked as it swung open slowly. I could sense Blake's unease in the place, but being alone with me filled him with aroused anticipation.

"So, what's the story with this place?" I whispered to him. He smiled and told me a creepy story about how a family used to live there, but then one of them went crazy and killed the rest of the family before he was killed by the police.

"And they say the axe he used is still in this very house; that you can see it changing positions around the house as the killer waits for any new victims that wander into the house." He took the opportunity to lean close and wrap a 'reassuring' arm around me.

"I've always loved a scary story," I whispered, playing along. I starred in most of the ones I knew.

"Is that why you don't mind living in that creepy Bathory mansion with the others? You're not related, are you? They've hosted many college girls there." He was concerned I could be one of them instead of the other staff he had known when they attended the college; some governesses and maids.

"No, I'm not related. I find the story of Countess Elizabeth Bathory to be quite thrilling and-"

"Creepy, disgusting, horrific," Blake finished. If he only knew that I was a thousand times worse than the Countess due to her son.

The boards creaked under our feet as he walked me around the house, telling me all the stories of different 'encounters' in those rooms. We walked into the old kitchen.

"And in here, a woman claimed that her boyfriend was murdered by a knife that just came at him and stabbed him to death. She was found screaming while she ran through the town."

I snorted and then asked incredulously, "Didn't they just peg her for the murder?"

"Apparently, his body has never been found."

"So why do so many people come here if it's supposedly that haunted?"

"For a thrill," he whispered in an ominous voice as he pulled me to him and started kissing me.

"Blake, we shouldn't." He pulled me back to his lips briefly and moved down onto my neck. His mind revealed that he had every intention to. Damn. "Blake, you and Natalie seemed pretty close. Are you sure she's not your girlfriend?"

"Definitely," his hoarse voice grunted.

"It sure seemed like that to me." His hands started wandering, and he backed me up against the old kitchen island, leaning me over with his ardent kisses and petting.

"She doesn't mean anything to me."

"And I do?" I laughed out in an incredulous tone. He had me on the island counter and was on top of me by this point.

"Absolutely." Typical.

I was only responding enough to not make him angry with rejection, but I wasn't sure what I would do to get out of this one. His lips wandered down to my bustline, trying to tease out a response from me. I was glad I had worn a corset instead of the low-line halter I had considered.

"Blake." He took that as encouragement and wandered down to my waistline, kissing just above the top of my jeans as he ran his hands all over my thighs. I felt him reach up and undo the button on my jeans, granting his tongue access to dip below the waistline. I gasped from surprise and a feeling of annoyance, but not from actual pleasure. I was about to make him black out using my power when I felt a presence in the room with us.

Blake was too busy to notice the apparition that appeared next to us. I locked eyes with Vladimir. His ghostly eyes took in the scene before him, first with surprise and then seething anger. I cried out in fright, only partially faked, and Blake's face snapped up to catch sight of the apparition just before it faded, wafting away. He screamed like a freaking pansy, eyes bulging, before he jumped back from where the "ghost" had been.

I decided to milk the opportunity and used my powers to have all the cabinet doors fly open, sending things crashing around him as I screamed in mock terror. I found an old chopping knife in one of the cupboards and sent it flying towards Blake to lodge in the wall next to his head.

Blake's eyes were saucers as he looked over at the massive knife stuck in the wall, the handle still wobbling from the force of the impact. His grimace of horror and rather high-pitched screams filled the room, and he shot forward, his arms waving around his body. He ran from the room terrified, abandoning me in the process. Perfect. I sent a few more articles flying around the main room, crashing into the walls near him as he scrambled out of the house, tripping on the entry rug before scrambling out of the house. I kept up the crashing inside the house and my screaming for effect until I could no longer hear him running down the street.

I stood up from the kitchen counter and looked down at my jeans, zipping and buttoning them up, as the rest of the old dishes fell out of the air wherever they had been suspended.

I looked up to the sound of delicious laughter.

Both brothers were in the entryway of the house looking at me. Jaxon was leaning against the banister, and Eben was against the wall there, both laughing hysterically at the situation. I smiled and walked over to them, joining in on the laughter. I brushed myself off from the dirty island as they continued to laugh; Jaxon was practically doubled over.

I smiled, and my eyebrows shot up briefly as I rolled my eyes. I said, "So much for chivalry these days." Both brothers burst out in a fresh round of laughter.

"I've never seen someone get the better of Blake so much as that," Eben said between laughs. I could hear his mind as his thoughts naturally expanded on how Blake was known for being a bully at the community college. Eben himself had never been a target as he was a Bathory and wouldn't have put up with the jock's attitude, but he had stepped in for a few others. Sweet, gentle Eben was also principled. I guess chivalry wasn't dead after all.

I smiled at Eben and said, "Yeah, well, he's a dick and deserved it. Not very brave for a Cavalier, that one." More laughter.

The three of us sped out of the house and headed back to the estate, still laughing at the moron. We walked through the entryway in a loud bustle, jostling and enjoying each other. Niklaus came wandering out of his study to see what the racket was about. Before we could recount the tale, a loud shriek came from upstairs from the twin's room. I rolled my eyes and was about to head up when Niklaus smiled, waving me off. He and Jaxon flew up the stairs to deal with it. I rolled my eyes and smiled at Eben, about to make another joke, when the sound of my cell phone ringing from my room cut me off. It was muted, being in my room, but it still filled me with dread. My smile faded.

I went still and turned to look over my shoulder at my room, afraid suddenly. I was in deep shit. Vladimir. Not only had he appeared and seen me with Blake, but I had forgotten my cell phone.

I turned and sped off into my room to answer the phone, but my fear had cost me precious seconds, and I missed the call. I unlocked the phone. Three missed calls. I felt that pulling, tightening sensation of fear in my chest. I put the phone up to my ear, trying to call Vladimir back, as I paced in the middle of the room.

I felt him in the room with me for only a second before a slap sent me flying to the floor, the cell phone sliding out of my grip to slide across the hardwood.

"Vladimir! It's not what you think," I stood up, trying to appease him. "Nothing happ-" My explanation was cut off with another slap that sent me sprawling back to the floor.

"I warned you, Sasha, no screwing around." This time, I thought better about standing and just looked up at him from where I was on the floor.

"I wasn't, Vladimir. I was just about to handle the situation, and you interrupted. He is a Cavalier."

"You said you weren't going hunting for a few days."

"Yeah, well, he called me. He's my source, and I have to keep him happy." Victor's apparition glared at me and reached down for me, putting a large hand around my throat, squeezing tight.

"You need to worry about keeping me happy, more, my pet. Don't let me catch you fooling around again." I shook my head in terrorized obedience. His form faded, releasing me from the hold on my throat. I sucked in a breath, coughing and sputtering where I lay on the floor.

"Sasha?" Eben's voice was cautious as the door opened, and his head leaned in. Still coughing, I put a hand to my throat and waved the other at him, trying to wave him away that I was all right. He looked horrified as he rushed to my side, kneeling down to pull me to him.

"Vladimir?" he asked anger in his voice.

"Yeah," I croaked out at him. I looked up into his blue eyes as they flamed angrily at his maker. When his eyes returned from their faraway look and connected with mine in the present, they softened and became sad.

"I'm sorry, Eben, you can go." I tried to stand, but he held me to him.

"What could you possibly be sorry for?" He asked. I didn't know what to say. For existing? For bringing my problems into their household?

"For involving you with my problems." He sighed and laid his forehead against mine, gently rubbing the side of my jaw.

"You're family, Sasha. This is your home, and we all care deeply for you and what you're going through. You're not alone anymore, so you should stop acting like you are." I reached my arms around him and hugged him to me, taking the comfort he offered me once again at Vladimir's cruelty. My eyes felt glassy as I laid my head on his chest. I closed my eyes with a sigh of defeat.

I felt Eben scoop me up into his arms, kick my door shut to drown out the screaming that was still happening across the manner and walk me over to my bed. He laid me down and looked at me. His eyebrows wrinkled, and an angry look crossed his face again as he turned my face to see the mark Vladimir had left on me. I was already healing, and it was fading, but it showed clearly at that moment. I pulled my face from him, feeling too vulnerable, and I rolled away from him.

This is where I would usually hug myself and try not to cry out loud in my room in Vladimir's castle before I could shut my heart off and turn back into the masked bitch he expected. My arms hugged my body as I lay there, staring at the wall, balling myself up.

And then Eben was there, wrapping his arms around me, pulling me back against him, his sweet scent enveloping me. A hand brushed my hair back from my face and a kiss was pressed to my temple, making my eyes close as the tenderness after Vladimir's brutality. I sighed at the relief it and he brought to me. My dark angel.

"Look at me, Sasha," he whispered with his lips above my ear. I swallowed and shook my head. "Let me in, Sasha," he whispered again, sending shivers over my body.

Eben really was going to be the most difficult brother, seeing into me even when I didn't want to open up to him. I swallowed and turned my head to look at him. He wore a sad smile as his beautiful eyes looked into mine, into my depths, searching for that hidden side. He gently turned me around to face him, not breaking the connection of our eyes. I blinked, wanting to break the uncomfortable connection of truth we had found. He could see me, the real me, the scared me, the one who should have cried after being slapped to the floor. A gentle smile tugged at his lips as he looked at me; he had found me. He brushed my hair back again and brought the same hand down to hold the side of my face as he leaned in to kiss me in his slow, smoldering way.

I pulled back, and my lips trembled from the tears that wanted to come. I had never allowed myself to actually cry tears when Vladimir hit me, but they poured out of me now at Eben's gentle touch that showed me that life could be different. His gentle smile touched his eyes with understanding and acceptance of my tears. I reached out and touched his face, looking in wonder at an embodiment of tenderness.

I pulled him to me to kiss him, fully accepting the moment between us at last. He responded, kissing me back and holding my jaw with a feather touch. The kiss deepened, and then I was smoldering, burning with an intense, slow heat at his touch. Slowly, I reached down, pulled his shirt over his head, and tossed it to the floor.

# CHAPTER 18

Eben's eyes were so soft and gentle as he lay over me, propped up on one elbow, gently running his fingers over my skin, intensifying the smoldering coals inside me. I ran my hand up his arm to his shoulder, caressing him there, moving over and up his neck to lightly touch his face. As my fingers reached his lips, his free hand came up to capture mine, holding my fingers to his lips so he could lightly kiss them while he caressed me with his eyes. Such tenderness had me feeling shy for once, and I was the one biting my lip with a nervous gesture.

He delighted in the slight flush he had brought to my cheeks, smiling at me. He brought my hand back up to his neck and bent down to make love to my mouth with those slow, scorching lips of his. I sighed into his mouth, allowing him entry to slowly torture me with his tongue. I savored this sweet sampling of my dark angel as my hands wandered down his chest and back up his back.

"Eben." He looked at me with such intense adoration I couldn't breathe for a moment, and then I sucked in a deep breath. He bent and kissed me again, making my body rise up to meet him.

His kisses trailed down my chin and throat as I put my head back and continued down onto my chest. His warm hands slid down my corset and braced my hips, lifting them, bowing me so he could press his lips to the thin line of exposed flesh above my jeans. His soft lips slid across the strip of exposed skin there, making me gasp and burn for more. The waistband of my jeans was pulled down just enough so he could close his mouth over my hip bone. He drew a moan out of me, and my hands went into his soft black hair. I gasped at the loss of his mouth there when he came back up to caress my face with the back of his hand. I shivered at the wet patch he had left there.

He smiled and then rolled us so I was above him, rubbing my back, brushing my hair back, and kissing my neck gently. He looked into my eyes as his hands slowly undid the lacing of my corset in the back. My need was growing so much I could hardly stand his gentleness.

"Eben," my voice sounded breathy with desperation.

He smiled and whispered, "I'm not going to let you rush this, Sasha. It's time someone taught you that tenderness can be even more intense and worth the wait." I groaned at his words and bent to kiss his neck while he slowly worked on the laces at my back, driving me crazy.

My hair fell about his face as he pulled me closer, slipping his hands up my back after finishing with the laces. My eyes mirrored his as he looked at me; desire, intimacy, love. I touched his face, still in wonder at what I saw there. He gave me a small smile, seeing my awe.

He tickled my shoulder blades, making small circles with his fingers, and then he reached up to slowly trail his fingers down my arms, drawing my corset with them. He slid it from between us, and it landed next to his shirt. His forearms slid along my upper arms to hold my shoulders, looking at me lying on his chest. His eyes were heavy with desire as he looked at me, pressed up against his chest.

His gentle hands slid to my neck and jaw, pulling me in for another scorching kiss. He rolled us back and pressed me into the bed with his slow but ardent kissing. His hands wandered down to caress my bare waist, one wandering up to gently cup a breast, making me gasp. His mouth turned its adoration there, causing me to cry out and arch my back, fisting his hair.

"Eben," I gasped out, starting to really pant now from the throbbing need he had flamed inside of me.

"Shhhhhh. Be patient, Sasha." I felt him start to remove my jeans, each slow movement intensifying the burn; the button flicked open, the zipper drawn, his fingertips on the waistband, the slow, gentle pull as his fingers brushed me on the way down, the brush of the jeans being freed from my toes.

His hands wandered back up my bare skin, up each leg. I drew my knees up as he reached my thighs, responding to his touch. He lay between them to gently plant kisses along the top seam of my panties as his fingers followed the inside ones around to tickle my backside a little. His hands slid under me to lift me up against his mouth, my fingers digging into his shoulders a little.

I looked down, and our eyes met. I saw a glimmer there of Eben's mischievousness as his teeth gently gripped the top of my panties to start pulling them down, his lips trailing down my skin as he went. His eyes never left mine, watching me burn for him.

His tongue slid from my ankle up to my knee, where he kissed his way up my inner thigh. I abandoned myself up to the moan that came as his mouth found me, taking me into his mouth, working me up into a fervor until I cried out. His tongue slipped inside my heat as his hands underneath me lifted me to him. I buckled and cried out as he worked me up into an orgasm before he went straight back to building up the smoldering intensity of heat he had ignited in me.

His mouth traveled back up my body, kissing my hip bone again as I felt him remove the rest of his clothes. His hands and mouth slowly came up to my face.

He stroked my flushed cheeks with the back of his hand, whispering, "You're so beautiful when you let me in here just like this." I couldn't hide from him, from his soulful eyes that saw the real me. I stroked his face as he looked at me. He bent to give me a sweet kiss, still looking in my eyes. With our faces still touching, he whispered, "No more hiding from me. The woman I see right now is stunning. I'm in love with her." I drew a breath at his words and stroked his face with my fingers.

"I love you too, Eben. No more hiding." His smile spread across his face, making my heart flutter. Here we were again; we had found that place of peaceful intimacy.

His adoring eyes took in all of my face, like he was memorizing how I looked at this moment to pull the memory out later. His hands found mine, and he brought them up to the sides of my face. Palm to palm, he laced our fingers and looked into my eyes, giving me a quick kiss, and then he watched my face as he gently breached my entrance. I gasped and closed my eyes, and he slid gently home. I squeezed his hands as he kissed my neck and slowly, oh so slowly, began to move inside of me. I moved, desperate to pull him closer, but his palms held my hands down.

"Shhhhh." I was dying, so unfamiliar with gentle, my body rising to meet his, trying to rush.

"Eben," I panted out, frustrated. He released one of my hands to bring it to my hips, which were responding of their own accord. He very gently but firmly held them, preventing me from rushing the moment.

"I'm going to take care of you, Sasha, Blossom." He started his slow, torturous movements again, holding me still. The building fire inside me was too much when he continued, "Right now and from now on."

I felt a building, coiling, inside of me like I never had before, and I trembled in his arms. He was slowly increasing his tempo, building the heat just like he did with his musical pieces, coming to a crescendo. My free hand gripped his back, digging my nails into his shoulder blade with the building heat. I had never known lovemaking like this before; such passion woven into tenderness.

At last, I boiled over and cried out his name as an overwhelming orgasm flooded over me, burning me as it consumed me. He continued his movements, driving the tidal wave on, finding his own release. We looked into each other's eyes as we burned. It burned on still as I trembled against him, a new flush of rose coming to my cheeks. He had been right; the long, intense orgasm still flowing through my system had been worth the torture of being patient. He had played me just like his greatest symphony, and I could do nothing but ride out the notes of pleasure now.

I looked at him, and with a smile of love, I pulled his neck to my mouth; I had to taste and savor him this way. I needed his decadent sweetness flowing over my tongue. He moaned as I bit down, gently sucking on him, taking my time. I heard him panting again, like he had in our moment earlier, as more pleasure entered his system. I felt him stroking my neck, trying to decide if he would taste me. He was always so gentle.

I pulled back from him and looked at him for a moment. I then closed my eyes and lay my head to the side, giving him silent encouragement. I felt his fangs pressing against my neck as he kissed me.

Gentler than I thought possible, he slid his fangs into my neck and, at last, tasted me. More pleasure hit our systems as he fed on me slowly with such gentle care. My hands came around him and slid up his back to embrace him as he took from me. My eyes closed, and I lay there in his arms at peace for once. When he pulled back, I opened my eyes to look into his that were flaming red. He had given me peace.

He stroked my cheek with his thumb and whispered, "That I could compose something to equal this moment; what I have found in your arms would take a lifetime." I died inside before I felt my heart open to new heights. I smiled at him, and he looked at me for a while.

Slowly, we worked our way down into the sheets of the great black bed that was now saturated in the scent of our lovemaking. Only the tiniest hint of faded Vladimir remained; Jaxon and Eben were both there with me, being breathed in as I fell asleep. Eben held me to him, stroking my hair until I fell asleep. I knew he would watch over me while we slept, preventing any nightmares of Vladimir that would threaten to take over my mind. I felt so safe, so beautiful in the vulnerability that Eben brought out of me, so loved. How had Vladimir ever managed to trap this beautiful soul? Vladimir, the embodiment of evil in my mind, harming my dark angel was a painful thought.

"I love you, Eben."

"I love you too, Blossom, my love." There were those hidden tears again. Oh, Eben. I would never be rid of him or his brothers. They would always be with me. This moment between Eben and I would be one I would never forget. It dulled the pain of Vladimir's cruelty, like pinning a tiny corner of a happy memory over the picture of a painful one. Jaxon's playful sweetness was also there, pinned over another tiny piece of Vladimir. I sighed, breathing in my sweet, dark angel, and finally gave myself over to sleep in his encompassing arms.

# CHAPTER 19

"Alright, move over! It's my turn!" Jaxon whined. I laughed heartily not releasing my hold, driving us even faster. Eben rolled his eyes.

"Give it a rest, Jaxon. You'll be back in control in no time. For now, just sit back and enjoy the ride. Sasha has hidden skills that I'm personally enjoying." I laughed again, flashing Eben a smoldering look over my shoulder. His hands reached out to caress my shoulder in response to the look I was giving him. Jaxon's jealous growl rumbled out over us as his hand snaked out to caress my thigh in response.

"Don't get in my way, Jaxon. I'm going to enjoy this." His hand stayed in place, so I just maneuvered my hold so he wasn't blocking me. His hand snuck over to try to remove mine and regain control, but I slapped him away.

He pouted and I laughed as he turned to look out the passenger side of his sports car. Eben joined in on making fun of his brother from the back seat as I looked at him in the rearview mirror. My hand pulled on the shifter as my tiny feet hit the pedals, pressing the throttle down even more, racing toward the winding mountain road we were heading toward. We hit the winding curves at full speed, the car turning like it was on rails in my expert hands. I down-shifted to maintain speed on the climb.

I looked in the rearview mirror and watched the Harley follow us, an evil grin spreading across my face as I demanded more from the engine. Sebastian shook his head at me and did his best to keep up. My eyes turned back to the winding road as we snaked through the mountain pass, heading to a remote location.

We had gotten word of a rogue wolf in the area from a remote wolf pack that was friends with Sebastian. The rogue had started drawing too much attention over the last week with 3 bloody slaughters close to Pine River. The Cavaliers had been on high alert this last week, and I hadn't been able to hook any, not wanting to draw attention to myself. I had been open with Vladimir about the situation going on in the area, and he had commanded me to deal with it.

Niklaus had insisted I take his two brothers with me when I went, not trusting that Sebastian would be enough to ensure I was safe. That, and that the wolves didn't bother me too much. Our species could be deadly to one another, so there was always tension, but at times, like with Sebastian and I, lines crossed, which could be intense. Wolves appreciated vampires' stamina, and they were always curious about the 'Vampire's Kiss.'

I turned the tunes on and enjoyed the radio, dancing a little as I drove, beating out a rhythm on the steering wheel. Jaxon was having difficulty hanging onto his pout as he watched me out of the corner of his eye.

I smiled as I remembered Niklaus's observation that the three of us could spell serious trouble as we got in the car. I had beat Jaxon to the driver's seat, and a few snarls had been exchanged, followed by a kiss that he tried to use to get past me. I managed to still slide into the driver's seat, flashing him a flirtatious but satisfied smile. Eben's laughter as he climbed in the back had only irritated his brother more; he had opted to sit in the back to remain close to me rather than take his Ducati. Niklaus had stood in the doorway of the manor watching our antics with an amused look, his mind enjoying our comradery and antics.

So, we sped along the mountain pass road, me expertly driving Jaxon's car. I snuck a sideways glance at Jaxon, and he looked over at me. I smiled, listening to his thoughts; he couldn't decide if he was more irritated or turned on with me driving his car. His thoughts were turning lustful as they watched me expertly handle the powerful machine. Both brothers were speculating where I had learned to drive like a pro. I smiled at Jaxon, sneaking another glance before looking back up again.

Sebastian was right behind us, following the curves on his Harley, running old memories through his mind as we zoomed along. He was thinking about how we had first met. Or how I had hooked him into a ruse from my perspective.

Finally, we pulled off the highway down a private, well-hidden, black-top drive with a security gate and fence. This particular pack stayed well-hidden up here in the mountains but would come into Pine River on occasion, according to Sebastian. He was directing me with his thoughts during the journey.

I slowed to allow Sebastian to lead the way, and then we went down the drive leisurely, the security gate closing behind us as we went. The closer we got, I could feel the tension in the car go up a notch. Both brothers were uneasy with being here; they had had far less exposure to being around wolves than I. I was actually relatively comfortable around them. I had had many dealings with them as Vladimir's weapon.

The tension continued to mount, so I said confidently, "Relax, guys."

We pulled up in front of what looked like a lodge with massive garages across the drive. I parked as far from the house as possible and threw the keys into Jaxon's lap before I opened the door and stood.

"Just relax, guys. I'll get the information we need and be right back." I shut the door and walked over to Sebastian, who was getting off his Harley. He wrapped an arm around me and pulled me close, rubbing the small of my back. Two muted growls could be heard coming from Jaxon's car. Sebastian laughed, smiling down at me, and then kissed the tip of my nose.

"I'm not sure that will ever get old," he laughed at my vampires' expense. He turned and pulled me along with him.

A small group of five wolves came walking out of the lodge and walked down the front steps to greet us. Sebastian dropped his arm from my waist to reach out and shake hands with the Alpha, named York, and his second.

"Shall we head inside to talk?" York offered. I heard a car door open.

"Sure," I said. Jaxon's growl was too low for the wolves to pick out, but I could hear it. Neither of the brothers had liked the idea of me going inside with a pack of wolves without them, but I had insisted that it would create too much tension because they were overprotective. They would be right outside if I needed them. I turned and mentally told them to chill out.

York turned, and the others followed him. Sebastian gently guided me after them inside with a hand on my back. We were brought to a large living room area.

"Can we offer you something to drink?" The second offered us out of habit, no doubt, turning to look at us.

Sebastian grinned shamelessly at the man's phrasing but answered, "Scotch." The man turned toward me with an askance expression. I smirked, and an eyebrow came up with a devilish look.

My eyes flickered to crimson, and I answered him, "Are you really offering me a drink?" The wolf's eyebrows shot up, realizing his blunder, but he was also extremely intrigued at my response; most vampires would shy away from a wolf, but those that didn't were 'highly prized' companions. He cleared his throat and laughed before getting Sebastian his scotch.

The glass was handed to Sebastian with one more fleeting look toward my glowing eyes as they started to cool.

Sebastian was chuckling again and wrapped his elbow around my neck to lean in close and whisper, "You really are a tease." Even wolves knew about the fabled 'vampire's kiss,' and most who had the rare opportunity to experience it would, along with any other benefits.

I looked at him, smiling in enjoyment with a hint of flirting, and leaned close to him to whisper, "Jealous, Seb?" His eyes changed a little as they looked at me when I pulled back from his ear.

"You bet. I have firsthand knowledge of what you're offering, remember?" I laughed at him, and he released me. The second stole a glance our way as he showed us over to the seating; he had heard every word.

Sebastian flopped himself down on one of their vast recliners, entirely at ease, and pulled me down to sit on the wide armrest, keeping an arm around my hip. All of the other wolves noticed my ease at his closeness; the Alpha's second, Lucas, in particular, seemed interested after my teasing him about taking a drink.

"We've spotted the rogue running the outskirts of Pine River. The most recent sighting was two nights ago. He is starting to draw attention from the Cavaliers."

"Then why ask us? You have a larger pack than just five and have plenty of numbers to deal with the issue. Why involve us?" I asked York. He looked at me, taking me in and glancing at Sebastian's arm again.

"The rogue is from our pack. He knows us all, and we would never get close to him. It's why I called Sebastian. Sebastian is the one who suggested that the two of you, mainly you, could help us." I said nothing.

"We can help. Do you have any scent that you could share with us?" Sebastian asked. One of the female wolves left and returned with a shirt, tossing it to Sebastian. She was uncomfortable getting near me and returned to sit in the crook of York's arm. Sebastian inhaled the scent and passed it over to me. I stashed a small piece of the fabric on my person to share with the brothers, just in case.

"So what's the story with this rogue, exactly?"

"Well, he's lost it."

I narrowed my eyes at York, saying, "That explains nothing. If I'm going to help, I want to know what happened." The Alpha said nothing. I could pluck it from his mind if I wanted to, but if he wasn't willing to cooperate, I wasn't sure I was willing to help. "Look, I have to deal with this problem with or without your help. It would just be nice to have as much information as possible; besides, why would you invite us here if you weren't going to tell us anything? Is he just running around in wolf form killing, or is he transforming back and forth?"

"He's going around murdering women out of vengeance. His desired mate got shot and killed by some couple that were out hunting in the woods illegally. He just lost it, and it has him going on a rampage. It happened a while back, but it's like he can't find a thrill anymore and has turned to murder," York finally explained.

"There's more to it than that, York," Lucas said. I looked at the second, and he sighed, saying, "He's my brother. He was second before the accident, and then his mental state just deteriorated so much after she was shot. He could never find another female he was interested in, and he blames me for the accident." That was an interesting tidbit.

"Why's that?" I asked him.

"She was out with me in the forest when she got shot." My eyebrows shot up, and I couldn't stop the look that crossed my face. His mind revealed that both brothers had been interested in the same woman; it had been a point of contention between the two for years because they had been very competitive.

I turned and looked at York, who had just turned to talk to Sebastian, "Look, we appreciate your help, but the vampire complicates things. What makes you believe she can help?" Sebastian had a feral-looking smirk on his face, full of confidence. I couldn't help but mess with York a little, so I mentally took my fingernail and drew the sharp point down the length of his spine while I looked at him. It felt as real as if I had used my real finger.

My hand framed my face, my pointer finger resting along my cheek as I smirked. I felt him shiver, and his mental hackles went up. Everyone in the room could feel it but didn't know why, though Sebastian knew I was the cause. York was staring at me as I smirked at him. I drew the fingernail around his ear and down his neck, turning my look to a sultry smirk. His nostrils flared a little as he intensely stared at me.

The female next to him picked up on what I was doing when the indentation of the invisible fingernail could be seen as I drew it slowly down his t-shirt. She shot out of her seat, coming at me, snarling. The rest of the pack wolves stood, alarmed, as she flew at me.

Neither Sebastian nor I moved as she sprang at me. I didn't bat an eyelash as I sent her sprawling backward onto the floor, swatting her like a fly. She jumped up again, snarling with teeth bared, and came at me again. This time, I rose slowly to meet her. She stalked over to me, taking a swipe at me. I caught her wrist in mid-air, reinforcing my natural strength with my magic, as I bared my fangs and viciously snarled at her, and then I sent her sprawling backward with a fist to her face.

"Keep your bitch under control, York, or we're leaving," I snarled at him. Sebastian, trying to hide his smile, wrapped his arm back around my hips as I sat back down. York jerked his chin, and one of the other male werewolves walked the female out.

York looked a little taken aback and I gave him a smirk. He was reevaluating me, and then a look of recognition came across his face.

He looked at Sebastian and asked, "This is your vampire?" A huge grin broke out over Sebastian's face in answer to York's question. Apparently, they had swapped conquest stories in the past. York's attitude changed toward me significantly, becoming instantly more at ease and trusting.

"Seems like Sebs been telling stories on me," I said, amused.

"Wait," Lucas held out his hand, looking between Sebastian and York and then at me. "This is Sasha?"

I smiled at him, saying, "Glad you've heard of me. If you're willing to help, Lucas, I believe we can trap your brother in a night or two."

"How's that?"

I flashed him a feral grin, saying, "We're going on a date."

# CHAPTER 20

The werewolf just stared at me. "A date?" I nodded. It was going to piss my vampires off to the max, but it was going to be the easiest way.

"That's right, Lucas. We're going to use your brother's competitiveness and grudge towards you against him. Shouldn't be too hard. He's looking for a thrill? Let's dangle one in front of him he won't be able to resist; a woman you're interested in." His mouth dropped open, shocked.

"Don't you believe he would find it tempting if he saw you out with me, acting like you're really interested? Don't you believe he would desire to take the ultimate revenge?"

"But you're a vampire. It's not like you're a werewolf or even human."

"All the more tempting for him, wouldn't you agree? If he believes you've found a woman you're interested in, especially a vampire, you don't think he would go for it?"

"Well, yeah, he would, but wouldn't that put you in danger?" I laughed a little.

"You're sweet." He got a small, embarrassed smile on his face. "It will be a little, yes, but I'll have you, Sebastian, and likely a couple of other vampires around to help deal with the problem." He swallowed, glancing around.

"Are there any social places that he frequents?"

"There's 'The Den.' It's a local werewolf club, a hub for supernatural creatures to hang out at without fear of being discovered. It's top secret, out in the woods outside of Pine River. You have to know someone and show *proof of entry*."

"Don't other wolves have an issue with the rogue? Why exactly would he go there?"

"It's considered 'pack business' so long as he doesn't start killing other werewolves. He's been sticking to the shadows, not really playing front scene. The Cavaliers make the others nervous but not enough to get involved when we are expected to handle it."

95

"And have you actually tried to deal with it?" I asked. Sebastian rubbed my thigh gently in a reminder to take it easy.

York answered, "We have. He was our best tracker and has evaded our attempts. He never lets us get close enough to really do anything. He's only let Lucas near him several times at that hangout. This has been going on for months, but it's only in the last week that he has started to murder women. Like Lucas said, he sticks to the shadows."

"Alright then, I guess we better draw him out. Seb, do you know the place?" He gave me a nod and smiled. I turned to Lucas, saying, "Alright, we'll meet you there tomorrow night. What should I wear?"

"What?!"

"Well, what would your brother like?" He thought for a moment and then looked me over.

"Probably something similar to what you're wearing, but a skirt instead of jeans." I nodded. Black corset and skirt it would be then.

We rose with a plan in place, and York and Lucas walked us out. Jaxon was leaning against the driver's door of his car, tracking us with his eyes. Eben was standing on the other side with the passenger side door open, leaning with one arm on the top of the car and the other on the open door; he also tracked our movements.

We stopped at Sebastian's motorcycle and turned to them.

"Seven alright for you, Lucas?" He swallowed, eyes wide, and nodded. A smile spread across my red lips as I looked at him. He was tall and broad, had black hair and eyes, and seemed sweet. "No need to be nervous, Lucas. Most men like it when I bite," I winked at him. Lucas' nervousness increased a little.

Sebastian looked at his reaction, and it struck him as funny. He wrapped his arms around me from behind, laughing while watching Lucas react. I looked over my shoulder with an affectionate smile for Sebastian and gave his cheek a light pat before turning back to Lucas.

"Quit teasing him, Sasha," Sebastian said into my ear, looking at Lucas with an amused grin. Lucas started to smile back.

"I wasn't." His smile dropped a little, making Sebastian laugh again, and Lucas really looked at me then. He studied me, deciding if he liked my flirtatious attitude or not. I intrigued him; there weren't a lot of vampires in Pine River that were so comfortable around their kind.

"Is it true that Sebastian first came across you on the racing scene?" I gave him a smile and leaned back against Sebastian, nodding.

"It was illegal street but yes. Of course, it wasn't by accident on my end, but that's a different story."

Sebastian laughed, "I was in Germany, studying the underground racing done by supernaturals, how their increased reaction times and senses affected the racing scene and flowed out into the area's culture. Sasha here challenged me to a race."

"And how did that lead to, you know?"

This time it was my turn to laugh and rub Sebastian's neck as I answered, "I kicked his ass and then told him looser buys dinner. The rest is history." All the wolves laughed heartily, and I even caught a few chuckles from the sports car behind us.

"Alright, well, I'll see you there at seven then," Lucas said, still uneasy. Sebastian shook their hands, and they turned to head back into the lodge. I sighed and turned to look at Sebastian after they were gone.

"This will never work unless he can actually act like he's into me." Sebastian smiled at me, casually wrapping his arms around me as he leaned back against his bike. I heard some rumbling from the brothers; they hadn't been filled in on the plan but didn't like what they were hearing.

"He already is." I rolled my eyes. "Sasha, I've known them a long time, trust me. You intrigue him; he's just not as forward as some."

"Well, he better work up some courage by tomorrow night, or we will never pull this off. I have a feeling his brother is very smart."

"That's a fact. You riding home with me then?" I smiled at him but pulled out of his arms.

"They're already going to be pissed with this idea, so I'd better not push it," I winked at him. He laughed and gave me an affectionate smile. "See you tomorrow." He nodded and got on his bike as I returned to the car. "Want me to drive?" I teased Jaxon.

"What idea, exactly, is going to piss us off?" I reached for the keys, and he jerked them out of my reach. I used the opportunity to press myself against him as I reached for them. His amber eyes sparkled at the contact, but he didn't relinquish the keys.

I gave up and went around the car to Eben, who climbed in the back again. Jaxon got in the driver's seat, and with a huge smile, I slid into the back of the car and shut the door. It worked and Jaxon was irritated once again.

"Since you won't let me drive, I guess I'll just have to snuggle up with Eben. Hop to it, chauffeur." The engine roared to life as Jaxon hissed at my words.

Eben put his arm around me, and I settled in close to him as Jaxon sped home. I took the opportunity to just lay my head on Eben, breathing him in as he gently stroked my face and hair in his tender, loving way. He ignored his grumbling brother as he looked at me, touching me. He had spent almost every night with me this last week, showing me tenderness and watching over me as I slept. Several of the evenings, he would come from playing his violin or piano after I had already fallen asleep, slipping in next to me.

It was evening when we got back to the estate. The three of us entered, and I motioned for them to come with me to Niklaus's study; I still hadn't explained what was going to happen. The three stood next to one another, waiting for me to explain.

"I'll be going out the next few nights with a werewolf named Lucas to lure his brother out. If Lucas acts like he is interested in me, his brother will most likely take the bait since they are competitive, and he blames Lucas for the death of his desired mate. He will want to take revenge through me." All three brothers scowled, not liking this idea at all.

"And Vladimir will have no problem with you messing around with werewolves? What happened to him being worried about us 'consorting with werewolves?'"

"Vladimir's issue was the 'wolf running around *his* property unchecked.' He doesn't care otherwise. He's sent me on many *assignments* dealing with wolves, including Sebastian. I just have to explain to Vladimir what's going on, and then he will be alright, I think, as long as we don't mention Sebastian specifically. That would be unwise."

"I don't like this," Niklaus stated. "It's perilous, Sasha."

"It needs taken care of. I don't see an easier way since the pack has already tried. Better me than some human."

"I don't like it. Are you going alone?"

"I'll have that other wolf with me and Sebastian."

"It's too risky. Take Jaxon and Eben, please. I would also go if I could, but I can't."

"Why is that, Niklaus? We both know you could take care of him easier than even me, given your past." He walked up to me and gave me a smile, putting a hand under my chin to look at me.

"It is precisely because I used to hunt werewolves, Sasha. I don't think it would be the best idea; they wouldn't let me anywhere near 'The Den' in the first place. It's not an unknown fact in their community."

I smiled at him and touched his face, amused, "You're legendary, but it's not the dark ages anymore, Niklaus. Relationships between our species have improved, even crossed lines."

He smiled back at me, "That may be, but some things will never be forgotten. I still think this whole thing is too risky, Sasha."

It was my turn to try to comfort him, "There aren't too many things that can hurt a vampire, Niklaus. I'll be alright."

"Werewolves are one of them, Sasha. Please be careful. Please bring Jaxon and Eben?" I was about to object when he added, "For me?" Well dang. I sighed.

"Alright, but they have to *behave*. No interfering. This won't work if a brawl is started over it."

I had switched my gaze specifically to Jaxon when I said the last bit. He looked to the side.

"Thank you," Niklaus whispered. I touched his face again affectionately.

"Only cuz you asked so sweet." I pecked him on the lips and made to leave, but he pulled me back for a deeper kiss before releasing me. One more caress on his face, and I left them to return to my room for the night. I was going to have to call Vladimir to explain.

I had just opened my door when a hand pushed it open for me, and Jaxon slid into my room with me, shutting it behind us. He had a funny look on his face, looking to the side, slightly embarrassed.

"What's the matter, Jaxon?"

"You're not actually going on a real date with that werewolf, are you?" He said, coming up to me, his eyes burning with irritation. I pulled him against me, kissing him, backing him up to my bed; my phone call to Vladimir could wait. I had his shirt and my jeans off before we even hit the bed. I straddled him, kissing him as his possessive hands wandered. I pulled back to look at him to answer his question.

"For all intents and purposes, yes. It needs to look real, but I'm not intending to take him home if that's what you're asking."

Jaxon's thoughts wandered to the bar for a moment, and he said with a smirk, "That didn't stop me, Doll Face. If Eben hadn't interrupted," he dropped off. I laughed.

"Jaxon, I promise I will always come home to you and your coven brothers. I might flirt, even pet a bit, but I would never take it farther than that with him. Sebastian is a bigger temptation, but I know who my heart belongs to." He got a pleased smirk on his face as he reached around to squeeze my ass, pulling me tighter against him.

His eyes hardened again, and he asked, "What about feeding from them?" I couldn't make promises in that area, but I knew that no one would taste as good to me as Jaxon and his brothers did.

I gave him a smile and bent close to his ear, whispering, "I will always come home to you. I will always crave you more." His hands tightened on me.

I slid my lips down his neck and bit him, drawing his spicy blood into my mouth and making him moan. I undid his belt and jeans as I fed from him. He snarled as I grasped him, teasing him. I released him and sat on top of him, feeling smug. His smirk returned, and he ripped the rest of my clothes off, much to my annoyance. He was going through my wardrobe at an alarming rate. He rolled me over with a possessive kiss. He bit down on me at the same time that he thrust into my body, making me moan. He held my hands over my head as he fed, bringing us to a demanding rhythm.

After my screams finally died away and he lay next to me, he pulled me snug up against him and whispered in my ear, "You're mine, Sugar Lips, and if you don't come home to me, I'll come after you."

# CHAPTER 21

I hopped off the back of Sebastian's motorcycle and waited for him to put the kickstand down and get off. We were in a secluded parking lot deep in the woods with nothing nearby. Jaxon pulled up in his car and got out just as Eben pulled into another parking spot on his Ducati. I had ridden with Sebastian for appearances' sake; we were going as a group, but it needed to seem like I was with the wolves, not the brothers. There were eyes even here in the parking lot.

Sebastian wrapped an arm around my waist as we walked over to meet up with Lucas, who was nervously waiting. I was struggling to believe this would work if he couldn't relax. The five of us sped off into the woods, me following the two wolves for a decent distance. We slowed and started walking when I spotted an absolutely massive man leaning against a tree with his arms folded. He turned toward us, looking each one of us over. A smile broke out over his face when he spotted Lucas as we got close.

"Well, look who's showing his face!" He offered a hand to Lucas and shook it, turning to Sebastian next. "Been a long time, professor." Sebastian shook his hand, and the man's attention turned to the vampires with the wolves he knew. "Unusual company you're keeping, Lucas," the man drawled as he looked the brothers over.

I took the opportunity to slide a hand over Lucas' shoulder, leaning against him with a wicked smile on my face for the bouncer. The man's attention turned to me as he looked me up and down. He liked what he saw, and I smiled with my fangs as my eyes lit up red in the dark, implying more was going on with Lucas than just being friends with how I leaned on him.

Lucas took a hint at last and wrapped his arm around my waist.

"These are my friends, Jaxon and Eben. And this is Sasha," Lucas said as he pulled me a little closer. The man murmured his approval as he looked at me. He looked to the brothers, waiting for proof of entry. He could smell vampires, but Cavaliers could wear enough scent to fool a nose at first whiff. Proof of entry was required before you got past the bouncers on the outskirts and at the door. They took no chances. The brothers' eyes glowed, satisfying the man.

He jerked his head, saying, "Head on in. Enjoy yourselves. Hang onto your vamp, Lucas. There's more than one wolf in there that would take your place eagerly, with opportunity. Even saw your brother inside."

We turned and ran another short way, passing another bouncer at a perimeter fence before we finally made it up to a small discreet door in the side of a mountain. The bouncer at the door again asked for proof, and we were finally granted entry to a descending flight of stairs to another door that opened up into the club inside the mountain.

There were several entrances and exits into 'The Den.' It was a popular spot, large and bustling with patrons and activity. There were all the amenities traditional bars and clubs offered: the bar, plenty of tables, private dark nooks, a dance floor, darts, card playing, pool tables, and even a large snooker table that caught my eye.

Patrons were laughing and hauling back drinks, dancing to the upbeat music, playing various games, and even a snarling scuffle broke out in a corner over a hand of cards, the wolves' eyes changing, canines descending. The dark private booths scattered about in the shadows were filled with couples using the seclusion or groups of wolves who wanted a private chat while they did shots.

I spotted another male vampire in the back corner playing poker with a round of wolves; his eyes glowed red in delight as he won a hand. He looked up at me, and I flashed him my fangs with a smile, getting a nod in response. The majority of the patrons were wolves, otherwise, but there were a few I had no idea what they were.

Eyes were starting to turn in our direction as we stood there; vampires didn't come all that often, and we were a curiosity.

"You play snooker, Lucas?" He looked down at me and smiled before leading me by the hand over to the table.

We set it up and started up a game. The brothers left to get us all drinks, leaving me with the two wolves. The rogue was here; we could all smell him, but he remained elusive; even his brother couldn't locate him with his casual glances.

I sidled up next to Lucas and draped an arm over his shoulder as he bent to take his shot and whispered in his ear, "Ignore him. Right now you need to focus on me and having a good time. Tonight is not about actually getting your brother to show himself. Tonight is about getting him to notice us. So relax." I pulled back from him, smiling at him like I had whispered something naughty in his ear. He gave me a crooked smile, still nervous, but he relaxed a bit before he leaned over again and took his shot.

I sighed inwardly; his reserve wasn't going to convince anyone. Sebastian came up behind me and wrapped his arms around me, and I reached up behind me to rub his neck in response while I watched Lucas with flirting eyes. I could feel more eyes darting over to us, taking in the open level of PDA between

Sebastian and me. Interest rose in the mental atmosphere of the club; vampire companions were a rare commodity.

The brothers had returned with drinks and started up a game of pool next to our snooker table. I pulled out of Sebastian's embrace to take my shot, making a point of bending over close to Lucas. Sebastian's eyes twinkled as he watched, and he flashed a naughty grin toward Lucas. Lucas met his eyes and couldn't help but smile back and laugh a little.

My turn ended, and Lucas wandered to the other side of the table, looking for a shot.

I chanced a glance over at the brothers. They were focused on their game, jeering each other and having a good time. The atmosphere was freeing in that we didn't have to hide at all; if you wanted to move to the opposite side of the table at vampire speed, no one would think anything. You didn't have to hide if your eyes glowed in reaction to something. The brothers were soaking up the freeing atmosphere. I could understand why the place was a popular hangout.

Sebastian drew my attention when he approached me, pressing me against the large snooker table. I smiled at him and wrapped my arms around his neck to lean in to whisper so only he could hear.

"I don't know what to do without completely throwing myself all over him. It's not supposed to look like I'm the only one interested. His brother won't give a crap about a woman interested in Lucas without him reciprocating. Would dancing loosen him up or make it even worse?" I heard Sebastian sigh. And then his mind had an idea. I pulled back and smiled at him with an appreciation and just a hint of evil delight. "You really do miss me, don't you?" I teased him. I heard him growl, not hiding it under his breath like usual. It could work, but the brothers weren't going to like it. They had done a bang job so far of not reacting but I had to warn them.

I walked over to Lucas, pulled him after me, handed his stick to Sebastian with a smirk, and started leading him across the room. Sebastian flashed the brothers a look that said 'Sorry guys,' and leaned the stick against the table to follow us across the club. Eyes all over the room tracked us as we crossed to one of the dark nooks. I knew that a particular wolf's was among them. I mentally warned the brothers to keep it under control, reassuring them of who my heart belonged to.

I pulled on Lucas' arm so he would slide into the booth first, following him. Sebastian slid in after me, pressing in close. Lucas was confused but had slid into the booth without objecting. Sebastian swept my hair back over my shoulders, kissing me there.

Lucas was still confused about what was going on, poor guy. I moved in close to him and slid a hand up his chest to his neck as my fangs descended, and my eyes lit up crimson. Lucas' breathing hitched a little before his heart sped up; he had caught on. I gave him a sly grin before leaning over to him.

"Relax, Lucas. Your brother is undoubtedly watching, and you're actually going to enjoy this. Let's see how much his interest increases when he watches me feed on two wolves." I kissed Lucas on the lips quickly and then leaned over to his neck, turning his head away from me with a firm hand on his jaw. I put my lips to his neck and then gently bit down. A loud gasp escaped Lucas, and his hands automatically came to my back to hold me while I fed on him.

Sebastian moved and extended his arm over to the table, almost like he was trying to give us privacy while I fed. Lucas' deep moans of pleasure and gasps were not missed by the ears in the room, though. I didn't pull much from the bite; I just took slowly from the bite, drawing out his pleasure to make sure that his brother could hear, regardless of where he was. It was about Lucas' pleasure, not feeding.

At last, I pulled back to look into Lucas' eyes as his face came forward to look at me. His eyes were glowing, and his hold on me tightened. I licked my lips clean and then leaned in to kiss him sensually. Fully aroused, having just been bathed in pleasure, Lucas' reservations were nonexistent, and he pulled me close to kiss me back. After a few moments, I pulled back with a teasing and slightly smug look. He searched my face, and then he met Sebastian's eyes, which were also glowing; I doubted there was a male in the entire club who wasn't turned on.

"Holy Hell, Sebastian," Lucas breathed for just us and let his head fall back as his eyes closed. "So that's the 'Vampire's Kiss.' Now I know what the hubbub is about. Damn."

I pulled out of his arms while he relaxed, and I turned to Sebastian. Sebastian couldn't hide his anticipation as he pulled me in for a kiss on the mouth.

"Careful, Seb," I whispered just to him, "You're on the verge of falling for me again. You know my heart is taken. I don't want to hurt you again." He laughed and put a kiss on my cheek in acceptance. I wasn't as gentle with him, but I drew it out just the same as he slumped sideways against the booth, also not hiding the pleasure I gave him. Lucas had leaned up to watch, no longer shy. His interest had turned genuine.

I released Sebastian and turned to Lucas, "Ready to go dance?" He licked his lips and nodded. Sebastian's idea seemed to work; Lucas no longer seemed hesitant to touch me. Quite the opposite. Good. Now, we might have a chance to convince his brother that this was real.

The three of us slipped out of the booth and went to the dance floor, where we started to dance, a werewolf sandwich with vampire filling. Sebastian helped spur Lucas on by becoming possessive of me and challenging the other wolf occasionally. It worked, and Lucas was soon pulling me up against him eagerly, not relinquishing his hold on me for Sebastian.

Another werewolf was eyeing me as we danced, and I gave him a little appreciative smile before turning back to Lucas. I was about to test just how comfortably possessive Lucas had become. The wolf moved in closer, and I moved away from Lucas just enough to allow the other wolf to slip in next to me, trying his luck at joining our little trio. Lucas reacted exactly like I was hoping and snarled at the man, shutting him out. A tense moment occurred, and vicious snarls were exchanged between the two over me while Sebastian pulled me back a couple of steps to protect me. I saw the brothers tense at the other side of the room. Jaxon looked like he might splinter the pool stick he held.

Lucas didn't back down, and the other wolf gave up, sent packing. I gave Lucas a big smile and ran my hands over him, dancing close again. He pulled me to him, almost forgetting that it was a ruse. My eyes peeking over his shoulder locked with another pair in the shadows. The pair stared at me, a glow of desire flickering to life in them. Desire for revenge.

# CHAPTER 22

He was close. He was watching us. He had taken the bait, hook, line, and sinker. He had ended up being smarter than I had given him credit for, but I hadn't realized it until it was too late that night. Thinking back, I should have been more careful and stayed closer to the brothers or Sebastian. Now, it was too late. If I had known what it would lead to, I would never have made such a costly mistake. Hindsight was a bitch.

It was the second night at 'The Den,' and I was on the dance floor again with Lucas. Sebastian was hanging back more tonight, giving Lucas more space with me. The trap was set, and I was about to set the hook. We had spent a fair amount of time dancing and playing pool against the brothers, and it was time to up the stakes.

I pulled close to Lucas' ear and whispered, "Your brother needs some more motivation, I guess. Take me to the back, and let's give it to him." He pulled back, his eyes igniting. He brought me to the back, looking for an open booth, but none were open.

I shrugged and nodded toward the stairwell to the side of the booths that led up to the exit. It would more than do. Lucas pulled me in and pressed me up against the wall there, kissing and petting me. I responded to him for a while, and then I pulled his neck to me and sank my fangs there, slowly drawing out his pleasure.

Wolves were interesting feedings; it was like tasting something wild. They each had their own flavor, but it was like comparing different kinds of wild game; deer versus elk versus bear. Lucas wasn't a terrible flavor, but I preferred Sebastian. However, no wolf could ever come close to the brothers; they were top-shelf.

Lucas was leaning over me, panting and moaning through the feeding that I was taking when his brother swooped down on us from farther up the stairwell. Lucas hadn't been hard to deal with, being so overwhelmed with

105

pleasure at that exact moment. A thick tree branch to the back of his head, and he had dropped instantly.

I had snarled at the man, coming at him to attack him, when a single needle came between me and victory. I remember looking over at the syringe the wolf had just stuck into me, confused, seconds before the drug hit my system, and my vision began to swirl. He had wasted no time, throwing me over his shoulder and disappearing with me.

Ugg. My head was throbbing. My whole being was weak, so weak. It felt like I was dying slowly. What was happening to me? Where was I? I let out a groan and moved, feeling dirt underneath my side. I then realized that I was bound, which confused me. The memory of my evening with Lucas hit me, and I groaned again. My brain felt foggy; I couldn't access my power at all. My body was so weak that the bindings on my hands and feet actually held me as I struggled against them. Why was I here? The memory of the rogue slipped into my mind. He had taken me and carried me off into the night before any of the others had even realized I was gone. He was going to kill me.

I struggled to sit up and look around me, but the drugs in my system kept pulling me under mentally. It was like I was fading in and out of consciousness. The little glimpses around had me thinking of some sort of shack out in the woods. I lay there for an indescribable amount of time, and at last, I felt the drugs starting to fade. It was like my mind clicked back on at that moment, and suddenly, Vladimir's apparition was there with me. He was fuzzy, fading in and out with my flashes of power flaring and fading. He looked like he was feeling the same way, drugged for some reason.

"Sasha." I briefly looked at him with heavy lids, and then he faded away from me. His link in my mind had just run out.

"Ahhh, you're awake," the wolf said, coming into wherever he had me. Fear gripped me. A fear like I hadn't experienced in a long time, the fear of death. Even Vladimir had never brought about this particular chilling grip on my heart. Vladimir was worse than death in many ways, but I had always known he would never kill me. "Come on, baby, you'd better feed, or the poison will actually do you in." I realized that he had picked me up and was holding me to his chest with my face right next to his neck. I felt tiny being held by this large, powerful wolf. And then I realized he was trying to get me to take blood from him.

I didn't want to feed from him, but my survival instincts kicked in, and I bit down, sucking hard to bring the life-giving liquid into my system. I was so drugged it was like an infant nursing, but he still gained pleasure from it, evidenced by his sighs and moaning.

"That's right, baby, drink as much as you can. You'll need it to survive the next dose." I pulled on him harder, drawing more of him into my mouth, and he cried out in his pleasure at it. "Maybe I won't kill you for a while if it's going to be like this," I heard him say. He set me down on the dirt again, and I looked up at him as he bent over me with a needle. The fear returned as he slid it into my neck and pushed the plunger down.

The fear of death and the drugs hitting my system pulled me down into the memory of the last time I had been this afraid, this certain I was going to die. The visions swam before my drugged eyes. I could see the torches all around me like I had on that night. The angry crowd screaming at me, spitting on me, even slapping me as I was dragged through them at the end of a rope.

The angry cries, "Witch! Demon! Burn her! Burn the witch!" I was drug through the crowd, tripping on the stairs leading up to the platform, my white nightgown tearing on the rough wood. "Burn the witch!" I was led to the pole in the center and painfully bound there as I cried out into my gag.

The man who had bound me came around to stand before me with a pair of sheep sheers. I cried out again as he yanked on my hair, cutting it short to the scalp and nicking me multiple times in the process. By the time he was finished, I was almost bald and bleeding. He left me, and my eyes took in the crowd, screaming at me. Bundles of wood were being laid against the small platform where I was bound. More torches and pitchforks.

"Kill her! Kill the witch!" Tears were pouring down my face as pitchers of oil were being poured out over the wood. I was about to die. Looking into the crowd, I saw my family there, their eyes cold and filled with hate, as they cheered along with the crowd to kill me.

A torch was slowly lowered to the bundles of wood, and the flames flew across them, hissing as they spread along the oil. The heat was overwhelming as the flames rose higher and higher, getting closer to me. The flames were starting to burn my skin as the fear of death swept its icy chill through my being. The smoke was burning my eyes and lungs.

"Burn the witch!" A cheer went out in the crowd as the flames rose higher.

The sound of thundering hooves. Swords being drawn and the clanging of steel upon steel reached me in my oblivion. Even where I lay on the dirt of the forest shack, I could feel the thundering, the drugs tricking my mind.

"Come with me, child," he had said to me, ripping me free from the binding that held me to the burning pyre. I threw myself into his arms, and he jumped back off the flaming pyre and onto his horse.

"Sire, what do you want us to do with the villagers?"

I clung to the man as he answered, "Kill them. Burn the village. Leave none alive. Do you have her parents?"

"Yes, Sire."

"And?"

"They informed us that her name is Sasha, and she is 12 years old."

"Very well. Kill them with the rest." Movement under me. A horse galloping while strong arms held me to him, tucked away safe in his cloak. The clattering of hooves over a bridge and then cobblestones. And then I was being carried in his arms.

The dirt under my palms moved; no, I was moved again. "Come on, baby, you need to feed again." I was laid against the wolf again. I did as he said. He was moaning and sighing again. "That's right, baby, take some more. Ahhhhh." I felt real tears flowing out of me as I fed on the rogue. My heavy, drugged mind skipped about in my memories. How I had been raised in the castle by my previous master, who had saved me from being burnt alive at the stake. How he had educated me not only in normal things but also in espionage, manipulation, and using my power. How he had kept me protected until the day I turned 17 when he had collared me and made me his in every way. How he had had a 'friend' come to attend one of his balls years later, introducing me to Vladimir at the ball. How the night of my 23rd birthday, Vladimir had turned me.

"Good job, baby. Until next time."

"No!" my mind screamed in its drugged state as another plunger slid downward.

I was utterly helpless, unable to move as my mind shuffled through old memories, not really seeing. The endless nights when my master would use me as a reward to his men that pleased him. The other times, he would have me kill the ones that displeased him. The night that Vladimir had stolen me away from my master.

I was being lifted again and carried, and then we were in the woods.

I heard the rogue again, "I'm not going to kill you, baby. The ultimate revenge on that bastard would be taking you from him and making you mine." *His.*

I was laid down somewhere soft. A bed? He was next to me then, pulling me to him again.

"Feed, baby." The drugs going through my system were so heavy, paining my body and mind. I had no choice but to feed from him. This time, he lay there next to me, holding me tightly to him, moaning his pleasure from my act of survival. His hands wandered over my body while I did so. He wasn't going to kill me; he was going to *acquire* me.

Somewhere deep inside my drugged state, my mind recognized that he had become addicted to my bite; I had become his new thrill, his new drug. Something to fill the void that he had been filling with murder. Another syringe. Was I dying? His feeding wasn't helping as much this time.

My mind was pulled back under, and my memories of an underground gambling house takeover came to my mind. I was hanging on the owner, as his new girl, when the shots rang out across the place. Screams and the lights went out. Vladimir had come to claim what he wanted, and it had been my job to be close to the man when he did so I could end him quickly. I drained the man, and he fell at my feet. More gunshots reverberated through my mind, somehow sounding so real and close to me. I heard a body fall. The vision was sounding and feeling so real.

"Sasha." Niklaus?

"Sasha? Sasha, can you hear me?" Eben?

"He drugged her!" An abhorred voice was heard through the fog. Jaxon?

"He gave her too much this last time. She's dying." Niklaus . . . .

# CHAPTER 23

A spicy cocktail. A savory meal. A dessert. I still felt foggy, but it had cleared enough for voices to reach me, including tastes and feelings. Where was I?

I heard a voice in the background, "Yes, Vladimir. She's coming round. It was a close one. Of course, we're feeding her, and we've already administered the antidote. It was the same as what the Cavaliers use on bullets, which are diluted and injected. She should be fine. Yes, I will help. I'm not sure. Yes, I'll call you in a few hours with an update." I felt a groan escape me. I felt terrible.

"I think she's coming to," I heard a different voice say.

The first person talking with Vladimir responded, "Yes, she is. I can feel her mind. She can already hear us."

"Why is it taking so long? We've always healed so fast."

"It's not like when you can just take the bullet out and administer the antidote. The poison is in her system. It's why it's taken this long, but at this point, it won't be long." Niklaus?

The same voice spoke close to me, "Yes, Sasha. I'm here." I felt gentle hands touching my head, and then I felt him there with me, inside my mind, helping to clear the fog.

"*Niklaus, where am I?*" I thought.

"You're safe at the manor, Sasha."

"*What happened, Niklaus?*" I thought again. I heard a sigh as he worked to overcome the remainder of the drugs that clouded my mind.

"You were taken by the rogue. He used a diluted version of the poison the Cavaliers use on their bullets. You were missing for two days."

"*Two days?*" I felt the metal fog finally creep away and drew in a deep breath, finally opening my eyes. I blinked slowly. Niklaus was leaning over me, his green eyes so caring and soft were looking back into mine. He smiled as I looked at him with recognition, and his hands slid down to the sides of my face from my temples.

"Welcome back," he smiled at me. He really was a vision, and I couldn't stop myself from reaching out to touch his face, still unsure if this was reality or another drugged mirage.

I heard another couple of relieved sighs nearby, but I couldn't look away from the beautiful man leaning over me.

"How did I get here?" I asked quietly.

"I had to go hunt a werewolf down to find you. You gave us all a terrible scare. Vladimir has been calling nonstop as well."

"Is the rogue dead, then?"

"Yes, I killed him." I sighed in relief, and then I smiled at him. He really was my white knight. How had I gotten so lucky? I caressed his face with my fingers as I looked at him, thinking about him. He had come for me. He had saved me when I needed him most. I had never needed anyone like that since the night my old master had saved me from the flames.

He smiled at me again and bent to kiss me before he whispered, "I will always come for you, Sasha." He leaned up away from me then, and my eyes took in where we were.

I was lying on the couch in the study. My eyes landed on Eben and Jaxon, standing nearby and watching me. Niklaus stood and made room for them to come close to me.

He smiled quickly and slipped from the room, saying, "I'll be right back." Eben kneeled near my head, and Jaxon sat on the couch close, both caressing me. I smiled at them, happy to have them close to me.

"You were both there too, weren't you?"

Jaxon smirked at me, saying, "I told you I'd come after you if you didn't come home, Doll Face. You really think I'd just let you run off with a werewolf?" I laughed at him, smiling, and pulled him in for a kiss.

I turned to Eben and laid my hand on his cheek, connecting with his azure eyes. I kept my promise to him in that moment and let him see inside me; the fear I had felt then, the relief and love I felt now. He brushed my hair back from my face with his hands and leaned in to give me a tender, loving kiss.

"I'm so glad you're safe," he said.

I looked at them both, and my voice was heavy with emotion as I whispered, "Thank you." I got two smiles back and rested in their closeness until Niklaus returned.

Niklaus pressed his way through to pick me up in his arms, saying, "Come on. You need to rest."

A shriek from upstairs, and the Governess was screaming at Lucy and Lucian again. I couldn't help laughing and rolling my eyes.

"I see that hasn't changed." Niklaus laughed as he carried me down the hall. I saw Eben and Jaxon slip out behind us to head up the stairs to manage the recent drama. Sounded like I was going to have to have another talk with the Governess and the twins.

Niklaus chuckled again as he opened my bedroom door, shutting it behind him. I expected him to walk me over to my bed to place me there, but instead, he turned and walked into the bathroom with me.

The sound of running water met my ears as he pushed the door open, and I spotted the huge bathtub that was almost full and covered in bubbles. Candles around the tub were flickering. I looked at him, surprised.

"You ran me a bubble bath?"

He smiled at me, saying, "Yes, I heard you liked them after a hard day. I think the last two qualify, don't you?" He had been listening in on my mind the afternoon he had gone to survey the Cavaliers with me. His attention to detail shouldn't have surprised me, but it still did. I wasn't used to being taken care of, especially in detailed ways like this.

I studied him as he gently set my feet on the ground and reached over to turn the water off.

I could hear his continuing worry and concern over me, wanting to do anything in his power that he could to protect and take care of me.

"Niklaus, thank you. For everything. I wouldn't be alive right now if you hadn't come after me when you did." I was emotional again, full of gratitude and the unfamiliar sensations of being on the receiving end of loving care; it seemed once the gates to my emotions had been unlocked, I was unable to prevent them from coming out. I threw my arms around his neck, breathing in his safety as his arms came around me to hold me. I heard him sigh at my closeness, his mind embracing the relief that I was there, safe in his arms. I couldn't disagree.

When I pulled back slightly, he leaned in and kissed me slowly at first, but then it was like his need for me overwhelmed him at that moment, and he deepened the kiss, holding me tighter against his frame. He gasped with emotion as he broke our kiss and caressed my face, looking at me like I might disappear.

"I thought we'd lost you, Sasha. I was so full of regret while I searched for you; I had never told you how I'm in love with you, and I regret that I denied myself your touch. I have never hunted a werewolf while holding such fear in my heart before." I looked in his beautiful green eyes, caressing his face with my fingertips.

"Fear?" I whispered, confused.

He held my face and kissed me again before answering, "I was so afraid of losing you. That you were lost to us. To me." I looked at him tenderly, running my fingers through his hair. "

"Well, I'm back now, thanks to you." We stayed quiet for a long moment, just looking at each other and listening to each other's minds. I felt so safe in his arms like I would have to worry for nothing. I could hear his mind embrace the thought.

The last man who had rescued me had turned around to enslave me and use me; the contrast between him and Niklaus could not be understated. Niklaus would never treat me poorly or use me; he barely allowed himself to touch me with all of his self-control and sacrifice. He was listening and couldn't stop the reaction of his breathy laugh and flushed cheeks.

"Was it difficult to find the rogue? To hunt him like you used to?"

He smiled slightly before answering, "He was a challenge, yes, being a very talented tracker himself. It was one of the reasons why I felt such fear when I was coming for you. He was challenging, and I'm more than out of practice in that area, I'm afraid. As you said, it's no longer the Dark Ages; things have changed for our inter-species relationships. By the time I found the old well house he had been keeping you in, he had already moved you."

I watched in his mind as he ran through the events of my rescue. How he had searched for me starting at the club, how everyone had been in a panic after I had disappeared, how Jaxon had called him, and he had come to hunt the wolf down, the other wolves at the club giving him a wide berth. He had spent a day trying to follow the rouge wolf's well-hidden tricky trail to the well house in the middle of the forest. I watched him enter and kneel on the ground, putting his hand on the indentation on the dirt floor there, exactly where I had lain, bound, drugged. He could smell the residual fear that I had left on the spot, the terror I had gone through at the thought that the werewolf was going to kill me.

I heard in his mind how he had been heartbroken for me and angry at the rogue at that moment. I saw him reach out where my head had lain in the dirt, touching it, whispering, "Hang on, Sasha, I'm coming." He then rose and started following the new trail the wolf had created in the woods.

The other two brothers were there, following him and helping as best they could, even though it was his area of expertise. How relieved he had been when he had found me. Killing the wolf. He picked me up in his arms and rushed me home, where I was safe with him and his brothers.

Listening to how much he cared, I suddenly wanted him to know everything about me. It was so strange; I had always been a private person by sad circumstances, but here I was, wanting him to know it all. To show him all about me and every piece of my life. I wanted to let him see the little good he and his brothers had brought to my life, the bad I had put up with over the years, and even the ugly subjected to me by Vladimir. I wanted to go over every moment of my life with him, knowing he would fully understand with his wise insight. To hear his thoughts on it all along the way.

He smiled, stroked my hair, and whispered, "There is nothing I would like better, Sasha, than for you to let me in completely. But that would take so long, your bath would get cold. You need to rest." I didn't want to let go of him. I had felt so unsafe in the last two days that it still brought shivers to my entire body. Niklaus's arms around me brought me safe relief, his understanding mind, and comfort. I wanted to know everything about him, too, to see into his past and his thoughts. "Your bath is getting cold, Sasha," he said with a smile and started to pull away from me to leave.

I backed up with him, not releasing my hold on him, as I reached out to turn off the bathroom lights.

The candles flickered around the tub, and I looked at him, thinking, *"Then we'd better get in."*

# CHAPTER 24

Niklaus's intense gaze held mine as my hand fell away from the light switch. So much passed between our minds at that moment. Was he going to leave? Did I know what I was asking? Was he going to let the moment pass for the sake of hanging on to that self-control? What about that regret? Was I sure that I wanted him to stay? How we felt about each other. How he wanted to touch me. How I would respond if he did. How I thought he was thinking a little too much. And finally, he reached out and took my face in his hands, kissing me like he had always wanted to, unhindered.

I backed away from him and slowly started undressing myself while I held his gaze, and I reached out with my power at the same time to slowly unbutton his black vest. His tunic came over his head and landed on the bathroom floor next to the vest. Our minds met on such a level, hearing one another's thoughts and arousal; it only served to fan the flames. I freed myself of the rest of my clothes and gave him a look before I turned to step into the water, sinking below the bubbles, out of view. I surfaced and smoothed my hair back out of my face, leaning back against the tub's edge. I had left him to finish undressing himself if he chose.

I closed my eyes and enjoyed the luxurious bath on my body. I listened to his mind as he finally made the decision to stay. He listened to mine as I ached with the need for him, to be wrapped up in his arms, feeling safe and treasured. The water in the tub rose as I felt him slide in next to me. It was like his passion was released once he had finally decided and given in. I opened my eyes as he pulled me to him.

His look was so intense as his wet hands came to my face, saying, "No more regrets. I don't want to waste another moment with you, Sasha." He pulled me to him, kissing me slowly but deeply with all of the pent-up passion he had denied himself. I melted into him. His hands left my face to hold my neck and stroke my back as I straddled him. My hands wandered up over his chest, caressing him.

I pulled back with a smile, looking into his soft eyes. We didn't speak, hearing so much inside one another's mind; how much we loved each other, how beautiful he thought I was, how grateful to him I was for saving me. How his fingers running up and down my spine were driving me crazy; how me pressing myself up against him was setting him aflame. His hand on my neck slid down to hold my shoulder, and the other reached for a luffa on the tub's edge. He brushed my hair back from my shoulder and gently started to wash me, cleansing me from my ordeal, gently kissing my mouth while he did.

He turned me to wash my shoulders and back, running the luffa slowly over my skin, driving me crazy as he did. His free hand slid around my rib cage, pulling me back against him with his arm just below my breasts. I leaned back against him, laying my head on his shoulder as his hands reached down to raise one of my legs so he could slowly, tantalizingly, wash me. His hand ran up the length of my leg, making my eyes close and a sigh to escape my lips, and then repeated the process with the other leg. I was on fire for him, aching with need. I felt him set the luffa to the side of the tub again when he was finished.

His right arm slid around me again, just below my breasts, to hold me back against his chest while the other brushed my wet hair from my shoulder closest to him. He bent his head to my shoulder, and his lips came to my bare, wet skin, kissing me there slowly, sending shivers down my whole body. I sighed with my eyes closed and my head lying against him. I covered his arm around me with mine, gently caressing him. I felt his wet hair brush over my shoulder as he kissed my shoulder and neck, his free hand wandering under the water over my hip and thigh to fan the flames that were growing inside of me.

I turned to look at him, and his sensual kisses traveled up my neck to just below my ear as his arm pulled me tighter against him, making me murmur his name. His free hand slid over my belly, journeying down between my thighs to gently tease me, making me gasp and lay my head back against his shoulder again. The orgasm that rippled through my body had been achieved so amazingly fast as his mind listened in on my reaction to his touch, knowing exactly how to coax it out of me. My hand reached up behind me to thread my fingers into his hair as I panted through what he was bringing out of me. He continued to kiss my neck and shoulders as I came back down.

I turned my face and kissed his neck, biting him as his fingers snuck up inside of me to start working their perfect magic deep inside. Pleasure flowed through him as I fed on him, his fingers dancing and stroking inside of me in just the right way, quickly building up another orgasm in me. I gasped on his neck as it burst through me and I felt him kiss me on my forehead, breathing heavy himself as he experienced it through my mind. I released my hold on his neck, and his hand came up to hold my jaw as he kissed my lips, his tongue slipping inside to take possession of my mouth.

The hand on my jaw wandered down to my belly, pulling me higher up against him, putting pressure there to meet his upward thrust as he entered me from behind. I moaned into his mouth as he repeated the process, again and again, knowing just how much pressure I needed and the perfect spot to hit as he did. I had never experienced such unique pleasure as this, our minds experiencing the pleasure that we were bringing one another, as well as our own, while we moved together. Listening to one another as our bodies united, we drew out the perfect line of pleasure without tipping each other over the edge, drawing out the moment.

He released my mouth with a sensual sigh, looking into my eyes with his that were heavily lidded with pleasure and love as we continued to move together. I could feel us both coiling, tighter and tighter. His lips slid down my neck, and then he bit down on me, feeding on me from behind as more pleasure took us higher. My head fell back over his shoulder with a scream as our orgasm undid us both, our bodies uniting as much as our minds to experience it all together. We rode the waves together, clinging to one another, trembling. Finally, he released me from his jaws and leaned his head to rest it against mine, both of us breathing heavily, coming down from the moment.

He could hear how I treasured the moment we had just shared, how perfectly romantic and sensual it felt. I had been dying inside for the need of his arms, and he had risen up to save me again, my white knight. I could spend the whole night in those arms, feeling him against me, in me. I loved him, and our moment had been perfect. I couldn't wait to make more with him, share old memories with him, and make new ones that we could treasure together.

*"I love you too, Sasha, my darling,"* he thought for me.

I pulled his lips to mine again with a hand on the back of his head, sighing with the pleasure of it. He brushed his hand along my body as he reached down and undid the plug on the tub; our water was getting cold. Still kissing me, he scooped me up in his arms and stepped out of the tub. His eyes were so full of adoration as he set me down on the rug, reaching for a towel to slowly dry me off as he kissed his way down my body; I held onto his shoulders to steady myself, massaging him gently. He came back up to kiss me as he dried himself off. He tossed the towel to the side, scooped me up in his arms, and carried me into my room and to the great black bed.

He held me gently with one arm and pulled the covers back, sliding our bodies between the sheets. He leaned over me, propped up on one elbow, looking at me as he stroked my face with the back of his hand.

"Niklaus, stay?" I whispered to him. His mind had started to think about how I needed to rest, and he should probably leave me so I could.

"You need to rest, Sasha."

*"Make love to me again, Niklaus. I need your arms more than I need rest,"* I pleaded for him in my mind. He was about to argue with me until I placed a hand on his face, begging him with my eyes as I thought, *"Please."*

He groaned, giving in, and bent to my mouth. My thoughts drifted to a place where I was determined to undermine all his self-control; I wasn't going to stand for him resisting me any longer. He laughed from above me as his hair fell about my face, making a curtain of sensual seclusion for our faces. I looked into his green eyes as a naughty look crossed my features. If I had to, I would pull out all the stops in the future. He kissed me again, hardly keeping a smile from his face long enough to really kiss me. I brushed his hair back and held his face, looking at him with love.

And then I gave him what he had always wanted; I unlocked my mind to him fully, inviting him to see whatever he wanted. He gasped at the gift I had just handed him; the keys to my memories. I pulled him into a kiss as I felt him there in my mind. My need was rising again, and he broke our kiss to travel down my body, intensifying the flames that were licking up me again.

"Niklaus!" I gasped his name as his mouth and fingers began driving me to madness between my thighs. A screech ripped from my throat, and then he thrust into me again, filling the bedroom and probably the halls of the mansion with my screams.

I awoke to Niklaus's voice, "No, Vladimir, she is recovering fine. We've been watching over her, yes. Yes, I'll make sure one of us is with her until she is completely recovered. Yes, or several. No, I haven't sensed you. Perhaps the distance and the drugs have something to do with it. She's sleeping, but I will tell her to call when she wakes." Great, just great. I mentally groaned. The last thing I wanted to do right now was call Vladimir. "No, I don't believe any more werewolves need to be 'taken care of.' Rest assured, I'll keep a close eye on the situation. No, the wolf was unhinged, and none of us would have thought he was capable of that. I'm sure she could have handled it and killed him were it not for him drugging her. Alright, I'll have her call when she wakes in a few."

I tapped Niklaus's arm for the phone. "Actually, she's just woken up, Vladimir."

I put the phone to my ear, saying, "Vladimir."

"I'm relieved you are alright, Sasha. I must say I'm slightly disappointed in you, my pet." That was to be expected.

"I'm sorry, Vladimir. I would have killed him, but he drugged me, as you know. It was so unexpected. I'll be more careful from now on. The Cavaliers won't be such a problem."

"You will get started on that by tomorrow."

"Yes, Vladimir."

"Are my sons taking good enough care of you?" I looked at Niklaus and smiled. The large black bed was covered in the scent of our lovemaking; the scent of Vladimir was wholly gone, replaced by Niklaus, Jaxon, and Eben. I breathed it in, soaking up the peace, love, and comfort I found in that.

"Yes, Vladimir, they are taking excellent care of me." There was a long pause.

"I think I'm going to come make sure."

# CHAPTER 25

Frantic thrumming. Fear-induced panic. I looked at Niklaus, and I swore I was going to faint.

"No, Vladimir, that won't be necessary. I assure you, I'm being spoiled. I want for nothing."

"I miss you at my side, Sasha, I want to see you. Our link is broken; it's time for a visit."

"Honestly, Vladimir. The entire reason you sent me here was so you didn't have to come. You coming now would be pointless. I'm fine." Silence. Oh god. He was still thinking about it. He was going to come, and then he would kill me.

"One night, my minx is different from having to stay the entire time. I will be there in two days." My heart stopped altogether.

"How about I meet you halfway?"

"You are supposed to be resting, under close watch of my sons."

"I thought you wanted me out hunting by tomorrow?"

"Hmmmm, you are right. Rest for now. You will pick back up with the Cavaliers right after I leave. I expect a *warm reception*. I will see you soon." The line went dead.

I stared at the wall of my bedroom, struggling to take shallow breaths, as the phone fell away from my face. I couldn't focus on anything. Vladimir was coming. Here. Vladimir was coming. He would smell the brothers' lovemaking all over this bed. He would kill me.

I flew out of bed, not looking at Niklaus, and ran to my closet. I dressed in a full black skirt and corset and then, at vampire speed, rushed out to the bedroom and started stripping the bed of everything. Niklaus could hear my mind, and he dressed and then moved to help me.

Niklaus began opening all of the windows and doors to my room. I stripped the bedding, throwing it in a heap on the floor. I was removing the bottom sheet when the initial shock wore off. I clutched the sheet between my hands and held it to my face as the tears started to flow; great sobs racked my body as I sunk to the floor weeping. Niklaus's arms were around me in a second, lifting me up to hold me as we stood in the center of the room. He could feel it all as I shook with sobs; the terror, the heartbreak, the disgust, the contempt, the despair. I would never be free. He would come. He would kill me or, worse, let me live. *A warm reception.* He would take me to his bed. He would have me feed on him. He would feed on me. He would touch me, possess me.

"Sasha! Sasha!" Niklaus was shouting. It wasn't until I heard the other brothers come rushing into the room, demanding what was going on, that I realized that I was screaming and thrashing in Niklaus's grasp. His hold on me stood firm, and I collapsed against him, crying again. Only his arms around me held me up; I had collapsed completely.

It was a mistake; all of it was a mistake. I should never have let them in. Then, this would only be normal life. I wouldn't have awakened inside tasting love and life. I would be dead inside still, able to deal with Vladimir like I always had.

"No, Sasha. Don't think like that."

"What is happening?"

"Tell us what's going on!"

Niklaus turned his head to his brothers and said, "Vladimir is coming. He will be here in two days." You could have heard a pin drop and then I could hear the stress response in their heartbeats. I could almost see them look at the state of the room, understanding dawning on them.

"What should we do, Niklaus?"

"The Governess and the twins will go on a short educational trip starting today. We clean the whole house, so he won't suspect anything, including this room."

"Our presence won't disappear that easily."

"Vladimir commanded us to look after Sasha and be with her around the clock until he arrives. He even instructed us to feed her. We will do as he asks, and it will cover what remains after a deep cleaning. He won't know."

"What about Sasha?!" There was no answer for that. We all knew it. My heart was aching, but I finally stood and pulled out of Niklaus's arms, accepting my fate.

I didn't say anything; I barely looked at them. I walked like a zombie to the bathroom and reached out. I was so numb as I dumped the ring into my palm and slid it onto my finger. I knew this was part of the *warm reception* that Vladimir wanted. I put the pouch back in its place, and my chest felt like a huge weight was on it. I walked back out into the bedroom, staring at the floor, and just stood there. Slowly, I raised my hollow eyes to look at the brothers. They were staring at my hand, glittering there at my side.

I couldn't bear it, so I shut them out of my mind, and then I turned to start working on the room at vamp speed. They were frozen for a minute, and then they snapped into action. Niklaus ran across the house to alert the Governess and the twins that they would leave in a few hours. The other two brothers left me to my work there and started cleaning the rest of the mansion. I went over the entire room, top to bottom, splashing chemical cleaners liberally. I swallowed as I looked at the bed; it had been bathed in scent I loved, and soon it would be covered in Vladimir. I made it up slowly, knowing there was no escape. I was at the mercy of Vladimir, who had none.

I sucked in a breath and grabbed my phone. I deleted the entire memory on it.

Jaxon tried to stop me as I sped out of the manor, but I was too focused to stop. Across town, I ran right onto campus. I only slowed when I had to walk through the college halls to reach my goal. A class had just ended, and I slipped inside the lecture hall. Sebastian spotted me and asked the gathered girls to come find him later if they still had questions. They left, walking past me and out the door. I sped over into his office to wait for him. He came in, looking so relieved to see me. My phone had shown dozens of missed calls from him.

"Shut the door, Seb. We have to talk."

He did as I asked, a concerned look crossing his face. "What is it, Sasha? I'm so relieved you're alright. I'm so sorry about what happened. I should have stayed closer! Please-"

"Vladimir is coming." Silence. I didn't look at him but whispered, "I think you'd better cut out for a couple days. He knows nothing about you being here, and I'd like it to stay that way. For you to be safe." I could feel his eyes on me. He walked up close to me and gripped my shoulders, angling his head to try to catch my gaze. I finally looked up at him with deadpan eyes.

"Sasha, I've been here before while he has come. I'll be fine."

"I wasn't here before; it could change things. If you lay low and steer clear of me, you should be safe."

His eyebrows came together, "What about you?" He was searching my face with his eyes. My heart pained so intensely that I had to close my eyes before opening them and not meeting his gaze again.

I swallowed and said, "I'll be fine, as always."

"Sasha-"

"Be careful, Seb. Don't call. Lay low, and he'll be gone in a few days." I sped out of his office, leaving him looking after me.

I walked at normal speed through the hall but sped through the outskirts of town back to the estate once I was out of sight. I entered the door and just stood there, looking at the mansion, which was sparkling clean and smelling of cleaning agents.

I heard Niklaus upstairs helping Lucy pack, answering her questions about how long she would be gone, and whining about having to listen to the Governess while she was away.

"Why does Sasha get to stay, and we have to leave?" Lucian asked.

"Because she has to, Lucian. Vladimir is coming to see her to make sure she is alright." I sighed and closed my eyes briefly before returning to my room. I entered the room.

Only the faintest scent of the brothers remained after it had been cleaned and aired out. I had also changed the mattress protector and cleaned the closet and bathroom. Any garments with a strong scent were thrown in the wash. It was now clean. It was now void of life.

I closed the room back up again and went to lie down on the bed. I could actually feel some lingering effects of the poison at this point. I was weak.

I lay there staring at the ring on my finger, my heart feeling like it had been ripped out of my chest. Vladimir was coming. Vladimir would be here soon. I was desperately trying to build my emotional walls back up again that had been beaten down. I would never survive otherwise. I didn't look up when I felt a brother lay down beside me. I was too transfixed on my ring, which represented an eternity of shackles, watching it sparkle on my finger as I slowly moved it.

A gentle hand crossed my body to cover the ring from my sight. I closed my eyes, not wanting to see the hand holding mine. I felt my lip tremble but bit down on it before fixing the mask back on. The hand drew my hands back toward my body and wrapped me up in an embrace, pulling me back against him. I stared at nothing as he held me, and he said nothing. There were no words of comfort that could be said. Another form came to lay in front of me, pressing in close. I barely noticed his gentle hand on my neck, caressing my jaw. I closed my eyes. I heard the third come into the room.

"I'm taking the trio to the airport. Try to get her to feed. She's weak at the moment." I couldn't stop the snort of irritation that came out of me at Niklaus's words. I turned my face into the pillow. It didn't matter how weak I was; I had no desire to feed. It was never wise to drink something sweet right before taking something bitter and acrid. It only made it that much worse when you did.

"Sasha," Niklaus drawled out in his impatient tone. "You need to, and Vladimir commanded us to. Would you like him to be angry with us that we didn't?" I snarled at him, using reverse psychology on me. The anger woke me up, and I sat up, pulling out of the embrace I had been in.

"Don't you dare try to manipulate me," I angrily growled at him.

"I wasn't, Sasha. It's the truth, and you know it. He will be angry at us all if we don't." He was right, but I was lashing out in anger. I shut my eyes and didn't look at him again. I was pushing them away; they all knew it. None of us seemed to know what to say. How exactly was I supposed to get through this without closing off my heart? I heard Niklaus sigh from across the room before he came over to sit on the bottom of the bed. I looked at him with distant, closed eyes.

"Don't close us out, Sasha. Let us help bear your burden, now and later."

My face grew pained, and I looked away from him, but I saw his compassionate look before I could shut him out. Eben reached out and turned me to face him, looking into my eyes. Mine were distant. His hands came to my face as he tried to connect with me.

"Sasha, you promised. Don't shut us out." I wanted to say, 'I lied,' but I couldn't get it out, not looking into his eyes like I was. He was so sad; they all were. I reached out and touched his face. He could see my misery; I was that wretched creature before him, lain bare once more. I could feel Jaxon rubbing my back as he pressed in close again. Niklaus was caressing, massaging my feet, from where he sat on the end of the bed. I looked back into Eben's eyes. His gentle kiss let loose the dam of emotions and I was lost to them as I cried. Vladimir was coming, and there was nothing any of us could do about it.

# CHAPTER 26

"Vladimir."

"Ahhhh, Niklaus. It is good to see you. The manor looks very good. Where is Sasha?" I was lying on the great black bed with Eben holding me. With a final caress to my face and a quick kiss, he moved away from me but remained there on the bed in a relaxed stance. Jaxon met my eyes from across the room, and I swallowed from the emotion I had seen there. All of us could hear the footsteps coming down the hall. Vladimir's mind promised violence for his disappointment with my failure. My breathing was shallow as the door to the bedroom, and Niklaus walked in to hold the door for Vladimir.

I looked at Niklaus first, and then my gaze shifted to Vladimir for a second before I swung my legs over the bed and stood to greet him. I was in all black like he preferred, wearing a long full skirt and corset. Eben got up off of the bed and walked over to the other side of the room to join his brothers.

I met Vladimir's approach by the foot of the bed and curtsied low to him, bowing my head and not making eye contact as I said, "Master." He was looking at me. Did I dare meet his eyes? I slowly raised my eyes to his. He was going to slap me. I offered him my hand in greeting.

He took it to kiss and then his eyes landed on the ring; I had offered up my left hand instead of the right. Possessive delight rolled through him at the sight of it, and he forgot about striking me as he brought the hand to his lips, eating me alive with his eyes. I bowed my head to him again. He used the hand he held to pull me up against him, and his other went to the back of my neck to squeeze as he brought me up to him for a possessive kiss.

We were fortunate that Vladimir was not a mind reader like Niklaus or me; he could work inside the mind to a degree, but not in the same way. Otherwise, he would have heard four strong reactions.

I realized that as terrible and horrible as this would be for me, it would be almost as hard on the brothers. They loved me as much as I loved them, and it went against everything in them to allow Vladimir even close to me. But what choice did any of us have? Vladimir was too powerful for even me to overcome. Each one of them was dying inside, watching him touch me.

Vladimir pulled back from the kiss and whispered, "I've missed you, my pet." He looked at me momentarily and observed, "You seem diminished somewhat."

I bowed my head again and said, "It is the poison, Vladimir. I'm sure I'll be back to normal once it's fully gone from my system."

"Mmmmm, yes. It was a powerful sensation to enter your mind when you were drugged. I almost felt drugged myself when I did." He planted another kiss on my lips. "You seem weak. Have you not fed? Have the brothers not been feeding you or bringing you someone to feed on as I requested?"

"They were, but I decided to just wait for you the last few days," I said quietly, looking down. I looked up into his eyes, and I saw a gleam of delight and arousal. He would have been angry, but my wording thrilled him.

"Ahhhh, my pet, I've missed you too." He walked past me into the closet, leaving me looking at the brothers.

The looks we exchanged at that moment were indescribable. The longing, the trepidation, the heartbreak, the deep pain at the situation; we were all feeling it together. I only broke eye contact with them when Vladimir returned. He had hung up his long cloak; being one of the originals, his dress was very traditional, even if he wore his hair in a modern cut; he would have been devastatingly handsome if he wasn't so cruel and evil. He came to me and grabbed my head with his hands, looking down into my eyes before he closed his. I felt him reestablishing the mental connection with my mind, fixing it to this latest memory.

I also felt Niklaus there, tracking what he was doing very closely, noting where it was and everything else he was doing. Niklaus subtly helped cloud my mind so Vladimir wouldn't see anything we couldn't afford him to.

At last, Vladimir withdrew from my mind and gave me another satisfied smile twinged with sadism. He could now keep a close eye on me again. He drew me to him and then picked me up in his arms, bringing me to his neck, expecting me to feed on him. I closed my eyes with a grimace before I opened them to meet the eyes of the brothers over Vladimir's shoulder. My eyes glassed over with tears as I looked at them. I didn't take my eyes off them as I turned my face and bit down on the side of Vladimir's neck. Each wore a pained grimace at his sigh.

I had to shut my eyes as the bitter, acidic blood touched my tongue. It was like swallowing bitter battery acid, bringing pain. It was so much worse than I had remembered after drinking from the brothers. My only consolation was that I hadn't just fed on them; it really would have been unbearable then. Vladimir held me to him as he turned around and sat on the edge of the bed to address the brothers. I could feel their hearts paining as they looked at us, but I knew they each wore a mask of indifference on the outside; they had to.

Vladimir was casual on the outside, but I could feel the deep pleasure the feeding was providing him. He wasn't audibly moaning or sighing, but his tight hold on me and heavy breathing were enough to show the brothers what it was doing for him.

"Tell me what happened with the werewolf. I want the entire story." Fear coursed through me, but I pushed it down; I could only warn the brothers not to mention Sebastian in the retelling. I had to keep him safe, or Vladimir would kill him and give him to the associate even all these years later.

The brothers filled him in on what had happened starting from that first night at the club. They weren't terribly graphic when describing the club activities; I was grateful for that. They focused more on how the wolf had drugged me and the resulting hunt that ended up in a successful killing of the wolf. They also focused on the large amounts of poison the wolf had given me, especially the last dose that had come close to killing me. They were trying to satisfy Vladimir with my performance in the case without actually defending me with their words, which Vladimir would not have taken well.

He still held me to him, encouraging me to take an extensive, prolonged feeding from him. The acid flowing down into my system had me wanting to cough and sputter as I listened in on his conversation with the brothers. My mouth and throat were already burnt by it, like coughing up stomach acid but swallowing it instead. His hands on me were possessive in a terrible, sickening way. I fisted his tunic to keep from shaking as his hands caressed me as I fed on him, still bringing him pleasure.

"And where are my witch twins? Where are Lucy and Lucian?" Vladimir asked the coven brothers, caressing me. His rough hand slipped up under my skirt to caress my bare thigh, causing me to gasp. My cheeks flamed at his touch; I was dying of shame as the brothers watched. Vladimir turned a predator grin down toward me and whispered, though the brothers could hear, "Patience, my minx. We will be alone soon enough." He had interpreted my gasp as a gasp of pleasure at his touch instead of shame and disgust; his self-assurance would never allow him to think otherwise. I was his in his mind, only his.

Niklaus cleared his throat before answering, "School trip, I'm afraid. The late notice made it impossible to cancel the reservations. You will just have to catch them the next time you are in town."

"Hmmm, well, that may be a while, I'm afraid. I have a lot of business over in Europe. So long as Sasha can keep things under control here, I unfortunately won't be back for a while." Mental relief was felt by us all. Another gasp from me, as his hand wandered over my backside under the skirt, had the brothers dying inside or burning with anger.

"And what of this new Governess? Is she doing well? I had hoped to *meet her*."

"She had to go with Lucy and Lucian on the school trip as a chaperone. It is working out so far, for the most part, but you know the twins. They don't make it easy on any of the Governesses." Vladimir laughed a little at the thought of his temperamental witch twins. He appreciated their volatile nature more than the rest of us.

"So, the human will be staying?"

"Yes, for now, she is working out." He nodded. "Keep her in line and silent, or I will come for her. She isn't to be involved with any of you. No more mistakes," his last comment was aimed more directly at Jaxon.

Jaxon hissed a little in response but gave Vladimir a curt nod.

"It's no longer a problem. Sasha made sure of that," Jaxon answered sourly. I could have applauded his acting if I wasn't so preoccupied with trying to swallow battery acid while Vladimir's hands were getting bolder under the folds of my skirt.

I started to pull back from his neck, but he turned to me and whispered harshly, "Finish." His attention turned back toward the brothers as I pressed back against him to finish taking a full feeding from his acrid vein. I was dying inside.

I could hear the smile on his lips as he answered Jaxon, "Yes, well, she is good at what she does, isn't she? What about the wolf? I do not want him back on my land again. I don't care what has to be done about it, but I'm assuming my pet also took care of that."

It didn't demand an answer, but Niklaus responded anyway, "Yes, it's taken care of. The wolf hasn't been back since the last few Governesses have left. There was some extra interest in the previous maids and Governesses but none in this one, so it hasn't been an issue. If it becomes one again, I'm sure Sasha will take care of it, and I will help her."

Vladimir's hand on the back of my neck squeezed tighter, his hand moving under my skirt sneaked up to grab my hip bone and press me against him. "Very well." I pinched my eyes shut tightly as his hand slid under my panties there, causing me to gasp against his neck again. I released him, finally finishing a full feeding, and he looked down on me smugly. His eyes were flickering to life, starting to glow a deep crimson as his finger wandered, and his mind started anticipating having me alone. I tried to remain impassive under his gaze. Apparently, I was successful because his heated gaze shifted to the brothers.

They could all see his intentions in his gaze as clearly as I could. He finally withdrew his hand from my skirt as he looked at each brother.

He finished his perusal, saying, "You may go." He sat me up off of his lap and stood, bending to kiss me on the neck a little. They saw the misery in my eyes as he did. Vladimir turned towards the bed and started undoing the buttons on the wrists of his tunic, ignoring his sons. They turned and slowly walked from the room. "Shut the door, Sasha," he commanded me.

I slowly walked over to follow the brothers to the door, looking at the floor, knowing what was coming. The brothers stood in the hall, looking back. My eyes raised to meet each one of theirs with a look of horrendous pain before I slowly swung the door shut with a 'click.'

# CHAPTER 27

I lay on my stomach at an angle over the black bed, the top sheet covering my lower half. My left arm stretched out above my head, glittering with the ring that rested there. My hair was swept up along that arm, and my other was lying near my face on the sheet, where I stared at nothing. My only response to my door being opened was a long, labored blink of my eyes. I could feel their minds taking in the state of things; me laying lifeless, the bed stripped of everything but the sheets, the room with the bedding and clothes strewn about, the smell. I breathed it in on every breath, Vladimir's rutting, my pain, my fear, the violence, the blood. You could smell it all wafting through the air of the black room.

Vladimir had left an hour ago to catch his plane, but I hadn't moved.

"Shit," Jaxon growled when his eyes landed on my exposed skin. His anger flamed so hot in my mind that it almost burned as he looked at the horrendous state of me. I already knew what I looked like, not needing a mirror to know; I had been through this enough times that I could picture the terrible coloring all over, scattered with bites, nail marks, and blood. So much blood. It was still flowing from me in certain places, particularly between my legs. I was healing, but the worse the damage, the longer it took. I had hoped I would be healed before they had come to find me, but the poison had slowed things for me.

I didn't look over at them, even as they neared. "That bastard," I heard sweet Eben whisper in deadly anger. Tears leaked from my eyes, but I didn't move; I couldn't without hurting. They were all horrified. They were all burning up in anger. They all now had a clearer picture of what it would mean for me to be Vladimir's Bride. To become the Bathory Bride.

I drew in a breath and shifted slightly, the sheet slipping to expose more of the damage. Bruises in the shape of handprints were all over. My wrists were so black there could be no mistake he had broken them during the night, holding me down.

"We can't move her for a bit. She needs to heal more," Niklaus told his brothers, his voice heavy with emotion.

I blinked again as I felt them carefully join me on the bed. They didn't touch me; they couldn't without causing pain. I felt Niklaus's comfort wash over my mind, causing me to take a deep breath and then sigh as I closed my eyes. The strength it must have taken them all to not come bursting in during the night must have been substantial indeed. Vladimir was never quiet, and his violence didn't allow for me to be. Listening in on their minds, I found myself wanting to comfort them.

I opened my eyes to see Jaxon lying in front of me. With great effort, I reached out with my hand near my face and slid it along the sheet to his face.

I closed my eyes, resting in their comforting presence, even if they couldn't comfort me with their touch. Niklaus's comforting presence in my mind lulled me to sleep, and I sighed at the relief as I slipped under.

When I woke, they were all still there. They had watched me slowly heal while I slept; only the worst bruising remained as yellow patches, and the blood spattered across my body.

"Can you move now, Sasha?" Niklaus asked me. I looked up at him and tested how I felt. I was sore in some places but well enough to move. I started to sit up when his gentle hand on my shoulder held me in place. "I'll run you another bath. The hot water will help." I nodded.

I sighed as I felt Eben very carefully move to spoon me, putting his face at the back of my head. Jaxon moved closer as the sound of the bath filling met my ears. Neither of them tried to really touch me; they just brushed their bodies against mine, too afraid to cause me pain with caresses. They brought me such comfort and relief nonetheless.

I brushed Jaxon's worried face and gave him a small but sad smile, saying, "I'll be alright. This isn't the first time. I always recover, right?" He said nothing, but I still wanted to reassure and comfort them.

"Your bath is ready," Niklaus said. "Can you walk?" I nodded. Probably by now.

The brothers sat up to help me do the same, and Niklaus carefully helped me off the bed and walked me into the bathroom, with the others following to help if needed. They had all seen me naked, but for some reason, I wanted to cover myself from their sight after Vladimir had touched me; I felt unclean and shamed. Niklaus grabbed a towel and wrapped it around me before he said, "This was not your fault, Sasha." It didn't matter. Vladimir was everywhere; his smell was all over me and my room. I could never be free of him.

"Shhhhh, he's gone now," Niklaus comforted me.

Still sore and stiff, I stepped away toward the colossal tub and dropped the towel, intending to step into the tub when I slipped a little. Three sets of hands reached out to catch me before I would fall, just in case, but I caught myself. Three minds wondered if I would be alright if I could be left alone.

"I'll be alright, I promise." I turned to see them giving each other looks. My face softened at their thoughts, how they wanted to take care of me.

Niklaus leaned over and kissed me on the cheek, saying, "I'll take care of your room." He walked out of the bathroom and started the same process we had done a few days ago.

I turned back to step into the tub when Eben's hand on mine held me back. I looked at him, askance. He gave me a sad smile and reached over with his free hand to slide the glittering ring off of my finger. He flashed it a look of anger before tossing it to Jaxon, who put it back in the pouch and tucked it away out of sight. I smiled at him and held his face with that hand momentarily. He surprised me when he started taking his shirt off and then the rest; they both did. Jaxon rushed over, scooped me up, stepped into the water, and slowly sank our bodies below the bubbles. I felt Eben get in on the other side of me.

Niklaus gave a chuckle from out in my room. "I suggested one of you. I don't think she actually needs both to steady her." He laughed again. I smiled for the first time in days.

Jaxon met my eye with his playful smirk and shouted at Niklaus, "There's still room for one more if you're jealous! I will enjoy a hot soak with our girl while you play maid." I laughed at his teasing and gave him an affectionate smile, running my fingers down his chin. Eben joined in on my laughter and caught my now-ringless hand to bring it to his lips for a kiss. I turned with a smile for him and gave him a kiss on the lips from over my shoulder.

Both brothers started caressing me in the water, gently washing me as they did. I smiled and closed my eyes at their gentle, loving touch. They were so careful with me. Their minds revealed they had no intention of taking advantage of the situation, even if their touch stirred something in me. We all knew I would need some time after the ordeal that I had just been through. I washed Vladimir from my hair as well as my body; I wanted nothing of him to remain when I was finished. My body was healing, but I was still weak from the night with Vladimir, blood loss, and the fading poison.

Niklaus walked into the bathroom, commenting on my thoughts, "The poison should be gone from your system in a couple days. I was thinking another round of the antidote might help, but the thing you need most right now is blood." The memory of the feeding I had taken from Vladimir had me gagging and retching while I turned away. My throat was still so raw, it ached. "I said blood, not red acid, Sasha," Niklaus gently teased.

I looked up at him but couldn't bring myself to smile. "You offering?" I tried to tease him back.

He looked at me and said, "Yes." I laughed then, giving him a smile. They were lifting my spirits little by little, so I decided to flirt a little. I raised an eyebrow and crooked a finger at him. It was his turn to laugh, and he started stripping.

He slid into the massive tub on the other side and reached for me, pulling me to him and gently wrapping his arms around me. I again expressed my gratitude to him in my mind and received a caress to the face in answer. He jerked his jaw to the side slightly and gave me a knowing smile, encouraging me to take from. I nestled in close to him as he settled, relaxing, as my lips went to his neck. I took another steadying breath, the memory of Vladimir still fresh in my mind, and then I bit down, drawing Niklaus' blood into my mouth.

Its amazing, savory essence was exactly what I needed to soothe my burning mouth and throat, and I couldn't help but sigh with the relief it brought me. Niklaus just held me, relaxing as I took from him until I pulled away and looked into his beautiful moss-green eyes, which were soft with love for me. I stroked his face.

"Thank you," I whispered. He kissed me passionately, followed by a nod, but then his eyes shot up toward Jaxon, and he laughed. I heard Jaxon's mental comment and shook my head with a smile.

Eben looked over at Jaxon, curious. "What? I just thought that was only the first course for her. Dessert's up next, bro, and I get to be the Aperitif," Jaxon answered with a wink for me. I laughed again.

Niklaus settled back in to relax in the hot water as Eben reached for me and pulled me to him. He took a moment to brush my wet hair back from my face with his hands and give me a gentle but sensual kiss. I touched his face and looked into his blue eyes, letting him see the real me. His resounding smile was small but so full of intimacy I wanted to memorize it.

I kissed him and then kissed my way down to his neck. I was slow and gentle with Eben, slowly savoring his decadent, sweet blood, just like you would any fine dessert, one small sampling after another. He sighed and stroked my hair, melting into the side of the tub to relax. I rested my face on his shoulder with a final lick. His sweet blood fully healed the burn, soothing me completely after Niklaus's initial healing.

The thought of Jaxon's spicy blood was appetizing now that I was healed. I peeked over at him from Eben's neck, and he smirked at me, giving me a wink.

He waggled his fingers at me, saying, "Come here, Sugar Lips. I know you want a taste." I smiled and laughed at him, letting him pull me through the water to him. He sat me on his lap to straddle him, and I gave him a look. "Don't worry, I won't do anything about that today," he smirked. I laughed and shook my head at him.

"You, showing restraint? That a first?" He looked to the side for a moment as his brothers laughed as they leaned against the side of the mini pool. His smirk returned before he closed his eyes and laid his head back, exposing his neck. I was a lot less gentle with him because of his snark, but it only made him laugh more as I finally bit him. Jaxon's spicy cocktail flowed through me, and he mumbled his appreciation of my bite. His hands wandered over my back, lighting a small flame inside of me. Niklaus scowled at him, but he only smirked back.

Niklaus rolled his eyes, saying, "She needs to rest, Jaxon. Keep working on that restraint."

He laughed but didn't stop his caresses, whispering, "We're going to have to do this again after you're rested." I was laughing again.

I pulled back to look at Jaxon, and he leaned in and kissed me. I kissed him back with a hand on his face. I smiled at him and rested my forehead against his jaw. I sighed in contentment, just resting in the comfort and care the three brothers were showing me. Hopefully, Vladimir would be true to his word and not return for a very long time. I was still his, though, no matter how far away he was. He even had a mental link on me again now. I wanted to stay here with the three brothers, loving them; I didn't want to move away from their embrace. But then the thought of Vladimir's command returned to me, and I sighed with irritation.

I had until tomorrow night, and then I had to start hunting Cavaliers again. I could barely stand the thought of another man's hands on me after Vladimir. I only wanted the brothers touching me, perhaps Sebastian. Sigh. I had no choice. The thought of going out on a hunt after the last one frightened me. I was terrified that the Cavaliers would do the same thing to me.

"What's the matter, Doll Face?" All three brothers had heard my heart pick up. Suddenly, the thought of hunting posed a danger for me.

# CHAPTER 28

I ran across the parking lot and threw myself into Sebastian's arms. His face went into my neck, nestling into my hair as his arms enfolded around me. He breathed a huge sigh of relief before he pulled back to frame my face with his hands.

He gave me a big smile, saying, "I'm so glad you're alright, Sasha! I was so worried about you."

"I'm glad you're safe, too, Seb." Sebastian was leaning against his motorcycle, waiting for us to go to 'The Den' with Jaxon and Eben. He pulled me back into another hug. I hugged him back, soaking up his warmth and the safety I felt in his embrace.

"Are you really ok, Sasha, after Vladimir's visit?"

I sighed. "Thanks to the brothers, I actually am."

The two brothers didn't even growl as Sebastian held me; either they knew how he felt and were giving him a moment, or they were actually getting used to my relationship with Sebastian. Or they weren't pushing their luck tonight; I had barely agreed to come out tonight, especially to this place. All three brothers had decided I needed some fun and to get out after my time with Vladimir. The brothers wanted to come here because we could actually be with one another, and no one would think anything of it; in the bars at Pine River, we couldn't associate too much, or the Cavaliers might catch on. I had to seem available and unassociated with them; they were persons of interest to the Cavaliers.

We pushed back from Sebastian's bike, and he wrapped an arm around my shoulders as we walked over to the brothers. They nodded at him and greeted him with small smiles. Interesting. What had gotten into them? We sped off toward the woods, greeting the first bouncer. It was the same one from the other night, and he greeted me warmly. We made our way to the club's door and greeted the third bouncer, who let us in after we flashed our crimson eyes at him.

Sebastian led the way down the stairs into the club. Too many eyes looked over at me for my comfort as we entered, but I did my best to ignore them.

We ordered drinks and then wandered our way over to the billiard tables. "Two on two?" I suggested. An evil grin spread across each one of their faces.

"Who with who?" Eben asked.

"I'm pretty sure the wolf and I can take you," I winked at the brothers. They laughed, accepting my challenge. "I'll break," I offered.

I bent over to break, and Jaxon leaned over to whisper in my ear. "You do know this is Eben and my favorite game, right? You're going down, Doll Face."

I sat up without breaking and glowered at him. "That so?" He just smirked at me. "Alright, then. Let's make a wager." He perked up, intrigued.

"What are the terms, Doll Face?"

What would goad him the most? He already knew I loved him, so that closed many doors. "If we win, I get to drive your car for the next week." My eyebrow raised in response to his glare. Eben laughed, coming up next to me to lean back against the table, watching our exchange with amusement. Sebastian was also amused, especially because he knew. Jaxon thought for a moment. It was almost like watching him shuffle through different files to see what he could get out of the deal. I smiled at him, draping my arms around his neck, waiting for him to decide.

"Alright," he said, pulling his car keys out of his pocket dramatically and setting them on the rim of the table. "If I win, we hit the back seat tonight." I couldn't help laughing at him.

"You're on," I agreed. Eben sighed but couldn't stop the laugh that made its way out of him. I released Jaxon and chalked the end of my stick. "You know, Jaxon," I said, turning to Eben to kiss Eben's lips sweetly. Eben accepted my affection and looked at me fondly, waiting for what I was going to say. "You don't give your partner much motivation to not throw the game."

Eben's mischievous grin covered his face, combining with his riding gear and flashing red jewelry to reveal the irresistible, dark danger he had, even if he was normally sweet in temperament. He flipped my hair over my shoulder and whispered in my ear so the others couldn't hear, "That's for sure." He planted a kiss on my temple and then backed away to give me room to break.

I turned and gave Sebastian a knowing smile, winking at him. He chuckled in anticipation and relaxed against the nearby standing table with his drink.

I bent over, purposely giving Jaxon a perfect vantage point to check out what he wouldn't be getting tonight. I flashed him a smoldering look which he returned. I turned back to the table and broke expertly. I then used my power to sink every single ball in the correct order for a win. Jaxon's smirk faded, and his mouth came open in surprise as he leaned on his pool stick.

Eben and Sebastian's laughter filled our corner of the club, as I reached down to grab the keys before jingling them in front of Jaxon. "Thanks," I said as I tucked them in the pocket of my jeans. Jaxon blinked and recovered, glowering at me.

He came over to me and pressed me up against the table, leaning over me, "Cheating doesn't count, Sugar Lips." I gave him a triumphant smile and reached up to quickly pull his fedora over his eyes. He did look delicious in his tank top, gold chains that matched his eyes, and leather jacket, but I wouldn't give in; I had won.

"You should have stated your terms before I broke, Jaxon. Deal's a deal. That car is mine for a week." He flicked his hat up with a finger and then pulled me in for a kiss.

"You'll never get away with that again."

"Usually don't, but it's always worth it the first time."

"Alright, you two. Let's play a real game. No more cheating, Sweetums." I gave Eben a sweet smile and gathered the balls perfectly into the triangle with my power.

"Break, Eben?" He nodded and chalked before taking his shot.

The four of us enjoyed playing a few games, jeering each other the entire time. In the end, the brothers won two out of three but narrowly.

I gave Eben a congratulatory kiss, saying, "Well played," after his winning shot in the third game.

Jaxon grabbed my hand and pulled me over to the dance floor. It was a nice slow beat, so he pulled me close. I wrapped my arms around his neck as his leg slipped between mine while we moved together to the music. Our faces were close, our eyes practically undressing each other, as our bodies brushed up against one another to the music.

I spotted Eben and Sebastian watching us as they talked and leaned against the pool table. They had started another casual game, by the looks of it. Still, they were more interested in watching us, most likely discussing us. I flashed them a red-lipped smile before turning my attention back to the blonde vampire whose hands were wandering over my body, setting me on fire. He captured my lips, and one of my hands settled on his cheek as I returned his kiss. His kisses bent my top half over backward as they moved downwards, my hair flying out behind me, and he slowly brought me back up to pull me close to him again. The two at the pool table had appreciated the view.

I gave him a smile, wrapping my arms around his neck again. I pulled him close and whispered for only him, "If you keep this up, you may win your end of the bet anyway." He growled his approval, flashing me his smirk. He kissed me again, and I settled my cheek along his cheek to keep dancing.

I observed a few different wolves eyeing us up here and there, and then my eyes traveled across the club to the private booths. A particular pair of eyes was watching us calmly, right next to another pair that held desire in them. I flashed my blood-red eyes at them, acknowledging their glances just as the music slowed.

I felt Eben come up behind me. Jaxon reluctantly released me to him, heading towards the pool table to take over Eben's game with Sebastian. I danced cheek-to-cheek with Eben, soaking up his tender closeness. I could still feel those eyes on me, even though mine were closed as I soaked up Eben. I smiled as he gently spun me out from him and back in as the song ended. He hung onto me for the next faster-paced one, but I couldn't stand it any longer. I kissed Eben and pulled away from him to walk over to the secluded booth with its observers.

The brothers were more protective and were right behind me; even Sebastian crossed the room to be close to me as I walked over to the area where I had been grabbed the last time. They relaxed a little when they saw who I pulled up in front of, but they stayed all the same. I slid into the crest-shaped booth next to the calm pair of eyes still watching me.

The seat was warm, like someone else had filled the spot just a little bit ago. I looked over at the pair that still held desire and nodded at them. Sebastian, followed by the brothers, slid into the booth on the other end to fill in the space by the pair of flickering eyes as they looked at me.

"Something I can do for you, York?" I asked the wolf who I was sitting up against. He smiled at me and motioned to a passing waitress, ordering us a round of shots.

"Not at all, Sasha. I just wanted to thank you for your help dealing with the rogue and apologize for the trouble it caused you."

I accepted his words with a simple nod and replied, "Thanks. Everything taken care of on your end then?"

"Yes. The brothers were kind enough to give us the location of his body so we could take care of it properly. He was a good man before he lost it. We honored who he used to be instead of who he had turned into." I nodded and hauled my shot back, which the waitress had delivered.

"Any idea where he came up with the idea or concept of the poison to drug me?" York drew in a deep breath and downed his shot, motioning for another round.

"I'm not sure exactly. He used to spend a lot of time around this place but there is also another bar in the neighboring town that he frequented, that wasn't a *private* establishment. It's possible that he located a source in that place. Otherwise, I have no idea. Perhaps he came up with the concept on his own, but I doubt it. I was told the original source was the same poison as the Cavaliers, correct?" I nodded in affirmation. "Then I doubt he made it himself. He hated them as much as the rest of us. Even if he had lost it, I don't see him associating with them."

Shit. Not good. Cavaliers running around with needles full of injectable poison was seriously bad news. I would have to look into the possible lead of a source at the bar in the neighboring town. York filled me in on the details of which bar over the next round of shots.

I listened to York, but my eyes wandered over to Lucas, who was sitting next to him and watching me closely. I gave him an indulgent smile before my attention returned to York. We were deep in discussion about different theories about the rogue's intelligence and the possibility of him coming up with the concept.

York had an arm around the back of the booth where I sat, talking with his other one. I was laughing at him and his theories, enjoying the discussion; I found that I enjoyed York's company. He was relaxed but intelligent, unafraid to have differing opinions from others but willing to listen to another view; I understood why he made a good Alpha for his pack. My guys were chiming in from the other side of the booth, arguing different theories in a friendly manner with him and even Lucas.

I was in the middle of an incredulous laugh when a snarl sounded from behind me, and quicker than I could turn, I was yanked from the booth by my hair.

# CHAPTER 29

"Blood-sucking Bitch!" A snarl reached out above the music, drawing looks from all over the club. I snarled in response to the comment as I landed on my ass on the floor, looking up at the same female wolf that had tried to attack me at the pack's lodge up in the mountains. "Think you can just come in here and move in on any wolf you want?"

She was snarling at me, her eyes changing as her face changed enough that her canines were showing. She was on top of me in a second, trying to scratch and bite me. A hand to her throat stopped her teeth's progress toward me and I sacrificed stopping her from scratching me, to slam my other fist into her face, *hard,* sending her flying back off of me.

I jumped up, snarling at her with blood-red eyes, fangs descended. She came at me again, springing from her crouching position, slamming into me from several feet away, knocking us both to the ground again as we crashed into an empty table. Her hands were flying out all over the place, trying to slap and scratch me as she snarled. I threw her off of me with my power and ended up on top of her, pinning her shoulders with my knees. I held her arms down, and she snarled from the floor where I had her pinned, thrashing her feet and head, trying to find a purchase.

"Who are *you,* calling a bitch?" She heard the implication in my words; she was a wolf, after all. She snarled at me, even angrier, as she struggled against me.

Our altercation had only lasted a few seconds before the guys had finally made it out of the booth to come break it up. I heard Jaxon's excited laugh in the background; he *would* love a girl fight. Sebastian's arms wrapped around my middle and pulled me off the wolf while York stepped in to prevent her from retaliating again. I calmly stood and let Sebastian hold me, looking at her snarling at me from York's grip. I sighed my irritation at the ridiculous drama, over nothing at all. It wasn't like she had caught me making out with her man.

She had just stilled when I shot out at York, "Better find yourself a different female with a little class, York. This one's just gonna breed hyper pups." Her infuriated snarl had me smiling as she resumed her struggle against him, trying to get to me.

Sebastian leaned close to my face and whispered through a smile, "Sasha, you are enjoying this way too much. Fanning the flame is not a good idea."

I looked back at him over my shoulder and shrugged before winking at him with a smile. "She started it," I laughed and turned around in his arms.

He laughed and shook his head, saying, "You're incorrigible."

"You gonna give me a dance tonight since your arms are already around me?" He sighed and laughed again, letting me lead him away from the fuming female to the dance floor. He held my hands, and we danced to the upbeat music while I kept my eye on the other woman arguing with York. I couldn't help the snort that escaped me when he sent her packing.

I held Sebastian's hands out to the side while I shook my hips to the catchy beat, moving in and out of his space. He gave me his crooked smile, enjoying the moment.

He tried to catch me closer to him, but I evaded, and he laughed, saying, "Tease." I gave him a broad smile as I moved back into his space. We both knew it was true where he was concerned, but we also enjoyed it.

I turned around to dance back against him and found my vampire brothers watching us. They were smiling at our antics, so I returned the smile, flirting with them, while Sebastian and I danced. They weren't worried about us any longer; they knew who I was going home with.

I looked from them to Lucas, who looked like he wanted to join us. I turned to face Sebastian again, hanging on him closer. I couldn't encourage Lucas' interest. Sebastian stole a look at Lucas and flashed him a glowing eye warning, wrapping his arms around me a little more. Lucas got the message and followed York back to their booth; they were talking animatedly about their ridiculous female's drama, by their gestures.

"Thanks, Seb."

"I told you that he was actually interested, poor guy. Guess your little ruse on his brother worked too well on him. He's got it bad."

I sighed and raised an eyebrow at him, hissing, "It's your fault! If you hadn't suggested I show him firsthand the 'Vampire's Kiss, ' we probably wouldn't have a problem."

He laughed in response and then leaned in to whisper, "It was so worth it."

I smirked at him, "For you. Poor guy won't be able to get that off his mind for some time to come." He laughed again, looking at me affectionately as we continued to undulate to the music. We cleared from the floor when the song ended and walked over to the brothers. I walked to them, and they both reached out to me, pulling me between them.

"Well, guys," I said, pulling out the keys to jingle them in front of Jaxon, "Your ride's leaving if you're not walking home. I think I've had enough fun for tonight." I pulled from them, holding the car keys in my hand as I led the way back to the parking lot. Sebastian's laughter at me goading Jaxon had me smiling.

We ran to the parking lot in the woods, and Sebastian came over to hug me and say goodbye. "If you need to talk about it, I'm here for you, Sasha," he offered, embracing me.

"Thanks, Seb," I answered and planted a kiss on his neck, nipping him just a little, making him growl and squeeze me.

I unlocked the car, sank into the driver's seat, and waited for the guys to get in. Instead of going straight home, I took us for a joy ride up in the mountains and eventually went to the neighboring town to check out the bar York had mentioned. I didn't stop the car; I just did a drive-by perusal of the place. It was dark and dirty, and something about the place made me wary. I would hit the place up the following night to see what I could dig up on the issues of poisoned syringes.

I sped the whole way home and even managed to swing the car around into Jaxon's parking spot before I shot him a smile and a wink. His glower couldn't hide the smirk, and I laughed at him. I tucked the keys into the pocket of my jeans and got out, heading up the steps to the house. The front door opened, and Niklaus looked out over to the car with a scowl; his mind revealed he thought Jaxon was screwing around 'hot-rodding' again. He looked surprised when Jaxon stepped out of the passenger's seat and looked at me. I gave him a big smile and a flirty wink as I walked past him into the house. He was laughing as he watched the other brothers get out of the car, and he turned to me, still laughing.

"He actually let you drive?" Niklaus asked, coming up to me.

"Not really, he lost a bet. The car keys were the price for a week," I laughed. Niklaus gave a huge laugh and laughed even louder when Jaxon entered with a pout. Niklaus pulled me in for a kiss with his hands on my neck and jaw.

When he pulled back, he smiled and whispered, "About time someone got the better of him. I think he's finally met his match."

"And have you, Niklaus?" I whispered, looking at him while I used my power to tickle him around his collar. His eyes lit up red in response, and I gave him a flirty smile. He couldn't hide his thoughts, though he didn't confirm anything with his words. I gave him a smug smile, pulling him in for a kiss.

A scream from upstairs broke our moment. It was well past the twins' bedtime. I sighed and waved off the brothers; it was time to have another talk with the two upstairs. I rushed to their room to find them screaming at the Governess, who was doing her best not to cower. Both Lucy and Lucian's eyes lit up red, and they went at the Governess again. I put up a wall of force in front of the Governess that the two ran into, knocking both down to the floor. They snarled and leaped to their feet, about to try again, confused, when Lucy spotted me in the doorway. Her rage turned on me, and she came at me, snarling with her fangs and claws.

I caught her around the throat with my hand and held her from me as I allowed the beastiality inside me to come out full force, roaring, "THAT IS

ENOUGH!" I used my power to shake the manor with my words as I roared with all my teeth and fangs, red eyes flashing. The Governess dropped to the floor, covering her head with her hands in terror, and Lucian stopped his advance on me to join his sister.

A sudden change came over both twins, and they went very quiet, their eyes fading to their standard color. I hissed at first Lucy and then Lucian for emphasis, and tears started to well in their eyes. I released Lucy and felt around in her mind for a moment. She was a spoilt brat, as was her brother, but I discovered in them both that they were starved for female attention, which surprised me.

These twisted, rather psychotic children were surrounded by men who spoiled them and Governesses who cowered in fear of them, unable to stand up against the two's tantrums long enough to offer any genuinely healthy affection.

"Come with me," I gently said, offering them my hands. Lucy just looked at me for a moment, deciding, as Lucian readily accepted and crossed the room. Lucy warily took my hand, and I led them both into their closet, which had a vanity. I pulled out a little nightgown for Lucy and handed it to her gently, doing the same with some pajamas for Lucian. I turned Lucy around and unbuttoned the back of her black and white dress, removing it, and she slipped the nightgown on over her head. She didn't know what to make of me being nice to her. I did the same for Lucian, helping unbutton his black vest and getting him dressed for bed as well.

I walked over to the vanity and sat down in front of it, gently pulling Lucy onto my lap as Lucian stepped up close. Lucy watched me from the mirror as I gently took her hair down and used her brush to gently comb out her long, dark hair. I didn't say anything as I paid careful attention to her. I met her eyes in the mirror and saw that nasty little smirk coming over her features, her eyes starting to glow like she was about to make trouble. My eyes flamed red in response, and I gave her hair a tug, giving her a look in the mirror. She instantly went back to normal, wearing a curious look on her face.

I finished with Lucy, set her off my lap, and then turned to face Lucian. I reached for a comb, wetting it, and brushed out his hair, giving it a nice part, before I finished. I then rose and, taking their hands, led them into the bathroom to brush their teeth.

Once they were ready for bed, I led them to their beds and pulled back the comforters so they could climb into each of their beds. I turned off the lights since we could both clearly see in the dark, and I sat on the edge of Lucian's bed, looking at them both.

"Are you ready for your bedtime story?" They nodded, still unsure what to make of me. "Once upon a time, a very long time ago, there lived a little girl in a village in the countryside of an evil King. She was different than other little girls of her age and was often forced to play alone. She became lonely but had dreams of being rescued by a prince who would ride away with her on a horse. As she grew up, she realized that she had special giftings. She thought it was a fun thing to have until the day she killed two young boys in her village with that gifting.

"The children of the village were out playing in the forest, and the little girl was being teased by the other children, ruthlessly. In a moment of anger, the little girl screamed and released a great force of power that caused a small rockslide. One of the boys who had been teasing her was crushed to death under the pile of rocks. The other children were afraid of this little girl, so they lashed out in anger, throwing rocks at her, until she became so enraged that she struck out with her out-of-control power again, killing another boy after he had hit her in the head with the rock. The rest of the children ran away, screaming from the little girl's anger that was hurting others. It wasn't very long before the villagers came for her so they could tie her up and burn her at the stake for witchcraft.

"It was at that moment, when she was about to be burned alive, that the evil King came and rescued her from all of the villagers, killing them and saving the little girl who was so different from others her age." Lucy and Lucian were absolutely enthralled by the story I was telling. Lucian even held his breath as Lucy's eyes widened. "You see Lucian, you see Lucy, sometimes lashing out in anger when you are gifted, can hurt other people and cause many problems in your life." They looked at me for a long moment. "It was you, wasn't it? You were the little girl." I smiled at them. "Lucy, Lucian, you are special and powerful, but your anger could hurt the Governess or any other staff." They absorbed my words but didn't react.

"Will you tell us more bedtime stories like that one?" Lucian asked.

I nodded at him, saying, "I will tell you bedtime stories, just like that one, if you promise not to attack the Governess any longer. Deal?" Lucian nodded and looked over to his sister to see what she would decide. Lucy took a moment, but at last nodded her agreement as well.

"Go to sleep, both of you, goodnight."

I felt a sudden change in our relationship that boded well for the future. The twins were curious about me but had found something in common with me that they could relate to. Both also appreciated that I wasn't afraid of them; most were, as the twins were so powerful.

I gave them one last smile before leaving them in their room. I walked out of their room, shutting the door, and turned to come to a sudden halt in the hallway. All three brothers were there looking at me in shock. I suddenly felt self-conscious.

"What?" I asked, blushing. Niklaus listened to their minds and shared a look with his brothers before turning back to me incredulously, whispering, "I think you may have just tamed the beasts."

# CHAPTER 30

Each of the men's minds was in a different place, but they were mulling over what they had found out about me through the story, and each of them was surprised at the twins' response to me.

I rolled my eyes, "Oh, come, now. The children just need a woman in their lives they don't view as a potential meal. I'm sure they'll be back to their impossible selves in no time, tantrums and all." They didn't say anything; they just continued to look at me. Their thoughts about me had me blushing; how I really was becoming a part of this family, how having me around would be good for Lucy and Lucian as well, how 'amazing' I was, how surprising it was that I was a motherly type.

"Oh, alright, stop right there! Good grief," I huffed and shoved past them. That was too far.

I walked down the stairs and crossed the entryway to the hallway that led to my room. I stopped before the massive black door and swallowed with the emotions washing over me. I reached out and opened the door, swinging it in as the terrible memories of Vladimir's night with me in this room flashed before my eyes. Tears actually pricked my eyes as my gaze fell on the bed. The room still smelled of him, reminding me that I could never really escape him. Would I always be his? Would I become his bride, that night with him becoming an almost nightly event? The shivers at the thought rolled through my whole body, making goose bumps break out all over my body as I stood there.

The thoughts of his abuse during the night had me absorbed in a mental hell as I stared at the bed, remembering. Vladimir's hands on my body, him inside of me, his teeth in my flesh, had me squeezing my eyes shut with a pained grimace. The screams from that night were still lodged in my soul; I could scream them for years and not run out of the grief that held me at the thought of being his every night. I was beginning to think I had made a huge mistake trying to bargain for my release from being his weapon. The idea of spending every night with Vladimir was entirely less appealing than being out doing his dirty work. But it was too late; the deal had been struck. I would be his.

I had stood there so long that everyone else had gone to bed. Thoughts and memories were still haunting me. Me screaming as Vladimir tore into my neck and body. No. I couldn't do it. I was seeping down into despair and a desire to end it all. I had tasted love, and perhaps that was all I was meant to have; a taste. I felt like I was falling into a vast abyss of horrendous memories that revealed my future. But could I actually do what was necessary to escape my inevitable future with Vladimir? Could I really fade into that abyss to never feel the love I had tasted?

The answer wouldn't be so complicated—the rogue had shown me that. A simple needle would become my escape, and it wouldn't be complicated to obtain either. If I simply left for that bar, I might even find my escape quickly. I turned where I stood and looked at the front door to the manor, a sickness in my heart. My steps slowly took me toward the door that would lead to my permanent release.

My miseries were flowing out of me through horrendous thoughts of eternal escape when I suddenly heard them embodied in music. My ear turned to listen, and then it was like I was floating through the mansion, following it across the entryway and up the stairs. I stood frozen, listening, closing my eyes. There it was, the sound of what I was feeling. Like Eben knew how I felt at this moment and was calling me to him, like the Pied Piper. And I was following, answering the call of his bow and strings just like the children had.

I stared at his door for a long moment, listening to his violin, deciding whether to return to my room or out the front door. Could I sink back into the shadows?

"*No more hiding, Sasha,*" Eben thought. I closed my eyes at his thoughts directed at me. He already knew I was standing there. I reached out and opened his door, sliding inside before I shut it behind me. He turned toward me, acknowledging me as he drew the bow across the strings of his violin. The sound was haunting as it reached my soul.

"Do you want me to leave?" I whispered. He didn't stop playing but shook his head, 'no,' while still holding his violin to his shoulder. I walked slowly over to his bed and lay down on the side closest to where he played. I took the pillow there and pulled it down to wrap my arms around it as I nestled my head into it.

I closed my eyes to listen to him play, breathing in his scent on the bed and pillow I clung to. I could feel his understanding; he knew exactly how I felt and had been there many times. His melody seemed to communicate precisely what I was feeling at the moment. I soaked it up, lying there. It was the balm that my sick heart needed at that moment, and I loved him for it. What would he think of me if he knew just how close I had come to reaching for the front doorknob instead of his? I didn't have the talent for expressing my sorrow like he did, but if I did, it would match his. He gazed at me while playing, moving my soul as his deep blue eyes delved into mine. They were full of patient understanding.

I closed my eyes, unable to hold his gaze, and held the pillow closer to me to prevent the tears that wanted to come. I felt lost. And then his melody changed, slowly transforming into something of pure beauty. I heard another piece of my heart in his notes that tasted of something profoundly complex and rich. It was how I felt in his arms, Jaxon's or Niklaus's. It was the pleasant ache that throbbed to be with them, to love them.

I slowly opened my eyes to meet his over the pillow I clung to. They weren't just looking at me; they were looking into me at that moment, as he tended to do. His slight smile reached his eyes as he looked at me, playing out a piece of my heart, reminding me of what I had found here at the coven.

I bit my lower lip, trying to stop the tears making my vision blurry, my eyes glassy. Eben's reminder made me want to find a way instead of just ending my story. Could I find a happy ending after it had been so terrible for so long? What was it going to take? I had no solutions, no answers for the future, but here in the now, I would soak up the love, just like Eben's notes rolling out over me. Would he mind so much if I stayed and listened? I didn't want to be alone. I didn't want to return to the vast, lonely black room that smelled of Vladimir and had horror scenes flashing in front of my eyes.

"Eben," I whispered, about to ask permission to stay when he stopped playing, lowering his violin to his side and coming to me.

He stroked my cheek with the back of his hand, my eyes drifting close at the loving touch. My lips parted on the pillow as he touched me. I opened my eyes to look at him, and I saw a look of such deep understanding it threatened to open up that weak dam holding my tears back. He leaned down and kissed me gently.

"Don't you dare take away my reason to play that second melody instead of the first for the rest of my existence."

"Do you read minds like your coven brother, Eben?" He smiled at me.

"No, but as you know, I can pick up on your emotions. Humans are easier, but with how strong yours were, it wasn't difficult."

"My dark angel. Not a mind reader but a heart reader instead." He had saved me as much as his brother had the other night from the rogue; only he had saved me from myself. "Eben, do you mind if I stay?" I was embarrassed to express my need. I so rarely voiced a need. He smiled at me and gently held my jaw with his hands, lifting my face from the pillow to kiss me.

"In whatever capacity you want, Sasha," he answered as he turned to place his violin in its stand before returning to me. Eben's tender lovemaking would be such a welcome contrast to the abusive violence that I had experienced at the hands of Vladimir. I pulled him to me, running my fingers into his hair, loving the sweet taste of his mouth on mine.

My arms went around his neck, and I rolled him onto his bed as I kissed him. I straddled him and pulled him up to me so I could pull his shirt up and over his head, throwing it to the floor as he laid back down on his bed. I just looked at him, soaking up his beauty as I ran my hands over him, tracing the lines of his tattoos and watching his eyes darken with my caresses.

"I love you, Eben. Thank you for pulling me back from the brink. I had been so close to," I just let it drop off while I looked at him. He gave me a smile that said he knew exactly what I had been about to do. "Don't you dare take away my inspiration, my hope, or this love we have found. I would never forgive you. You've only just begun to bloom, my beautiful blossom. I cannot wait to see what other beauty you reveal as you feel safer here with the coven."

I smiled at him then. I held his gaze as I slowly reached down across my body and pulled my halter top up over my head, whipping my hair out to the side. I smiled at the spark that I saw dance in his blue eyes as he looked at me. His hands wandered from my thighs to my waist, rubbing my sides. I bent to him to give him a slow kiss as I reached down between my legs to undo his belt. I gave him an alluring smile as I drifted down to pull off the rest of his clothes, dragging my long, soft hair down his body behind me. He sighed at the feeling of its gentle, tickling caress sliding down his body.

I returned to straddle him, looking down into his azure eyes that were so beautifully dark with arousal and love. I began slowly running my long black nails over him with the lightest touch. His eyes drifted close as my nails wandered across his skin, slowly starting to build up the burn. Now that I had tasted tenderness, slow, I planned on showing him that two could play that game. I watched the pleasure reflected on his face as I slowly drew my nails up his side, shoulder, and neck and lightly up onto his face to trace his lips, following the smile that tugged at them. I slid them down his chin, back down his neck, and slowly down his chest to tickle his navel. My nails wandered down his thighs and back up, bringing out a quiet moan from him.

I smiled as his hands moved to undo my jeans. I let him slide them from my legs and drop them to the floor. The clunk of Jaxon's keys in my pocket made me laugh a little. I laid down on Eben with our faces close, still teasing him slowly with my nails as I started kissing his jaw, dragging my parted lips along it to under his ear. I sucked on his neck there as my nails moved lower to really tease and taunt him, making him moan louder.

I kissed my way onto his torso, straddling him again. His eyes fluttered open to look at me. I watched his face as I slid my body down onto him, his eyes closing and his lips parting with a sigh of pleasure. He was caressing my thighs and back and opened his eyes again to look at me. He reached for my face to draw my lips to his, kissing me passionately as I started to move on top of him. He rose up to meet me as I leaned down to his neck and gently bit him, increasing his pleasure while I continued to move over him.

I stopped feeding from him to bring my lips to his ear, whispering, "I'm going to take care of you, Eben. Right now, and from now on." His arms surrounded me, and he hugged me to him in response. My mouth returned to his neck, slowly feeding on him, taking my time as my body built up his burning need until he cried out my name as I tipped him over the edge.

# CHAPTER 31

"Eben, did you want a ride, or were you walking or planning on taking your bike today?" Jaxon's voice came through Eben's door. Eben pulled up from my neck, his red eyes looking at me with a naughty little smile as I pulled him down to my lips instead. "Eben?" I laughed as Eben kissed me, my arms wrapped around his neck. I felt Jaxon's mind as he heard me behind the door with his brother. I could almost see the glare he was shooting at the door.

I smiled at Eben, who was lying on me, while I answered Jaxon, "You're walking too, remember?" I gave another laugh, and Eben joined me. Jaxon's growl from outside the door only made me laugh harder.

The door to Eben's bedroom opened, and Jaxon stormed into the room. Eben rolled over, annoyed, and took me with him, so I lay up against him, the sheet covering us. I settled into the crook of Eben's arm, putting a hand on his chest, and smirked up at Jaxon.

"I think I'm a bad influence on your brother, Jaxon. He might be skipping class this morning instead of you." He was irritated about the car but also for finding me in Eben's room, instead of his.

"Where are they?" I smirked at him until he stalked over towards us, looking for my jeans. He spotted them, but just as he was reaching for them, I used my power to pull the keys from the pocket lightning quick, catching them in my waiting palm. I blew Jaxon a kiss with that same hand, and then the keys disappeared beneath the sheets.

"Off you go. Enjoy your walk," I laughed.

His smirk returned as he said, "You think that's going to stop me?" My smirk faded as he sprang onto the bed on top of me, and I screeched and tried to move out of his reach.

Eben growled in irritation, "Get off Jaxon. Get out."

Jaxon ignored his brother, focusing on me. He straddled me, fishing for the keys under the sheets. We grappled for a few minutes, me keeping the keys away from him, him sneaking a couple feels, when he finally found purchase on the wrist of the hand that held the keys. I closed my fist around them, laughing hysterically, as he growled, first in irritation and then triumph, as he tried to open my fingers to get the keys.

Eben's irritation had faded as he watched me taunt Jaxon, laughing. He folded his hands behind his head, wearing his mischievous look as he watched, amused. Jaxon had left the door open, and I was relieved the Governess had already taken the twins to an early morning educational outing, even if I had managed to stay covered under the sheet.

I used my free hand to reach up and tickle Jaxon, causing him to release my wrist for a second, long enough to resume the struggle. We were both laughing by this point, enjoying the tussle. I hid the keys behind my back as he pinned me and bent close.

Jaxon looked at my neck for a moment, which had a drop of blood on it, and then whispered, "You Eben's breakfast, Sasha?" I smirked at him. He smirked back and leaned closer to my ear to whisper, "I didn't know you did *breakfast in bed,* Sugar Lips." He sat up to look at me.

I wiggled out from under him and moved back over to lay back against Eben, offering up my shoulder and neck to him. "Yes, well, you interrupted, so you'd better get walking if you don't want to be late," I said as I reached back to rub Eben's neck as he lowered his lips to my neck to bite me again. I gasped at the pleasure, closing my eyes for a moment before I looked up at Jaxon. His eyes lit up at the sight.

I smoldered at Jaxon, taunting him through the pleasure that was washing through me. He flashed me a fangy-snarl before he growled. He was on the other side of my neck in an instant, biting down on the other side, making me moan and throw my head back as my back arched. My other hand dropped the keys and fisted Jaxon's blonde hair. Another moan tore out of me as I held onto them both, riding the waves of overlapping pleasure. I couldn't stop the sounds coming out of me as they both pulled on me, making me throb all over. The sound of an irritated sigh from the doorway drew my heavy eyes.

Niklaus stood there with a scowl and folded arms. I saw a flash of red in his eyes as he watched his brothers feed on me, making me moan, but his scowl remained.

"You're supposed to be a *good* influence on these two, Sasha. Missing classes isn't part of that. We have to keep up our image in the community for the humans." I smiled wickedly as I looked back at him for a second before another moan parted my lips and closed my eyes.

Jaxon finally released me and said, "He's just jealous he's not in on it." Eben released me, laughing at his brother's snark. I looked at Niklaus. His mind revealed that Jaxon wasn't far off the mark. I raised an eyebrow at him, and his eyes flashed crimson. "Told ya, Sugar Lips," Jaxon laughed as he looked at Niklaus.

"Alright, you two better head on out," Niklaus directed to Jaxon and Eben.

Jaxon got off the bed. "You really gonna make me walk?" I smiled at him. Niklaus had stepped away from the door, and Jaxon stepped into the hall, looking at me and pouting.

I winked and answered, "I'll meet you at the car in five."

"Fifteen," Eben said as Jaxon was closing the door. Jaxon growled as my laughter echoed through the closed door, followed by pointed silence and a moan.

I pulled the sports car into a parking spot outside of the bar that I had driven by the previous night. Its boarded-up windows flashed with neon signs, and you could hear muffled music coming from inside the establishment. It definitely wasn't my usual scene, but you had to follow where the lead was.

I stepped out of the car in my knee-high boots, black leather pants, and black corset. My hair hung loose and straight down past my waist, and I had added silver hoops to my ears. I wasn't sure what to expect from this particular establishment. Several pairs of eyes turned to look at me while I walked past toward the bar.

"Hey girly, you looking for a good time?" I flashed the unkempt man a smile before I stepped in closer to him.

I whispered, "I'm looking for a special kind of good time that I heard can be *acquired* here. Know anything about it?" He looked me up and down for a moment, licking his lips.

"I might. For the right price." I could feel he knew something, but I wasn't sure if he was referring to a human substance or the one I sought.

"I'm looking for *something special,* not the usual stuff." Recognition flashed in his eyes. He did know. I flashed him an alluring smile. "Where can I find someone who does know something?"

"Like I said, I can tell you, for the right price."

"You mean, tell me the name of someone else who knows or the name of the source?" His mind flashed up a man in his mind at my question.

"The source."

"That's alright, I think I'll take my chances in finding him." I left him there, staring after me as I walked up to the door and went inside.

The place was as dirty inside as it was out, complete with a greasy-looking bar, run-down jukebox, low-hanging lights that occasionally flickered, and a pilling pool table. I heard the ker-chunk of the balls hitting one another as someone sunk one into a corner pocket.

Multiple eyes turned in my direction and took me in with their eyes, but I was distracted entirely by the scent of the place. Vampire. There was at least one other vampire here. I began wandering, searching for the man from the other man's mind. My eyes found him sitting at a table in total darkness of a corner of the bar. His eyes met mine in the dark as I smiled and walked casually over to him, the darkness of the corner swallowing me from the sight of the other patrons. Here was my vampire. Interesting. He was also the source, supposedly. He angled his head to look up at me as I stood over him.

I flashed my eyes at him and saw him flash me a fang in response since the other patrons would have seen his eyes as he faced the bar.

"Hey there, big boy. I heard a rumor that you might be able to show me a *thrill*." He gave me a knowing smile, complete with fangs, and gestured for me to take a seat near him.

"That could be true on multiple counts, sweetheart." My red lips spread into an alluring smile, and I leaned towards him.

"What are the options?" His predatory grin made one option very clear. His mind revealed that he hadn't been with a female vampire for years and was going to try to negotiate some *quality time* for the other.

"Well, there's always a good time without other aids, and if your other style is something else, I have something that could drown out your sorrows for a couple of hours all the way up to forever. What's your pleasure, princess?" Interesting.

"So, do you mix this *good time* yourself? I want to know what I'm buying is legit stuff."

He laughed. "I have a couple of associates, and we mix it together. Small batches, hand-mixed to perfection."

"Really? Is it certified organic, too?" I said sarcastically while flirting with him.

He laughed again, leaning towards me. "What you looking for?" I looked him up and down, returning my gaze to his.

"Are your *associates* as appetizing as you?" I asked in an alluring voice, batting my eyes at him. His mind showed me two other faces as he compared himself to them.

"Perhaps one, but the other wouldn't be your type." Another vampire and a human; very interesting.

"Well, do you have any first-time specials?"

He laughed, saying, "I'll tell you what. You give me half an hour out back, and I'll give you an entire syringe of something that will send you on a trip for a few hours, with a milder dose thrown in for free." I flashed my eyes at him and gave him a smile, showing my fangs.

"Lead the way, Casanova."

I looked behind me to check out the rest of the bar quickly as I followed the man out the back exit into a deserted alleyway. I needed to get him farther away from here.

"Look, I'm not so much a back ally kind of woman, Casanova. How's about you follow me?" I walked up to him and ran my hands up his chest to encircle my arms around his neck while I waited for his answer.

"Alright." I released him and sped off into the night, far away from other people. I found an old abandoned cemetery on the edge of the town. Kinky. I liked it.

I took hold of his hand and pulled him after me toward a large crypt. I could feel his sense of anticipation and delight in my chosen venue. I pulled the door shut after us and turned around at lightning speed to start kissing him while I pulled his jacket off and threw it over a coffin. I pushed him, still in vampire speed mode, up against the back wall while I tore his shirt off of him, snarling like I was aroused. He was thrilled.

"So," I panted in a husky voice, "If I was interested in more *thrills* with this associate, where might I find him?" I kissed him before he could answer but then nipped my way down his neck, driving him wild.

His mind revealed what I wanted to know while he said, "Why, when you got me?" I pulled back and smiled at him.

"I like diversity."

I didn't let him comment before I started undoing his belt as I snarled and sunk my fangs into his neck. He was overwhelmed with pleasure, having not had another vampire feed on him in years, and his head fell back on a moan as I fed on him. But I kept feeding on him. And soon, he was to the point where I would drain him if I didn't pull back.

"Alright, sweetheart, I'll take what else you've got to offer me." I didn't release him, and he snarled in annoyance.

I suddenly bit deeper, and with a vicious snarl of my own, I ripped his throat out. His blood flowed down over his body as he gurgled and looked at me. He was about to pass out from being completely drained, even though he would heal.

"Sorry," I whispered to him as his eyes grew wide, and he fell at my feet. I felt a pinch in my calf before he dropped limp on the crypt floor. Perfect. Now I needed to tear him apart and burn him, crypt and all. It only took seconds before I stood before the blazing crypt, holding his jacket, which was loaded with his syringes, over my arm.

And then I felt a pulling on my mind. I looked down, and my eyes fell on a syringe sticking out of my calf. Damn. I was sinking to the ground as I whipped out my cell phone and pressed the speed dial. He picked up instantly. "Niklaus. . ."

# CHAPTER 32

Snuffling getting closer. And then, a hot, wet tongue started licking my face, making me giggle uncontrollably as I stared up at the stars through the forest canopy.

"Scheb - beeeee, that you?" I giggled again, my eyes finally looking over at the great black wolf as he transformed down into the shape of my friend.

"Over here!" he shouted, and I heard others coming. I grabbed Sebastian's face and brought him down for a full kiss on the mouth.

"I misch do, Scheb. Wanna schtay with me, heer? Luck at the schtars!" More giggling as I looked up. They were floating around in the night sky as I looked at them, transfixed.

"What the hell are you trippin on, Sash?" I felt him gathering me up in his arms.

"The jacksnett, please," I waved my arm around at the ground as I lay limp in his arms, my limbs and head hanging back watching the forest spin around us. I saw the brothers coming toward us and was confused about why they were upside down. I smiled at them, still hanging upside down, laughing, and glared at Niklaus. Pointing a finger, I said, "Ahhhh, Nicky, come to ssschold me hugh?" I giggled some more until it turned into hysterical laughter and ended with a snort. I heard muffled laughter.

"Well, it doesn't look like she got a serious or threatening dose," I heard Niklaus comment as he laughed a little. More laughter. I flashed him a smirk before I turned my head and suddenly wretched all the blood I had taken from the vampire all over the forest floor.

"Jeeze, Sasha," Sebastian said as he jumped back from the flow. I flopped back, limp again, giggling. Was it possible to feel this terrible and high in an unstable way at the exact same time?

"I'm rather impressed with how far she was able to crawl away from the fire," Niklaus said.

They started walking with me, and I shouted, "Jacksnett!"

"Grab the jacket there, would you?" Sebastian asked one of the brothers.

"Here, give her to me, and you can get dressed. We don't want to start a commotion with you walking around as you are," Niklaus said. I murmured my approval at the thought, and I heard Sebastian chuckle.

I was passed over to Niklaus and I heard the sounds of Sebastian getting dressed. My head flopped against Niklaus's chest.

He looked down at me and I grinned like a fool and reached up to touch his face saying, "Yur so handschome, Nicky." I heard more laughter. I looked over, my head flopping back, and saw both Jaxon and Eben walking with us. They were the source of the laughter.

"I told you one of us should have gone with you, Sasha," Niklaus said as he carried me.

"Get the keys out of her pocket," I heard Jaxon say. "I'll go get the car. We really shouldn't walk her through town with her covered in blood."

"No! I won da bate." More laughter.

"Well, you're not driving like that, Doll Face." I felt him take the keys, and then he was gone.

"I'll take these samples back to the college with me to get them analyzed, and we'll see what other information comes of it. I'll drop by your place tomorrow evening or the following with the results. Glad you're alright, Sash," I heard Sebastian say as he gave me a quick kiss on the forehead.

Jaxon pulled up in the sports car, and Eben opened the door for Niklaus to maneuver us both into the back seat, still holding me in his arms. I relaxed against him as we drove back to the estate. I was carried into my room, and he held me still as he undressed and bathed me, me giggling the whole time.

Once I was clean and dressed in my nightgown, he pulled back the covers of my bed and put me between the sheets. I pulled him down for a kiss, and he swept my hair back before holding my face and kissing me again.

"You need to be more careful, Sasha," he whispered. I gave him a smirk and pulled him back to me when he tried to leave. I need to go call Vladimir, Sasha. He knows." I moaned, my high sinking a little.

Niklaus left the room, and I closed my eyes, hating that I could still smell Vladimir in my room. I most definitely didn't want to fall asleep in this state with his smell around me; the nightmares would be horrible. My door opened, and I looked over at Jaxon, who came over and flopped on the bed next to me. I didn't even wait for him; I just pulled him to me, kissing him, pulling on him while I giggled.

I heard him laughing as he said, "I like this version of you, Doll Face." I shoved him over and crawled out of the sheets on top of him. I laid down on top of him, practically purring, as I sampled his lips again.

His hands were on my thighs, rubbing them as my long black nightgown rose and fell with his hands, creating a pleasant sensation there. I couldn't stop laughing every time he touched me, so I grabbed his hands and held them over his head, smirking at him. He tried to move and I used all of my strength, reinforced with my magic, to hold him in place. I bent over and teased him with my tongue on his neck and ear before returning to kiss him with a drugged growl.

The door opened, and Niklaus walked in, talking on the phone, "Yes, she is definitely not acting herself right now, but I'll try to keep her out of trouble. No, I sent Jaxon to watch over her while I called you." He looked up at us just then and exclaimed, "Dammit, I gotta go."

He actually hung up on Vladimir and started coming over to us, but before he could even reach us, Vladimir's apparition appeared. Jaxon's eyes widened, having never seen the magic before, and he struggled to get away from me, but I held him down, still laughing. Niklaus reached out and pulled me off of Jaxon while I laughed hysterically; the drugs combined with the fear making me loose it a little.

Vladimir took in the situation rather calmly. His form drifted over to me, still held by Niklaus. He grabbed my chin roughly and made me look at him through my drugged eyes.

He bent and kissed me and then said, "Niklaus, try to keep her under control in this state, will you? Give her the antidote quickly since I'm not there to enjoy her like this."

"Yes, Vladimir," Niklaus answered him.

I smirked at Vladimir and laughed, reaching up to run my fingers along his chin in a seductive way. He growled his approval and kissed me again before fading as I laughed and waggled my fingers goodbye at him.

"Now I know you're trippin'," Jaxon said after watching my interaction with Vladimir.

"Go get some antidote, will you?" Niklaus asked, and Jaxon sped from the room. I turned around to look at Niklaus. Jaxon returned with the antidote and Eben.

Niklaus held the bottle up to my lips, and I glared at him, "Gonna be a spoilsport, Hugh Nicky?" The other brothers laughed, and then he tipped the bottle to my lips, and I took it.

Niklaus held me as the antidote hit my system, sobering me up very quickly. It also brought on the aftereffects of the poison of feeling terrible for a few minutes. I winced and held my head as I moved to sit on the edge of the bed. It was as close to a hangover as I ever wanted to come. I moaned and flopped back on the bed. Jaxon was laughing at me again.

"Jerk," I shot at him with a smile. He laughed harder and came over to lounge on the bed next to me. "Was it just me, or did Vladimir take that rather well?" I moaned. The brothers chimed in an affirmation.

"You know, he seemed strange to me on the phone when we talked before I came in. He even chuckled at me describing your state of mind," Niklaus said, his mind turning very quickly with this information. "Sasha," Niklaus looked at me, "Did you notice anything different about Vladimir the last time you had the drugs in your system?" My brow wrinkled as I thought about it for a while.

"I'm not sure; I was so out of it when the rogue had me, but if I actually remember, he seemed strange when he came to me in that magical form, yes. Why?"

"I think that his mental link with you has something to do with it when you're drugged. I'm not sure exactly. I'll take some time to think about it for a while. We'll see what Sebastian has to say when he brings information on the samples. How are you feeling now?" Niklaus asked.

I sighed and opened my eyes. "Much better, thanks," I said kindly at him. He and Eben came to lounge on the bed with us.

"No more looking into this alone, alright?" Niklaus gave me a look while he said it.

I sighed, "Ok, no more alone on *this*." I looked at Jaxon lying next to me and reached out to pull him to me. I kissed him while my hand slid from his face to his hip, where it tucked into his pocket to pull out the car keys. I enclosed them in my hand before he could stop me and sent them into my nightstand drawer with my magic. "I don't need a designated anymore, thanks. But I could use a drink," I winked at him.

His eyes lit up as he looked at me, still resting on my lips. "Wouldn't want to stain this," I said pulling his white sweatshirt off him. I ran my hands all over him, kissing him. I practically sprang on top of Jaxon, straddling him.

"Sasha, don't you think you should rest?" Niklaus chuckled at me. I put a finger across his lips to stop him.

"Not at all," I smirked at him. "If you're too tired, you can go; otherwise, don't stop my fun. Besides, you yourself said 'no more wasted time,' remember?"

I leaned over to Niklaus and kissed him. His hand came to my face to hold me there for a moment before I broke the kiss. His look darkened as he listened in on my mind, filling with naughty thoughts. I flashed him a smirk as his mind couldn't help but respond to mine. My smirk grew into a completely feral grin, fangs and all, as I used my power to pull his vest and tunic off of him, adding it to the growing pile of clothes on the floor. Jaxon's mind was ticking away, his arousal growing as he watched me work his brother up a little. I bent back down to Jaxon and gave him a kiss as his hands returned to my thighs. I murmured my approval.

I turned to Eben, who was leaning against the headboard on Jaxon's other side. I gave him a flirty perusal. "If you don't want to stay, you'd better leave now." His sweet smile slowly faded into a smoldering look as he looked at me, his blue eyes turning dark. I smirked at him and took my fingernail, drawing it up along his chest as my power slowly pulled his shirt up and over his head, freeing him from it completely. "That's better," I winked at him. His smoldering look didn't falter as he looked me up and down. I pulled his face to mine, leaning over to kiss him, tasting his sweet flavor. I looked back to Niklaus, saying, "Should we take this back to the tub?"

# CHAPTER 33

I walked into the bathroom after Niklaus said the tub was ready. Niklaus was already in the water, looking at me as I ate him up with my eyes. I turned as Jaxon, followed by Eben, came into the bathroom. I angled my head, leaning over to kiss Jaxon as I slowly raised my arms above my head. Jaxon smiled for a second as he kissed me and reached out to pull my nightgown up my body and over my head, whipping my hair with the speed. I reached out and started undoing his belt, helping him out of his jeans. He picked me up, pulling my legs around his waist as I clung to him. He started stepping into the tub with me as I looked behind him and helped Eben out of his clothes with my magic.

I straddled Jaxon with my legs wrapped around him, and we sank below the bubbles. I kissed him from above his face until I sunk down on him, taking him inside me as he growled. I moved on him for a couple minutes, enjoying his snarls, before I leaned forward and sunk my fangs into his neck, taking him even higher as I fed and moved on him simultaneously. His hands on my hips helped me finish him off after a bit, just as my first orgasm rolled out over me, making me bend away from him backward, my long, almost-black hair filling the water's surface. My arms stretched out behind me as I rode out my pleasure, hissing. Jaxon held my waist as he bent forward and kissed my stomach.

A hand snaked out and pulled me from Jaxon, and then I was lying with my back against Eben. My arms bent around him backward as my head turned to feed from his neck. Eben's head fell back over the edge of the tub as I maneuvered myself for him to breech me from behind, feeding from him. His arms wrapped around me as I moved with him, his hand slowly slipping down my front to drive me crazy for a while. I had to release him from my jaws, on an open-mouth hissing moan, as pleasure ripped through my system, pulling his from him as well. I heard Jaxon's approving growl as he watched. I could feel Niklaus's mind as he mentally rode the waves with us.

I stayed on Eben's lap, leaned forward, and pulled Jaxon across the tub to my lips with my magic. I released him with a wicked smile. I returned to Eben's lips as I reached behind me, lovingly rubbing his neck. His tongue slipped inside of me to drive me crazy, making me moan. Jaxon leaned forward and started kissing my neck before his mouth traveled down to tease me just above the water's surface. I looked down at Jaxon and lifted his chin to kiss him again before sending him back with a magical shove and a playful wink. I gave Eben one more caress before my eyes turned to Niklaus.

He pulled me to him, and I sat on his lap. My eyes were heavy with desire as I looked at him. I would never tire of the coven brothers; I would never get enough, even if I lived out the rest of eternity with them here in the mansion. I leaned forward and sunk my fangs into Niklaus, feeding on him, making small noises with the pleasure I found there. His fingers snuck up inside of me to work their magic on me as I leaned over him. I ran my hand up his chest and held his neck to me as I fed through the orgasm he brought on so quickly. I hissed when he entered me, returning to my feeding as he started working me up again. I finally released him from my bite.

I bent over backward again as he held my waist and started to drive me to abandon. My eyes met Jaxon's as he watched, and I reached out behind me toward him and Eben. They came to me as I sat up a little, giving them an alluring smile. Jaxon's eyes were glowing red as I looked at him. Eben moved in close enough for me to lean against his chest as I pulled Jaxon's lips to mine with a hand on his jaw. Niklaus's thrusts from below added to the sensuality of the kiss I shared with Jaxon, and I felt Eben's lips at the side of my neck from behind. And then he bit down, and I moaned into Jaxon's mouth.

Jaxon released my mouth to move in on my neck on the other side, drawing on me as Eben fed on the other side. I reached up behind me to fist their hair as they fed. I arched my back and let out a shriek as Niklaus finished me off. But then he bent forward and sunk his fangs into me, just below my ribs, making me throw my head back in a scream of overwhelming pleasure. I thought my body and mind were going to explode from the overwhelming amounts of unending pleasure rolling through me as all three brothers fed on me at the same time; the orgasm Niklaus had coaxed out of me was still rolling into the mix.

I would never have enough of them. As horrible and evil as Vladimir was, the trio was the opposite but just as strong. Where Vladimir drew pain, they coaxed pleasure. Where Vladimir used you for his own gain, they supported and gave. Where Vladimir abused, they healed. Where Vladimir was full of malice, they were full of love. They were all I needed. They were all I wanted, all I would ever want. I only wanted to live here with them, loving them and being loved. To be Vladimir's Bride would be an eternity of torture and horror. To stay and be the brother's Bride would be pure heaven. The contrast couldn't be overstated.

My senses finally returned to me as they stopped feeding on me, one at a time. I drew a deep breath, so relaxed and sleepy it was unbelievable. I felt complete with them. I gave them each a lazy smile.

Niklaus pulled the plug on the tub, and we all got out and dried off. I slipped my nightgown back on and sent each of them a mental message. I entered my room and slipped into the middle of the great black bed to wait for them. I listened as they each returned to their rooms to change into their pajamas and slowly returned to me. Niklaus had checked on the twins before coming back.

He lay down at an angle, and I leaned my head and shoulders back against him, feeling sleepy. Jaxon and Eben each claimed a side of me, gently caressing me for a while as I played with their hair with my hands. Niklaus's arm lay across my collarbones, holding me in a gentle embrace as we slowly dozed together on the great black bed. Surrounded by them and their scent, Vladimir was once again drowned out. Eventually, our caressings stilled as we fell asleep there, each of their embraces comforting me, making me feel safe and whole. I really would want for nothing if I was theirs.

I went from total peace to confusion as I suddenly found myself in a different room. My eyes looked around me, taking in my surroundings. It was familiar but confusing. How could I be here when I had just been with the brothers? My eyes landed on Vladimir's bed in the castle's master bedroom. I looked around me again, taking in the dark state of the room, and my eyes looked back to the bed. He was there, sleeping in the center of the bed, his arm slung over the back of a naked woman lying next to him; the sheet covered their lower half. I took in the sight of his naked, powerful frame lying in stillness.

Vladimir's arm was possessive even in his sleep, his deep breathing moving it slightly at the shoulder and chest. I took a step toward the bed but remained in the shadows. I walked slowly to the edge of the bed, looking down at them where they slept. I glanced around me again, expecting something to change for some reason. I walked around the corner of the bed to where he lay with his back to the side of the bed. It surprised me to see him looking so peaceful; I had never seen him sleeping before because he had never slept when he was with me. I felt surprised and curious, but also a huge sense of wariness.

The sight of Vladimir sleeping was in stark contrast to him when he was awake. Could the man in front of me, so silent and still, really be the same Vladimir I knew? Was I trapped in some dream? I stole another glance around me, expecting the real Vladimir to come flying at me from some other angle, sinking his fangs into my neck. The woman drew in a breath, shifting, and Vladimir's arm tightened over her for a second. Her face came into view; Missy. I looked back at Vladimir. I had to be dreaming; this couldn't be real.

My hand slowly reached out, pausing for a moment, on its track toward him. My fingers paused again, only a fraction above his skin. If this was a dream, surely I would feel nothing. My fingers floated there as I tried to decide if I would touch him. I swallowed and then brushed my fingers against his skin. I jerked my hand back; his skin had been taught and warm. I felt frozen with fear. Surely, I hadn't actually felt him. My hand shook as I slowly reached out again and touched the back of his neck with the lightest of touches. His head moved a little at my touch, and I jerked my hand back again, my eyes growing wide.

I backed away from the bed, truly frightened now. I carefully walked around to the other side of the bed, looking down on a sleeping Missy. I reached out and touched her hand. I could feel her, too. I jerked my hand back with a small gasp. She didn't move, but at my gasp, her blood-red eyes flew open to stare at me, mine growing wide as she stared right at me. Her look was so intense before she opened her mouth, exposing her fangs on a wicked hiss. My eyes grew wider, and I hurriedly backed away from the bed. She sat up, still hissing, then sprang at me with her claws and fangs bared.

I jerked awake with a scared gasp, shivers running throughout my body where I lay on the great black bed of the mansion. I felt the brothers look at me; my heart was pounding, and my sudden jerking awake had awoken them.

"Did you have a nightmare, Blossom?" Eben asked, concerned.

I stroked his hair, saying, "I'm not sure what it was, honestly. I was there with him, with them. I could feel him." I was almost muttering to myself as I said it, still so confused about the entire thing. "I could touch her too, and then she awoke."

"Who?" Jaxon asked.

I looked down at him with frightened eyes, "Vladimir and Missy. They were sleeping in his bed. I was there in the dark, looking at them. I walked up and could feel him, touch him, while he slept. I touched her hand, and I could feel her, too. She opened her eyes and saw me. She attacked me, but then I awoke and was back here."

Niklaus had been quietly listening, watching the replay in my mind while I talked about it. Niklaus reached over with his hand that wasn't wrapped around me and started stroking my hair in a comforting gesture.

"You weren't just having a dream?" Eben asked. I looked into his blue eyes and reached out to touch his beautiful face for a moment.

I whispered, "He felt as real to me as you do right now."

# CHAPTER 34

We all sat around the study, waiting for Sebastian. I heard him pull up on his motorcycle and went outside to meet him. He gave me a big smile and pulled me into a hug.

"Good to see you back to normal, though I rather liked you like that, except for the blood part. Not cool, Sash," he winked at me, pulling me into another hug. I wrapped my arms around him and leaned into him fully, settling my head against his shoulder.

"Thanks for helping find me the other night," I said. "And sorry about the blood. Out of my control." He laid his head on top of mine for a minute, still hugging me to him.

"Well, I've got some interesting news to share with you guys," he said.

I pulled back and held his hand as we walked into the mansion together. I led him to the study, and he greeted the coven brothers. Sebastian sat on the edge of the couch, leaning on his knees with his elbows. I felt nervous for some reason and chose to remain standing as I waited for what he had to say.

"We ran the samples. A particular associate of mine who is familiar with our world did the work. It turns out that the syringes were loaded with a mixture of Cavalier poison derived from vervain and werewolf venom; they were mixed in different quantities depending on the desired effect. There were syringes with straight poison that would kill, all the way to ones that were mostly werewolf venom with a little of the poison.

"The more the poison, the longer and deeper you would go; the more the werewolf venom, the shorter and higher you would go. It just depends on the mixture. Sasha obviously got stuck with a syringe that had ample amounts of werewolf venom and a little of the poison. The two work together to create the effect. For example, the dose Sasha got only created the high through the venom because the poison first allowed her system to absorb it. It broke through her natural healing abilities to allow the venom to affect her but in a less serious manner. The mixtures with more poison open up the effect to be taken deeper, which is why it lasts longer but also creates a deeper effect on the mind, like what the rogue used on Sasha when he kidnapped her.

"The last syringe he used on her was as close a mixture as you could take without dropping a vampire instantly. It almost killed her because of the previous dosing she had received from him," Sebastian finished, looking up at me.

"Is there anything else?" Niklaus asked.

Sebastian shook his head, saying, "Until we find the source, no. My guess is that they just created a new market for this. How they got ahold of the Cavalier poison is a mystery. My guess would be the venom may have even come from your rogue, but I have no way of knowing. Sasha, you know where to find the associate?" Sebastian asked me.

"Yes, but it will take some time to locate the exact place; all I got was an image, not directions," I laughed as I looked at him. He smiled at me and stood. I nodded my thanks and sighed, "In the meantime, I need to get back to hunting Cavaliers to keep Vladimir appeased. Maybe I can do some snooping and see what I can find out about how our pushers got their hands on the poison in the first place. Either way, I have to get back to hunting. Excuse me, I have to go give Vladimir a call." I stepped out of the room and walked to my room, picking up the cell phone on the nightstand. He picked up almost instantly, as usual.

"Feeling better, my pet?"

"I'm back to normal, Vladimir, don't worry. I'll be heading back out again tonight to start hooking more Cavaliers, if that pleases you?"

"Good. All this werewolf and poison nonsense has distracted you from dealing with the main problems. Any news on that front?"

"I'll be working to track down the samples and their source. They were Cavalier poison as we thought," I said. For some reason, I couldn't bring myself to tell him that werewolf venom was involved; I couldn't put my finger on exactly why it mattered, but for some reason, my intuition told me to keep that part of the revelation hidden from him.

"Good, but stay focused on the Cavaliers. If the source does end up being the Cavaliers, this could be very bad. Report back to me when you're finished tonight. How are things with Lucy, Lucian, and the Governess?"

"The twins and I have come to," I paused, trying to think of the right thing to say, "an understanding. Things have become more peaceful around here between the three of them because of it. The twins rather enjoy stories of your conquests as bedtime stories." He actually laughed in enjoyment. He always had appreciated his twins' tenacity, and I knew telling him that I was using his horror stories as their bedtime stories would please him.

"Ahh, my minx, I miss you at my side."

The phone line went dead, but suddenly, he was before me. I dropped the phone from my face and put it in my pocket. He came to me and grabbed hold of my jaw, jerking my face toward him, bending down to kiss my lips. I apparently had pleased him even more than I had originally thought. His other hand slipped around me, pulling me close to his form.

The door to my bedroom opened, and Sebastian was about to walk in. He froze, seeing Vladimir's form. I looked at the door and slammed it shut with my power as Vladimir turned to look at who was entering my room. I quickly reached up and pulled him back to my lips as a distraction, and he growled with his approval.

"Ahh, my minx, you make me miss you. Perhaps you will need to come home for a visit soon."

"Vladimir, I am settled here, and you know very well that I'm in the middle of dealing with all of these things. It would be unwise to leave before the Cavalier poison especially has been dealt with, even for a short visit."

"One night now and then, Sasha, will be enough."

"Coming all the way to Europe takes more than one night, Vladimir."

"Mmmmm, yes. Well, I will think on it. Business sometimes takes me to New York. I have a trip there in a few weeks. I would like you to meet me there." Shit.

"As you wish, master," I replied obediently with a curtsy, as he would expect. I said, "Hopefully, the Cavalier poison is manageable by that point and hasn't spread. That would be bad news for our kind, including your creations and holdings."

I could almost hear him thinking over what I had just said before he replied, "Yes, well, we will see how it's going as we get closer. Call me once you're finished tonight." I curtsied again, and he squeezed my jaw. He turned my face back up to kiss me possessively again. He faded away, and I was left alone in my room, terrified at the horrible notion that I might have to go to him in New York. At least he wouldn't come back here if that was his decision; it meant safety for the brothers and Sebastian. It meant that Lucy, Lucian, and the Governess wouldn't need to flee. It also meant that I would be at his mercy and alone to deal with it. I shuddered.

I left my room, and Sebastian still stood there, frozen in shock and fear of what he had just seen.

"Seb," I said, smacking him lightly on the face, "Snap out of it." He blinked and looked at me, coming back to the present.

"What was that, Sasha?!" He asked, alarmed. I pulled on his hand, leading him back to the study where the brothers still were.

"It was one way that Vladimir communicates with me; keeping an eye on me. You were very lucky he didn't see you, Sebastian. If he had seen you," I trailed off for a moment, looking down. "Vladimir can pop up any time, unfortunately, so you even being near me is a risk."

We had just walked into the study, as we were still talking. "Honestly, Sebastian, any one of you," I gestured to him and the brothers, "Being near me, with me, is a risk because of that. The day I'm caught will be my last."

"Why does he care? I mean, I know that he wants me dead, or his associate does, but what does it matter if the brothers are near you, with you?" I sighed. I had never told him about the deal I had made with Vladimir. I felt Niklaus walk up behind me, putting his hands on my shoulders in a supporting way. I took a deep breath. I wanted Sebastian to know.

I turned and looked at Jaxon, saying, "Would you mind going and getting it?" He knew instantly what I meant and gave me a nod before disappearing in vampire speed. He returned, and I held out my hand toward him, not breaking eye contact with Sebastian. I felt Jaxon slide the ring on my finger as I said, "Vladimir cares, Sebastian, because he intends to make me his for the rest of eternity." I brought my hand up next to my face, with the back showing off the ring. Sebastian's eyes shifted to the ring and he froze with a look of stunned horror on his face as he stared at it. I swallowed, not looking away from him as he was transfixed on the ring. "He intends to make me his Bride. The Bathory Bride."

Sebastian's eyes changed as he looked at the ring, unable to control his deep emotions at what I had just revealed to him. His wolf eyes turned to meet mine, and he saw the pain in mine. I couldn't hold his gaze and squeezed my eyes shut, a grimace coming to my face. I dropped my hand but crossed my arms to hold myself, rubbing my arms, seeking comfort. Niklaus pulled me gently back against him and pressed a loving kiss to my temple, soothing me with his gift. Jaxon and Eben walked up close to us.

I swallowed and finally met Sebastian's eyes again. He was looking at me just like the brothers had after they had found out; deep concern, fear, and horror.

"Sasha," he said. "Holy hell. How did this happen?" I pulled from the brothers to wrap my arms around Sebastian's neck, trying to comfort him. He wrapped his arms around me. I felt him sweep my hair back before he pressed his face to the side of mine. I rubbed the back of his head in a comforting way. He still loved me, even if he knew that I was in love with the brothers. He still worried about me, and discovering that Vladimir was going to make me his Bride was tearing him up inside. He had become my best friend, I realized.

I pulled back enough to look at him and tried to explain, "I made a deal with Vladimir. I was trying to negotiate to no longer be used as his weapon, doing things like what he had made me do to you. He set the condition of me becoming his Bride, agreeing that he would no longer use me as his weapon but that I would become his Bride and remain at his side, in his bed. He sent me first to square things away here before I am to return and become his Bride for the rest of eternity. So you can imagine why me being in love with his sons is a problem."

"So he can just pop up anytime he wants to check on you?" Sebastian clarified.

"Yes, he could pop up now and see you."

"There's no way to stop him from doing that?" Sebastian asked.

"He has a link on my mind that allows him to do that as he likes. If Niklaus destroyed the link on my mind, Vladimir would know. Niklaus weakened it last time so it would fade faster, but then he came to town and renewed it. With him commanding me to come to him in three weeks, he will just renew it again."

All four of the men in the room reacted strongly to the news. "What!?" Several of them almost shouted.

I released Sebastian to look behind me at the brothers, explaining, "Vladimir's business is bringing him to New York, and he has commanded me to meet him there for another night."

I looked down, whispering, "At least this time you won't have to listen. You won't have to see me after he's finished with me." Niklaus's arms were around me, tucking me into the safety of his arms, but even that comforting embrace wouldn't stop Vladimir from taking what he wanted from me again.

"My god, what does he do to you, Sasha?" Sebastian asked, mortified at my words. He looked up and met Niklaus's eyes. Niklaus's scowl didn't fade, but I heard him sharing exactly what Vladimir did to me the last time; the image of the state of me when they had found me lying on the bed sticking in his mind.

A snarl so vicious it made me cringe ripped its way out of Sebastian at the image shown to him by Niklaus. I opened my eyes from where I was nestled in Niklaus's arms to look up at Sebastian. His wolf eyes were almost glowing. He wanted to rip Vladimir to pieces after this new information. He had always known that Vladimir had used me to infiltrate and manipulate, but he had never really thought about how else Vladimir used me, how his cruelty extended into that realm as well.

And then I heard his mind ticking away before it clicked into place, and he asked, "What did he do to you when you left me and returned to him without delivering me?"

I closed my eyes and turned my face into Niklaus's chest, whispering, "It doesn't matter, Seb. Drop it."

"Sasha?" I could hear him asking Niklaus in his mind.

Niklaus was about to show him when I stopped him with a hand on the face, saying, "No. He doesn't ever need to see that."

Niklaus's patient gaze landed on mine, saying, "Don't you believe he has a right to know?"

"I don't want him to carry the guilt, Niklaus. It doesn't matter in the long run."

"Sasha, please, I need to know," Sebastian pleaded.

"Seb, no," I pleaded back. I could see the determination in his eyes, so I stepped up to him to touch his face. "Sebastian, it can't be unseen, and you don't need to carry the guilt. It was my choice, alright. He punished me; that is all you need to know, alright?"

Sebastian looked at me, caressing my face, and answered, "I need to know, Sasha." I couldn't understand why he did, but I gave Niklaus a look that showed I had given up trying to convince Sebastian otherwise. I turned, walked past Niklaus, refusing to watch the exchange, and walked to the other two brothers.

Eben took me into his arms, cradling me to him, while Jaxon stood close, looking into my eyes. I refused to look at Sebastian as Niklaus started sharing the vision of me in Vladimir's office. I shut off my mind so I wouldn't have to see. I already knew, and I had never planned on Sebastian knowing. The first snarl from Sebastian had me cringing and shutting my eyes, clinging to Eben. He had barely gotten started on the memory.

# CHAPTER 35

I trembled in Eben's arms as I listened to Sebastian's reactions, to the replaying of the memory of Vladimir punishing me for saying 'no' to him and refusing to return to hurt Sebastian. I could hear Sebastian's pain, and I ended up fisting Eben's shirt and squeezing my eyes on the gut-wrenching howl of pain that escaped Sebastian. Eben's arms tightened around me as tears slipped out of my eyes to roll down my cheeks. I would never have chosen to show Sebastian; I would never have revealed the truth because it could only bring him pain. I heard Niklaus shift his stance and move.

Sebastian had walked up to where I stood in Eben's arms, being held by him. "Sasha," Sebastian's voice was raw with deep emotion. "Why? Why didn't you just deliver me?" I finally opened my eyes to look at him, turning my head to look at him full in the face.

"You know why, Sebastian."

"You should have just delivered me, Sash."

"I would make the same choice, Sebastian, even had I known what he would do to me. I would make the same choice if it meant protecting the brothers or you. Without hesitating." Eben's arms tightened around me in response to my words. I turned more towards Sebastian and reached up to take his face into my hands, looking into his eyes so he wouldn't miss what I had to say. "Sebastian, I love you. You're my best friend. And I would give my life to protect you if it called for it."

His face was so pained as he looked back into my eyes, and slowly, he drew me into his embrace, Eben relinquishing his hold on me. I hugged him back as his face went into the crook of my neck.

"I'm so sorry, Sasha. I'm sorry I was angry at you for leaving. I'm sorry I treated you unkindly that first day here in my office."

"It's ok, Seb. You didn't know, and I had planned on never revealing it to you. It was my choice; you bear no responsibility of guilt." I felt him shaking a little as he held me to him. "I will always make the choice to protect you and the coven brothers if I can, Seb. If that means I return to Vladimir," I swallowed with emotion, "then I will."

The four of them rejected my words with hissing, growls, and even a few 'no's.' As if to emphasize my words, my phone jingled that I had received a message. I didn't release Sebastian completely, but I took one hand and dug my phone out to look. It was a text from Vladimir, containing flight information. He had booked me tickets to New York, in just over two week's time for one night. Another text came in as I looked at my phone, containing information about where he was staying and where I would need to go. I closed my eyes and put the phone back in my pocket.

"Sasha?" Niklaus asked. I hadn't reopened my mind to anyone, including him.

"I leave for New York in eighteen days," I whispered.

Sebastian's arms tightened around me as he whispered back, "No, Sash." I hugged him before pulling out of his embrace.

"I have no choice, Sebastian. If I don't go, Vladimir will come here, which is bad for everyone. He would only take it out on me, being even worse. Excuse me. I have to go get ready to go out tonight."

I stepped around him and sped off toward my room at vamp speed. I walked into my closet and started trying to pick out a dress, but I couldn't handle it. I was going back to Vladimir's bed in a little over two weeks. I pulled a red number off of a hook but broke down crying, holding it to my face. Never free. Not even being half a world away from him. Not even out on a mission away from him. Not even after tasting real love. I would never be free.

The dress was taken from me, and Jaxon's spicy aroma washed over me as he held me. He held my face with his hands and kissed me gently while I cried. I kissed him back, soaking him up despite the salty tears running down my face and into the kiss. He swept my hair back from my face as he continued kissing me, caressing me gently.

"It's going to work out, Doll Face, in the end," he offered me. I wanted to believe him, I really did, but I just couldn't see how.

Jaxon invaded my mouth, pulling me tight up against him. I responded by growling and pushing him onto the floor of the closet, stripping him on the way down; I was going to use him to drown out my sorrow, and I knew he would have no problem with that. My clothes were soon on the closet floor with his, and he rolled me over to be on top. His tongue captured mine, teasing and coaxing, driving me to abandon, making me moan as his hands were all over, making my skin light on fire at his demanding touch. His hands at my waist bowed my back as I arched against him, his mouth traveling to my stomach.

Tears were still flowing down my face, but I didn't care. I wanted him and wasn't about to let the moment pass. I pulled him up to me and sunk my fangs into his neck, and he did the same for me, both of us bringing each other to a high of pleasure. I pulled him into me with my legs wrapped around his waist while we fed on one another. I felt so raw from emotion and so drunk with pleasure at the same time. I refused to release my hold on his neck, even if his demanding movements inside of me drug out moan after moan and sigh after sigh.

It was only when we came to our completion that I had to release him on an open-mouthed hiss, my fangs pointing toward the ceiling as my head flew back, my back arching, my red eyes rolling up into my head. He kissed me gently on the neck, stroking me, and we stayed like that for a while. I clung to him, the heartache dulling a little at his comforting embrace.

"I'll be there tonight, at the bar, if you need anything, Sugar Lips. I'm sure Eben will join as well," Jaxon offered, caressing my cheek.

"What I need tonight can't be offered or achieved in public," I smirked back at him. I pushed him off of me and rolled on top to straddle him. His eyes practically sparkled at my naughty words.

"That's debatable. The back of the bar works just fine," he smirked as he said it, angling his head where he lay on the ground.

I smiled and leaned back over to his ear, "I think the three of us stark naked, doing what I have in mind, would draw a little bit of attention that even the dark corner of a bar wouldn't conceal." I could hear him mentally groan with desire at my words that taunted him.

"I'm going to hold you to that, Sugar Lips. When you get back tonight," he threatened. I laughed and sat up.

"Yes, well, I'm not so sure Eben would be up for that," I teased.

"I wouldn't be up for what?" I heard Eben say at the doorway of my closet. I looked up at him, and that naughty look he would get crossed his features. He was enjoying the sight of me sitting on Jaxon.

"Sebastian left but promised to be at the bar tonight if you needed him," Eben offered. I gave him a nod. "You didn't answer my question," Eben stated.

Jaxon laughed, caressing me. "Your little Blossom was having naughty thoughts about sharing tonight, Eben," Jaxon teased, looking up and behind him at his brother. Eben met his eye and then he looked up at me. I unashamedly met his inquiring gaze before I smirked and bent over to kiss Jaxon.

I sat up and grabbed the red dress I had pulled off a hanger. I stood, grabbed a fresh lingerie set, and approached Eben. I wrapped my arms around his neck and kissed him before continuing into the bathroom to get ready.

Once I was ready, I found both brothers relaxing on my bed, waiting for me. "You two better go get changed; I'm heading to the bar right now," I said.

"You sure you don't want to hang out here for a couple hours before you go?" Jaxon said with a smirk. I looked at him and then at Eben, who still smiled wickedly. Mine grew.

"I would love nothing more, but hour-wise, now is the time to go hook a Cavalier. Raincheck?" I said, meeting first Eben's eye and then Jaxon's. They jumped off the bed, sandwiching me between them.

"You sure you can wait, Sugar Lips?" Jaxon teased me as his lips ran from my shoulder into the crook of my neck from behind while Eben captured my lips, pushing his way inside. They were lighting me on fire, and I wasn't so sure anymore. I could feel my eyes light up as I started to throb. I had to escape them, or I wouldn't go hunting Cavaliers tonight.

"After, I promise, but first I need to appease Vladimir." His name was like a bucket of cold water on all of us, allowing me the head space to squeeze out from in between them.

"I'll see you there," I said, speeding off, vamp speed, to head off to the bar.

I walked inside and headed to the bar first to order a drink. I spotted Sebastian sitting in the far corner, so I approached him, leaning in close as he wrapped an arm around my waist.

"Hey," I said.

He gave me a deep, affectionate look and answered, "Hey, back." I planted a kiss on his cheek, and he rubbed my waist. Our friendship had grown deeper just over the last afternoon, having the truth revealed, I realized. I really loved him, and he was the closest friend I had ever had. "So," he whispered just loud enough for my vamp hearing, "Who's the lucky guy tonight?"

I laughed a little and then turned my eyes to peruse the bar. My eyes landed on Blake in the corner and I gave a snort as the blonde was all over him again. I moved my gaze just as he noticed me. Another Cavalier was in a pack of guys watching sports, and a third was in a back booth with another group. This one wasn't set up ideal, but his mind captured my interest; it was so dark and violent.

"I think I'm going to need some help on this one from you and the brothers. He is a man who wants to take, not be offered, so my goal will be to get his attention by seeming unavailable. Wanna play pool?" Sebastian smiled at me, and we carried our drinks over to a table near the booth.

Eventually, the brothers came and joined our game. I flirted with all three of them, openly teasing and taunting them under the casual scrutiny of the Cavalier. Blake wandering over to try to make up for the last time, and me shooting him down hard, only added to the ruse I was laying out before the man in the booth. I used my attention toward Jaxon to send Blake on his way but then turned around and teased Jaxon once he was gone. The brothers knew what I was doing, and I explained it to them mentally, so they just played along. The man was watching everything I did.

"I'll be back, boys," I winked at them.

I walked toward the back of the bar, brushing past the man's booth on my way to the restroom. I heard him get out of the booth, casually following me to the back. He would be waiting for me in the dark to leave the ladies' room. I acted distracted as I came out of the room, pretending to be talking with another man on the phone, leading him on that he was the only one and that we would move on in our relationship soon but that I wasn't ready to sleep with him yet.

Looking down, I slowly moved back toward the dark corner that held the exit door. It only took a second for the man to come up behind me once I hung up and started putting my phone in my bag. His hand covered my mouth, and his other arm pinned both of mine as he shoved his way out the exit door to the dark alleyway out back.

# CHAPTER 36

I pretended to struggle against the man as any woman would. I could just see Jaxon from the dark as the man pushed the door open. Jaxon's eyes flared red when he saw, his jaw muscles locking, his mind revealing he was dying to come and kill the man himself. At last, the man pulled me behind him, out the door, and into the dark alleyway that didn't have another person. I continued to struggle as he pulled me down the alleyway to a door past the nearest dumpster.

I felt a gun shoved into my ribs as he said, "You're going to be quiet, you understand?" I forced a whimper, and while I nodded, he released my mouth and reached for the door.

It was a door that led down to an old cellar in the run-down building behind the bar. My eyes caught movement in the shadows of the alleyway as he forced me down the stairwell. I was in a difficult situation. He was a Cavalier with a gun, and I had no idea what kind of bullets he had in the chamber, normal or poisoned ones.

He kept the gun shoved into my ribs, and I was honestly wary of him now as I watched him reach to start undoing his belt and pants. After successfully undoing both, he pressed me into the wall and started pushing my dress up.

I was trying to decide what to do, probably using my magic, when I felt a breeze, and a pair of hands reached out around the man's head and instantly broke his neck on a snarl. The man dropped to the floor of the cellar, the gun still in his hand, and my relieved eyes met Jaxon's blazing red ones as his chin flew up in defiance and anger at the man. I gave him a grateful smile and rushed into his embrace.

"He's lucky that's all I did to him after touching you like that," he whispered. I snuggled up against him, soaking up the safety of his arms.

"Thanks, I wasn't sure what he had in that gun," I whispered back. I felt him look down at the gun.

He released me and bent down to pick it up. Dropping out the clip revealed that it had been loaded with poisoned bullets; our eyes met. The man actually could have killed me. Appreciation for Jaxon's protectiveness washed through me, and I let him feel it. Jaxon slammed the clip back into place and put the gun in his belt, covering it with his jacket.

"Where do we need to take him?"

"Do you have your car?" I asked. He nodded. "Pull it around here in the alley, and we can load him up and take him out to the woods. I'll go get Eben and update Seb, and we'll meet you back here. He gave me a nod and a kiss on the forehead before we both sped off.

I came in from the back to make it look like I had returned from the restroom to confuse his friends in the booth. I leaned over and whispered what had happened into Eben's ear as I leaned on him; Sebastian was taking the last shot of the game, sinking the eight ball in the corner pocket. I smiled and went over to him, acting like I was just congratulating him when I was updating him. He was petting me a little and then jerked his head like we were going to leave together. I nodded and followed him out the front. Eben went to the bar for a couple minutes and then left out the front, where his Ducati was parked.

Jaxon had the car waiting, and Sebastian stood watch as we loaded up the body into the back seat. I hopped in next to it, and Jaxon got in. Sebastian waved before we sped off, followed by Eben, and headed home on his motorcycle.

We headed up into the forest to a marked area and buried the creep deep underground. Jaxon held onto the gun. You could never know when it might come in handy. Jaxon drove us home with Eben following on his Ducati.

We walked into the mansion, and Niklaus came out of the study to greet us. "Everything ok?" He asked, seeing our faces. Their minds revealed what happened as Jaxon drug the gun out from his waistband and handed it to Niklaus for safekeeping. I turned and left to go to my room.

Eben was hot on my heels and said, "Don't call Vladimir just yet. He doesn't appear when he thinks you're out hunting, right?" I looked at him and nodded. "Perfect," he whispered, taking hold of my face to kiss me.

And then my door was shut, and Jaxon was behind me, kissing my shoulder and neck again from behind. I teased Eben with my fingers sliding around his waistband as I kissed him back. I whipped his shirt off of him and returned to kissing him, teasing him with my fingers. Jaxon reached up and swept my hair over my right shoulder, kissing me as he slowly drew the zipper to my dress down my back, letting his knuckles caress me on the way down.

He brushed the loosened strap over my left shoulder and kissed me there.

I didn't release Eben's lips, but I reached behind me to pull on Jaxon's shirt, turning slightly, pulling it over his head, and taking his hat with it to the floor. Jaxon's hands slipped inside the open back of my dress to caress me, as Eben reached out to tease me through it at the same time. His kisses wandered down my neck, and he slowly peeled the dress from my form, his hands sliding down my shoulders. Eben's kisses traveled down the front of me as he slowly peeled the dress from my form. He didn't come back up but repeated the process with my panties. I felt both brothers rid themselves of the rest of their clothes.

I moaned when Eben's hot mouth found me while Jaxon unclasped my bra, dropping it to the floor, kissing my neck as his hands reached around to caress and tease my breasts. Moans and sighs were unceasingly coming out of me, between them working me up into a frenzy. My head fell back against Jaxon's shoulder when Eben pushed me over the edge, making me gasp. Jaxon chose that moment to bite down, and I reached up to fist his blonde on another heavy gasp. Jaxon leaned back, lifting me slightly as Eben stood, bringing my legs with him. Jaxon drew out the feeding on me as Eben entered my wet heat, my legs around his waist.

I reached back and clung to Jaxon's shoulders as Eben held onto my waist, securing me to meet him on each thrust, Jaxon's bite only serving to drive me even higher. I felt that wonderful coiling sensation starting as Eben moved inside of me, hitting me just right each time. Jaxon's arms tightened around my ribs when he felt me finally shudder with the release of the orgasm Eben had worked me up into. I cried out and gasped as Eben continued to move, pushing the orgasm on. He bent over and kissed me as I felt him reach his own climax. Jaxon finally stopped feeding on me and turned us toward the great black bed, pulling me after him as I released Eben from my legs.

We were kneeling on the bed, Jaxon behind me still. Jaxon reached around to the front of me to start teasing me, working me back up until I was panting, while Eben sandwiched me and kissed me, cupping one breast and running the other hand up and down my thigh. I leaned forward and broke my kiss with Eben to sink my fangs into his neck, making him moan before he did the same to me, just as Jaxon entered me from behind with a powerful thrust, filling me completely in one swift movement. I moaned into Eben's neck but didn't stop feeding from him as my body jerked with Jaxon's strong movements from behind.

I took draw after draw from Eben, timing them with Jaxon's thrusts as the tension built again. Eben and I were sighing and moaning our pleasure as Jaxon set the pace for both of our noises. Jaxon bit down on me again as the heat built up inside of me. After ample amounts of incredible pleasure, it was finally released on a blazing wave that swept out from my core, encompassing every nerve ending. When the wave reached my neck, I had to pull away, laying my head back on a deep moan, as my cheeks flushed and I kneeled there, panting through the rest of the amazing orgasm while the brother's feeding pushed it on.

Before I had even fully come down from the moment, Jaxon drug my limp body below the sheets. Eben followed us under and moved in close to me. I relaxed with my eyes closed as Jaxon held me from behind with an arm around my ribs, just under my breasts. Eben slid a leg between mine, pulling my leg up towards his hip, caressing my thigh. Our faces were almost touching, and Jaxon's was nestled in the back of my neck. I had one arm slung over Eben, and the other covered Jaxon's that was around me. I didn't want to move from their embrace, so I used my magic to pull my phone to me.

Vladimir answered on the first ring. "What news, my minx?"

"Another Cavalier has been dealt with."

"Good. Did you have any trouble this time?"

"No. A broken neck was all it took. The Cavalier had a gun loaded with poisoned bullets, but it's all taken care of now. I'm going to get some sleep now, and I'll try to go back out tomorrow or at least look into some things as far as the poison goes. There is a frat party happening on campus tomorrow that I'm planning on hitting up to make a few younger ones disappear. Shouldn't be too much trouble to get a few in one night."

"Did you get the information I sent you?"

"Yes."

"Good. Call me tomorrow, my pet."

"Yes, Vladimir."

"Are you keeping my sons in line?"

I met Eben's eyes and said a simple "Yes."

The line went dead as I smiled at him, tossing the phone onto my nightstand before slinging my arm back over Eben to relax. I caressed Eben's back and Jaxon's arm while I closed my eyes to relax, pulling the black sheet up our bodies so we could sleep.

"Niklaus's gonna be sad he missed out on the fun, Sugar Lips," Jaxon teased. "Maybe next time we should invite him." I laughed and patted his arm before nestling down into their embrace to get some sleep.

A thought occurred to me before I drifted off, so I spoke to Jaxon, "Thank you, Jaxon, for your help tonight."

"No one touches my Doll Face like that and lives," he murmured into the back of my neck.

I smiled and turned my sleepy eyes to Eben's beautiful blue ones. I took my arm from his side to gently caress his face as I looked into his eyes. I leaned in and kissed him gently.

"I love you," I whispered to him.

"I love you too, my Blossom," he whispered back, giving me another kiss.

I took the hand on his face and reached behind me to run my fingers into Jaxon's blonde hair, turning my face up toward him and saying, "Love you."

I felt him smile into my neck, and he nestled deeper into my hair, saying, "Love you, Doll Face." I released him and returned my arm to stroke Eben.

I reached out with my mind to Niklaus, who had just put Lucy and Lucian to bed and was walking toward his own room. I mentally caressed him, and he returned the caress.

"I love you, Niklaus," I thought for him. I felt him sigh at my words as he walked into his room.

"I love you too, my Darling. Sleep well." I smiled and let him feel it.

"I'm coming to you tomorrow night if you don't find me first. Good night, my white knight."

I felt him laugh as he slipped into his bed. I cast my own apparition to bend over and kiss him good night, caressing his face, before I drifted off to sleep in the arms of Eben and Jaxon. Tomorrow night was a frat party on campus that would be full of hormonal men eager to take me up to their rooms, but for now, I rested in the arms of two of the three I was in love with.

# CHAPTER 37

I walked up to the frat house, buzzing with life, even on the outside. It was night, and the party was in full swing. I had had an idea that morning on how to avoid suspicion of multiple deaths, feeling inspired, and had done some preparations earlier in the day, stashing what I needed on my person. Jaxon had managed to score an invite to the party and was already there. The whole invite thing amused me. Predators facilitating predators to converge in one area, like a watering hole, and any female with a nice ass was welcomed inside to be converged on. This is precisely why I chose a mini skirt, knee-high tight boots with a tall heel, and a deep blue corset that provided ample cleavage for roving eyes.

I walked up to the front of the house, flashing the door guards an alluring smile while I ate them up with my eyes. One of the guards wanted to leave his post to follow me after I ran a finger along his chest, walking by. I would have been tempted to enjoy him before the brothers; he was very good-looking.

I passed into the house without a problem, taking a drink from a guy who offered it. Several other alphas merged on me, and I enjoyed flirting with them while my eyes casually took in the party, looking for my first target. I spotted him and excused myself from the group of guys around me.

My target was a popular one, having several girls around him already. Nothing like competition to stir interest in a male, so I walked up to him to set the trap. The girls around him shot me dirty looks, trying to claim their hard-won territory.

"Excuse me, but have you seen Blake? I thought he was going to meet me here tonight, but I haven't seen him," I said innocently, knowing full well that Blake wasn't at this party at the moment. I would have smelt him if he was.

"No, sorry, haven't seen him." I sighed disappointedly, saying, "He's the only one I know! Huh, ok, well, thanks anyway."

After giving him an innocent smile, I slowly turned and returned to the group of guys I had left. They enthusiastically welcomed me back into their

175

fold. Now that I had the baby Cavalier's attention, he was picking up on the attention the other guys were showing me. Suddenly, the girls surrounding him were boring because they were easy. I was openly flirting with a couple of the guys, in particular, the biggest alphas of the group who were responding. I felt him come up behind me and talk with the guy I was leaning into, flirting.

"Better lay off, Derrick, or Blake'll beat your head in. She's here for him."

I turned and scowled at the baby Cavalier, saying sharply, "I never said I was here for him; just that he's the only one I know who was supposed to be here. I'm not Blake's." I gave him a dismissive perusal before I turned back to the group.

He reached out and touched me, saying, "Look, I'm sorry, I misunderstood, ok? I thought you were his girl if he had invited you here."

I snorted and challenged him, "I decide who's girl I am, even if just for the moment. And since he decided to stand me up, I'm here on my own and can be with whoever I want if I think they can handle me." I leaned in towards him and whispered the last part for just him before I turned away from him.

"That so?" He challenged me.

I gave him another perusal, "That's right." I turned back to the guy standing next to me, who was getting an ego boost from my dismissal of the baby Cavalier.

"You dance as well as you can verbally lash?" He challenged me again. I turned and looked at him like I was evaluating him at last.

"Better, but can you?" I challenged him back. He gave me a self-assured, crooked smile and dragged me away from the other guys towards the communal room set up for dancing. It was darker in that room, with flashing lights roving around that did nothing to inhibit the activities happening in the dark.

I got right up in his space, provocatively moving against him, to the pounding tempo that filled the room and reverberated throughout the rest of the house. Reading his mind at what drove him crazy and what didn't affect him, I quickly narrowed down what he wanted. I had him already groaning in need before the end of the song, rubbing up against him in just the right way to tease him.

My vampire eyes could see clearly in the dark, and I picked out Jaxon from the crowd. He was dancing with some other girl but kept an eye on me while at it. I gave him a predatory smirk as our eyes met in the dark. He flashed me a fangy grin as I perused him with my eyes, secretly flirting with him while I worked my baby Cavalier up into a frenzy.

The baby Cavalier's voice was husky as he leaned over me whispering in my ear, "You up for a private party up in my room?" I gave him a wicked smile and pulled him to my mouth, kissing him just how he liked it, making him lose his mind with desire. I smiled again; even Jaxon could smell the hormones flowing out of the baby Cavalier I was working over.

"Let's not spoil my fun by walking up the main staircase. Is there a back way?" He nodded. I already knew a second set of steps in the kitchen went up.

He took me by the hand and led me out of the room. I gave Jaxon a smile and a wink as we passed them on the way.

We snuck up into his room, and he locked the door before turning back to me and pulling me to him. I gave him some time to enjoy me a little before I started backing us up to his bed. I pulled his shirt off of him, running my hands up his jock's chest before I pushed him on the bed. He found it exciting that I was taking charge, so I went with it and straddled him, kissing him. I moved down to his neck and bit down, pulling on him hard to overwhelm his mind with pleasure as I dug something out from under the back of my corset. He was moaning his pleasure loud enough for someone outside the room to hear. He barely felt the needle that I inserted into the crook of the inside of his arm, pushing the plunger down.

I fed on him, drawing his pleasure, until I could taste the drugs that I just put into his system. By then, they had taken his mind, and I released him without a fight or problem. I watched as the corrupted drugs entered his system to instantly OD him. The light went out in his eyes, and I wiped the syringe clean and positioned his own hand on it, staging it to look like a self-given dose. I picked up his shirt, threw it in his closet, then turned to sneak out of his window, leaving his door locked, and crawled back into another unoccupied room. I snuck back into the hallway and down the kitchen stairs.

I joined the other dancers in the common room, giving Jaxon a quick kiss on the neck as I passed. I walked back out of the room and was pleased to see my next target had joined the group of guys that I had just left. I openly perused him for a second before turning back to the guy named Derrick.

Derrick turned to me, saying, "Well, there you are. Was he not up to the challenge?"

I laughed like he was so witty and said, "Apparently, I'm just too much for him to handle. I left him on the dance floor, looking for a good time from another source." It was a hint that would make sense to them come morning. The Derrick guy smiled at me and flashed me a predator's grin, which I returned, much to his pleasure.

"Blake's really missing out on you?" Derrick asked, shaking his head.

"Yeah, well, I guess he wasn't up for the challenge either. Who's your friend, Derrick?" I asked jerking my jaw in the other baby Cavalier's direction. He was openly perusing me, and I smiled at him.

"That's Bryan, but a spicy thing like you wouldn't be interested."

"Why's that?" I asked, not taking my eyes off of the little Cavalier.

Derrick leaned over and whispered, "Because I'm here." I flashed him a look. Hmmmm, if I could show Derrick a good time, I would have an in for future parties.

"Better show me your room, then," I whispered back so the others couldn't hear. "I'll meet you upstairs in five." He nodded and smiled, his eyes eating me up, lingering on my cleavage.

Derrick casually dismissed himself from the group, and I moved closer to Bryan, giving him another perusal. He looked at me, curious.

I leaned in close to him and whispered, "Derrick seems to think you couldn't handle a woman like me. That true, Bryan?" He looked at me then, fire crossing his eyes at the challenge. I smiled at him and whispered again, "Don't agree, huh? You up for proving him wrong? Find me on the dance floor, and let's see."

I wandered off to the common room and blended back in with the crowd at the far end of the room. It only took a minute before the little Cavalier took the bait I had dangled in front of him. He grabbed onto me, and we started moving together.

I worked him up and slowly moved us to the very edge of the room in a corner. I pushed him up against the wall and started making out with him before I bit him, exploding his mind with pleasure, while I slipped another needle into his arm and gave him a full dose. He went slack in my arms, and I carefully arranged him in the corner, slumped over with the needle lying next to him. Jaxon had watched the whole thing with a growl of approval for just my ears. As I walked by, I gave him a playful pat on his rear, heading to the kitchen stairs again. I went up and found Derrick's room, entering it.

I found him waiting for me by the door, and I was on him in a second as he reached over and locked the door. Derrick wasn't a Cavalier, so I had no plans on actually killing him; I was just going to use him for an 'in' later. I pulled his shirt open in the front, running my hands over him as I kissed him and backed him up to his bed. I let him shuck his clothes and force me onto the bed as I kissed him. Before he could actually do anything, I sunk my fangs into his neck, drawing on him, and I used my power to enter his mind, altering his consciousness, making this moment completely fuzzy for him but bathed in the overwhelming pleasure my bite caused him.

When I had finished feeding on him, I had him black out. I stashed him between the sheets and made it look like we had a great time. I slipped my black thong down my legs and stuffed it partially under his pillow. I then unlocked his door and slipped out of his room.

Jaxon was leaning against the wall, right outside of Derrick's room, waiting for me. "Did you enjoy that?" He growled at me playfully.

"Actually, yes," I laughed back at him as he pressed me against the wall, kissing me. His fingers snuck up my mini skirt to tease me quickly, showing me he had listened in on my antics.

"Come on, let's go home," he whispered.

I laughed. "I'm Niklaus's tonight," I whispered. "Sorry."

He growled and said, "When you get home, maybe, but if I should happen to get you in my sports car and pull over before we get there, there's nothing he can do about it." I laughed at him.

"Alright, but first, let me find my last target for the night. He's got a needle that's calling his name, and I'm not one to disappoint." He gave me a feral grin, and we turned to go find my last baby Cavalier victim for the night.

Jaxon distracted him while I snuck up behind him and bit down, sinking the needle in his arm as I dragged him into a bathroom. I locked him in and snuck out the window, meeting up with Jaxon outside.

True to his word, Jaxon pulled his car over before we got back to the estate and made good use of my lack of underwear. We walked into the mansion, and I kissed him good night and headed to my room. I opened my door to find Niklaus sleeping in my great black bed, waiting for me, and I shut it behind me.

# CHAPTER 38

I silently slipped into my closet and changed into a short emerald green nightgown. I brushed my hair and removed my jewelry, leaving it on the bathroom counter. I walked out, slipped between the sheets of the great black bed, and slid over to Niklaus. He opened his eyes on an intake of breath and found me with his warm moss-green eyes. I leaned over and caressed his face, kissing him lovingly. His hands came to my face, and he kissed me back passionately but with tenderness.

"I'm glad you're home, Sasha," he whispered.

"Me, too," I answered him.

To my delight, he was already shirtless, and I moved to lay on him. I folded my arms across his broad chest and laid my chin on them, smiling at him. He looked at me tenderly, tucking my hair behind my ears as he listened in on the night's events I showed him, commenting along the way in his mind. He laughed out loud at my deception with Derrick, especially at how I had left a black thong for him. He pulled me to him to kiss me, enjoying the playfulness I had shown him.

"You enjoyed that a little too much, I think, Sasha," he said with a smile while gently flicking the tip of my nose with a finger.

I laughed, but my mind turned serious, thinking about how I had missed his embrace lately. In reality, it hadn't been that long, but it had felt like ages since he had held me. I laid my face on his chest as his arms came around me at the thought. He started stroking my hair, caressing the back of my neck with his fingers as he went. I closed my eyes, enjoying the intimate moment as he shared his day with me. I drew patterns on his chest with my fingers while I listened. His replaying of the twins' bedtime had me laughing; they had been nagging for me to come and tell them another horror 'bedtime story.'

Niklaus's mind revealed just how much he appreciated my new connection with Lucy and Lucian and that I would go and spend some free moments with them, growing our relationship. He credited my relationship with the two as the source of their dramatic behavioral change; they were even nice to their nanny. As nice as the two terrors were capable of.

His thoughts drifted back to the previous night, where Jaxon had intervened to save me from the armed Cavalier. He knew that I could have handled the situation, but Niklaus's firm belief was that I shouldn't have to all the time; he was grateful for his brother's protectiveness and action at the moment when he hadn't been there to help me.

I pressed a kiss to his chest, thinking about how it was ok that he wasn't there, that he couldn't always be the one to be there for me, protecting me as he liked to do. He smiled and pulled me up for a gentle kiss, accepting my consolation but still wishing he could. I felt his growing dread at the thought that I would be leaving for New York in a couple weeks. He was thinking about following me there so he could be there after Vladimir left and help me home. I smiled at the thought but also wanted to cry at it. I didn't want him to see me like that ever again; the image of the last time still hung in his mind.

My eyes were glassy as I held his face and kissed him with all the longing I felt for him. His arms tightened against me, bringing me closer to his lips as he kissed me back. I opened for him to slip his tongue inside of me. I couldn't decide whether I wanted him to take the lead and make love to me or if I wanted to bring him all the pleasure I could. I opted for the latter and left his mouth to trail kisses down his chest, reaching to remove his pajama bottoms and staying there to tease and pleasure him with my mouth. Just before I brought him to completion, I returned to his mouth to love on him there, giving him a moment, caressing his chest with my hand.

I could sense the moment he was back under control, so I slid on top of him, taking him deep inside of me, making him gasp as his green eyes became heavy with the pleasure I watched across his face. I listened in on the pleasure I was bringing him as I moved on top of him, changing angles with his need, walking the fine line between drawing out his pleasure and tipping him over the edge. Moving over him, I couldn't reach his neck, so I settled with biting him on his chest, drawing out more pleasure for both of us. I drank from him, even though I had had plenty at the frat party. That blood quenched a need, but it would never come close to the flavor that Niklaus presented me with.

I loved this nobleman so much I could barely stand it. No one had ever taken care of me like he did, and I couldn't help but delight in the pleasure I had in taking care of him like this, in loving him back. I finally moved just right and tipped him over the edge, moving more, driving him on as I watched the pleasure capture his beautiful features with my eyes.

I stilled and relaxed on top of him, soaking up the closeness, the beautiful image of his moment of encompassing passion. I had ridden it all with him, my mind experiencing it along with him. He was relaxing with his eyes closed as he started stroking my hair again, brushing my neck, while his other hand gently drew a light trail up and down the arm resting on him.

I shared with him some more memories of my childhood, and he watched them with pure enjoyment, commenting along the way and even laughing at my antics. He kissed the top of my head when I shared some hard ones of my adolescence growing up in my first master's castle. A great yawn captured me, and I slid off his body and snuggled up next to him. He turned and threw an arm across my middle and settled against me, in the crook of my arm, surprising me. Typically, he was the one to hold me, but I loved returning the sentiment and started brushing my fingers through his soft hair. I pulled the covers up over us and was just settling down to sleep when I felt his whole body stiffen against me.

"Vladimir is coming, Sasha!" He whispered, almost panicked. I used my power to lift the covers over him, moving many pillows around to disguise his form. I closed my eyes and pretended to sleep as Vladimir's form appeared. My heart was hammering in my chest as fear took hold despite my calm outward appearance. I had turned on my side, moving away from Niklaus, who wasn't even breathing.

Vladimir's form reached out and ran a possessive hand down over my body, and I opened my eyes to look at him. Before he could look at the bed and glean anything, I reached out with my power and had Vladimir's ring shoot across the room onto my finger. Vladimir looked at it as I held it up.

"Would you like me to wear this when I come to you in New York?" The pleased but still predatory gleam in his eye intensified, and he bent down and kissed me.

"That and nothing else, my minx. You forgot to call me," he warned in a deadly tone. I closed my eyes with a grimace.

"I'm sorry, Vladimir. I got rid of three Templars and created another 'in' for future parties."

"Three! I guess that would explain why you're so tired." He grabbed my chin and jerked. "Don't forget to call me again, or I'll have to come and really remind you. Do you understand?" I nodded in fear and submission.

He was about to look behind me at the bed, so I pulled him to my lips and whispered, "Good night. I promise to call, and I'll see you in New York." He was so pleased by my show of affection that he simply gave me a wicked grin and faded away.

Once he was gone, I let out a pent-up breath and could hear Niklaus do the same. My heart was still hammering, and I felt ill with the fear that had washed over me. I flipped the covers back and looked at him.

"Niklaus, how did you know he was about to appear?"

"I was in your mind at the time, Sasha. It was like the memory he had fixed it to flared up for a second. I had watched him place the link, so I knew where it was. It was strange to see the memory of that light up in your mind, even though you weren't thinking about it directly at the time. That was too close, Sasha," he breathed in relief. I moved close to him, and we embraced each other, each offering the other comfort for the close call. "Sasha," Niklaus said, thinking. "I believe I could make it so you would have warning the moment the link flared up. It would be like the memory actually coming to your mind instead. It would only give you a few seconds' warning time, but it just saved us and could be of use in the future. What do you think?"

"Niklaus! That's amazing. Yes! I would never have thought of that." I sat us up and opened up my mind to him completely. He placed his hands over my temples to work inside my mind, focusing on the link and how it worked. Viktor would know if Niklaus destroyed the link or even weakened it at this point, but he wouldn't sense Niklaus changing it to give us a warning.

I could feel him working inside my mind on the link. The moment felt intimate, and pinpointing why took me a few moments. I realized it was because I fully trusted Niklaus now; I wasn't trying to hide anything from him, and I had no fear about him being in my mind in such an unrestricted way.

He was about to withdraw from me when I shared with him the image that I had gleaned from the other drug-pushing vampire's mind of where his associates would be. Niklaus examined it for a long moment, studying the image in full color for clues as to where it could be. He had several possibilities that came to his mind that we could check out together the following day.

I liked the idea of him coming with me; he had told me I couldn't go on my own when looking into this anymore, so one of the brothers had to, and the other two had college classes to maintain their image. He leaned in and kissed me, happy I wasn't fighting him to ensure I would be safe. He laid us back down in the covers and pulled me close to him, holding me in his arms, cherishing the moment. I swept his hair out of his face as I looked into his green eyes.

I got a smirk on my face and whispered, "You're so handsome, Nicky." His head was thrown back on one of the biggest laughs I had ever heard from him; it was pure heaven to listen to. When his face turned back to mine, his eyes twinkled with delight, and he smiled at me. He pulled my lips to his, still smiling.

Niklaus sighed, "You're good for my soul, my darling Sasha." I kissed him again and then settled down to drift off to sleep.

I remembered I needed to show him the men we would look for the following day. I brought up the image of the human man the other vampire had shown me. Niklaus had never seen him before, but he was curious if he was a Cavalier, being the source for the poison. It was an interesting idea, and it was likely.

Then, I brought up the image of the vampire associate for Niklaus to see in preparation for the following day. His arms tightened around me as he hissed at the image that flashed before him; he knew him, and this particular vampire was a dangerous one.

# CHAPTER 39

I stared down at the morning Pine River local newspaper, the headlines reading, "3 DEAD AFTER OVER-DOSING AT FRAT PARTY." Perfect. The entire community had bought my little ruse the other night, and I had to admit that I was pleased with my handiwork. I had just walked into the lecture hall at the community college and headed straight into Sebastian's office.

He was standing just inside, reading something in one of his texts. I smirked at him when he looked up and smacked him in the chest with the newspaper before I went to lounge on his couch. My smirk didn't leave my face as he unfolded my weapon and read the headlines.

Surprised, his face shot up to me, saying, "You?!" My smirk deepened, and my eyebrow shot up. He gave me a slightly disapproving look back before he turned to read what the article had to say. Without looking up, he said, "I didn't know your hunting was branching out to students, Sasha."

"Cavaliers are Cavaliers, Seb. Baby or not." He narrowed his eyes at me before tossing the paper on his desk and returning to his text.

"You need something?" He asked me.

"You," I smirked. His eyes shot up to lock with mine as his brow furrowed. "You finally coming on to me, or did you need me in a different capacity, witch?"

"Ouch," I drawled out in mock hurt. "Someone's crabby. What's got your hairy knickers in a wad, wolf boy?"

He glared at me before returning to his text, answering, "I'm busy. I've got a lot of work right now." I took a magical finger and pressed it against his forehead, pushing his head back in a slight shove.

"That wouldn't get you so pissy; what gives, Seb?" He sighed, irritated, and tried to focus on his reading, but his mind betrayed his deeper thoughts. My upcoming visit to Vladimir and his lack of complete understanding about me becoming Vladimir's Bride were stewing under the surface. I sighed. Revealing the truth had brought us closer, but it also made him worry about me more now. "Seb," I drawled out in a caring tone.

"Stay out of my head, Sash," he warned in response.

"Hey! Enough with that. Just talk to me about it, alright. Stewing and pushing me away, since I'm the one you're worried about, are not going to help," I scolded. Sebastian sighed, irritated because I was right, slamming his book closed and tossing it on his desk.

"I'm sorry, Sasha. What can I help you with?" In a second, I was in front of him, brushing his hair out of his face and looking at him tenderly. I stepped into him and gave him a hug until he finally returned the embrace.

"Well, I was kinda hoping to use your nose tonight, if you wouldn't mind."

He pulled back and looked at me. "How so?"

"We need to locate the place where the vamp's associates are making the drugs, and I was hoping that maybe you could help me look in the areas of town that Niklaus said were the most likely to contain the right place."

"I'm happy to help, but I don't even have a scent on either of the two that you were shown," he pointed out.

"Well, I was thinking that there might be a rare possibility of you picking up on vampire combined with werewolf; specifically, our rogue's, even if it will be way old. Your nose is that good, right?"

Werewolves had excellent senses, just like vampires, but their noses were even better than ours. Their noses could pick up the faintest scent weeks old when ours couldn't. Ours did fine with old scent if it was saturated, like Vladimir's room had been.

He smirked at me and said, "It's a long shot, but I'm willing to try. What do I get if I find them?" He pulled me up against him tighter, teasing me.

I rolled my eyes, saying, "A dog treat?" I couldn't stop the wicked chuckle that escaped my lips, developing into a loud bit of laughter at his mock glare. He gave me a quick wap on my ass for that and released me.

"I'll settle for a drink and a dance later," he said.

"No prob. At 'The Den?'" I asked. He gave me his half smile and nodded.

"Sash, about New York," he started, but I cut him off.

"Seb, I have to go. I have no choice. I'm sorry you're worried about me, about the trip, about the whole thing."

He sighed. "I know that, I just feel frustrated."

"At what, exactly?" I asked.

"Well, feeling helpless to stop it for one thing."

"You're not alone in that. Get in line behind the other four of us," I said with a bitter edge.

"It's more than that, though, Sasha. Something doesn't add up for me in this."

I furrowed my brow at him, "Like what?"

He rolled his eyes and gave an irritated growl, saying, "If I knew, it wouldn't frustrate me so bad. I mean, why now? Haven't you asked Vladimir before to not send you out on missions?"

"Yeah, I suppose I've asked him a few different times over the years. He's always refused until now, so I took my chance while I could."

"Something just doesn't add up, Sasha. Vladimir is many things, but random is not one." Sebastian shook his head and gave another frustrated sigh. His mind revealed that he was going to think about it some more. Whatever helped him sleep. "I'll see you tonight, ok? Meet me here," I said, placing an address on his desk.

It was totally dark as I leaned against the old brick building, waiting for my wolf companion to join me. I was in the vicinity of the first possible area that Niklaus had pointed out. We had gone during the day, scoping out the different places and narrowing down our search, but we needed Sebastian's nose to get further without searching each and every warehouse, which would take forever. It might still come to that, but I had a lot of faith in Sebastian's nose.

"Not cool, Seb!" I said into the dark. I heard him snort and come out of the shadows around the corner, his great wolf form moving silently as his yellow eyes lit up the dark.

"Just checking if you're letting your guard down," he thought. I rolled my eyes.

"You know how much that creeps me out when you hunt or stalk me. The hair on my neck is still standing up, you dick," I glared at him. I saw a smug look cross his wolf features. I put a hand on my hip and motioned down the alleyway with the other, still scowling, giving him an impatient look. He put his nose to the ground and started perusing the area. I got a pop shot in saying, "Good boy." He turned and growled at me, his lips rippling with the deep bass warning. It was my turn to wear a smug look. He returned to his perusal of the area, and I followed along.

We moved on to the next area Niklaus, and I had checked out as a possibility, and still nothing. It was getting late, but we agreed to go hit up one more area on the outskirts of town. We arrived, and even I could pick up the scent of vampire in the area, though that didn't really prove anything. But then Sebastian picked up a trail. The rogue had been in the area.

I followed Sebastian closely, watching his back as he followed the scent around the area. Multiple scents converged on one location; the rogue, a human, another vampire, and the vampire I had burnt the other night.

"Yeah, no mistaking that scent after you practically threw up his blood all over me that night," Sebastian thought sarcastically.

"Well? Where to, Seb?" I whispered so his hearing could just pick it up. This was a meeting place for sure, but it was not where they were actually making the drug. He turned and started following a trail; he now had the scent of our vampire and human that he could pick up in other places and follow if needed.

The trail led down alleyway after alleyway and started heading out of town. We were soon sprinting through the woods, following an old road. We entered a gate across the road, passing into a fenced area with signs saying things like

'Keep Out,' 'Private Property,' 'Danger Zone,' etc. We ran along the road for another mile or so and came to the edge of a clearing.

We hid in the trees, looking where the trail led. I looked over the old quarry, which was eery in the moonlight. My hand landed on Sebastian's side as I looked out over the bottomless old pits, now partially filled with water, old equipment, and an old tunnel that went underground. This had to be it. I looked over at Sebastian, and our eyes met in the dark before we turned back to look at it. I pressed the speed dial on my cell.

"Sasha? Have you found something?" Niklaus asked.

"Yes, the old quarry West of town seems to be the place. The vampire's trail led here. We're looking at the place now and may follow the scent in closer to double-check that this really is the place and not just somewhere he's spent time."

"Sasha, you need to be careful. He is very dangerous. In fact, why don't you just stay put, and I can-" he said, but I cut him off, catching movement coming out of the old tunnel.

"I gotta go, Niklaus, he's here." I hung up on him and put the phone away, moving more behind a tree to conceal myself. Sebastian crouched down into the underbrush of the bushes to hide his presence. Luckily, we were on the right side of the current breeze, so he wouldn't smell us. Part of me wondered if I couldn't just walk up and try to make a deal with him. His mind revealed he was irritated with someone, and he brought his phone up to his face.

He began arguing with someone about another shipment, supplies were running low, and how he had sent a shipment of the final product out to some key cities as samples for the vampire communities there. Not good.

And then he smiled as he said, "It's almost ready to be put into production; we just need to find a couple wolves to try it on. Yes, soon. I expect you to have another box ready for me in the next couple of days." He hung up his phone and looked around the quarry for a moment. He slowly turned and made to walk down into the tunnel when my freaking cell phone decided to go off. Dammit! I should have put it on silent. I pushed the ignore button and silenced it, but it was too late.

"Shit! Stay here, Sebastian. I'll see if I can smooth this over like I'm trying to make a deal and get a hit. Stay in the shadows and don't attack unless he does," I thought for him to hear.

I sped over to the road out of sight and started walking toward the quarry like I hadn't been trying to hide my presence there. The large vampire's eyes lit up red in the night when he spotted me coming his way, so I returned the gesture. He was pissed, and I wasn't sure about how smoothly this was going to go, but I needed to try. Maybe we could get the jump on him if I could get him off his guard. I walked slowly and casually, letting him peruse me with his flaming, angry eyes.

"Who are you? What are you doing here?" he demanded. I flashed him a confident, knowing smile that conveyed that I wasn't worried.

"I'm here looking for another fix since that bastard at the bar decided to get me hooked and then just up and disappear on me when I try going back to get more multiple times!" He glared at me as I walked up closer.

"How do you know about this place?"

"He told me about it during one of our exchanges. Bragging up a storm about how he and his associates were going to be filthy rich and blah, blah, blah. I must say, though," I paused and openly perused him before continuing, "His assessment that he was the good-looking one was totally wrong."

The man's red eyes narrowed at me, still pissed, but I caught the tiniest flare of interest at my words before the anger returned. He was extremely tall, powerfully built with broad shoulders and frame, and had short black hair and rugged features—essentially a very deadly-looking knockout.

My flirtatious smile transformed into a look of fear as he sped to me, grabbing me around the throat and backing us up to the edge of the quarry pit. My hands were on his wrist as he squeezed my throat and leaned me over the edge of the quarry, glaring at me with his blazing eyes.

"He would never have told anyone the location of our work; you lie, little girl. Now you're going to tell me why you're really here," he whispered in a terrifying threat as he precariously leaned me back over the edge of the vast pit.

# CHAPTER 40

The night breeze blew my hair about as it hung out below me, over the vast dark abyss. I looked back at the vampire's enraged eyes as he held me over the edge, squeezing my throat.

"There are plenty of old trees down there to run you through when I push you over the edge, girl, so you'd better think twice about how you answer me. What are you doing here?"

I choked out, "I told you! I'm here looking for more." I pulled out an old syringe we had saved from the man's jacket with one hand while my other one still held his wrist.

I didn't have to fake my fear, which showed on my face and made the needle shake as I held it out toward him like a peace offering. He was more dangerous than I thought, and his mind revealed just how much. Perhaps we should have just made a run for it, waiting for some more backup. I was a vampire, but so was he, and he had me outmatched in strength and probably speed, but I had my power.

"Sounds like you were one of the last ones to see my associate before he disappeared," he implied much with his tone. And then his mind turned to getting information out of me instead of sending me flying down into the abyss.

He dragged me away from the edge and started backing me up toward the tunnel that went underground, using his hold on my throat. I started struggling a little, trying to see if he would change his mind; if he got me down in that tunnel, I was dead because he had a defensible position in which to easily kill me. He was going to drag me down there and torture me for information about his associate.

We were almost to the entrance when I vamped out on him, my eyes glowing red as my fangs came out on a ferocious snarl. And then I really started to fight him.

I dropped the needle and, quick as a flash, used my hold on his wrist and my other free hand to reach up and snap his arm, freeing myself from his hold.

He snarled back at me, his fangs descending as he reached over and snapped his arm back into place. I was on the defense, outmatched, I knew, and he was all confidence.

He attacked me so fast I could barely brace for his frame, slamming into mine as he swiped at me with his hands, baring his teeth. I sent a powerful wave of magic back at him, knocking him a distance away from me, but he was so powerful it didn't move him as much as it could have.

Lightning fast, he reached behind him, plucked a pole from the ground that had been an old sign, and swung it around at my head. I only had time to reinforce my face with my magic and put my hands up, trying to protect myself, as the pole slammed into my head, whipping it to the side and knocking me to the ground. With a snarl, I turned back to him and ripped the pole from his grasp with my magic before slamming it back into him. He caught the pole with both hands and, using brute strength, forced it up over his body to fly over the pit's edge. I had gotten up while pushing the pole onto him, but he sprang on me the moment he was free of it.

We slammed into the ground, grappling with one another, snarling ferociously, snapping our jaws at one another. I was doing what I could to lean away from him, even as he was on top of me. My hands gripped his wrists while my magic was the only thing holding his head away from me. If I hadn't had my magic, I would already have had my throat ripped out by his salivating, snapping jaws, but he was slowly getting closer.

Our fight had only lasted a few seconds at vampire speed, and I could feel Sebastian racing over the clearing to help me. I felt a snap, and my left arm flopped helplessly to the side on a searingly painful break.

He found purchase on my neck then, strangling me, as my remaining hand and magic held his face and deadly jaws away from me. Vladimir had strangled me many times before but never like this; this man was squeezing the life out of me, my vision starting to darken around the edges as I struggled against him. Vladimir had only ever strangled me to make a point by hurting me or threatening me; he had let his rage get the better of him one time and strangled me until I had passed out, but this was different. This man was going to kill me, crush me as I started to weaken, my eyes starting to go bloodshot with the pressure he was putting on me. As I weakened, so my magic weakened, and his huge fangs began inching closer to my neck.

I was just about to black out when Sebastian's snarling wolf form flew out across the space, landing on the vampire and knocking him off of me. I went flying a short distance with the force of it and hit my head on a large boulder. I heard vicious snarling from both creatures as they fought nearby but out of my sight, as it was slowly returning to me.

I was hurt, but mostly I was just pissed, which helped me rise to my feet. I reached over and set my broken arm on a snarl of my own. My vision was clearing enough to see the fight waging in front of me; werewolf against vampire. Sebastian lunged and found purchase on the vampire's arm, shaking him as the vampire's granite fist slammed into Sebastian's face.

As I ran toward the fight, I used my magic to protect Sebastian from another hit. I went for the vampire's throat, but he pulled me off of him and threw me back towards the boulder, turning back to Sebastian to free himself. I saw the man reach out, and with his free hand, he pulled out a pistol, and a shot sounded, followed by a whine. The gun was then turned on me, and another shot rang out just as Sebastian lunged at the man again. The bullet hit the boulder next to my shoulder; I could smell the Cavalier poison on it- gone were the days of slow bows and arrows of poison when they tried to hunt us in ancient times. I snarled and sprang at the vampire, grappling with the hand that held the gun, trying to get him to release it. I jerked my head to the side as he fired off another shot, narrowly missing me.

I heard three other distant snarls at the same time that I heard a roar of pain come from the vampire; Sebastian had succeeded in ripping his arm off at last and chucked it to the side before lunging for the vampire's leg. The vampire pulled me to him and, in a flash, head-butted me, sending me to my knees and freeing his pistol-wielding hand. He pistol-whipped me, sending me to the ground before an expertly placed kick broke my leg as I screamed. I looked up to see him turn the gun on the enraged brothers who were running toward us, firing multiple times, before he had his leg swept out from underneath him by the massive black wolf. I used my magic to pull out his other leg, sending him to the ground just in time to avoid another bullet aimed at me, his pistol hand flying toward the sky.

The brothers were on him in a second, the gun being ripped from his hand and thrown aside as they converged on him, tearing into him with their fangs and hands. Sebastian was shaking and tearing at his leg, growling viciously, his eyes glowing. Eben went for the pistol arm, tearing it off, as Jaxon went for the vampire's neck with his fangs, ripping his throat out, and Niklaus gripped and twisted, pulling the vampire's head clean off of his body. The four of them proceeded to tear him to pieces, and soon, what was left of him was set ablaze. Jaxon sped off as the other three came to me. I noticed that Eben had taken a bullet and was weakening as he sat down next to me.

Niklaus approached me and looked me in the eye as he reached up and set my leg quickly. My eyes slammed shut as I screamed with the pain, but it was over soon, and my healing was already kicking in. He gently turned my chin to look at my neck where I had been strangled, but I knew that was healing, too. He checked in with me mentally to make sure I was alright otherwise. I was more worried about Eben and Sebastian.

Jaxon's sports car came blaring down the road and pulled up close. He hopped out to help Eben inside as I held Sebastian, who had changed back into his human form. I picked him up in my strong vampire arms and started limping to the car with him. They both needed help quickly.

"Jaxon, take them back to the mansion quickly and treat them both," Niklaus instructed. "Sasha and I will remain here to deal with what we can find and meet you there."

"Jaxon," I called for his attention, and he looked at me, "Put Seb in my room as he heals up. It's going to take a little longer for him compared to us. Make him rest!" Jaxon nodded at me before he sank into his car and sped off.

I sighed and turned to Niklaus. He was scowling at me, frustrated that this had happened at all. I showed him exactly what had happened, and his scowl softened some when he realized I hadn't just rushed into things; my cellphone ringing had given us away.

"Vladimir called me, Sasha, when you ignored his call, but I was already on my way here. I couldn't pick up either at the time," he informed me. Fliiiiiip. Vladimir hated being ignored and was going to be pissed. He rarely saw reason in these circumstances, and I had a sense of foreboding about his reaction.

Niklaus and I checked the place out completely, setting what remained of the facilities on fire and destroying what we didn't set aside for samples and study. We garnered as much information as we could, including some files he had on the drugs, future projections, and all those involved. No wonder he protected this place so much. We both carried a box home to the estate as we sped around the outskirts of town to get there.

I set my box down in the study and turned to Eben, sitting on the couch, waiting for us. He was already better, and he let me know that Jaxon was finishing up with Sebastian in my room. I gave Eben a huge hug, feeling relieved that he was alright. He wrapped his arms around me as I whispered my thanks for coming to my aid and that I was relieved he was okay. He stroked my hair and then released me when I pulled back. I turned and thanked Niklaus as well and headed out of the study. I wanted to check in on Sebastian and thank him and Jaxon for their help with the crazy vampire.

I sighed and started walking down the hallway to my room. My hand was just reaching up to my door knob when my memory of Vladimir standing in my room, holding my head, flashed before my eyes in vivid picture. I gasped and mentally called Niklaus's name. I stood frozen at the door. I didn't want Vladimir's violence on display before the brothers, but I couldn't open my door either, revealing Sebastian to him, so I just stood there with a pounding heart, waiting.

Vladimir manifested behind me, and I was yanked back from the door by my hair, Vladimir's apparition bending over me with a snarl to tear at my exposed throat, blood running all over the floor, as I heard the brother's running out of the study.

# CHAPTER 41

Vladimir's apparition tore into my neck viciously as I struggled against him, my blood running down my neck and back, creating a thick puddle on the floor. I could feel both Niklaus's and Eben's horrified eyes on me as Vladimir attacked me. He wasn't actually able to feed on me, so it was running all over me and the floor, but he made his point before pulling back and standing me up, again pulling my hair back as my gaping wound continued to bleed.

"How dare you ignore me!" He screamed at me, pulling me close to him even in my contorted position. He released my hair, and a painful slap sent me sprawling to the hardwood.

Vladimir's furious gaze drifted to his sons, standing only a few feet away. He started walking over to them, and even though the magic was through me, he could still use it to harm them if he wanted.

"Vladimir!" I screamed at him, and his enraged form turned back to me; I had successfully diverted his attention away from them. He slowly stalked back towards me. "Vladimir, I couldn't answer! You blew my cover in the forest when I was tracking down the drug-wielding vamp, and he heard the phone ring, revealing my presence. We just got back. I was going to call you, I swear!" He reached down and dragged me up off the floor with a hand to my throat, suspending me in the air by it.

I knew struggling would only enrage him more, so I went totally limp in his grasp but still maintained eye contact, trying to show that I was being honest. I saw his rage slowly settling, and he finally set me down.

His fingers dug into the open wound on my neck as he leaned in close, hissing at me with his fangs, "Be careful, Sasha, or I will have to come there and teach you a lesson. I won't wait until New York if you ignore another one of my calls like that again, my pet. A missed call is one thing, but you ignoring me is unacceptable." And then he released me and turned his glare on Niklaus, saying, "That goes for you as well." And then he faded as I collapsed to the floor in a pool of my own blood, shaking and coughing while I held my throat.

Both brothers ran over to me to help me up. Eben picked me up in his arms after I wobbled a little, and they headed down the hall with me still holding my neck and wheezing. I had just about had my fill of being strangled for one night. Niklaus involuntary chuckled at my snark even while I was hurt. I gave him a smirk that transformed into a grateful smile.

I was never more grateful for the warning I had had of Vladimir's appearance when the door was opened to Sebastian lying in my bed, Jaxon just finishing up the bandage on his shoulder. If I had stepped into the room, Vladimir would have seen my friend.

Both looked up, surprised and concerned at the sight of me being carried by Eben, drenched in blood, holding my neck, with fresh marks on my body.

"What happened? He was dead!" Sebastian almost shouted.

Eben carried me into the bathroom to get me cleaned up while Niklaus stopped by the bed, bitterly saying, "Vladimir happened." I heard both Jaxon and Sebastian growl.

Eben carefully set me down on the sink vanity and helped my shirt off. He started cleaning off the blood with a rag, but we both agreed that a quick shower would be easier. He helped me remove the rest of my clothes and stayed close as I showered, ensuring I was stable. Eben gently helped towel me off, looking at my healing wound with a concerned scowl, and then he slipped a nightgown over me. He kissed me gently, then walked me out to sit on my bed. I crawled over to Sebastian, lying down, and brushed his hair from his face.

"You big oaf, what d'ya get shot for anyways?" I teased. His beautiful golden eyes found mine on a smile, and he laughed, pulling me into a hug on his chest.

"I'll be good as new by tomorrow morning, don't you worry," he winked at me. I planted a kiss on his cheek.

"Thanks for saving me, Seb. You too, Jaxon." I turned my eyes on him, and he gave me a smirk with a look of deep affection. I turned back to Sebastian, whom I was almost lying on, and said with narrowed eyes, "Are you going to be good if I sleep on the other side of my bed?"

Sebastian grinned and laughed at me, teasing, "I don't know. I might not be able to control those wolfy urges." He waggled his eyebrows at me for emphasis, making me laugh and caress his face with a smile.

"Sasha, you should feed," Niklaus said. I turned my eyes on him, and they lit up red. I slid over to the other side of the bed and crooked my finger at him with a smile.

He bent over and picked me up, saying, "Why don't you just come sleep in my room?"

I smiled at him, saying, "Don't trust Sebastian, do you?"

Niklaus raised an eyebrow at me, "Not one wolfy bit." We all laughed, and I put my arms around his neck as he carried me from the room.

"Night, Seb," I called over Niklaus's shoulder before we left the room.

"Night, Sash," he said before settling down to sleep.

The other two brothers followed us across the manor and stood at Niklaus's door. Niklaus held me with one arm and pointed at Eben and then at Eben's room, saying, "You, go rest." He turned to Jaxon and pointed at him and then at his own door, saying, "You, inside. Open the door." Jaxon complied and went to sit on the edge of Niklaus's bed. Niklaus handed me to him.

Jaxon pulled me close and exposed his neck for me to feed from him. His arms tightened on me as his eyes drifted close on the pleasure that flowed through his system at my bite. When I was finished, he stood and returned me to Niklaus with a slightly envious look.

"One of these days, I'll get you in my room, Sugar Lips."

I smiled and said, "Soon." He smirked at me and left, shutting the door behind him as he went. Niklaus pulled the covers to his bed back and slipped me inside, turning to cross the room and change into his pajama bottoms for the night.

He returned to me and pulled me to him, encouraging me to feed from him as well. He drew in a deep breath when I bit down and caressed my face, kissing my forehead as I fed from him slowly, drawing out his pleasure. His mind had already revealed he was going to force me to sleep after this instead of anything else, so I drew out our pleasure through the bite for as long as I could.

He gave me a gentle kiss before tucking me into the crook of his arm, whispering, "Good night, my darling, Sasha, my love. I'm so glad you're safe." I slung an arm and a leg over him and drifted off to sleep, feeling completely safe once again.

It was very early the next morning, and I slipped from Niklaus's arms and room to go check on Sebastian.

"Now, where are you off to, Sugar Lips?" I jumped and turned to see Jaxon leaning against the wall with a smug look.

"Going to go check on the patient," I sneered before turning and walking toward the stairs.

He was behind me in a flash, wrapping his arms around my middle, his hot breath on my ear as he whispered, "Sounded like you actually slept last night. If I had you in my room, that would be the last thing on the agenda." I enjoyed the shivers that ran from his lips against my ear down my back. I turned my face toward him and reached up behind me to stroke his neck. My eyes closed at the feeling of his lips on my neck, just below my ear, kissing and sucking lightly. A sudden gasp had us both looking over.

The Governess was standing in the hallway near her door, looking at us. She had been suspicious before about things happening, but this was the first time she had actually seen Jaxon show me affection and touch me. Her mind blazed in hot anger at the situation; it was one thing for Jaxon to just not be interested in her any longer, but the truth that he was with me now, the one who had told her to stay away, infuriated her to no end. I turned and left, Jaxon following me, but before I left, I could hear her determination to 'steal' him back in her mind. Great, more drama.

I quietly walked into my room and saw Sebastian was still sleeping. I gently crawled across the bed to lay beside him, barely moving the covers. Jaxon relaxed in one of the chairs, keeping an eye on us. I almost laughed as his mind revealed that he still didn't fully trust Sebastian to not try to win me back or change his status from friend to more. He was comfortable with us in public, but this felt more intimate, and he wasn't above keeping an eye on Seb. I smirked at Jaxon and raised an eyebrow; he had the good sense of looking to the side and going a little pink. I used my magic to caress his chin and kiss his lips, drawing his eyes to mine.

I gave him a loving smile before I turned to Sebastian. He looked better, and I couldn't smell any new blood, so I was reasonably sure he was healed underneath his bandage. I breathed and sighed, nestling close to him to wait until he woke.

My eyes went to the door when Eben joined us after a while; he went and sat in the other armchair after checking in with me mentally. I finally felt Sebastian stir, so I looked at him, sweeping his hair from his forehead. His eyes opened and found me, and he smiled, reaching up to caress my face. I leaned over him and peeked under his bandage, gently removing it when I saw he was healed.

"You okay, Seb?" He gave me a smile and nodded.

"Perfectly fine, thanks. What about you?"

"Always. I'll be heading out soon. Don't you need to head to the college?"

He nodded, saying, "Where are you headed?"

"I'm heading back to the quarry to see if I can pick up a trail for that human. He still needs to be tracked down and taken care of."

"Not alone, you're not," I heard Niklaus say as he entered my room.

"The rest have classes, so unless you're willing to come with me, alone it is. Vladimir is pissed enough after yesterday, and I have to get back on his good side before New York, or I'm really going to pay for it." I saw looks of concern on all the brother's faces; they knew I was right.

"Of course, I'll come with you," Niklaus answered.

I planted a kiss on Sebastian's face and left the room. Lucy skipped up to hug my legs, with Lucian only a second behind. I hugged them both back and bent down to them. "Headed somewhere, you two?"

"Yes, the library. Why didn't you come to my room last night? I wanted another story; the Governess tells ones about princesses, not murder. They're boring," Lucy whined as Lucian nodded in agreement.

I laughed. "I promise I'll come again soon, okay?" She nodded, and they both turned to Jaxon. He was apparently driving them and the Governess this morning before heading off himself. He leaned over and kissed me goodbye before reaching out to take the twins' hands and walk them to his car. The Governess followed with a sullen set to her lips, giving me a glare on her way out of the door.

I watched them until Eben stepped into my line of sight. He looked delicious in his dark clothes and leather jacket. I smiled at him and reached up to caress his face as he looked deep into my eyes. "Be careful today, my Blossom," he said.

I gave him another smile, whispering, "Niklaus will be with me. I'll be fine." An arm around my waist pulled me to him for a gentle, smoldering kiss.

Eben whispered, "You've had too many close calls lately." I nodded at him. On that point, I couldn't argue.

I kissed him once more and said, "Have a good day." He turned and headed out the door to his Ducati, a helmet under his arm.

Sebastian gave me a hug goodbye, and I promised to update him when we found anything else out. I gave a sigh as my mind started thinking over just how ordinary and nice the last few moments had been, kissing the brothers goodbye for their day and hugging Lucy and Lucian. This really was a family, one I was desperate to be a part of permanently.

"You're not used to normal family moments, Sasha," Niklaus said, walking up to me.

"No, I'm not. You know that better than anyone," I admitted. Niklaus walked up close to me and held my face as he kissed me, slipping his tongue in my mouth and making me tremble. I put my arms around him, kissing him back. He nipped my lip, making me sigh, while he looked into my eyes.

"It's about time you started getting used to it. You already are part of this family," he said, smiling at me.

"For now," I thought. Niklaus gave me a scowl.

"We'll find a way, Sasha. Have some faith. Maybe someday you'll be the central point to this all instead of Vladimir."

"You ready to go?" I asked him. He gave me a nod, brushing my hair over my shoulder. It was time to go track down a Cavalier.

# CHAPTER 42

I watched Niklaus bend down and touch the dirt, evaluating the tracks on the ground. It was fascinating to listen in on his mind as he was, and I was learning a lot; every minute detail had meaning for him and played into the bigger picture of what it meant. We took off through the forest again, following the trail, heading back toward town. The trail eventually led us to the back of the Cavalier compound, where we hid and observed for a while.

"So, it's definitely a Cavalier then. See where he was sneaking in and out of the compound there," Niklaus thought, pointing to a particular spot that seemed to lead into a building that had been one of the ones we had noticed the last time we had observed the compound.

But how to get a look around? How to locate our Cavalier and take him out? I blocked Niklaus from my mind just as a thought manifested.

"Sasha," Niklaus used my name as a whispered warning.

"Come on, let's go. We've spent most of the day here and seen nothing. I may have an idea, but I haven't thought it through yet, and you're not going to like it, I'm afraid," I said. We flew across town, back to the estate. I went into his study; this was going to take some convincing.

"Alright, Sasha. What is this idea that I'm not going to like?" Niklaus asked.

I got a sheepish look and shrugged, "A party."

Now, he was confused. "A party?"

"A private party with a particular blue-eyed Cavalier," I said, looking at him.

"No, Sasha, absolutely not! There would be no way for any of us to protect you if you got into trouble. You would literally be walking into the nest of all the Cavaliers alone. It couldn't get any more unsafe than that! I don't think that even Vladimir would approve of that, Sasha."

"Well, I guess there's only one way to find out," I said. Before Niklaus could object, I brought my phone up to my face to give Vladimir a call.

He picked up immediately and spoke coldly, "Report." Yup, still pissed at me.

"Niklaus and I were able to track the human scent to the Cavalier compound. The human involved in the drug scene is a Cavalier." Silence. O-kay. Pissy pants. A laugh escaped Niklaus, but he started coughing to cover it. "I have an idea for how to get an inside look into the compound by using my previous source, but it would mean going into the compound, to his apartment with him, by myself."

"No screwing around, Sasha. I already warned you not to. Are you forgetting who you belong to? After yesterday, I'm starting to really think that, my pet."

"No, Vladimir. I could never forget that. I wasn't suggesting that I would-"

"No screwing around, especially with a Cavalier."

"So, you don't have an issue with me going into the compound alone, so long as I don't sleep with the Cavalier?"

"Lead him on, flirt, do what you need to if it gets you results, but don't you dare take it farther than that. Go, look around, discover what you can, but never forget who you belong to." The line went dead. I rolled my eyes.

I looked at Niklaus, who was scowling at me. Vladimir might not care if I went in there alone, but Niklaus certainly did; it was one of the reasons why I loved him. He was always looking out for me. When we returned, I had already let him back into my mind, and he could hear all those thoughts and my determination.

"Sasha, you can't just go waltzing into the middle of the Cavaliers, even if you are hanging off the arm of their golden boy. It's not safe."

"Which golden boy are we talking about," Jaxon smirked from the doorway. Eben was right next to him. They had just gotten back from classes.

"I'm going out tonight," I said.

I turned and left the study, heading toward my room to get ready. I felt the three of them following me: Niklaus was determined to change my mind, and the other two had questions about what was happening. I left my door open and walked into my closet. I pulled on my black skirt above my knees in the front and fell to mid-calf in the back, a pair of lace pantyhose and black boots, and topped the ensemble with a deep blue strapped corset that laced up the front. I pulled my hair up and started pinning it into a waterfall of cascading curls, meeting Niklaus's eye in the mirror as he walked up behind me in the bathroom.

"Sasha, this isn't safe, can't you understand?"

"What's not safe?" Eben asked, his concern covering his features. I looked into his beautiful azure eyes in the mirror and smiled. The corset I had put on exactly matched them.

I turned back to my hair but answered, "Niklaus doesn't like the idea of me going out with Blake." Jaxon and Eben both scowled.

"It's more than that, Sasha! You would be going with him alone to his apartment in the Cavalier compound." The other two brothers hissed their disapproval, both scowling.

"Look, it's the only way. It needs done, so I'm going to do it." I finished my makeup and turned to leave but found myself trapped by the three of them.

"Please don't make this hard on me," I said. "This needs to be done, and you all know it. If there's a better plan, then please, speak up!" I looked around at the three of them; nothing. "Very well. Come to the bar if you like. Follow us to the compound. You could even watch the back entrance that the Cavalier uses, in case I need you and you think you can sneak in, but don't interfere with Blake and me. If I can work it right, he'll be hooked for good, and I'll have an invite more often than I can go." Niklaus scowled, crossing his arms. Jaxon's eyes went red, and he growled. Eben got an angry scowl and heaved a sigh. I rolled my eyes.

"Vladimir already reminded me to not screw around with him. Don't you start, too. I have no intention of letting it come to that, and my power of persuasion will affect his memory, as it happened with Derrick at the frat party." I sighed when they didn't move. I glared at them. "Move. This is old, and I have no time or patience for it."

"I don't like him even believing he has a chance with you, let alone taking you back to his place and you making him think he scored, Sugar Lips," Jaxon growled.

I sighed, "Fine. I'll get him drunk as a skunk and make sure he passes out, okay? He might get in a feel or two, but I won't leave him thinking anything happened. Deal? Besides, tonight is just setting the trap up. I won't be going back with him tonight."

I tried to press through them, but they converged on me. Jaxon captured my mouth, his arms coming around my waist to pull my hips to his. He flashed his brothers a look before he smirked at me and silenced my protest with his mouth again. I started to push away from him when his devilishly skillful tongue snuck its way into my mouth, driving me to distraction. I felt my hair get swept from my shoulders on both sides and then both Eben and Niklaus claimed a side of my neck with their fangs, making me hiss and pull from Jaxon's mouth.

Jaxon pulled me against him as my head fell back, and I felt his lips trail down from my chin. Pleasure was rolling through me from Niklaus and Eben's bites, but I still sucked in a breath, feeling the tingling trail that Jaxon's lips left as they slid down the front of my throat, down my collarbone, to just above my breast. I gasped and fisted his hair as he licked me there and then bit down. My mind was overwhelmed with pleasure that overlapped one sensation on top of the other; time meant nothing to me at this moment, and I released any hold I had over it. Riding the waves of ecstasy, I moaned and sighed. I began throbbing, desire for them taking over my mind, my breathing coming fast and shallow.

Jaxon released me, and slowly, the other two followed. He leaned over me to look into my eyes.

"Vladimir thinks you belong to him, but we know better, Sugar Lips. He doesn't make you vibrate like we do. Remember that when you're out with Blake, come home to us." All three flashed out of my room, leaving me standing there, still aching for their touch. Jerks. I guess I deserved that, and he was right; I would be thinking of them and aching for them when I was out tonight.

I sighed, wiped off the remaining blood, and headed for the front door. I had to rekindle Blake's interest, and I knew exactly where he would be: the usual bar.

I zipped my way there and slowed when I came around the corner. Walking at human speed everywhere would be so annoying; I could barely remember what it had been like so many years ago. Dang, I was old. Come to think of it, I was one of the oldest female vampires that I even knew about. Most were younger, like Missy, being killed for reasons above my understanding. Maybe my powers had something to do with me still being alive, or perhaps it was how overprotective Vladimir had been of me over the years, keeping me secret.

I knew of one other female in the underworld close to my age; she was now the Bride of one of Vladimir's associates, Darius. Darius had kept her like Vladimir had kept me, serving him in the underworld, until recently making her his Bride. I rarely saw her, though; he kept her hidden away from almost every other person in that world. Only Vladimir had spoken with her in the last five years. Perhaps that is where he had gotten the idea to name those terms even? I would have to talk with Sebastian and offer up this idea to help settle his mind on the subject since he seemed so unsettled about the timing of it. Maybe it would give him some peace.

The other female vampire had different skills, just like I did. She was also a witch but one useful in divination. There had been times, years and years ago, when we were younger when Vladimir and Darius would trade us back and forth for the use of our skills. Though Darius was far from kind, he lacked the cruelty that Vladimir breathed, and so those times were periods in my life when I felt freer until I was forced to return to Vladimir. It made me think of the last time that Vladimir had been willing to trade me for a time, how he had kissed me when I returned to him. It had been the most gentle and affectionate he'd ever been with me. It was then that I had realized that he had come to be attached to me. He loved me in his cruel, destitute way.

Was he going to lock me away, too? The thought just occurred to me. Damn, I hoped not. I heaved a sigh. I so desperately wanted to talk with Sebastian about all of this.

I pulled the bar door open and walked inside. Scanning the bar, I spotted Blake in his usual scene, hanging out with a bunch of girls around him, hanging on him. Hmmmmm. What would grab his attention in this situation? An evil grin spread across my face as I spotted exactly what I needed, crossing the bar with a couple drinks. No Alpha male could resist two females fighting over him; Blake would be no exception.

I turned my eyes from my target and started walking swiftly toward her path. I reached the exact spot I needed half a second before she did and turned, spilling one of the drinks all over her front.

"Oops," I said in a mockingly innocent tone of voice. "Didn't see you there, Natalie."

# CHAPTER 43

The preppy blonde cheerleader was fuming at me. I heard her mind as she was about to pour the other drink down my front, so I reached out and took it from her faster than she could track.

"Aww, Nat, don't spill Blake's drink. He wouldn't like that. Should I carry it to him instead since you can't seem to keep it in its glass?" I said all this sweetly, flashing her an innocent look like I was trying to help. "Accidents happen. Maybe you should go clean yourself off in the restroom? I'll deliver this," I said in that same tone, turning to walk the drink over to Blake. Natalie was fuming and decided to follow me. Perfect.

Her attempts to trip me were pathetic, and I easily avoided them as I sauntered over to where Blake was. I walked up to him and he looked up at me with surprise.

I gave him a friendly smile, with just a hint of fire in my eyes, as I bent over, giving him a good view as I handed him the drink, saying, "Natalie had a little accident carrying the drinks and needed to go clean herself off, so I offered to bring this to you." He looked me up and down, lingering on my cleavage for a moment before he took the drink. I leaned close to his ear and said, "Get a better waitress next time." Natalie took the bait and pulled on my arm, yanking me back from Blake and turning me to her.

"You did that on purpose!"

"Brought him his drink after you spilt the other one, yes, how observant of you, Nat. I must say you have a gift for the obvious." Some laughter from the others around us made her go pink but settled her resolve to get me back.

"You bumped into me, spilling the drink on purpose so you could bring him the other one! You're just jealous he's here with me and not you this time."

I gave her a patronizing smile, but then I leaned in close and whispered so no one else could hear, "You forget, pompom queen, I've had him alone when he was pulling down my panties, making me gasp."

She gasped in shock, leaning away from me before angrily turning red. She scowled in hatred and let out a screech, bringing up her hand to slap me. "You whore!" she screamed as her hand sailed through the air.

I let her get the slap in before I returned the favor, drawing the eyes of most of the patrons in the bar at Natalie's high-pitched scream of rage. Her claws went for my eyes as she threw herself at me. I caught her wrists and leaned away so she would put even more strength into trying to reach me. Once she was applying enough strength to not be able to catch herself, I turned to the side and let her go. She went flying across the open space, crashing onto the small coffee table covered in drinks, landing on the floor looking up at me.

She was really a mess now, and she came at me again, but Blake stepped in her way, his ego sufficiently stroked.

"That's enough, Natalie! Geeze, you'd better go get cleaned up or go home and change; you're a mess." I snorted and then turned and walked across the bar to join the others on the dance floor like nothing had even happened. I caught sight of Natalie arguing with Blake, gesturing angrily toward me. I turned and continued dancing as she started walking out of the bar.

I knew it was only a few seconds before Blake would come to me. I felt his hands on my hips pull me back against his frame as he bent over close to my ear.

"I thought you weren't interested anymore? You shot me down hard last time I came over to say hi." I leaned back against him, bringing an arm up to stroke his neck.

I turned my mouth toward his ear, saying, "You freaking left me in a haunted house, Blake. You deserved it, and you know it."

"This mean you forgive me, then?"

"Not yet, but I'm willing to let you try to make it up to me." His hold tightened on me, so I moved against him, driving him crazy.

He was a bit breathier as he asked, "And how do I do that?"

"Go out with me tomorrow night, and we'll see where it goes from there? You did promise me a private party at one point." I felt his heart rate go up a little at my words.

We danced for a few dances like this, not talking with me, driving him crazy. At last, I turned around in his hands to flash an alluring smile as I ate him up with my eyes. His eyes were like blue flames sunk into a predatory smirk. I pressed myself against him more as we moved to the music, and he didn't hesitate to hold me tighter against him as well. We were dancing so close that our faces were almost touching, our breath mixing. I leaned forward ever so slightly to brush my lips against his, still looking into his eyes. I then smiled and stayed close, still looking at him like he was the most desirable man in the world. Too bad he wasn't even close, but what he didn't know wouldn't hurt him.

He leaned back down and kissed me, moving his hands over my back. I kissed him back, sliding my hands up his chest to surround his neck. He finally released my lips, and his look left no mystery about his thoughts, even if I wasn't a mind reader.

"Why don't we just get out of here now, Sasha?" he said in a husky voice. There would be no getting him drunk when he was already like this. I needed an excuse, and then I smelt it entering the bar. A quick message, and he was right behind me.

"Mind if I cut in?" I turned, releasing Blake, and smiled at Sebastian.

"There you are! I've been waiting for you," I said in genuine delight. He reached out and pulled me to him as the next song came on. I turned to Blake, saying, "Tomorrow, okay? I have to talk with the Professor about something, but we're on for tomorrow night, okay?"

"Don't forget that drink you owe me, Sasha," Sebastian chimed in.

"Right, that too," I added, smiling at Sebastian. I looked at Blake with a look that said I still wanted him. "Night, Blake." He gave me a smile and a nod before wandering away. I turned back to Sebastian and said, "Thanks. So, how did you happen to end up here tonight?"

He laughed, saying, "A few vampire brothers may have called me, asking me to come make sure you were alright."

"Wow," I said in true amazement. They really had started to trust and accept Sebastian.

"Looks like I made it just in time too. By the way he was looking at you, he was about to take you out back," Sebastian laughed.

"Mmmm, yes. Tomorrow night, I'm going to get him stark drunk. Any recommendations?"

"Sure. Did you actually need to talk with me about something, or was that a ruse?"

"Actually, I do." Our conversation on the dance floor was so quiet that no human ears could pick it up over the music, making it completely private. Even a secluded booth couldn't offer us the same privacy as we talked, so we stayed where we were dancing together while we talked. "First, I want to say thank you again for saving me yesterday. I would have been a goner if you hadn't been there, Seb. I'm sorry you got shot, too."

He smiled at me, saying, "Don't worry about it. I'm just glad I was there to help. Something else on your mind?"

"Well, you know how you feel things don't add up in the whole Bride department?"

"Yeah, still haven't worked that out yet."

"Well, I think the timing may be simpler than you think."

"Oh yeah?" He looked a little surprised, but then an expression of intrigue crossed his features. He always had been a curious one; it's why he was so good at his job and why he traveled all over the world researching all the time. His curiosity got him into trouble sometimes, but he was also a wealth of knowledge.

"Well, Vladimir's associate took a Bride some years back. I think it may have given Vladimir the notion in the first place. The other female vampire is also a witch; several times, they would switch us back and forth for skills exchange. The other vampire finally made her his Bride, but now he keeps her locked away from everyone else." Sebastian's mind accepted what I said about the notion coming from the other vampire's Bride, but he seemed more confused than ever with my details of keeping her locked away. He had a strong desire to go and do some looking into things.

"What's the name of the associate and Bride?"

Suddenly, I felt awkward and cleared my throat. Sebastian looked at me, furrowing his brow. "What's the matter?"

I cleared my throat again and said, "The associate is Darius, and his Bride's name is-"

"Beth." I looked at him, surprised.

I knew he would know Darius because it was the same associate who'd demanded his head as the blood price for doing another favor for Vladimir. He was the entire reason I even knew and loved Sebastian at all. It's why I had been sent to lure Sebastian in in the first place. I still wasn't sure how Darius even knew Sebastian at all or why he had ever wanted his head. None of it had made sense to me, but I was less inclined to ask questions about things back then. It was before I had even felt something for Sebastian, so it hadn't really mattered at the time.

"How do you even know her name? I know you know Darius because of the whole 'blood price' thing with me and all that past history, but how do you know Beth's name? I'm confused, Seb. Why did he want your head in the first place? Why were you the 'blood price' he had demanded anyway? What did you do to cross Darius?"

Sebastian looked at me, a little astounded. "You mean they never told you why you were even sent to lure me in?"

"I didn't exactly ask questions back then, Seb. I did what I was told, and it normally didn't matter. But that was before I cared about you. So?"

"Well, I was doing research into Originals, including Elizabeth Bathory and other older vampires at the time. I met Beth at a party and made a connection with her. She was unguarded and open to talking with me. I met up with her a few times right after that, and we spent a lot of time talking; she gave me a lot of information she had gleaned over the years. More than her master would have liked her to, I know. I kept researching and looking into his business and various aspects of vampire traditions, culture, and customs, particularly older vampires. After a few weeks of looking into things, he caught me with her talking in the gardens. We were actually discussing her becoming his Bride because he had just told her. He saw me before I fled, and so he wanted me dead after that," he explained.

"Always getting into trouble, aren't you?" I teased him. He growled and pulled me closer. I smiled at him and hugged his neck to me, closing my eyes to lean my face against the side of his. "Well, in one way, I'm glad you got caught; otherwise, we wouldn't be here dancing together today, and I'd be missing out on all of this, including having you as a friend, Seb." He hugged me.

"Me too, Sash. I'm sorry for what it cost you, but I'm glad you're here now. Now, what's this about you going out with Blake tomorrow night?"

I laughed, answering, "Tomorrow night, Blake is taking me inside the Cavalier compound, to his apartment, so I can sneak a look around and try to locate our drug Cavalier." Sebastian stiffened, his mind jumping to how risky it would be.

# CHAPTER 44

I stood over Vladimir's sleeping form, watching him. He was sleeping alone tonight. I reached out and gently touched him; he still felt as real as the last time. It was fascinating to watch him sleep; the contrast between him awake and when he was like this was amazing. He could be anyone like this, someone simple and friendly who cared about others. A charming, handsome man who devoted his life to helping others. He could be the freaking pope kissing babies. I backed into the shadows, hiding myself from him just in time. The cell on his nightstand started ringing, waking him. He picked up the phone and started talking.

I held my breath as I watched and listened. So this was real then; there was no question about it. Vladimir hung up, setting the phone back on his nightstand. He was about to lie down when he paused, and his eyes started roving the room like he could feel someone was there. I almost sucked in a breath in fear. I quickly left before his eyes could land on me, returning to where I was physically sitting on the couch of the manor's study.

I sucked in a breath and opened my eyes to look at Niklaus. He stared back at me as he dropped the phone from his face, which he had just used to call Vladimir.

He could see in my mind that it had been real, but for the other brother's benefit, I said, "It was real and current timing. He picked up the call while I watched and spoke with Niklaus. I could still feel him when I touched him before Niklaus called. The link works both ways." We all looked around at one another, unsure what that could mean for us in the future, but it could be invaluable information. "It was like he sensed me, though, right before I came back. He had hung up and was about to lie back down when he paused and started looking around his room."

"Did he see you?" Niklaus asked.

"No, I faded from the room before he could look in my direction. I didn't want to risk being seen." Niklaus nodded his head.

I looked at the time and sighed. I had to go. Our little experiment occurred right before I was supposed to leave to meet Blake.

I approached Jaxon, who gave me a warning look and handed over his keys. "Better not scratch it. And I hate the fact that Blake will be riding in it."

"I'll take good care of your precious car, Jaxon," I smirked at him.

"You better bring it back in one piece, no scratches," he growled, grabbing me to pull me close for a kiss. I got the sense he wasn't really talking about his car at all. I swept his blond hair out of his face and kissed him.

"Thanks," I whispered. He nodded.

Niklaus hugged me, saying, "I'll be outside the compound with Jaxon, back where the Cavalier sneaks in and out, in case you need us, alright?"

"Sure. I'll be fine, Niklaus. With you that close, I'll be able to stay connected with you, no problem," I answered him, gently touching his forehead. He nodded and leaned in to give me a quick kiss.

I walked toward the study door, and Eben stood up from the couch he had been sitting on next to me. "Be careful, Sasha." I smiled at him, letting him see the calm in my eyes.

"I can handle Blake, remember?" He laughed at the memory of the last time Blake had tried something with me, and I had sent him screaming from the haunted house, fearing for his life.

"I know. It's the rest of them, being in their compound, that is the real worry," he offered. I reached up and caressed his face. He answered by reaching for me with both hands, gently pulling my face to his for a slow, loving kiss.

"I'll see you all when I get home, okay?" I said before stepping out the front door to go meet up with the Quarterback.

I walked into the bar and sat down to order a drink. I smelt him enter the bar and tracked his footsteps as he came up behind me to whisper in my ear, "I thought you wanted a private party back at my place? It looks like you're planning on staying a while."

I turned and smiled at him, getting a sexy smirk on my face. Then, reaching out, I fisted his shirt and pulled him to my lips in an unexpected move. I released his lips but kept our faces close, my eyes sparkling with mischief.

"I told you, Blake, you need a woman who can hold her liquor. If you think you can outdo me, I'll let you take me home right now." His eyebrow raised at my challenge.

"Alright," he said, taking me up on the challenge and taking a seat. He motioned to the bartender.

"You know," I said to him, "I even brought a couple special bottles to take back to your place, so don't think the challenge ends here." He gave me a confident smirk.

The trick was to get him just inebriated enough here so I could continue once we got back to his place without him getting too distracted or trying to get into my pants. I had worn tall black leather boots, leather pants, and a black corset for ease of movement and stealth if I got to explore the compound later.

I finished my first drink simultaneously as Blake and motioned for a round of shots. What Blake didn't know was that alcohol didn't affect me to even the same degree as it did a human. He could be stark drunk to the point of throwing up, and I might be buzzed a little. Which is why I would be driving us back to his place. After several rounds of shots, I pulled him to dance with me for a little while.

After several dances, I said, "I'm ready for that private party now. Come on." We left, and I motioned him to the sports car.

"Jaxon's car?" He asked, seeming impressed. I laughed, getting in.

I knew where to go, but I let him give me directions so he wouldn't become suspicious of anything. We pulled up to the gate, and Blake leaned over to the guard, introducing me. We were waved in, and I waited for him to direct me to the apartments. I parked, and we got out. I followed him to his apartment, carrying my arsenal of high-end liquor in a bag.

He let me into his apartment, and I looked around at the modern decor with interest.

I walked the bottles to his coffee table and turned, "Glasses?" He gave me a predatory smirk and went into his kitchen to bring some out. I met him in the middle of the living room and took the glasses from him, letting him bend down to kiss me. He wrapped his arms around me, deepening the kiss. I pulled away from him, saying, "Tsk-tsk, Quarterback. You haven't won the game yet. If you can keep up with me, you'll get a prize, but not before." I pulled away from him completely and sank on his couch. He went and turned some music on.

I poured us some drinks and handed him his when he sat down. After the third one, I started acting tipsy to encourage him. He leaned over and started kissing me, caressing me with his free hand. I pulled back with a look and poured him another. His mind was beginning to get a little impatient, so I pushed him back against the couch and grabbed the bottle, sliding onto his lap to straddle his hips with my knees. I leaned over him with a devilish look and tipped the bottle into his mouth. He pulled me up against him with his hands on my hips, caressing me. If his hands on me had belonged to one of the brothers, I would have already been on fire, but Blake's left me cold.

I smiled and took a swig from the bottle, offering him another before I bent over to nibble on his bottom lip. I was slowly lighting him on fire as I alternated between kissing him, pouring more liquor down him, and letting my free hand wander over him. I tipped the bottle, which was almost empty, into his mouth while I started unbuttoning his shirt to reveal his jock's chest, slipping my hand inside to caress him. I leaned in and kissed him, teasing him with my tongue before pulling away and pouring the rest of the bottle down his open mouth with a wicked grin. I leaned back, arching my back, thrusting my chest out as I reached for the other bottle.

He took the opportunity to bend over and kiss me right between my breasts, and I sighed for his benefit as I came back up, pulling his lips up to mine for a kiss. He was almost there, so I kept working on him to drink more. He reached up and pulled on the laces on the front of my corset. I let him loosen the top two rungs before I moved to kiss his neck, making him moan. I sat back, grinned at him, and took a swig with a raised eyebrow, challenging him. I offered him the bottle with the same look, and he took it and downed a large shot, actually impressing me. He bent forward and started kissing down my chest to where he had unlaced me.

I heard a mental growl in my mind, and I thought, "Relax, boys." Niklaus was obviously keeping tabs on exactly what was happening and showing Jaxon; they didn't like what they were seeing in their minds.

I pulled Blake's lips back up to mine and checked in with him mentally, completely drunk. Perfect. I started moving on top of him, getting him excited, essentially giving him a quick lap dance, before I bent to his neck and bit him. He moaned and panted his intense pleasure while I moved over him, his mind soaking up the moment. He barely noticed me tipping more of the alcohol down his throat. I continued until he finally passed out, laying his head on the back of the couch. His memories would be fuzzy at best; mission accomplished. Great.

I started digging around in his pockets for his keys and found them. I reached out with two fingers and touched his forehead, adding a little of my magic to make sure he wouldn't wake from his drunken state. I set the bottle down on the coffee table and reached down to do up my laces again.

Once I was put back into order, I slipped out of his apartment, locked the door, and snuck off into the dark of the compound. I reached the back of the apartment building and very carefully started moving along the outer fences in the shadows toward the building that the Cavalier had gone into from his escape in the back.

I slid along the back wall of the building next to the apartment building, heading toward my goal. I was in total darkness, but with my vampire sight, it posed no problem. I moved silently along, creeping closer. I pressed up against the wall when I heard a guard walking toward the front of the building I was behind. My eyes were the only thing that shifted as I pressed myself against the wall, finding the brothers concealed outside of the fence from where I hid. That guard wasn't a true concern, being on the opposite side of the building, and soon was gone.

I started edging closer to the alleyway between the building I was against and the one I wanted to be in. I glanced at the brothers again; they were closely tracking me and the area. I glanced down the alleyway, and then my ears picked up on footsteps and another sound ahead of them. I was still peeking when the source of the different sounds came around the corner, making me whip my head back around the corner and press my body against the brick wall, fear on my face. My eyes met the brothers' in the dark, their fear mirroring mine. A low growl emanated from the massive Doberman as I heard a second pad up next to him, picking up on my scent. Shit.

# CHAPTER 45

The two Dobermans growled from up the alleyway as I heard their handler walk up behind them. "Suche!" I listened to the handler say, and the two Dobermans began advancing on my position from down the alleyway. Their deep bass growls sounded down the alleyway as they stalked toward my position. I started creeping away from the corner to the center of the wall. I could feel the brothers' panic at the approaching guard dogs; they were trying to think about how to help.

The two Dobermans rounded the corner, but before they could signal their handler, I reached out with my magic and captured their minds, having them come to me like I was their handler. I reached out and changed their minds around, reversing their training so that I was now their handler and the Cavaliers the enemies. Niklaus's mental surprise rang out in my mind.

"Sitzen," I commanded them quietly, just loud enough for their ears but not their Cavalier handler, who continued on his rounds, waiting for their return or signal that they had found something. Both sat obediently next to me. I edged closer to the alleyway and looked down. They were exactly what I needed for a distraction. "Krängen," I commanded the dogs to heel. They dutifully took up a side each and followed me closely as I crossed the alleyway and finally reached the building.

I snuck up to the door and noticed it only had a simple lock. Either the Cavaliers had too much faith in their perimeter, or the drug lord had arranged for a simple entrance—maybe both.

"Beschützen!" I commanded the dogs to guard me, and they turned to watch my back. "That is so hot, Sugar Lips," I heard the faintest whisper from the woods and smiled in response.

"Should I bring them home, Jaxon?" I teased him, just loud enough for vampire hearing. I heard two chuckles.

"Maybe," he answered me.

"Or do you want me to go dominatrix on you?" Aroused silence was my answer.

I dug my lock-picking kit out of my boot and set to work on the door. When it clicked open, I swung it open, revealing a dark back entry hall.

I turned and looked at the two Dobermans, saying, "Suchen und angreifen!" They took off to find their old handler and attack him just as I slipped in the back door, closing it behind me.

I zipped around the room carefully but at vampire speed, observing and taking in what I could about the place. I saw various weapons loaded with poisoned bullets, stacks of boxes of the poisoned bullets, vials of the poison itself, and one entire half of the room set up in a lab to fabricate the poison.

I checked the logs and noticed one man's name, in particular, who handled the poison shipments. A quick perusal of the stock and the manifest showed discrepancies. This had to be our man; his scent was everywhere, matching the scent from the quarry and the meeting place Sebastian had found. I would need to look for him outside of the compound so I could kill him and make him disappear. Doing it inside would only cause problems.

I took pictures of records and even the recipe for the poison; it had developed over the ages and changed, and this was a rare golden opportunity to know what they were using so we could update our antidotes. The current ones worked, but they still took a long time. I was about to leave when, as an afterthought, I reached out and stashed a couple of vials of the poison on my person.

I locked the door on my way out and began sneaking back to Blake's apartment. I could hear the dogs attacking their handler and more Cavaliers rushing to help. I used my vampire speed to get to the stairs. I threw Blake's keys inside and locked him in, heading down to Jaxon's car. I got in and backed out of the parking space in time to see a few Cavaliers rushing the dogs. I pulled up to the gate and rolled down my window. The guard was so completely distracted by the dog attack happening in the courtyard that he barely noticed me as he opened the gate for me. I looked in my rear-view mirror to see the dogs avoiding more Cavaliers coming for them. One drew his gun, preparing to eliminate them. What the hell?

"Kommen Sie!" I mentally ordered the dogs as I waved my hand at the guard and pulled out of the compound. I drove down the street and turned a corner, idling in the alleyway. I opened the passenger side door with my magic just as the dogs came around the corner. They jumped in, and I shut the door, taking off and turning a corner before the Cavaliers, who were following them, could see the car.

I drove back to the estate and swung Jaxon's car into its parking spot with a sharp turn of the wheel. The front door opened, and Eben looked over at me, relieved. His mind revealed he had been worried about me.

I left the car door open for a second as the dogs hopped out, then shut it. "Krängen," I commanded them again, and they each took up a side as I started walking up to the house.

Eben took in the dogs for a second with surprise, and then I saw his blue eyes darken as I walked up to the house with them. It seemed he shared Jaxon's opinion. I walked up to him and, reached out to stroke his neck and pull him to me for a kiss. I couldn't resist it when he looked at me like that, those dark blue smoldering eyes that burned into my soul.

He wrapped his arms around my waist and kissed me before he whispered, "Where'd you get the dogs?"

I smiled wickedly and said, "Consolation prize from the Cavaliers." He laughed and turned to walk into the house, following me.

"Niklaus isn't going to like this," he laughed.

"Yes, well, it's not every day you get to commandeer specially trained guard dogs that are used to supernatural creatures. Wouldn't want to waste." Eben's gentle hands slid onto my hips, and he leaned in to kiss me as I wrapped my arms around his neck. I didn't move from his lips even as the other two brothers entered the front door. I heard Jaxon's laugh as he spotted the dogs and me kissing Eben. His mind came to the correct conclusion that Eben also found it sexy as hell. Niklaus was a little less enthused about the prospect of the dogs, but the image of me in all leather with the two Dobermans at my command also stirred him.

"Sasha, really? Now we have to feed them. Where will they stay, honestly," Niklaus huffed. I smiled on Eben's lips and turned to look at him.

"We feed the Governess too, Niklaus, and they will stay in my room. Who knows? Maybe they'll come in handy?" Jaxon choked up at my first comment and couldn't stop the laugh that left him afterward. Niklaus scowled at me. "Please, can I keep them, Nicky? I'll take care of them all by myself," I teased him in the tone of a little girl asking to keep a puppy she had found. The other two brothers started laughing, and Niklaus couldn't hold his scowl; it melted into a smile, and he even went a little pink before he rubbed his neck and laughed along with the others.

"Fine, you win, Sasha," he said, still laughing. I smiled at him but closed my eyes as Eben's lips kissed my neck. I squeezed him with my arms and then released him.

I walked the two steps to Niklaus and kissed his lips, saying, "Thanks." He shook his head in disbelief at how easily he had let me have my way. I had him wrapped around my finger, and we all knew it.

I left them and walked up the stairs, heading to Lucy and Lucian's room with the dogs still staying close. The twins, at least, were going to love them. I walked into their room, and they were just getting into bed. Both saw the dogs and let out excited squeals, rushing over to us. I mentally encouraged the dogs to be affectionate and loving with the twins as they petted and doted on them.

"They are not for eating, you two," I clarified. "Alright, into bed. They will be here when you wake, and you can even go play with them outside tomorrow."

"Will you tell me another one of your stories, please? I want to hear a good bedtime story."

I smiled and answered, "Sure. Hop into bed, and I will come and sit with you." They eagerly complied, and I sat on the edge of Lucian's bed.

"A very long time ago, a young woman was living in the castle of the Evil King, studying under many different tutors in all manners of subjects. She even had tutors in the various arts of fighting, swordsmanship, waging war, and horsemanship. One day, this young woman was out for a ride in the countryside when a bandit swept down on her, trying to overtake her on the horse to rob her of all the fine clothes and jewelry the Evil King had adorned her with.

"She rode her horse far and fast, away from the man, but he eventually caught her and captured her. When he realized who she was, he decided to hold her for ransom instead. He held her captive for a full week, and over the time together, they became friends. By the end of the week, the man professed his love for the young woman." Lucy's eyes had gotten big, and Lucian was leaning forward, both enthralled with the story I was telling them.

Lucy asked, "So the robber fell in love with her?"

"Yes, that's right. He professed his love and that he wanted to change his life so he could marry her. They spent another week in the forest talking about their future life together, how he could farm or become a tradesman and have a home and a family together.

"The young woman was very young, and her heart was quickly swept away by the idea of love. They were going to run away together the next day, using her jewelry as a start to life, but that night, the Evil King's guards discovered them and captured them, beating the man viciously in front of the young woman. They were dragged back to the castle and thrown before the Evil King. The Evil King was furious that the young woman was willing to throw away all he had given her for the 'foolish love' of a robber with no future. The young woman cried and begged the Evil King to release her, saying she wanted to go with her love, but the King refused.

"He wanted to teach the young woman a terrible lesson: that she wasn't allowed to love anyone and that it hurt to love others. So, he had her tied up to watch him slowly torture her love to death right in front of her, and on the final thrust of a sword to kill her love, the Evil King told her that if she ever loved anyone again, he would do the same thing to him; every man that she ever loved would have the same fate.

"So, the young woman turned her heart off then and there and never dared to love another until hundreds of years later, she met a very special man she had been sent to hurt. She couldn't hurt him because she had come to care about him, so she returned to her new master, and he punished her terribly. And then one day, her new master sent her to go and take care of his three coven sons and his two little witch twins, and she learned how to love again and found her family." I heard Niklaus sigh mentally. He had been listening, sharing with the brothers what he was hearing.

Lucy and Lucian were asleep in their beds before I had finished the tale. I silently got up and left their room, the dogs following me. I closed their door, and my mind's attention was drawn to the Governess. She was pacing her room, deciding if she would try to seduce Jaxon by waiting for him in his room. I rolled my eyes. Seemed another little girl needed to learn a lesson tonight. An amused and slightly evil smirk crossed my features as I entered Jaxon's room. He was still downstairs with his brothers.

I went and lay down in the center of his bed to wait, crossing my ankles. I put a hand on my face, my pointer finger running up the side of my cheek; my other arm was across my body in the crook of my folded elbow. I mentally commanded my dogs to stand right in front of the door, and I smirked at the door, waiting for her.

# CHAPTER 46

My evil smirk with a raised eyebrow remained as I looked at the door, and the handle started to turn. The door swung open, and the Governess meant to sneak into the dark room when she froze at the sound of two viscous, low-rumbling growls. My left arm reached out and turned the bedside lamp on, my other hand remaining on my face while I watched her eyes slowly adjust to the sight in front of her. Her eyes took me in first, lying on Jaxon's bed. My eyes flared red, my fangs descended, and an evil smile spread across my face. Her eyes darted to the two Dobermans directly before her when they growled again, baring their teeth at her.

I turned my gaze down to pick at my nails while I spoke, "You know, I warned you, Barbie. You're not here for Jaxon. You're here to care for the twins and be a human liaison as needed. Seems you need a reminder of where you belong." As I said the word 'reminder,' both dogs started snarling, and I finally looked up from my nails with my red eyes.

She was shaking in a mixture of fear and anger as she looked at me and the dogs. She screamed at me, "Jaxon was happy with me before you came along and screwed everything up! I knew that you just wanted him for yourself, but he chose me first! I'm what he really wants. If you weren't keeping him away from me, he would have already been back with me."

I sighed and then laughed. "Oh, blondie, I hate to break it to you, but you were just an amusing plaything. If Jaxon had really wanted you, don't you think he would have gone behind my back to try to stay with you? He is known to sneak around to get what he wants, from time to time."

"That doesn't prove anything, you bitch! Jaxon loves me! Not you!" She screamed again. I sighed again and rolled my eyes. Such drama.

"I don't have time to play this little game all the time. Jaxon is where he wants to be, but I'll make you a deal." I said calmly. I rose from the bed, and the dogs started snarling at her, snapping ferociously and backing her out of the room step by step, me following behind the dogs. She backed out of his room slowly and across the hall until her back came up against her door.

The screaming Governess had drawn the brothers' attention downstairs, and I felt the subject of my discussion with the Governess walk up the stairs to stand down the hall, taking in the scene. They had all heard her screaming his name. I smirked at her as the dogs stopped their advance, standing right in front of Jaxon's door. I walked forward to stand between them as I flashed my fangs and red eyes at her.

"What deal?" She asked, trying to control her shaking voice. I leaned against his door frame, with my left arm extended high on the frame, reaching down to stroke one of the snarling Dobermans.

"If Jaxon wants you, he can come to you in your room tonight, and I won't stop him." She gasped in triumph. I raised a finger on my right hand to let her know I wasn't finished, "But, if he doesn't come to you tonight, you will drop this, once and for all, lest I have to start making good on my warnings. Do we have a deal?" I looked at her, and her eyes were flaming as my smirking gaze traveled down the hall to where Jaxon was standing, watching. Her gaze followed mine, and she finally noticed Jaxon standing there. I turned my gaze back on her, and she turned to me with her jaw set, all confidence. I smiled at her sweetly before I opened her door with my magic, sending her sprawling onto her backside inside.

I followed her to her door frame and whispered in a quiet, threatening voice, "If I have to make good on my threat, Barbie, you can count on being my next meal. Have a good night."

I stepped back, shut her door, and commanded the dogs to heel before I turned and started walking down the hall.

Jaxon watched me advance on him, his eyes eating me up as I got closer. I perused him up and down with obvious approval, smirking at him. I walked up close, and he looked down at me with his devilish smirk. I ran my fingers down his jaw, turning his face as I continued by him, heading for the stairs.

He turned to watch me walk down the stairs and whispered, "Is there a door number two, as well?" I looked over my shoulder at him with an alluring and appreciative smile.

I looked him up and down again before I whispered, "Across the hall or across the mansion, you choose." I caressed his face again with my magic and headed down the stairs.

"What was that about?" Niklaus asked me as I was about to pass the study. I walked inside to see him and Eben sitting on the couches as if they had been discussing something before he asked.

"Apparently, the Governess needed another reminder. I mean, I thought I had made myself clear that first time, but I guess not," I said, shrugging. Eben's mischievous look crossed his features as he looked from me to Niklaus. Niklaus shook his head, but he had an amused look on his face.

"And how exactly did you remind her?" Niklaus asked.

I looked up, thrumming my fingers on my lips like I was thinking, and said, "Actually, I think I was reasonably understanding, considering. Next time, I won't be so nice." Eben laughed.

I reached down with my hands and stroked the dogs at my side, scratching their ears. My face softened as I looked back at Niklaus and said quietly, "Good night."

I turned to leave, but Niklaus stood and reached out to me, pulling me to his chest and wrapping his arms around me. I sighed and melted against him, soaking up his embrace. He stroked my hair, thinking about how much he loved me and how much I had changed since coming to the manor. He was right. If the Governess had attempted something like that, even a couple days after she had tried to confront me that first time, I would have literally eaten her alive. Not that I wouldn't make good on my threat now, however. I meant what I said.

"Good night, my darling," Niklaus whispered to me. I turned my face to look at him, gazing into his beautiful green eyes and stroking his hair.

"Good night, my love," I said back to him and stood up on my toes to kiss him. He released me, and I leaned over to Eben and kissed him goodnight as well. I turned and walked down the hall, bringing my cell phone out to call Vladimir and update him on how the night went. He picked up immediately, as usual.

"Sasha." Well, that was at least some improvement.

"Hello, Vladimir. I'm back from the Cavalier compound." I opened my bedroom door and walked in, shutting it behind the two dogs that entered with me. I got a comforter out of the closet and threw it on the floor in the far corner of the room while I talked with Vladimir. "Blake brought me to his place, and I got him drunk enough to pass out, and then I was able to sneak into the Cavalier's poison room and check it out. I gathered a lot of information and now have the name and scent of the Cavalier involved in our little drug issue; it should be resolved soon." I covered the phone's mouthpiece and commanded the dogs to lie down on the comforter.

"Who on earth are you telling to lie down in German?" Vladimir demanded of me.

"I may have also acquired two of the Cavalier's guard dogs in the process."

There was silence on the other end of the line, and then he actually laughed. "Sasha, my minx, you amuse me." I was surprised at his good mood.

"Lucy and Lucian are in love with them." He laughed again. They had always been a soft spot for him.

"What about my sons?"

It was my turn to laugh a little, "Yes, well, Niklaus is a little less than enthusiastic about them staying here, but it's all squared away. They've already proved useful."

"What is your next move?"

"Well, I will be tracking this specific Cavalier down to deal with him. Hopefully, I'll have him squared away before I come to New York this Friday. Perhaps not, but hopefully."

"Very well, my pet. Call me, and I will see you in a few days."

"Yes, Vladimir." I put the cell phone on the nightstand and wandered into my closet to strip. I then wandered into my bathroom and stepped into the shower to wash any remaining scent of Blake off of my body and hair.

My bedroom door opened; I had a visitor. I heard him come into my room and then come to the bathroom. I kept my eyes closed as my face was under the stream of hot water, but I couldn't miss the sounds of his clothing hitting the floor before the door to the shower opened, and he was with me. My wet body slid against his in the most amazingly provocative way, my soft curves molding to his hard frame as his hands slid over my body. His fiery kiss captured my lips, possessing me in a demanding way, and he pulled me up against him.

A hunger for him began to consume me, washing through my body in such a powerful wave, originating from where his lips moved over mine, possessing me with his tongue. A growl escaped me, and I forced his tongue back, invading his mouth with mine, as I shoved him back against the shower wall with my vampire strength, making him let out a breath. I growled at him again and drew my nails down his chest slowly, as I owned him for the moment. I climbed up his frame, fisting his hair to pull his head back to look up at me as I clung to his torso with my thighs; him supporting me from underneath with his arms. I looked into his eyes with a possessive hunger all my own.

My gaze landed on his amazing lips, and I leaned my face down to suck his lip into my mouth, to nibble on him. I let my lips wander to the corner of his mouth before I took my tongue and licked the water off his jaw from center to just below his ear. I kissed him there, nibbling on his ear before I returned to look down in his eyes again. I smiled wickedly, pulling on his hair again and exposing his neck. My teeth slid down his jaw and neck to stop over his throbbing carotid. I drew circles on his neck with my tongue, making him gasp and hold me tighter. I pressed my fangs into his taught skin, not releasing my hold on his hair.

"You're mine, Jaxon," I whispered. He squeezed me in reply, and then I bit down, drawing his spicy blood into my mouth. His jaw fell slack on a moan as I pulled on the bite and his hair simultaneously. I maneuvered my hips to wrap my legs around him, sinking down on him, squeezing him while I fed from his neck. He let out a growl and pushed me back against the neighboring rock wall, starting a demanding rhythm inside of me while I still maintained my hold on his neck and hair. At last, I had taken my fill, so I released him to grip his shoulders. He captured my lips and again possessed me with his tongue, teasing me and working me up.

He released me, withdrawing from me, his demanding hands holding me in place against the wall. He looked into my eyes with such intensity before mischief crossed his features, and he flipped me around, pressing my chest against the rock wall.

He leaned into my ear, pressing me against the wall even more, and whispered, "And you're mine, Sugar Lips." His hands slid around me to grip my hips and angle me perfectly so he could possess me from behind. I moaned as he filled me, stretching me just right. He withdrew to plunge into me again as his hot breath fanned my ear. I heard his growls and pants at his movements, his face right next to my ear. "I will always choose you, Sasha. Even if I did enjoy you marking your territory earlier." Another thrust. Another moan.

"Jaxon," I sighed his name as his kisses traveled down my neck while he continued to move inside of me. He bit down with his next thrust, and even more pleasure invaded my system, making me cry out with it. I barely heard his moaning, my pleasure enfolding me so much. He timed his thrusts and his pulls on the bite together, making me sigh or moan with each one. He was all I needed at that moment, my head and long, wet hair falling back over his shoulder as he worked me up into a blazing inferno. My panting was on every breath now; he had me so close. With one more thrust, he released the white-hot flame that locked my muscles up on pure bliss, before a scream was released from me, announcing his choice to the rest of the estate.

# CHAPTER 47

I sighed and stirred. I heard Jaxon murmur underneath me, holding me in the great black bed. It was Monday morning, and Jaxon had spent the last two nights with me, not sleeping all that much. I heard my bedroom door open and sighed, snuggling into Jaxon's embrace more. I just wanted to stay here; sometimes, I hated the ruse of them attending community college, but I understood their need to fit into the community and be less suspicious, especially to the Cavaliers. My sleepy eyes found Eben standing beside the bed, grinning playfully at us.

"You're such a hog, Jaxon. Keeping her all to yourself the rest of the weekend," he teased.

"You could have joined," was Jaxon's lazy answer. He didn't move or open his eyes. I smiled at him and turned my smirk on Eben, letting out a little laugh. Eben smiled back and shook his head, enjoying Jaxon's reply.

I sat up from Jaxon's embrace, letting the black sheet slide from my form. Eben's look instantly turned dark and smoldering. Underneath that calm, sweet demeanor was a wild soul and majestic lover. He didn't fight me as I dragged him to me with my magic. I pulled him to my lips and rolled over on top of him, pressing myself against his bare chest. His hands came to me to caress my soft skin with his tickling fingers. I knew they had to leave, but I couldn't help it- I wanted to taste him.

"Niklaus will be coming to scold us soon," Jaxon lazed as his hands folded behind his head, watching me.

Looking into Eben's eyes, I nodded an affirmation to Jaxon's words, saying, "Yes, he's already thinking about it." I kissed Eben again, showing him a look that conveyed the depth of my love for him. He returned the look right before I leaned to his neck and bit him.

His decadent blood slid over my tongue, filling me with such pleasure I closed my red eyes. Eben groaned in ecstasy and tightened his hold on me, the rest of him relaxing into the massive black bed. I felt Jaxon slide out of the bed and find some clothes, still watching me feed on Eben. We all heard Niklaus's relaxed footsteps coming down my hallway, and I heard him lean against my door frame, probably crossing his arms.

I finally released Eben and turned my blood-red eyes on Niklaus. He was smiling instead of scowling, one hand on his hip, the other he was using to lean against the door frame, with a quick conversation passing through our minds about Jaxon and Eben needing to leave as I climbed off of Eben. I slid back into the sheets of the great black bed and gave Niklaus a smug look that changed to desire as I looked at him. He angled his head a little as he looked at me, his gaze deepening as he listened in on my mind.

"So, this is what you two do all day while we're gone," Jaxon said, waving a hand between us looking at one another.

Niklaus's look faded into an irritated scowl for his brother. Jaxon smirked at him and turned to wink at me before he slid out of the room, satisfied that he had goaded his brother a little. Eben slid out of the room after giving me a smile. Niklaus turned to watch them go.

He waited a few minutes until I heard the other brothers leave, then he turned back to me, saying, "What are your plans for looking into that Cavalier? You shouldn't go alone, Sasha."

"I'm going to find him. I'll start my search at the Cavalier houses to see if he's there, and tonight, I will start perusing the bars searching for him. I was also going to head back to the quarry to see if there was any fresh scent there. It might be a pain to try to actually locate him outside of the compound."

At that moment, a thought occurred to me, and I sped off into my closet to get dressed. I chose my black leathers and sped out of the room to the boxes in the study that we had packed up from the information from the quarry. I dug through a box until I located what I needed. Excellent. This could possibly be so much easier. I sped back to my room and closed the door. Niklaus was waiting inside.

I opened the vampire's cell phone and looked through his contacts for the name I had discovered in the poison room inside the compound. Bingo. There it was, confirmed as the last call he had made. I pressed the 'send' button and brought the phone to my ear.

It rang a few times, and he picked up, tentatively saying, "Hello?"

"I'm sure you must be expecting him, but as you can tell, it's not."

"Who is this? And why do you have his cell phone? Where is he?"

"Slow down, I have a deal to offer you. I was going to replace your other associate at the bar after he went missing, but then your other vampire friend decided to double-cross me. So, I'm here to offer you a better deal than he ever did if you take me on as your new partner. I even have a werewolf friend who can supply us with what we need to keep producing." On an afterthought, I added, "And he'll open up the new market you had been discussing branching into with your previous vampire associate."

"What happened to him?"

I let him hear my smile as I said, "I killed him. He double-crossed me and got what he deserved. I can't stand it when people don't stand by their word, don't you? He was about to cut you out anyway, so I did you a favor, Cavalier." I heard his muffled intake of breath.

"How do I know you're not just lying?"

"Why don't you go check your warehouse? He mentioned something about another source that was giving him a better deal on the poison. Two vials were delivered the night I discovered his treachery."

"He never mentioned you."

"Backstabbers are rarely honest. Call me back when you've verified and want to cut a new, better deal." I hung up on him and looked up at Niklaus. "With any luck, he will come to us, and I won't have to hunt him down," I said nonchalantly.

"You absolutely cannot go to that meeting alone, Sasha," Niklaus said.

"I won't, Niklaus, don't worry," I said, stroking his cheek. My debonair worrying vampire.

"Debonair?" He said, a small smile coming to his face as his eyes darkened.

"That's right. Would you prefer suave instead?" He stalked up to me, looking down at me as he got up close. My eyes lit up red as I looked at him, my mind revealing how much I wanted him at that moment. "What should we do while we wait for the return phone call?" I said in a breathy voice. A hand on the back of my neck brought my lips to him as he leaned down to meet them.

He reached behind me and slowly unzipped my black leather corset, throwing it back into my closet. I rid him of his top as well, launching myself around his hips as soon as it left my hands.

"You know, I think Jaxon had the right idea earlier," I said in a husky voice. His hands wandered up my back, and I leaned forward, biting him without warning. He stumbled toward the bed and caught us on the pole of the four-poster with one hand, leaning his head against it while I brought him to ecstasy with my bite. I pulled back on a hiss toward the ceiling, my fangs and mouth red with his blood. He fell onto the bed on top of me.

He took both of my hands in one of his and raised them above our heads, holding them there as he kissed me. He kissed his way down my neck and, still holding me, bit me, feeding on me, making me moan and strain against him. His free hand went to my bared chest and teased me, driving me crazy. His fingers slid along my side, making me squirm and shy away from his tickling touch. He smiled on my neck briefly before he drew from me again. His free hand slid into the waistband of my leather pants. He used that same hand to then remove them as he fed on me. I was in such a state of pleasure I didn't notice him removing the rest of his own clothes.

He released me and looked down at me. He still held my hands above my head as his mouth sank to my breast, sucking and pulling moans and gasps out of me; his free hand slid down my hip to hook under my knee and raise my leg a little. His fingers found me while his mouth paid homage to the other breast, and soon, he had me over the edge with his perfect mind-reading skills. He pulled the leg up into the crook of his arm, his hand caressing my thigh as he slowly breached me, hitting an amazing angle with my leg in the air.

"Niklaus," I said, gasping, as he gave me a wicked smile, knowing exactly how right he felt to me.

His quick, commanding thrust tore a gasp from me, and I looked at him, hardly able to keep my eyes open with the pleasure rolling through me. I gave in as a moment of stillness covered me before he again hit the perfect spot on a sharp thrust. He kept up the perfect sensation of stillness and sharp thrusts until he could feel my need building to where I needed more and quicker. He held my leg up, my ankle resting on his shoulder as he worked me perfectly until I was screaming his name before my orgasm had even hit. When it did, it was like a moment of losing control, and I abandoned myself to it, the mansion shaking for a brief moment at my release, my power shuddering at Niklaus's power over me.

He continued to move in me, knowing exactly how to drive my pleasure on, lengthening it as he sought his own release. My fingernails dug into his shoulders when he released my wrists, unable to hold them up through his own pleasure that exploded through his system. He finally let my leg drop as he leaned over me, breathing heavily.

I wrapped my arms around him, holding him to me as he rode his own waves of blinding pleasure. I stroked his back, laying my cheek against the top of his head. Yes, I could get used to doing this every day, during the day, while it was just us at home. He laughed at me before sliding off me to lean over me, holding the side of his face in his hand, his arm bent at the elbow. I smiled at him, reaching up to tuck his long, soft hair behind his ear. We looked at each other, listening to each other's minds and commenting on each other's thoughts.

The cell phone on the nightstand started ringing, and I reached for it. At the same time that my arm reached out to pick up the phone, the memory of Vladimir in my bedroom, holding my head, flashed before my eyes. Niklaus saw it, too, and he met my eyes. Vladimir was coming.

"Run!" I whispered to him, my eyes wide in fear. Niklaus sped out of my room, grabbing his clothes on the way out at vampire speed. The door had just clicked shut as I brought the phone up to my ear, jumping out of bed to gather my clothes.

Vladimir's apparition manifested next to me as I answered, "Yes?"

My eyes met Vladimir's as I listened to the Cavalier say, "You were right; two vials are missing that I can't account for. Where do you want to meet?"

"The old quarry should do, don't you think?" Vladimir was listening in on both sides of the conversation with interest.

I started sliding into my clothes as the Cavalier replied, "Yes, that will be fine. Meet me there in two nights at 9pm. Bring your werewolf friend."

"See you then." The Cavalier hung up, and I put on my corset, acting like I was getting ready to go out for the day.

Vladimir's eyes narrowed at me, and he said in a deadly quiet tone, "Werewolf friend?"

# CHAPTER 48

"Uh, yeah. You remember the wolves I helped with the rogue issue? It was part of my ruse to get an in with the Cavalier. I'm pretending to cut him a deal and become his new partner in the drug business to get him to come to me. In two nights, I'll ambush him at the quarry, and hopefully, this whole thing will be over. Was there something else you needed, Master?" I saw a little tug on his lips at me calling him Master, and he stepped up to me. He pulled me to him, squeezing the back of my neck to claim my lips. I was so grateful he couldn't read minds, or he would have heard me comparing his touch to Niklaus's from only an hour ago; the stark contrast between the two and my response to both.

"What does a wolf have to do with this drug business?" He asked, seemingly satisfied with my first answer.

"The vampire, talking on his phone, had mentioned something about expanding into a new market using werewolves. I used that tidbit I had overheard as a corroboration to my story and offered to bring a wolf friend with me to help expand our market."

He squeezed my jaw, roughly stroking my cheek, and gave me a wicked grin, whispering, "My minx. I'm looking forward to New York very much."

"Master," I said simply, as I couldn't think of anything else to say to him. New York was approaching rapidly. His face bent to mine, and I leaned up to meet him for the kiss; I had to get back on his good side before New York. I heard him sigh, and his eyes searched my face momentarily before he faded on a satisfied smile. Sigh. First, I had to focus on my problems here.

Wednesday night rolled around faster than I had thought possible, but here I was, standing at the burnt quarry with Sebastian at my side, waiting for the Cavalier to show.

"Thanks for coming, Seb. I'm sorry about all of this; it seems I've wrapped you up in some dirty business a lot lately. Putting you in danger, getting you shot. I don't feel like a very good friend right now," I admitted in a whisper to him while we waited in the dark. His arm came around my waist, and he pulled me close.

"Sash, you're the best of friends. You saved my life, even knowing that the price could have been yours, even if it could have made me hate you. You still love and care about me and are one of the most loyal people I know. Quit putting yourself down before I have to spank you," he teased at the end. I rolled my eyes and laughed, giving him a quick kiss on the neck.

Both of our faces whipped around toward the road. A black SUV was coming down the lane. We watched it approach, both of us on high alert; he could come out, guns blazing, and just mow us over if he wanted. This was the riskiest part of this entire trap. I heard the brothers draw in a breath where they were hiding.

The Cavalier left the SUV running but opened the black window enough to look out into the darkness. I stepped forward into the glow of the headlights so he could see me and gave him a confident smirk.

"Glad you made it at last," I said, putting one hand on my hip, the other hanging at my side, the headlights creating a glean on my leathers. He rolled down his window a little more and momentarily looked me up and down.

"How did you kill him? You're no match for him."

"I had help," I gestured in the dark, and Sebastian came to me. I felt around inside the car with my mind to ensure he was alone.

"Alright, what are your terms?" he asked, his eyes shifting around. He was obviously nervous, but I couldn't tell if that was just because I was a vampire in general or because I had killed his previous associate. He was a Cavalier, so their mistrust of my kind couldn't be overstated. He had had dealings with the other vampire, but I was new to him, so he was extra distrustful. Crap. How was I ever going to get him out of the car?

"That's my question. I promised you a better deal, so you tell me," I offered. Normally, this wasn't the shrewdest business move, but I wanted him off guard; hopefully, his greed would settle in.

"Well, our last deal was a clear cut fifty-fifty so . . ." He trailed off, thinking as he spoke. Not true. His mind revealed that his last associate had only offered him a twenty percent cut of the profits.

I smiled at him and said, "Come, come. I know that wasn't really your deal. You only got twenty percent. Would an even thirty-three satisfy you?" He looked at me, reevaluating me for a minute. He actually had started to believe my story at last.

"I want a full forty or no deal," he said back, nervous about pissing me off but willing to risk it to get more out of the deal.

"Hmmm, greedy, aren't you? Alright, forty percent, but you better not jerk me around, or I'll do worse to you than your vampire friend, you understand?" He nodded at me with wide, wary eyes. "Shall we shake on it?" I asked in a friendly but still serious voice. His mind glanced around the dark, looking for a sign of any trouble. His eyes landed on Sebastian standing there and then shifted to me. He slowly extended his arm out of the SUV. Damn. I was hoping to get him out of the car.

I sauntered over to him and looked at him for a second. He was nervous but also extremely interested in me. I gave him an alluring smile and slowly reached out my hand to grasp his. He shivered at my touch, but it was less from repulsion, as I would have expected, and more from aroused curiosity. I didn't release his hand and tilted my head at his perusal of me, my eyes lighting up red as I looked at him.

My alluring smile spread a little bit in enjoyment as I whispered to him, "I'm the first female vampire you've ever seen, aren't I?

His lips parted in surprise, and he said, "How did you know?" I laughed in genuine enjoyment at his fascination with me.

"The way you're looking at me. You want to be disgusted, to hate me, but you just can't help being attracted to me. You're fascinated by me, which I guess is understandable since there aren't many of us out there," I simply said honestly.

"There aren't. I hope I haven't offended you?"

"Not at all. Curiosity doesn't always kill the cat," I said with a smile. I had to get him out of the car, or we were screwed; my mental attention went to where I still held his hand. It was all I had. I leaned forward and whispered to him, gently firming up my grip, "Sometimes it's the curious little mice that get caught."

I hissed and pulled on his arm, trying to pull him out of the car, but I had forgotten one thing: humans wore seat belts. His body jerked against the belt, and he slumped out the window for a second. My grip faltered on him as the belt held fast because I hadn't pulled hard enough to break it. He pulled back into the SUV with a look of horror and slammed down on the accelerator after flipping the SUV into reverse.

I hissed and leaped onto the vehicle as the tires buzzed, shooting gravel at the sudden acceleration. I reached in, grasping for his seat belt, to rip it off of him as the SUV flew backward, heading for the trees. I had my feet on the step, and my right hand held me on the vehicle using the luggage tie down on the top while my left reached in to reach for the belt. The trees were coming up fast, but he turned the wheel sharply, trying to throw me off.

My grip held firm, but my feet flew out to the side of the car at the turn, my hair whipping about me, getting in my view of my goal. I hung from the car, my feet skittering along the gravel, trying to find purchase on the SUV again.

At last, my feet found the step once more, and I snarled at him as I reached inside and tore the belt from him, throwing it over my shoulder out of the window. I reached back in on another snarl, intending to rip him from the car when a gun came whipping out, aimed at me, and I had to swing out against the back window, hanging from my one arm again, to avoid the shot that rang out in the night. I cursed and tried to swing around to grab his gun when it disappeared into the dark SUV.

He pulled on the wheel again, and I saw the window going up. I snarled again and swung around, putting as much force into it as possible, slamming my left fist into the window just as it was almost closed. The glass shattered, sending a sprinkling of tiny pieces inside the SUV and into my fist. I reached inside again for him but had to dodge another bullet. The back window next to me shattered with another shot that had been so close to me. Yikes.

We were still flying backward down the lane, approaching the tree line, when I saw them. The brothers had left their hiding places and stood in the road, blocking the SUV. The Cavalier noticed and slammed on the brakes, sending me flying toward the back of the SUV.

I managed to snag the back of it just as he hit the accelerator, going forward this time. A couple shots rang out, shattering the back window as I ducked, hiding below the glass line on the back. I saw the brothers start running for the SUV as I turned my attention upward. I coiled and sprang, launching myself onto the roof of the SUV, finding purchase again on the roof rack. I started pulling myself forward as we raced along. He knew I was there, and he jerked his wheel this way and that, trying to get me to lose my hold on his vehicle.

At last, I managed to crawl right over the driver's side, focusing entirely on the vehicle below me, trying to maintain my hold and reach my goal. He was right below me, and he must have heard me. A shot rang out, piercing the roof and making a hole right between my arm and my face. I cursed again and rolled over on my back, just in time to avoid another shot that went up through the roof, me swaying dangerously as the SUV sped along unstably.

I gritted my teeth, snarling as I balled my left fist again. Using all my strength and the momentum of rolling back into place, I slammed my fist down through the roof of the SUV, right into the top of the Cavalier's skull; blood spattered everywhere inside the vehicle, and I felt his body slump forward inside.

The SUV continued speeding along, the pressure from the slumped body continuing to hold down the accelerator. I ripped my fist back out of the top of the SUV and grabbed the luggage rack to steady myself. I looked up just in time to see the ledge of the bottomless quarry pit pass under the front tires of the SUV that I clung to.

I heard shouting behind me, but it was muted to my ears as my eyes were locked on the dark abyss that I was being hurtled down into. My hair was flying out behind me as the vehicle screamed over the ledge, heading toward the darkness below—darkness full of long, pointed wooden trees, just ready to act as a stake through my heart.

# CHAPTER 49

How in the hell did I always wind up getting myself into these types of situations? The wind on my face stung my eyes as my hair whipped out behind me, the darkness beginning to swallow the SUV and me. In slow motion, I remember turning my head to look behind me, my eyes finding the four men I cared most about in the world, watching in terror as I sailed beyond even their supernatural reach; not even a jump from the ledge could rescue me now. I wasn't sure what they saw in my eyes before I turned my face back to the abyss before me. Their minds were consumed with the utter horror and pain of having to watch me die, unable to help me in any way.

I knew that I had only one chance. I held onto the SUV with my hands and pulled my legs up beneath me, moving into a crouching position. The SUV had just started to turn hood down, and it would be my only chance. I focused on summoning every ounce of strength I possessed, building my magic for a split second before the SUV hit just the right angle. I pushed off with my whole being and magic, propelling myself forward, deeper into the abyss before me. My arms shot out before me, and I clasped them together to form a point, sleeking my body down as much as possible to allow me to sail as far as possible into the night.

I closed my eyes, feeling the wind on me as I sailed through the open expanse of night. I felt my body start to angle down, so I tucked my knees up to my body for a split second, changing the orientation of gravity's pull. Then, unfolding my legs, I started hurtling downward into the darkness.

Out of the corner of my eye, I saw the huge black SUV crash down on the trees. Great spikes of dead wood impaled the vehicle, and the rest of its windows shattered. The pierced gas tank began leaking fuel all down the vehicle and dead trees. A screeching sound of metal hitting rock sent off a spark, and suddenly, the entire side of the quarry pit was illuminated by the great fire that engulfed the SUV.

My attention returned to my own fate, and I looked down, just as the blackness swallowed first my feet and then the rest of me, as I plunged down into its bone-chilling depths, fading from sight and sound. The ice crept into my very core, stealing all breath that I might have had at that moment, and I tried to scream to no avail as I flailed about. Panic set in, my lungs empty as I floated down into the void, a painful burning settling in. Finally, I opened my eyes and saw only darkness all around me until I looked up. There was a golden flickering there. My arms and legs began reaching and straining for the little glimmer of hope. My fingers reached for it, straining, desperate to escape.

At last, they broke the surface, and my head followed, allowing me to gasp and take in a deep breath of cold night air as I treaded the black waters of the quarry lake. I turned in the water toward the flames burning the side of the quarry, my beacon that had allowed me to see where to swim. I coughed up ample amounts of water for a minute before that settled down, allowing me to swipe my long, wet hair out of my face.

I felt Niklaus's great relief as he heard my mind. I took a deep breath and turned to start swimming toward the side of the quarry. I heard him telling the others I was alright, and all felt relief.

I pulled myself out of the frigid waters on the side of the quarry and looked around me for a way out. I was desperately cold, but I was unhurt. I coiled my legs and jumped as high as I could, grasping the next level of the quarry. I did this over and over again until I was just below the edge of the top. Several pairs of hands reached down for me, and I smiled at them, allowing them to pull me up into their embrace.

I was surrounded on all sides by warmth; I was freezing. If I had been human, I would have gone into shock, and hypothermia would have already set in. I sighed in relief to be surrounded by them. At least this mess was over, right?

"Well, that makes hunting regular Cavaliers seem just boring now," I chattered out. There was laughter from my guys, and I heard Niklaus sigh at me before he, too, joined in. Their caresses and gentle kisses told me, as much as their minds, how relieved they were that I was okay.

"Let's get you home and into a warm bubble bath. I think this qualifies as one of those difficult nights, don't you?" Niklaus teased. I smiled at him and started walking toward home.

We took off at supernatural speed back to the estate together. Sebastian reached over and kissed me on the forehead before he walked over to his bike, which was parked inside the gate.

"See ya, Sash. Come find me to say goodbye before you leave for New York, okay?" I nodded and smiled at him.

After reassuring the guys that I was alright, I walked into the house and headed for my room. I was just going to have that bath and go to bed. I was freaking tired after that adrenaline rush and frigid swim. I soaked in hot water in my huge tub for a while, then slipped into my nightgown and went to bed.

True to my word, I slept like the dead until daybreak. I didn't dream or even stir until my two massive Dobermans came crashing through my bedroom door, right onto the bed, licking me and acting like two ginormous puppies. I looked up and smiled at Eben; he had taken them out for me in the morning, letting me sleep. I closed my eyes and drifted back to sleep after wishing him a good day at college.

I woke a little before noon and got up to get dressed. I would go to the campus for Sebastian's lunch hour to say goodbye. Tomorrow morning, I was getting on a plane to New York to go meet Vladimir. I was terrified.

I walked into Sebastian's office and saw him drinking a coffee at his desk. I set some takeout on the desk for him, and he smiled up at me.

"Thanks, Sash," he said with warm affection.

"Sure," I smiled back, plopping into the armchair before his desk. I suddenly didn't know what to say, so I just sat there and looked around his office while he ate. What were you supposed to say on the eve of going to a tyrant's bed?

I would leave tomorrow, and if I was lucky, I would be back by Saturday night. Niklaus and I had discussed him coming to New York and following me so he could be there for me. I finally agreed, but we both knew he couldn't actually save me from my fate there with Vladimir.

"What are you thinking about, Sasha?" Sebastian asked me, pulling me out of my thoughts.

"About how I have to leave tomorrow. Niklaus will follow me, but" I just let my words drift off as I looked down at my lap. I heard him sit up and reach out to me, pulling me up and around his desk to come sit on his lap so he could hold me.

I snuggled up to him but had no words to describe just how heavy my heart was. His thoughts echoed mine, along with the desire to go back through his research on Elizabeth Bathory, the Originals, and other older vampires, still trying to settle his mind on some things. He decided to look into it when I was away.

"Sash, come find me when you get back, okay? I wish I could," his words also dropped off, but I heard his mind finish that he wished he could stop all this from happening.

"I will, Seb," I whispered. I spent the rest of his lunch hour with him before leaving for the mansion to pack and prepare for my departure.

It was night, and I was pacing in my room, glancing at the packed suitcase waiting for me. My left hand sparkled under the moonlight, streaming into my room, my two Dobermans watching me with their eyes as they lounged in the corner. I was never going to be able to sleep tonight. I was far too anxious and full of terrible dread. My breaths were coming rapidly as my mind worked itself up.

"Sasha." My head shot up from the floor, where I stared as I was pacing, probably wearing a line on the black rug. "Sasha." I closed my eyes and listened. "Sasha, come to me." His thoughts were strongly bent on me, my mind hearing them. I sucked in a breath and started walking out my door, across the manor and up the stairs. I opened his door and stepped inside, his calm, soothing melody rolling over his room.

I shut the door and looked at him briefly before whispering, "You were thinking quite loudly, Eben." His beautiful smile showed over his shoulder as he continued to play his piano.

"I'm glad you were listening and that you actually came." He turned back to his piano, and I quietly approached him. I leaned against the side of it to watch him play.

"Did you need something, Eben?" I asked.

He smiled up at me, whispering, "I could feel your distress from here, my Blossom." Oh, Eben. Sweet Eben. I didn't say anything as I watched him play. His melody was smooth and calming; no accident, I knew.

I sighed, accepting his sensitive care of me and loving him for it. I reached out and caressed him with the back of my hand. My dark angel always watching over me. He looked up at me while he played, caressing me with his beautiful azure eyes. I was absorbed in thoughts of how much I loved and appreciated him and his tenderness. But my train of thought was tainted as the knowledge of Vladimir's looming cruelty crept into the beautiful picture; it sent cracks ripping through my mind, the fear and trepidation of what was coming blackening my calm. Tears swam in my eyes, so I shut them. Eben's fingers stilled on the keys, and I heard him push his piano bench back.

His gentle hands reached out to capture my hips and slide me along his piano to him, making me sit on the keys with a tinkling sound. My heart was dying inside, beating frantically at the thought of leaving here. Eben wrapped his long limbs around me, laying his head against me.

"Sasha, your heart sounds like it's going to take off," he whispered, sitting up to look at me.

I framed his face and let him see into me as I whispered, "I'm scared, Eben." The tears finally escaped my eyes and rolled down my face.

I could feel his agony match my own at the thought of me leaving to go be with Vladimir. We still didn't know if I would be returning here to the estate. Eben closed his eyes and leaned forward to plant a kiss on my stomach while I held his head. I felt a fluttering there at his gentle touch, so I raked my fingers into his soft black hair, turning his face up to me. I looked into his eyes and bent to kiss him, not breaking eye contact, communicating my misery of being taken away from them. My eyes were sad, letting him see into me.

"I love you, Eben," I whispered, caressing his lips with my thumb. He gave me a sad smile and reached up to pull me back down to him. My mouth opened on a sob, and he gently invaded me, drowning it out. My hands came to his face, trembling with all my emotion. Eben slowly stood, not breaking our kiss, and then he was above me where I sat. His fingers went up into my hair, gently holding my head; his kiss held a desperate edge to it as he tasted me. Tears still ran down my face as he kissed me, my sorrow at having to leave his touch, his brothers', to go engulf myself in abusive misery.

"Eben," I sobbed out when he pulled back to look at me. My hands reached out to pull his hips to me, running my fingers along his waistband, making him gasp.

His eyes darkened as he looked into mine, but they were guarded as he whispered, "Sasha, I'm not sure—" My eyes were sad, but deep in them, he could see my need for him—the love and utter desperation I had.

The truth was I had no idea if I was coming home; if Vladimir would insist, I come back with him now that the drug issue was over. It was a strong possibility. I just looked at Eben while I slowly lifted his shirt over his head. If this was the last taste of tenderness and love I would ever have, I wasn't going to waste it.

My lips trembled slightly as I looked up at Eben. My lips parted in anticipation as I saw him bend his face to mine, gently retaking possession of my mouth. I slid a hand up his chest to his neck to pull him to me, deepening our kiss, while the other slid around the soft skin of his back.

"Love me, Eben. If I never come back, I want to remember."

"Shhhhh, my Blossom, don't think like that," he said over my lips as he gently pressed me against the back of his piano. My eyes found his again, and his intensity matched mine before his mouth came down on my lips to sweep me away on a river of longing. I moaned his name when his hands bent me forward so he could reach behind me and slowly undo the laces of the corset I wore.

His kisses wandered down to my neck so he could nipple on my ear, sending shivers down my whole body as he worked on the laces. I felt his mouth move downward, and then he, oh so gently, bit down as his fingers finished unlacing me.

My head lolled back, and my hands went to my sides to balance myself, making the keys on his piano tinkle again. His fingers traveled from my jaw, tickling their way down my neck to my shoulders, slowly leaving trails of goosebumps on their journey to remove my corset. I reached out, desperate to feel his skin against mine, as he leaned over me, gently feeding on me.

I drew my fingers up his back, his muscles stretching and cording, as he bowed it to lean over me. I reached forward to undo his belt, gently teasing him with my fingers as I slid them around his waistband, dipping below to follow the beautiful V of his hips. He gasped on my neck, and his hands slid over my body, turning the shivers and goosebumps into a slowly building burn. I couldn't hold back the moan that slid out of me as my head fell to the side when his hand reached up to cup my breast and tease me with his thumb. His other hand was holding my neck to him.

His hips between my thighs held me in place on the keys of his piano, pressing me back against it. I felt him release my neck, and I turned my head to look at him with heavy eyes. His eyes were a beautiful shade of red, and his mouth still had my blood on it. My eyes tracked a single drop of blood that fell from a fang before he could lick it away, and my eyes transfixed on it as it landed on a porcelain key next to me. My blood was on his piano. I stared at it, contemplating its significance for a moment. I felt his caress on my skin, driving the smoldering coals in the pit of my stomach to a new level.

I turned back to him and leaned in to kiss him, reaching out to rid him of the rest of his clothes. The keys of his piano tinkled underneath me at my movements. His mouth traveled down me while his hands slid up my thighs to bunch up the skirt I wore around my waist, his hands preventing me from sliding off the keys. Every touch was gentle but full of a burning passion, a driving need we had for one another. He kissed his way down me, one hand holding me in place, the other reaching up to make me burn, as he slowly drew my panties down my legs. His hot mouth on the inside of my knee had me almost buckling, a few notes ringing out from the piano.

"Eben, shouldn't we move to your," I was interrupted by an involuntary gasp as his kisses rose higher along the inside of my thigh. I fisted the piano beneath me, more notes sounding, as his amazing mouth found the center of my throbbing need, making me cry out and fall back against the piano again; I would have slipped from it entirely if his strong hands hadn't been holding me in place.

I squeezed the piano again and heard him chuckle between my thighs, "Don't break my piano, Sasha." I released my death grip on it but clamped down again when he returned to driving me crazy with his mouth on me.

"Eben," my voice was hoarse and desperate. He kissed my thighs, massaging them with his hands.

"Shhhh. I thought I already taught you this lesson?" He half whispered, half laughed. I groaned. I was going to die before I could get there, his slow build of caresses and teasing driving me out of my mind. He gave me a small taste of release that I was begging for but continued right into building up the next one; the tightness and need only magnifying. I groaned and gave myself over to him completely as his fingers invaded me, working with his mouth, making me cry out while they danced inside of me like he was playing the most complex musical piece. His mouth wandered over to my hip bone, sucking and nibbling.

He came up to my mouth, and I pulled him to me, desperate for his lips on mine. He sampled them, nibbling on them, teasing me to intensify my need, my desire. It was like I was slowly filling my lungs to capacity, one tiny gasp at a time at each one of his touches and movements, but still unable to catch my breath. His teasing kisses wandered to my neck, drawing another moan from me while he leaned against me. A moan so sensual it surprised even my own ears slipped from my lips when he gently pressed into me, making more notes ring out behind me.

His mouth on my neck wandered to my ear, and he whispered as he started to slowly move, "And I can think of no better place to make music with my heart's melody than right here."

I slumped on his chest, helpless before his gentle rhythm that continued to drive us higher. I was gasping again, filling my lungs once more to capacity, as I felt the build. Each sensual thrust made the keys on the piano ring out alongside my gasps and moans. I couldn't take in any more air, going absolutely silent as he held my hips with the perfect angle, pushing me heavenward.

And then I knew what all that air was for; as soon as the dam holding back my pleasure burst, it caused me to throw my head back on a scream that turned into a deep, long moan as the pleasure smoldered on. It felt never-ending, flushing my cheeks and making me feel limp and boneless; only Eben kept me from sliding from the piano as the keys struck the chords I hit with my pleasure. They tinkled again at Eben's climax.

He held me there, against him, even as I sunk my fangs into his neck. It was his turn to slump against me and the piano as I fed from him. His blood was so rich, so hot and sweet; perfection. He sighed and gathered me around him while I fed to carry me to his bed. He lay down on his back, holding me to him as I gently fed from him. I laid in the crook of his arm, and he drew my knee up over him, caressing my thigh, relaxing into his bed while I slowly sucked on his neck. I would hang onto our moment tomorrow. It's what I would picture the following night. What I would keep in the forefront of my mind, leaving my body as Vladimir used me, hurt me. When he told me I wasn't coming back.

The thought of leaving these arms around me had me sad again. The idea of Vladimir's being around me soon brought tears back to my eyes, and I had to stop feeding on Eben because of the sobs that started escaping me. Eben turned on his side and fully drew me into his embrace, tucking me under his chin, just letting me cry. I could hear his heart breaking as much as mine was at the thought of what awaited me tomorrow. I cried myself out and fell into an exhausted sleep in Eben's arms while he watched over me, stroking and kissing my head until sleep claimed me. My dark angel.

# CHAPTER 50

I pulled my small suitcase behind me as I walked up the steps to the massive estate on the outskirts of New York. My thoughts were on the moment when I had left the manor. I had bent down to give Lucy and Lucian a hug, telling them to take the dogs out to play and to take good care of them while I was gone. They scampered off to the back gardens, the dogs following them, eager to play.

Jaxon had stood next to them. His look was so sad and broken, his amber eyes delving into mine. I swallowed with the emotion I felt as I wrapped my arms around his waist and laid my head against his chest, listening to his heart. His arms held me tight before he cupped my face and looked down into my eyes. "I love you, Doll Face. Come home to me," he whispered, utterly devoid of any playfulness.

I leaned up to kiss him before I said, "I love you too, Jaxon." One more quick peck and he released me into the embrace of Eben.

Eben caught me with one arm around me, the other coming to hold my head to his shoulder. He bent and kissed the top of my head. He laid his cheek there for a long moment, his mind communicating so much pain in me having to leave. I held his face and gave him one last slow, smoldering kiss, whispering on his lips that I loved him.

"I love you too, my Blossom." I hugged him again before I let go and grabbed my suitcase, walking to the door.

Niklaus opened the door for me, and I stood before him, looking into his worried gaze. His moss eyes took in my face, his mind listening into my despair. He reached for me and pulled me to him for a hug. I released the suitcase to lay against his chest, my hands splayed out next to my face. He could feel me trembling all over as a small sob escaped me. He held me, using his gift to do his best to soothe me, while he rubbed my back.

"I'll be a few hours behind you, Sasha." He looked down and I met his eyes from where I rested on his chest. "Be strong, Sasha," he encouraged me and gently kissed me.

I reached up and touched his face, whispering, "I love you, my white knight." He smiled and kissed me again.

"I'll be right behind you, my darling," he reminded me as I had turned and left the manor.

Now, here I was, climbing the steps to Vladimir's huge estate here in New York, each step taking tremendous effort as it brought me one step closer to Vladimir.

At last, I stood before the massive door, reaching up with my left hand, which sparkled, and using the grotesque knocker to alert the household to my presence. The butler opened the door and showed me inside. My suitcase was taken from me. I was escorted down the long hall to Vladimir's personal study. The butler knocked on the door and stepped in to announce me after Vladimir had acknowledged him.

"Mistress, Sasha, Sir."

Vladimir turned, and his eyes met mine. They slowly traveled down the length of me as he dismissed the butler with a wave, who backed out of the room and shut the door, leaving me alone with Vladimir. I had put on a black corset with lace overlay detailing, a matching skirt that sparkled while I moved, and black jewelry, including chandelier earrings and a striking black necklace. My makeup, even my lipstick, was black with the tiniest bit of red set against my pale skin. I set my jaw and didn't let any nervousness or emotion show as I looked back at him. The only color on me was a slight rainbow twinkle on my left hand as my finger moved.

When his gaze slowly wandered back up me and met my eyes, I dropped my gaze to the floor and curtsied slowly for him, saying, "Master." I felt his arousal in his mind, but there was more there; anticipation, satisfaction, pride, and elation. I wasn't sure what to make of it. Was it only the ring and me becoming his Bride, or something more?

He slowly walked up to me, his eyes still roving all over me with such intensity as a smile of satisfaction spread across his face. He reached down and took my hand, thumbing the ring that rested there, before bringing my knuckles to his lips to kiss them. It stole my breath.

"My dark Queen," he whispered above my knuckles. I had a hard time holding in my surprise at his words. I didn't know how to respond, so I looked into his eyes. "I have something for you." More surprise; Vladimir rarely gave me gifts. He turned back to the mantle of the great fireplace and guided me over to it, still holding my hand. He lifted the lid on a mahogany box that was lined with felt. Inside rested a gothic tiara of sparkling black diamonds. He released my hand and stepped up to stand over me, gently placing the sparkling tiara on my head with a sinister smile. "You look ready to rule, my minx." His hands came to my face, surprisingly soft, as his eyes started to glow red. He bent down and kissed me possessively but not painfully for once. I still wasn't sure what to make of him as I raised my face to meet his kiss; I couldn't afford to get on his bad side right now. He growled his approval of my response and looked down at me. Did he just caress my face?

"I have a business associate, one you know well, that should be here any minute. I must conclude my business with him before we can be alone." His arm came around me, pulling me tight up against him, and he kissed me again. "I would like to take you home with me. It sounds like you have things under control in Pine River, and there isn't a reason to send you back. It is time you returned and became my Bride, Sasha, and you look ready." I was dying inside. I knew those goodbyes back at the manor would be my last. I could feel his determination. A knock resounded on his study door.

"Enter."

He didn't release me until the butler bowed and announced his guest, "Sir, Master Darius is here to see you."

"Show him in," Vladimir commanded the butler as he released me, taking me onto his arm like I really was his Queen.

Darius walked into the study and gave a polite, formally low bow, which Vladimir nodded at, and I gave him a curtsy. Darius' eyes were drawn to me, and I could see his openly admiring appraisal of me. Vladimir's smile spread at his associates' gawking directed at me.

"How is Beth?" Vladimir asked. Darius' eyes switched to Vladimir, and he smiled.

"Very well," he toned back and looked me up and down again.

Something was off, but I couldn't figure it out exactly. There was more behind their words, I knew, but something else was nagging at me. After a moment, I realized it was because I couldn't hear their thoughts. I hadn't realized I couldn't hear Vladimir until Darius had entered the room. It took specific magical efforts to block me out of the mind, and Vladimir was doing so for his mind and Darius'. This phenomenon distracted me so much that I almost forgot the dread I was feeling at the fact that Vladimir had decided to take me home with him. What was going on?

Vladimir reached for me and pulled me off of his arm to come and stand before him. "Go wait for me in the master suite. I will conclude my business with Darius once the third party arrives and will be with you soon, my Dark Queen." He pulled me to him again for another kiss and released me.

I curtsied and turned to leave the room, shutting the door behind me and leaning against it. My mind was reeling. Why block me from their minds? Why the secrecy? More often than not, I sat in on Vladimir's meetings because I was a part of his plans. What was he doing that Darius was involved in?

Still leaning against the door, my hearing picked up Darius's voice. "Does she know?"

"No, and I made sure to seal off our minds at her arrival. She is unaware for now, but all will be made clear after I've escorted her under guard back to Europe."

"Have you already succeeded then?"

I stared at the ground, unmoving, but my mind was spinning. What was going on? What was I missing? What had been happening in my absence? Why under guard?

The great doors to the manor being opened cut off my train of thought. Another tall figure dressed all in black with a long black trench coat blowing in the wind, revealing multiple weapons, entered the hall. His tall leather boots left puddles on the marble floor as his powerful stride carried him into the hall, ignoring the butler attempting to escort him. His red eyes landed on me as I leaned up from the door, hurriedly moving down the hall towards him.

"If it isn't the royal witch herself, looking as appetizing as ever," his scarlet orbs perused me up and down, lingering on my crown and then cleavage. "You look good enough to get on my knees for."

I narrowed my eyes, holding out my left hand, which he took. I greeted him with a slight sneer, saying, "Otis."

"Sasha," he whispered back through a half smile, his eyebrow challenging me as he leaned over my sparkling hand to kiss the back despite me practically shoving the ring in his face. If I had to wear it, I'd use it as a shield as it suited me.

"What are you doing here?" I demanded of him, rolling my eyes, my tone swathed in sarcasm. "Is there a war going on?" He chuckled a little too much in delight.

"More than you know," he intoned. "Have a nice vacation at my old stomping grounds?"

Otis Bathory, once one of the soft coven brothers, was now Vladimir's head of security. He rarely left Vladimir's main estate in Europe. If Vladimir was traveling, Otis would send a security detail of powerful vampires along unless instructed otherwise; Otis never came himself. Outside of Vladimir and myself, Otis was one of the deadliest vampires in existence now that Vladimir had corrupted him. Otis' presence alone would have tipped me off that something was going on.

"You're as magnificent as always, Sasha. I'd love to take you upstairs myself, but I'm afraid I have a meeting," he smiled.

"I doubt Vladimir would allow that now that his plan is in motion," I sneered back. Otis' eyes darted up to the tiara sparkling on my head for a moment before their red returned to look at me with mild amusement. He studied me momentarily.

"I beg to differ. And yet, you don't seem to object. Are you sure you know what you're getting yourself into?"

"Do you?" He scoffed at my retort in amusement.

"I'll enjoy following you around every moment of every day, Sasha. After the announcement, you're mine. You might be his Bride, but you'll be my charge, my good little girl," he smiled, slowly kissing my hand he held. He sharply pulled me close, his lips almost brushing mine as he towered over me. His sour smell drifted towards me, revolting me. He was like the warhead of the vampire world. "Would you like a taste now, Sasha?" Was he offering for me to feed from him?

"That would make you late for your meeting, Otis. You know how understanding Vladimir is of tardiness," I retorted. He glared and released me, stepping around without another word to head down the hall and enter the study.

I sped up to the master suite, entered it, and quickly shut the door. I had one chance to tell the brothers while I was alone upstairs in Vladimir's bedroom.

Like his bedroom in the manor, it was all black, but this room was absolutely massive, and the black bed was in the center of the room, just waiting for me to writhe and scream on it. I sighed and reached into the pocket of my skirt. I knew it wasn't the wisest thing to do, I had no idea how long Vladimir's business would take, but I had to call Niklaus and let him know I wouldn't be coming back, that I would never see him again. My chest was in a vice as I dialed his number; I was on the verge of tears when he finally picked up.

"Sasha? He can't have left already."

"I. I'm calling to say 'goodbye,' Niklaus. Some very strange things are happening, and it's unclear, but Vladimir has some big scheme going on in Europe, and part of his plan involves me in some way. He's taking me back to Europe tomorrow."

"What?" Alarm strained his voice.

"Vladimir has informed me that he will take me back to Europe tomorrow. I'm not coming back to Pine River, probably ever again. When we return, he intends to make me his Bride, his Dark Queen. I. I overheard him speaking with Darius about me not knowing something about Vladimir succeeding at some secret plot, but I couldn't glean more because he blocked me from all their minds. I can't help but wonder if he sent me to Pine River to get me out of the way, like he had planned this all along and knew I would take the deal he offered. And the way Darius greeted him was also strange as if he was Vladimir's subservient instead of his equal."

"That is odd. Do you know what they're meeting about?"

"No, but there's more. Otis is here." Shocked silence was the reply before he asked me if I was sure. I told him everything Otis had said, even the offering for me to feed on him.

"Could they plan to lock you away, like Darius' bride?"

"Perhaps that is why."

All was lost to me. My home, my friends, my family, and the love I had tasted. I was sinking back into despair, similar to the dark abyss I had flown into a few nights earlier. It swallowed me, chilling my very soul, just like the black water of the quarry; starting with my feet, it flowed upwards to swallow me into a place where I couldn't breathe and didn't know how to escape. I was being taken, my bleeding heart would dry up, and the screams of terror in my heart would ring forever inside of me. I was Vladimir's. I was only his now. Now and forever. A slave. A prisoner. A Bride to the cruelest creature I knew while I was in love with his three coven sons. That was the definition of pure agony.

"Sasha," Niklaus' voice brought me back, "I have to tell you that the Cavalier numbers have been swelling rapidly since you left. They've called all their reinforcements back and it seems like even other bases are sending them here. Something is happening on our end as well. They're acting like they're preparing for war."

"Whatever this is going on, it's much bigger than a war with the Cavaliers, Niklaus. It's like there's a war going on, on both fronts, especially with the way Otis laughed at me saying that. Something is coming, Niklaus, and we're about to be caught up in it. Worse, I know I'm never coming home to you or your brothers. I'm lost to you. Please don't ever forget how much I love you all. Be safe and protect one another. Goodbye."

"Sasha!"

I ended the call and wiped the phone's memory. I reached inside and took out the SIM card, so he couldn't call me back, showing a record of it.

Were the Cavaliers preparing to go to war with the brothers? What was I being dragged into back in Europe? What was Vladimir really up to, and why was Otis here? Was I really lost to the brothers and the love we had discovered? Was all hope lost?

I turned to the door expectantly as footsteps approached down the hallway. My fate was coming for me.

# ABOUT THE AUTHOR

A.P. Raven is a novelist and a dedicated mother of three, known by her growing fanbase as a talented writer who keeps you coming back for more, begging for sequels through her literary works including this book 'The Bathory Bride' and its sequel. Her work has long been praised by her fanbase but is newly available for a wider audience now on Amazon. A.P. Raven lives in several places all over the world, including Illinois state, and in an African country with her husband, three children, and their animals. She enjoys writing, reading, gardening, and raising chickens.

Don't miss out on the
action-packed sequel!